THE LEVELING

ALSO BY SHANNON DENISE EVANS

What the Mountains Know: Life, Unstuck

VELVET MOON CHRONICLES
VOLUME ONE

THE LEVELING

A Novel

Shannon Denise Evans

Lamplighter Publishing House

Lamplighter Publishing House, LLC

New York, New York

Lamplighter Publishing House, LLC
New York, New York

ISBN 978-0-9995351-3-4 (hardcover)
ISBN 978-0-9995351-4-1 (paperback)
ISBN 978-0-9995351-5-8 (e-book)

Story & content edited by Michael Mendiola
Copyedited by Meghan Pinson and Rhonda Erb
Cover concept by Firewire Creative
Cover composition by Dragon House Creative Ltd. / Christina Cucco
Interior concept & layout by Firewire Creative
Additional interior artwork by Dragon House Creative Ltd. / Christina Cucco
First Edition, February 2020
Printed in the United States of America

This book is
dedicated to my
dear friend, editor,
and creative partner
in crime,

Michael Mendiola.

My words have
never been as safe
as they have been
in your hands.
Thank you for your
patience, creativity,
intelligence, and
determination.

TABLE OF CONTENTS

PART ONE

What is life?

It is the flash of a firefly in the night.

It is the breath of a buffalo in the wintertime.

It is the little shadow which runs across

the grass and loses itself in the sunset.

—Crowfoot

1

A WINTER NIGHT'S DREAM

Zoë stood watching the rain hammering against her bedroom's large bay windows, the torrent streaming down the glass, making her feel as if she was in the depths of an unforgiving sea. It was 3:33 a.m., and although exhausted, she would do anything not to fall asleep. To slumber meant to dream and to dream meant being imprisoned in a nightmare with a spectral presence that, real or imagined, had nearly choked the life from her a few nights prior.

What she needed was a way to slip into sleep's oceanic Underworld while still attached to a line of safety. Having read that dreams were influenced by whatever was last anchored into the subconscious, she sought the purest and most steadfast choice to serve as a lifeline: her mother.

Picking up an old photo of her and her mother from the vanity table, she traced the edges and felt her mother's steady, grounding presence soak into her hands like water into parched skin. She'd been gone nearly two decades, yet Zoë could still feel her, sense her.

The photo was taken by her father on her first day of school, third grade. Her mother was kneeling beside her and pressing her cheek against Zoë's while focusing on the camera as though it were an old friend. Tranquil radiance emanated from her like sun shining through a set of silky curtains. Even though her mother was full-blooded Cherokee with black hair and dark eyes, she had angelic, white-stone pale skin, which she attributed to being "born at night when the moon's kiss was far stronger than the sun's."

Shifting her gaze to her younger—and decidedly awkward—self, Zoë studied the collage of characteristics passed down from her mother: fair skin, high-set cheekbones, slight widow's peak, and raven hair. Absent were her mother's earthen eyes and composed demeanor, and in their place, her father's stormy blue eyes and fiery Irish temper had taken up full and fat-bellied residence.

Continuing to study the picture, she felt disconnected from herself, seeing as the elegant and reserved woman she'd become was far removed from the unlovely yet true-hearted girl in the photo. Past eclipsing present, her life's timeline reversed in her mind's eye until she was eight years old again and marred by an eggplant-colored birthmark covering her right cheek.

It was after school, and Ben Johnson had her pinned up against a tree. Ben was handsome, popular, and until that day, hadn't paid her an ounce of notice. Feeling a flitting sensation in her stomach, she imagined thousands of butterflies were taking flight and fluttering against the inside of her skin as he stepped toward her.

"Close your eyes…I'm going to kiss you."

After doing as he'd instructed, she parted her lips, and when he pressed his body against her and put his hands on her hips, she felt her skin flush with heat. Hungrily his lips brushed hers before he pulled away and slapped the left side of her face with something foul-smelling and wet.

With the sting of his slap reaching all the way down to her toes, she opened her eyes and stared at Ben while a horde of his friends emerged from the surrounding trees, all of them doubled over with laughter. Like a predator toying with stunned prey, he reached out and rubbed another handful of feces-laced mud into her left cheek.

"Now both sides of your face look like shit, you ugly little bitch."

A rumbling clap of thunder yanked her back into the present. Inhaling, she recalled that many years later, she'd found out Ben's father used to beat him—once so badly he'd been hospitalized. In that moment, she had realized that Ben had been cruel because he was broken; he hadn't known kindness, therefore, he wasn't capable of giving it.

She refocused on the now-pristine right side of her face where just a trace of her birthmark—what her mother called her "warrior's mark"—remained. So, as the story goes, duckling had indeed become swan, but beneath the surface of downy white was a blackened undercoat reminding her that she was her mother's warrior—who, for a time, traveled her path with a face others had found offensively unbeautiful.

As she put her mother's photo back on the vanity, the weightiness of sleep summoned her into its arms. With her limbs growing heavy, she turned off a small lamp on her vanity, stood, and guided by the moon's watery light, walked across the room and slipped into bed.

Nestling beneath the covers, she watched the flames dancing inside the marble fireplace while the warmth of her bed burrowed into her bones. Soothed, she took in a deep breath and held the air in her lungs, hoping it would keep her unrest at bay. When she let herself exhale, her breath felt stale and heavy as it drifted into the dim room like fine ashen dust.

"You still awake?"

Lula's thick Scottish brogue hung midair as she made her way to the canopy bed, her presence lifting the weight in the room and parting the sea of darkness as if she were a steady, light-bearing vessel. To Zoë, Lula was three in the body of one: mother-in-residence, keeper, companion.

Lula put a cup on the night table at the side of the bed. "It's chamomile with cinnamon." Easing herself down, she patted Zoë's leg. "Brought you something."

Zoë took a large, well-worn hardback from Lula and read the title to herself: *A Tale of Two Cities.*

Lula watched her for a moment before commenting. "Nothing better when you can't sleep than a good story—and I know you love Dickens."

Zoë felt her heart warm and expand as the darkness parted further. "I can't wait to read it."

Lula leaned forward and gave her a motherly kiss on the forehead, the scent of her Oil of Olay filling the space between them. Lula rose from the bed and crossed the room, leaving a trail of lightness in her wake. Stopping just outside the doorframe, she turned and spoke. "Sweet dreams." With kindness in her eyes, Lula gave her a tender smile, then closed the door behind her.

Running her hand over the large book and sensing the richness of the words seeping through the cover, Zoë felt it beckoning her to lose herself within its worn pages. But unable to keep slumber at bay any longer, she set the book down next to the tea Lula had left for her.

Nestling beneath the covers, she heard the wind picking up until it shook the windows inside their old wooden frames. The rain pounded harder against the glass, causing her heart to thump in her chest while the rustling trees outside cast ill-omened shadows into the room like greedy beasts demanding her attention.

Her mother's words crept into her ears: "You belong amongst the shadows, and when they take you, you'll be forever changed."

Silently, Zoë countered as darkness pulled at the edges of her consciousness:

I don't like change, Mother.

My eyes are forced shut. Against my will, I travel.

I feel dank air fusing with my skin and wonder if the spectral presence has again taken me hostage so as to have a companion, a source of light to illuminate its pervasive darkness. Perhaps I will awaken unscathed, but if past foreshadows future, I fear my death looms.

These are my nights of late—traveling through blackness, feeling like I've gone from being whole to an array of moving pieces, a million fragments in unified motion creating the misty outline of a person. Inside my consciousness, I demand to know what's happening, as it seems my nightly travels are controlled by something malevolent and possessive. But there is no response to my plea; I hear only the echo of my own voice as it mixes with the sound of pounding rain.

Seemingly forced downward by invisible hands, my pieces plummet as my mind merges back into my body with a deafening crash, the jolt of hitting what I assume to be the ground fusing my pieces together, charging the base of my spine and bringing my nerves into one cohesive, streaming current. In response, my eyes fly open, but I can't see through the haze of my watery vision, so while my sight sharpens, I lay stone-still and wait for the sensation of pins and needles to leave my legs and feet.

Digging my fingers into the soft earth, I concentrate on my senses and take in a deep, saturating breath. A sweet floral taste coats my tongue as the woodsy scents of cedar and pine travel to my brain and coax my vision into full clarity.

There is a fine pollen-like dust floating in the air that shimmers as it drifts through beams of moonlight. I send my gaze upward along a stream of light to a canopy of tree branches reaching toward the night sky, which is starry indigo with flat clouds lilting through it like wisps of creamy paint.

Hearing the sound of lapping water, I sit up and shift my focus to a large pond where a mirrored reflection of the clouds on the water's surface make me feel like the world has flipped upside down, the pond now a platform of sky.

In my peripheral vision, I notice broad-leafed tree branches swaying and dipping downward in a gesture that suggests they're acknowledging my presence, a convivial wave from the bark-skinned giants lining the pond's shore.

Feeling the touch of velvety leaves brushing against my arm, I examine a majestic-looking tree next to me, the bark of its trunk lined like a dry riverbed and covered in vines all the way down to its gigantic root system.

I'm sitting between two of the tree's python-sized roots on a bed of tiny, paper-thin wildflowers that feel like pieces of silk against my skin. Patches of moss interspersed throughout the blanket of flowers give the ground a checkerboard illusion, and if I stare long enough, the forest floor appears to come alive with motion.

The richness of the forest stings my eyes with its vibrancy, yet as real as this dreamscape seems, I know I'm forming the world around me like a cinematographer creating a scene on film. Once awake, I'll remember very little—only remnants of what I've seen, felt, and encountered.

Sitting here surrounded by the undeniable strength of the trees, I want to cocoon myself in the comfort of the forest as I did when I was a child. I've always felt safer in the woods than I did in real life, a feeling that was also shared by my mother. I'm certain trees are prominent in this dream because she loved them—to her they were old friends—and encircled by one of my mother's favorite things, I feel her presence like a whisper.

I can almost see her running toward the still waters of the pond, bits of refracted moonlight painting her smooth skin as she dives into the water and disappears below its dark, glittery surface. Like a sin-ridden soul seeking baptism, part of me wishes I could follow her and submerge myself beneath the moon's liquid reflection just as she and I had done in a similar pond when I was a child. After exhausting ourselves in the water, we'd lay beneath the trees while my mother told stories of our ancestors, our Clan, and how everything she knew had been passed down to her from my great-great-grandmother, a gifted medicine woman.

Having failed to carry on the traditions of our Clan, I find these memories so far from my current existence that they seem like someone else's life, and to look at me, you'd never know I have Cherokee blood in my veins. I'm focused on the feeling of shame leaching into my bones, knowing I took my mother's teachings for granted, when my thoughts are interrupted by the sound of something moving through the trees along the pond's shore to my right.

The underbrush at the base of one of the trees shakes, and I struggle to my feet. In a blur of movement, two small creatures scurry from the bushes, slip into the pond, and vanish beneath the water's surface. Then one by one they reappear, and with the moonlight shining on their fur, I realize they are otters.

I can't help but smile and recall how I used to beg my mother to read the Cherokee tale of The Rabbit and the Otter over and over when I was little. As though commenting on my recollection, the otters make soft sounds as they play, rolling around one another before disappearing beneath the dark water.

Without their chatter, the breeze drifting through the trees sounds like the forest is speaking, gentle words meant only for me, and as I inhale the fragrant night air, the forest's voice mixes with that of my mother: "The forest knows you better than you know yourself. When it speaks, you must listen."

The echo of her words merges into the sound of someone breathing behind me, and when I feel something brush up against my back, I turn, but no one is there. Now facing away from the pond, I scan a narrow moonlit path a few feet away, and while searching it for movement or any indication of who or what may be nearby, I hear violent thrashing in the water behind me.

After whirling around, I study the pond and surrounding woods only to find everything dead-still—even the water's surface is glassy smooth and without so much as a ripple. With the air condensing, my stomach twists into knots and my muscles contract from the surge of adrenaline racing through my system.

Wetness seeps between my toes and I smell the unmistakable iron-laden stench of blood rising from the forest floor. I look down and my heart breaks: the otters lay at my feet, blood leaking freely from wounds on their necks, their dark eyes lifeless and their faces distorted from the fear of whatever just assassinated them.

With the sour scent of burning sugar wafting toward me from the pond, I watch a dark mist float along the water, then stop in front of a bank of trees on the shore. Swirling, blackening, and taking on a solidified human-like form, the mist materializes between two trees before blending back into the night like a specter.

For a split second, I see it again—closer this time—then it's gone. I'm starting to sweat and the anxiety rushing through me is strangling my will to run. I know it's close to me, as I feel my cells being crushed by the weight of its darkness.

When a slight movement catches my eye, I look toward a tree a few feet away. It is there, thin beams of light shining down on the right side of its body, revealing the muscular detail of its imposing semisolid shape. Illuminated by the moonlight, its full form is clear: male, strong, and formidable.

It, or rather he, pulses with pure, unrelenting sexual aggression, the incarnation of testosterone so potent it's ignited and plumed into the disembodied, smoke-filled form of a man. He is searching me and drinking in every part of my body like I'm the antidote to whatever poison has eroded the flesh I sense he's desperate to regain. With his eyeless stare boring into me, my blood thickens and hardens as if the liquids inside me are refusing his desire to consume them.

Then, like a vaporous ghost, he fuses with the night and rushes toward me, the odor of singed sugar slamming up my nostrils. His very presence demands my submission. He needs my spirit inside his, and I'm certain he'll not rest until he's made it so: I am the day to his night, he the black moon to my sun.

Everything about him is calculating, and as my thoughts dip into blackness and my mind separates from my body, his smoky hands wrap around my throat. But before my thoughts go blank, he cuts off my flow of air, then purposefully stops short of strangling me to death.

"Zoë? You all right?"

Heated and sweating, she sat up and felt her body tense as Lula pounded on the bedroom door. Swinging her legs over the edge of the bed, she halted at the sight of dried blood covering her feet. A twinge in the pit of her stomach echoed Lula's nervous knock as she bellowed, "I'm awake, Lula!"

"You okay, dear?"

"I'm fine."

She knew she'd failed to quell Lula's anxiety, a fact evidenced by the tone of Lula's voice as she probed. "Why'd you lock the door?"

While surveying the keyless brass lock beneath the doorknob, she could feel Lula's concern ambling toward her through the closed door like a love-starved kitten. Steadying the tremble in her throat, Zoë spoke. "Just getting in the shower."

"Well, breakfast is on the table."

"I'll be down in a bit." A pregnant silence filled the space between them, and as Lula tried the door one last time, Zoë sat motionless until Lula descended the stairs.

Part of her felt guilty for withholding the details of her dreams, as under normal circumstances there was little she wouldn't share with Lula. Yet how could she explain something to Lula that she didn't understand herself?

Standing on her heels, she eased weight onto her stained feet, then walked toward the bathroom. After taking a few steps, she noticed the missing brass key lying on her bedside table. Having picked it up, she unwound a piece of ivy from around its handle while a disjointed film replayed in her mind: the forest, the dead otters, the smoky demon—all still part of her, like shadows.

In an attempt to disarm the images reaching out from her dreams, she closed her eyes and whispered, "Breathe, Zoë. Just breathe." Pressing herself back into the safety of her architected world, she felt the tension in her body begin to wane.

Out of necessity, she had carefully constructed her life, making sure every thought and action had an exact purpose. Such discipline allowed her to anticipate her clients' needs without having to expose the private aspects of herself. Whether sexual or intellectual, the psyches of others were what she sought to unlock, leaving little time to delve into her own; but she liked it that way, as it kept things simple and anchored her in the lives of those who required her care.

Feeling calmer, she made her way toward the warmth of the heated bathroom floor. Once there, she removed her nightgown, looked at herself in the full-length mirror, and felt her blood run cold. Stepping closer to the mirror, she discovered a set of soot-inked handprints around her neck.

Somehow, the remnants of a supposed dream had slipped through the cracks of time and space into her waking life. A flash of panic gripped her as the foundation of her structured world weakened.

The shadows have come for me, Mother, but I will not be taken.

2

'TWAS BRILLIG...

The cab slammed to a halt. "Here, lady."

She handed the driver two twenties, knowing the ride cost far less. After opening the door, she stepped out of the cab as someone cried out, "Watch it!"

A firm hand yanked her from the path of an oncoming car and pressed her against the side of the cab, making her realize she'd exited street-side rather than on the sidewalk.

Catching her breath, she turned and focused on the petite Asian woman standing beside her. The woman's doll-like features belied the fierceness of her stare as she sized Zoë up with slate-colored eyes. But before Zoë could thank her, the woman got into the cab and closed the door.

Zoë watched the cab pull away, then crossed the street and stepped onto the sidewalk. Walking down Park Avenue, she fumbled through her purse in search of the sticky note with Dr. Lawson's address. Locating it, she discovered that as usual, she was going in the wrong direction and would now be late.

Whenever close to being tardy, she'd hear her father's accented voice roaring in her head: "Zoë Maria Hall, bein' late is the sign of someone unkempt, mentally disorganized, and unable to plan properly. It's shite. A true lady should always be prompt, polite, and polished."

Thoughts tousled, she reached Dr. Lawson's building and made her way around the corner to the private entrance, which was marked by a plain brass nameplate. Part of her felt like Dorothy outside the Wizard of Oz's royal palace as she pushed the jade-colored buzzer next to the door.

Once it clicked open, she turned the brass doorknob and entered. Hearing the door close behind her, she gathered her resolve and approached a sleek desk to her right, behind which sat a middle-aged receptionist who was slim, tiny, and tidy.

After a thorough once-over, the woman addressed her. "Good afternoon. Please take a seat. He'll be with you shortly."

Studying the receptionist, Zoë deduced that this was the type of woman who cut the crusts off her sandwiches, shined her patent pumps daily, and even went so far as to iron and starch her underclothes. Try as she might, she couldn't stop staring.

The little woman's overly lined lips grew tight. "Is there a problem, dear?"

"No, not at all."

She walked to a white leather couch in the waiting room, then sat and crossed her long legs while twisting the bracelet on her wrist—a nervous habit she'd had since childhood. Stroking the braided leather and copper wires intertwined beneath her fingertips, she found the scarlet stone at the bracelet's center.

Tracing the carved "L.D." in the stone's center, she smiled at the secret nickname given to her by her mother: Little Dragon. A childhood memory played in her mind's eye like an old vignette film, and like an outside observer, she watched her younger self kick a fir tree in the backyard of her house.

Having thrust her foot into the unsuspecting tree a second time, she was winding up for a third when her mother appeared out of nowhere. "Little Dragon, he can help you if you stop kicking him."

She turned to face her mother. "*Him?* Him who?"

With a gleam in her earthen eyes, her mother explained, "A tree is unyielding, strong, and able to withstand the cruelest of weather. It puts deep roots into the ground, gaining nutrients from the soil, while its leaves gain sustenance from the sun. It has learned how to live in both worlds—the world of light and the world of shadows." Feeling her mother's wisdom pour over her like warm water, Zoë was calm, clear, and steady.

"You have much fire, but it must be tempered with earth—you can learn from this tree." Drawing in closer, her mother whispered, "Besides, you're hurting his feelings."

A sudden gust of wind whipped down the little hillside behind their house and wrapped her mother's thick black hair around them until nothing existed but her mother and their secret world.

"May I get you a glass of water?" The tiny woman tilted her head, waiting for a response as Zoë came back into the present.

"I'm fine, thank you."

The receptionist eyed her for a moment, then returned her attention to the razor-thin computer screen sitting on her desk.

In theory, seeking therapy to explore her dreams had seemed like a sensible pursuit, but Zoë wanted to run and escape this stark lobby with the too-tidy lady at the front desk. Panic rose in her throat like an icy liquid monster but stopped in its tracks as a warm voice inquired, "Ms. Hall?"

"Yes?"

"I'm Dr. Lawson."

She stood and shook his hand with such vigor, she swore his eyes bulged. "Zoë. Nice to meet you."

Following him across a black-and-white mosaic-tiled floor into a narrow hallway, she found herself zigzagging behind him like a drunken bird ill prepared for impending flight.

When they reached his office, Dr. Lawson stood at the door and beckoned her inside. As if in slow motion, Zoë brushed by him close enough to see the flecks of amber in his hazel eyes.

The doorway seemed to suck her in, then throw her into a soft leather chair as he inquired, "Can I get you anything?"

"No, thank you."

Taking silent notes, she appraised him. He was handsome and well-manicured, with soft tufts of grey hair at the temples, and as he leaned over to get a pen from his desk, she noticed that the argyle of his socks matched his sweater. Yet something was off. His ensemble, so well thought out, seemed incongruous with his professorially messy hair and visible five o'clock shadow. For reasons that escaped her, she felt the icy monster reform in her throat.

Dr. Lawson settled into a firm, boxy chair and focused on her. "Ms. Hall, where would you like to begin?"

Dr. Lawson watched Zoë wind a strand of raven-colored hair around her pale finger as her perfume snaked its way across the room and flirted with his nostrils. Most of their session had been consumed by her sly circumvention, her bright smile not quite concealing the fear in her eyes. With their time almost at an end, he wondered why she seemed determined to keep herself from revealing even the plainest of details. Considering himself a patient man, he was surprised at how she'd managed to step on his nerves.

"Ms. Hall, how do you feel I can help you?"

Parting her full lips, she inhaled and glanced at him sideways like a dog hearing a strange sound. "Maybe they're not enough…"

She sank deeper into the leather armchair as he probed. "Who?"

Looking out the window of his office, she responded as if speaking sideways would diminish the intimacy that was threatening to develop between them. "They're my business—men. It's all I know."

He prodded while his pulse quickened. "How long have men been your business?"

Hesitating just enough to let him know the subject was raw, she opined, "For a long time—and perhaps I need more." She stopped winding the strand around her finger.

"What does 'needing more' mean to you?" he inquired.

"Honestly, I'm not sure." She searched his face with a stormy, blue-eyed stare.

Attempting to coax her toward him, he inferred, "Is that why you're here?" He felt her forced silence encircling him like cellophane. "Outside of your men, do you have other relationships?"

Fidgeting with the bracelet on her wrist, she twisted it while responding, "Yes. A few."

"But you prefer interacting with men."

Brightening, she quipped, "Don't you?"

Leaning an elbow on the arm of his chair, he searched his thoughts before replying. "It depends."

She stopped twisting her bracelet. "What made you choose your profession?"

With unflinching honesty, he answered, "My mother was mentally ill." He pressed her. "And what made you choose yours?"

Her eyes glassed over as she spoke almost to herself. "I can't really say. My grandfather, I guess. Maybe that's why my dreams are…"

Watching her body tense, he swore the heavy silence in the room coated the office walls. "You feel your grandfather and your dreams are related?"

She continued. "Tangentially, maybe. A twisted side of masculinity morphing into a nightmare."

He delved further. "How often do your nightmares occur?"

A flush of pink crept across her skin. "Nightly. Savagely."

Jotting down a few notes, he questioned, "What do you mean, 'savagely'?"

"Violent. Deadly."

The obvious self-reliance she possessed waned enough for him to see how terrifying the nightmares were for her. What he needed to determine was what part of her waking life was causing the unrest, as he suspected it to be the origin of her dreams. "With your men, who is in control?"

She crossed her legs. "I am."

"Within the encounters, what's your role?"

"I'm not sure what you're asking."

"With men, are you friend, mother, seducer—"

She interjected, "Seduction is a selfish act. Feeling wanted or powerful by manipulating someone's emotions—I've no interest in that."

To him, she was becoming clearer: fiery intellect, barriers of steel, and a heart she hid from almost everyone. What he wanted to know was why. "Then, at its core, what's your role?"

Placing a gentle hand on the arm of the chair, she expounded, "I'm a living journal for those without the courage to write. Their secrets, their fears, their desires are safe with me."

In observing her attempt to describe her role, he understood how crucial it was for her to have one. She needed to be defined and she demanded things around her be as well, all a telltale sign that her safety had at one point been in question. On some level, she had been betrayed, robbed of a childhood, tricked by fate; at least, that was his instinct.

She continued. "I suppose it's not really 'a role,' but 'roles.' Caretaker. Servant to the lost. Keeper of sorrows."

"Part woman, part vault."

Light seemed to shine out through her eyes as she replied, "A raw distillation. But accurate."

They observed one another for a moment as she smiled. He felt as though a rush of pure oxygen was pushing into the room. "So where does a vault go to unburden?"

A veil of sadness draped her face. "Maybe it's eventually crushed by its own weight. Releasing its locked secrets counters its very purpose."

He surmised the nightmares were a derivative of what was leaking from the vault she held inside her. In his gut, he felt she was a good-hearted woman, but he was quite certain she didn't see herself in that light. "Don't you deserve the same right to unburden as those who seek your care?"

She shifted her gaze toward a small vase sitting on the coffee table between them. "Well, in keeping with our metaphors, you could say that a vase only seeks something to hold. The vase itself doesn't seek to *be* held."

The look in her eyes informed him that she'd divulged as much as she was willing, at least for now.

Reaching down, she retrieved her purse. "Our time is up."

Although she stood, he remained seated in his chair while watching her walk across the room. Once in front of him, she offered her hand and confirmed. "See you next week?"

Returning the firmness of her handshake, he replied, "I look forward to it, Ms. Hall."

Once she'd left the room, he leaned back into his chair and replayed their conversation in his mind, wondering if she would actually return for a second session.

3

HIT & RUN

Leaving the snow-dusted concrete of the street behind her, Zoë walked up the stairs to 66 Jane Street feeling frustration gnawing at the base of her spine. A series of questions plagued her thoughts, heaviest amongst them being why she hadn't been able to tell Dr. Lawson details about the presence in her dreams. Perhaps discussing it, or rather him, aloud made the nightmares real and gave him life; images haunting her nights need not be disentombed during the day.

A blast of arctic wind whipped down the street and froze her thoughts midstream. She stiffened against the cold while like an icy knife, her mother's voice pierced her thoughts: "There are two wolves within us all, the black and the white. The wolf you choose to feed is the one who wins."

Then I will starve them both.

Once at the top of the stairs, she opened the thick wooden door to her house and welcomed the warm air colliding with her chilled skin. "Lula?"

"You're late."

Walking into the kitchen where Lula hovered over the stove like an alchemist, she noticed that Lula's bright-red hair, which was usually pinned up in a French twist, resembled an abandoned bird's nest.

Lula spoke over her shoulder. "He'll be here soon. You'd better get to it. I'll be up in a jiff."

Making her way toward the curved mahogany staircase that led to the second floor, Zoë was about to pass the sitting room to her left when a lightbulb housed in one of the Victorian sconces popped and went dark.

Lightbulbs were a common casualty she'd always attributed to the house's old wiring. Yet even after the electrical system was replaced last year, she still couldn't keep the sconces and lamps lit. Lula always said, "You and this house have fiery wires. You two better learn to negotiate light. You know I hate the dark."

Almost at the top of the stairs, she watched Lula's enormous orange tabby cat, Lucille, appear from the darkness and make her way down the stairs. But instead of her customary behavior of darting by and dismissing her, Lucille stopped mid-stair and softened her face as she twitched her fat butterscotch tail from side to side.

As had always been the case, Zoë and Lucille tolerated one another for the sheer purpose of keeping harmony in the family. They were like two sisters who, if not for familial relations, wouldn't give one another the time of day. Normally with Zoë this near, the hairs on Lucille's back would stick straight up, but in this moment, she was calm and relaxed.

Zoë stood still, crossed her arms, and stared into the cat's downy round face, finding it peculiar that although Lucille had been with Lula since they first met twenty years ago, she hadn't seemed to age a day. Maybe it was because Lula pampered Lucille like a child. God forbid the damn thing eat something out of a can like a normal cat.

Without warning, Lucille crouched down, launched herself claws-first onto Zoë's purse, and began shredding its tassel to bits with her needlelike teeth. Hissing, Lucille hung from the purse, her front claws tearing into the virgin leather. Zoë was about to snatch Lucille from the bag and hurtle her down the staircase when Lula called to her from the foot of the stairs.

"Lucille!" Lucille's eyes were like saucers, bits of red leather tassel hanging from her chin. Lula tromped up the stairs and grabbed her. "Bad kitty."

Lucille leapt from Lula's grasp, bolting down the stairs like her rear end was on fire.

Furious, Zoë shot a sideways glance at Lula. "Lula, so help me—"

Lula watched Lucille tear around the corner and into the kitchen before ushering Zoë up the stairs, speaking in a bossy, mother-knows-best kind of tone. "Up you go! You need to change."

They walked up the final few steps and crossed the hallway into Zoë's bedroom, where she switched on the light and dropped her mangled purse onto a sage-colored satin chair. Beginning to undress, she shifted her focus toward the high wood-beamed ceilings and studied the room's lavish Victorian décor.

There was something exceptional about 66 Jane Street. It was her sanctuary, her friend, and in many ways, her protector. To her, living warmth emanated from the walls, a quality that made her feel the house wasn't just a construct of wood and steel, but rather, one of flesh and bone.

Lula lit a pile of kindling, replaced the fire screen, then zipped across the room, leaving Zoë to watch the fire breathe its first tiny flames before shooting so high it licked the outside of the marble mantel.

Rummaging through an antique wardrobe, Lula retrieved the vintage 1940s dressing gown and embroidered scarlet corset that Zoë often wore for her most fastidious client. As was customary, Zoë gripped the bedpost while Lula fitted the corset around her tall and curvaceous frame.

"Go."

Wrapping the corset's laces around her fingers, Lula pulled so hard Zoë almost toppled over. Lula let out a hardy laugh. "Don't know my own strength!"

Inhaling a quick breath, Zoë prepped herself for the next heave of cinching as Lula gave a final tug, then tied off the laces and tucked them in. Placing the dressing gown over Zoë's shoulders, Lula turned her around.

"A vision. Now, give us a smile."

Zoë replied dryly, "I would if there was any air left in my body."

Moving away from the bed, she walked across the room and sat at her vanity, then let down her hair and applied her signature red lipstick while

Lula stowed her day clothes and tidied the bedroom.

The doorbell chimed and Lula quipped in response, "The Prince of Darkness has arrived." She winked, then scuttled from the room on heavy feet. She had the endearing yet annoying habit of walking on her heels. There was no wondering where she was in the house: HEEL toe, HEEL toe…

After hearing the front door shut, Zoë listened to Lula chatting up Mr. Llewellyn as he came up the stairs. "Winter's certainly come in like a lion, hasn't it?"

His voice was self-assured and calculated. "It has."

Walking to the chaise lounge, Zoë saw a blur of orange fur as Lucille ran by the door and down the hallway. Lucille loathed Mr. Llewellyn, and by past accounts, the feeling was mutual.

Sitting on the chaise, Zoë felt her focus pulled by the weight of Mr. Llewellyn's presence as he came down the hall, his walk confident and the rhythm of his steps succinct, like strong punctuation in a sharply constructed sentence.

Despite her efforts, he'd only revealed the obvious: he was powerful, intelligent, and controlled. But behind his dominant façade, she sensed a buried secret and was sure that at some point in his life he had been disassembled. A broken toy soldier left in the attic, once fresh from the box, now armless, headless, and without identity.

While thinking of Mr. Llewellyn's plight, she felt a kinship toward Dr. Lawson, seeing as she, too, fixed people. Sex and the subsequent money were inconsequential, as she needed neither; her true passion was for reassembling and liberating the men who came to her.

Draping herself on the chaise with one bare thigh revealed, she angled her back toward the door, knowing that her cancellation of his appointment the previous week would result in displeasure he was certain to express.

The door to her bedroom creaked open, then closed, and as he approached from behind, she could smell his woodsy cologne and shined shoes. Feeling her face flush, she turned to find him picking imaginary lint from his suit while boring a hole into her with his pointed stare.

"Why did you cancel our appointment last week?"

In the firelight—tailored suit, blond hair, and fair skin—he was striking, magnificent in an almost brutal manner.

She sharpened her gaze. "I had other business."

Removing his suit jacket, he walked toward the chaise, then took off his tie with enough force to cause a lock of hair to fall from its molded position and come to rest on his long lashes. There was a hint of fire in his eyes as he moved closer, but it wasn't born from lust; rather, it was something more menacing—hatred?

Now in front of her, he threaded his hand through her hair until his palm came to rest at the base of her neck. A few of his fingers dug into her skin as he pulled her to a standing position before running his strong hands down the sides of her body and letting them come to rest on her hips.

It was unusual for him to touch her, and over time she'd grown accustomed to his measured, cold demeanor. Yet in the moment unfolding between them, she swore he was contemplating kissing her, an act he knew she'd never permit.

Sensing her silent refusal, he pulled his leather belt through the loops of his slacks, shoved it into her hand, then turned and lowered himself onto his knees in front of her.

"Hit me."

They'd flirted with semi-violence in the past, but he'd never asked her to hit him.

He rotated his head enough to make eye contact, then stared at her with a seriousness she found disturbing.

"Don't hold back."

It was clear that his request wasn't a want, but a need, and with that as her impetus, she positioned herself closer behind him. "Where?"

He demanded, "Anywhere."

Putting a firm hand on his back, she pushed him forward until his chest was pressing against the chaise's velvety surface.

He peered up at her with a steely stare. "As hard as you can."

Seeing the insistent look in his eyes, she hit him. A small, helpless breath escaped his lungs as he ordered, "Again."

Clutching the belt, she raised her arm and hit him with a force she didn't think herself capable of exhibiting. With his eyes closed and mouth open, his frantic breath scorched the air around them while a guttural groan left his lips. "Harder."

Turning the belt around, she readied the buckled end, then raised her arm again and cracked a series of vicious blows.

"Make me bleed."

Sight narrowing, she hit him so hard and with such force that time seemed to stop, the only sound resonating in her ears being that of metal on flesh until he collapsed to the floor.

Seeing blood seeping through the back of his stark-white shirt, she placed her hand on his leaking wounds, unable to remember how many times she'd hit him. Part of her wanted to take him in her arms as a way of counteracting the violence he'd suffered at her hand, but she knew that wasn't something he'd want. Instead, she continued standing over him with her hand on top of his blood-soaked shirt.

He rose from the floor and retrieved his suit jacket and tie. Never looking at her, he pulled a wad of bills from his pocket and laid them down on the chaise before exiting the room without a word.

Back aching, he descended the stairs into the foyer while Ms. McKenna came clomping down the hallway to escort him out, her bright, shiny face irritating him in his present mood.

"Good evening, then, Mr. Llewellyn. Always a pleasure."

Noticing the vein pumping in her neck, he wanted to reach out and bring it to violent cessation.

"Ms. McKenna."

He was harsher than he'd meant to be, but she didn't seem to notice.

"Please, call me Lula."

He wanted to dislike her, this eccentric gatekeeper to Zoë's house. He'd been seeing Zoë for a while now and still couldn't reduce Ms. McKenna down to her base; there were just two people by whom he'd ever been stumped, and they both lived in a brownstone on Jane Street.

Ms. McKenna helped him put on his heavy wool coat, then handed him his gloves. She opened the front door.

"Nighty night!"

He stepped outside, the intense cold seizing his breath. Finding her jovial smile maddening, he watched Ms. McKenna close the door behind him.

Walking down the icy stairs, he realized how warm Zoë's house had been and once he was on the sidewalk, the wind came thrashing down the street and almost froze his feet to the pavement.

He climbed into his black Mercedes and settled into the leather seat, jerking forward when his bloodied back met the stiff cotton of his dress shirt. A jolt of searing pain shot down his spine like lightning.

He closed his eyes. It was bliss.

4

A NIGHTMARE ON JANE STREET

Depleted, she filled the bathtub with water, feeling desperate to sink herself into its cleansing abyss. Placing her bloodstained fingers beneath the faucet, she watched the stream of water turn a temporary shade of fleshy pink while a flash of the leaking wound on Mr. Llewellyn's back raced through her mind. As the iron-laden scent of his blood mixed with the hot steam, she felt ashamed by her loss of control and unapologetic brutality. Yet she'd done what he'd asked: he begged her to hit him.

She undressed, then climbed into the hot water and sank into its liquid haven, her heartbeat creating small ripples that coaxed her to relax. Letting herself succumb to the peacefulness of the moment, she felt her thoughts becoming tranquil and her mind clearing while strands of her hair floated around her shoulders and swayed with the water's rhythmic waves.

Shifting her focus upward, she looked out a small round window on the far wall. Powdery snow gathering on the outside ledge caused moonlight to filter through the window and across the bathroom floor in a muted beam of light.

Bathed by the moon's starry stream, she inched her body deeper until her chin touched the water's surface. Reflected candlelight from the pillar candles lining the bathtub turned the water into a creamy golden sea. When she gazed into the candles' flames, everything around her seemed to disappear.

Her father used to say, "There's magic in a flame," a statement she'd failed to grasp until now. It did indeed appear there was a touch of the divine in the flame, its glowing light a welcome distraction from the dread she felt creeping along the edge of her spine.

Closing her eyes, she forced herself to take a deep breath while shadows crept in from all sides.

I'm thousands of moving pieces in inky blackness, forced through what feels like empty space, my body refusing the commands I'm giving it: to open my eyes, to wake. Cool air whips around me and I feel the pieces of my frame splaying outward as if I'm a conscious, propelled form of snow.

In my mind's eye, I see the misty outline of my frame moving through the darkness like phosphorescent plankton in a cold, lightless sea. Then the particles making up my form slam into what feels like a wall while my mind crashes back into my body.

The musty smell of damp stone fills my nose, and as my sight comes into focus, I find myself standing upright. As if my limbs have been asleep for hours, they struggle to return to life. The feeling of blood regaining its flow in my arms is painful, so I open and close my fists, hoping to speed the process. As my legs find their way back to normalcy, I exhale and notice that when my breath hits the cold air, it turns into a thick cloud of steam.

I watch the steam floating through rays of watercolor moonlight filtering downward along the curved walls of the circular cathedral in which I now stand. Studying the cathedral's gothic architecture, high stone walls, and exposed wooden beams, I find they combine to form a kind of royal gesture and for a moment, I feel I'm alone in the private sanctuary of a queen. There's a sacredness about this place, a purity that emanates from the stone walls as if they are sentient and breathing. And were I to delve into the base of my gut—although it's disconcerting—I'd say this place is familiar.

With my spine feeling its bone turned to ice, my skin forms tiny bumps; in response, I wrap my arms around my torso and realize I'm naked. Looking around the cathedral, I search for anything I may use as makeshift clothing, and upon seeing a long silken tapestry hanging on a wall, I put one labored foot in front of the other until I'm standing in front of the tapestry.

I pull on one of the corners, and with just a few tugs, the rod breaks free on one side and releases the tapestry onto the stone floor along with a cloud of fine dust. Having retrieved the fabric, I wrap it around my body and tuck in one corner at the top like a towel.

Although grateful for the warmth the tapestry offers, I'm in need of relief from the bite in the air and scan the cathedral for any indication of an adjoining room or potential source of heat.

Looking to my left, I see the thin outline of what looks like a door built into the wall. Yet upon closer inspection, I see it's not a door, but an inset stone panel covered in ancient, symbol-based writing.

Glancing around the room, I notice there are twelve similar carved panels and that the only portion of wall without a panel is where the tapestry had been. That section of wall is smooth save for an embedded iron latch and several lines of etched cursive writing above it.

Enough light shines down through the glass ceiling for me to get a clearer look at the writing:

> Asdans four, though you be blessed,
> You brothers endure at her bequest.
> Inside these walls it begins and ends,
> For within her veins is the power to bend;
> Time, matter, and elements grand,
> All rest within the palm of her hand.
> Bloodstained skin and wolven born,
> The thirteenth rose will rule by thorn.
> From a distant place of one and three
> Comes our life, our death, our destiny.

Reading the poem again, I feel the words seeping into my skin. Continuing to let my eyes pass over each word in slow motion, I realize the longer I read, the more deeply the letters appear to carve themselves into the stone's surface.

After taking in the poem's last line, I shift my focus to the embedded latch, noticing it's connected to a lock-like mechanism housed beneath it. Taking a moment to examine the lock's intricate gears, I'm unable to stop myself from smiling. Looking around the room and taking in its details a second time, I understand the elements of this dream and do something rare where my father is concerned, which is to think of him with even an ounce of fondness.

Represented by the room's cathedral style and structure are my father's rooted Irish Catholic beliefs, while the tapestry around me represents the most beloved role my father ever played: Hamlet. I still see him reenacting the scene when Hamlet kills Polonius, who is concealed behind a tapestry—Father using that scene as a parallel for every life circumstance with which I was presented.

I turn my gaze back to the iron latch in the wall and hear my father's thick Irish accent bouncing around in my mind: "Every man has a beautiful tapestry he shows the world. It's what's behind it you should worry about." Yet another life lesson to be learned from the pages of a play, and in this moment, I'm aware that Shakespeare was more of a father to me than my own.

I lift the latch and feel something sharp slice into the side of my finger, causing me to withdraw my hand. The cut isn't as deep as the amount of blood would indicate, and in so knowing, I refocus on the wall.

I watch my blood drip from the top of the latch into the lock's gears and, like oil to a rusty machine, the gears turn counterclockwise. The sound of grinding stone fills the room, and I turn around just in time to see each of the carved panels begin to slide sideways into the wall like giant pocket doors.

In unison, all twelve panels retract into the wall, revealing the large gates that had been concealed behind them. The gates are constructed of thick iron bars with welded Roman numerals at their centers, and the terrain beyond each gate appears to be of varying types.

My father would often present me with puzzles and mysteries to solve as a child, and with this dream draped in his memory, I suppose this is a recreation of sorts. I find this situation irritatingly relevant to my father; the gates are closed, and I assume locked, yet the only apparent way out of the room. Like a ripple in time, I hear my father's gruff voice in my head: "The answer's usually staring at your arse while you're lookin' in the other direction!"

Determined, I walk to each of the gates and rattle the bars to confirm they're locked. Cold and frustrated, I look up and deduce that without the superhero ability to leap through the domed stained-glass ceiling above, I'm trapped.

The air in the room thickens, and when it drifts into my lungs I feel like I've inhaled sludge-laden smoke. Pulling my focus from the ceiling, I'm about to try the gates once more when behind me, I hear creaking iron. After turning around, I find one of the gates ajar.

With trepidation, I walk toward the gate—which harbors a massive inset Roman numeral IX—while examining a dark, sinister, tree-lined path just beyond its unforgiving iron bars. The forest surrounding the path is not the same lush green of my previous dreams, but rather gloomy and grey with blackened trees that are leafless, smooth, and misshapen.

The sickly sweet scent of burning sugar slithers over my shoulder and begins creeping into my nostrils. Heart racing, I turn away from the open gate and watch as a fine black mist floats along the stone floor of the room.

Panic rises in me while with every passing second the mist grows denser and takes on a formidable male form. In the confines of the enclosed circular room, I realize how large he is, and before my mind can protest, I slip through the gate.

In the grips of adrenaline and fear, I bolt down the path knowing in my gut this decision wasn't the right one. I'm unable to navigate for lack of light; and the farther I run, the more the moonlight is sucked up by the blackness of the forest.

My instincts are telling me to veer off the path, which I do with a heavy dose of reluctance. I make it a short distance before realizing the terrain beneath my feet is too difficult to traverse barefoot. Not knowing what else to do, I duck behind a tree, then lean against its gummy bark as my skin begins to crawl.

From the direction of the cathedral, the scent of burning sugar is weak but getting stronger. I feel him stalking me and, worse, I'm sure he knows my exact position. Exhaling, I attempt to clear my mind and settle my nerves enough to find a way out of this nightmarish forest. Hearing a twig crack behind me, I look over my shoulder, and although my eyes aren't yet adjusted to the darkness, I'm certain I see someone standing a few feet away. I can tell by the person's outline that it's not him even though his scent continues growing stronger—closer.

Whoever is moving toward me looks like a ghost, their wispy frame and pale skin visible even in the darkness. In response, I tense the muscles in my legs, readying to run.

An urgent whisper shoots through the trees: "Don't move."

A woman's pale face comes into full view, her long white hair glowing against the fabric of the dark robe she wears. Her stature is lesser than mine, more delicate and fragile, but there's no mistaking the raw power radiating from her.

She turns to me, her eyes so large they look almost inhuman, and if ever my mind were to create the image of an angel, she would be it.

"Come." Her whisper is controlled and calm, all the things I am not.

Taking my hand, she leads me forward, navigating the forest without fear; and in this, I presume she must know something I don't, because my senses tell me we are being stalked by the devil himself.

We're back on the path now, walking toward the cathedral structure, and for the life of me I can't understand why we aren't running in the opposite direction, as all my instincts are telling me to turn around and get as far away from the cathedral as possible.

I catch a glimpse of him materializing at the end of the path like a black stain smudging itself into existence, his scent pungent and singeing the inside of my nose like sugary acid. We're mere feet from the structure, and I still can't wrap my mind around why she would be leading us toward him. But after we take a few more steps, he vanishes, absorbed by the murky night.

Once we reach the cathedral, she ushers me through the open gate and back into the circular room. I turn around, expecting to see her following me, but instead she's closing the gate and trapping herself on the other side.

Echoing her spirit, her gaze is kind and expressive. We're connected in a way that leaves me feeling desperate to help her. I rush toward the gate and yank on the bars, but it's locked.

Her hands are soft and small, and as they grip mine between the bars, I feel an unbearable electric current racing up my arms. There's no doubt in my mind that this is the end of her life, and by the look in her eyes, she knows it too.

"Zoë, I choose you. But you must choose them." Although her voice is calm, there is sadness in her face. "Their fate rests in your hands."

Before I can process what she's said, I see him appear behind her, a hell storm rising. Swelling and twisting like a nuclear plume, he pulls her entire body into the center of his cloudy blackness until they are one.

I back away from the gate and watch in horror as her eyes fill with a thick dark mist. Every inch of her skin turns black, as if death is consuming her from the inside out until the bones in her face sink inward and it looks like she's beginning to rot. I'm watching her decompose while she's still alive.

Appearing connected to her both in life and impending death, the structure around me quakes and large chunks of stone break off from the walls and crash to the ground. Rushing to the center of the room, I turn in time to see her burst apart, everything moving in slow motion as the walls crumble and shards of colored glass plummet from the domed ceiling. Having no way to escape, I drop to my knees and shield my head while the entire room explodes around me.

5

THIS WAY COMES

Zoë felt sharp claws digging into the flesh of her chest, causing her to shoot up into a sitting position as Lucille leapt onto the wet tile. Soaked and naked, Zoë inhaled and leaned against the outside of the bathtub wondering how she ended up in the middle of her bathroom floor.

After taking a moment to gather her thoughts and bring her mind into the room, she stood and grabbed a towel. Drying off, she glanced down at Lucille, who stared at her while sitting dead-still, disquiet etched into her ginger face. Lucille's whiskers were bright-red at the ends where she had brushed Zoë's lipstick, tiny paintbrushes readying themselves to color a dark and bloody bit of artwork.

Hearing Lula's soft knock, she threw the towel around her body while Lucille raced across the room at top speed, slid on the floor, and hit the door with a thud.

Lula opened the door and looked at Lucille, who was shaking her head and sneezing. "Was that you hittin' the door, you poor thing? Were you trapped in here?" She picked up Lucille and rocked her while eyeing Zoë.

"What happened?" Stroking the little white tuft of hair under Lucille's chin, Lula continued, "I called you for dinner at ten of eight. It's almost half past now."

"I fell asleep." Zoë made her way out of the bathroom to her bed and crawled beneath the covers.

"I've been cookin' all day. Aren't you hungry?"

"Not really."

The thick silence in the room was pushed aside by Lucille's bulldozer-like purr. Lula insisted, "Better get ready, then. He'll be here shortly."

Lula left the room, then closed the door as she cooed and cuddled Lucille.

Alone and surrounded by only dim firelight, Zoë felt her focus drawn toward the corner of the room by her vanity. She could almost sense the veiled presence of the mist-filled demon, causing her flesh to rise and form tiny bumps.

Like an old warped record playing inside her thoughts, the angelic woman's words seeped into her ears: "Their fate rests in your hands…" Her mind replayed the woman's gruesome death like images looping through a faulty camera until she forced her eyes shut and willed her mind to produce only clean white space.

Pulling the covers up to her chin, Zoë wanted to cancel her next engagement. She had a strict policy against two clients in one day, but her next appointment was a referral from Mr. Jackson Tate Lewis, or J.T. Although no longer a client, J.T. was her friend and financial advisor and had been since she was eighteen.

Lying on her bed watching the firelight dance on the ceiling, she realized that night with J.T. almost two decades ago had been the last time she'd ever let a client kiss her. Wanting to be alone, she reminded herself that J.T. had never sent anyone to her before; willing or not, she owed it to him to keep the appointment.

The man had called her a week prior, his voice confident and strong. They talked for a few minutes before she inquired, "What's your name?"

Silence worked its way through the phone and nibbled her ear with its cottony mouth. "Bill."

"Just Bill?"

He laughed, which relieved her. "St. James."

Toward the end of their conversation, she asked one of her customary questions. "Anything special you'd like me to wear?"

"I've always had a thing for Cyd Charisse."

"Well, you're in luck."

"See you then."

She had to admit that despite herself, her interest had been piqued. So with little time to get ready, she got out of bed and hurried to her wardrobe.

After dressing, she sat at her vanity and heard whispering down the hall. Straining to listen, she could only make out a few hushed words.

"No. I'm telling you I've seen them. They're in the walls—"

Who the hell is here?

The whispering continued until she heard Lula's footsteps coming toward her room. Zoë rushed from the vanity and flung the door open. "Were you just talking to someone?"

Looking puzzled, Lula shoved her hand into her apron pocket. "Of course not. Who on earth would I be talking to?"

Lucille sat next to Lula's feet, wide-eyed and twitching her tail as Zoë sized the two of them up.

Lucille continued staring while Zoë spoke. "Send him up when he gets here. Sorry about dinner."

Lula flashed a warm smile as she entered the room and walked toward the bed. "We'll eat when the Rookie has gone." She had a propensity to code-name all of Zoë's clients, and it was clear the Rookie was Bill.

Having grabbed a log from the metal basket next to the fireplace, Zoë tossed it onto the fire, causing soot and sparks to fly into the room.

Lula stopped straightening the bed linens and turned around. "I'll do that."

Zoë brushed the wood splinters from her hands, then walked into the bathroom to wash up. Standing in front of the pedestal sink, she felt her feet melting into the floor until the cold tiles seemed to become quicksand, sucking her downward into blackness.

"Zoë!" Lula was kneeling next to her. "Good God, are you all right?"

Shocked to find herself flat on the bathroom floor, Zoë responded, "I'm just lightheaded."

Lula helped lift her from the floor. "You should've eaten."

She was about to reply when the doorbell rang.

Lula pressed, "You sure you're okay?"

"I'm fine. Honestly."

Lula looked at her for a moment, then left the bathroom.

Leaning over, Zoë turned on the faucet and dabbed her forehead with cold water. Catching her reflection in the mirror, she studied her face and attempted to convince herself that she was fine and just needed rest.

Looking closer, she watched her pupils grow smaller until they were black specks amongst irises of blue, two tiny boats in a vast ocean. She felt weightless, dazed, and like her consciousness wasn't quite her own.

Lula crashed into her trance like a bird into a glass door. "The Rookie's here."

Zoë left the bathroom, walked across her room, then sat on the chaise while Lula probed, "You sure you're up for this?"

The truth was that she wasn't, and rather than lie, what she wanted to do was tell Lula about her dreams and the presence that inhabited them. Instead, she prodded Lula for details on the visitor waiting down-stairs. "And?"

Lula smiled as she spoke. "Handsome, but out of place. Should I send him up?"

"Yes."

A gentle knock on Zoë's door brought a welcome reprieve from her thoughts. It had taken him ages to climb the stairs. She called out, "Come in."

After a few minutes of waiting, she stood, opened the door, and found Bill standing in the hallway. Leaning against the doorframe, she watched him taking in the curves of her body.

"Nice dress." His boyish smirk revealed a dimple on his right cheek, but absent was a dimple on the left.

Backing up, she ushered him into the room and closed the door, realizing she had been wrong about his appearance when she'd pictured him. In reality, he was tall, well past six feet, with thick, russet-colored hair, blue eyes, and a blushing, fair complexion.

Bill walked past her to the fireplace, then sat in one of the velvet chairs. Shifting his weight forward, he put his hands toward the fire, causing his tailored navy suit to strain at the back seam.

Sitting in the chair across from him, she leaned back and watched his mind churn.

"I'm not entirely sure why I've come." He turned to face her, and as he scanned her body an inch at a time, it was evident why he'd come: to forget someone.

Feeling that touch would be more soothing than words, she leaned toward him and slipped his hand beneath the crinoline of her dress. Without hesitation, he skimmed her thigh with his fingers, then pulled one of her garter clips apart and sent it crawling up her leg like a satin serpent.

Their eyes locked and his breathing elevated just enough to let her know the feel of her skin was affecting him. Yet rather than continue inching his fingers upward, he removed his hand from beneath her dress. "I don't know if I'm—"

Placing a tender hand on his cheek, she watched pain streak his face. His ache was one of loss, of love gone. And as her thoughts drifted to Evan, she understood—with raw lucidity—how he felt.

6

SOLITUDE

Bill walked across the sprawling lobby of 825 Fifth
Avenue as the doorman called after him, "Have a good
evening, Mr. St. James."

He spoke over his shoulder. "You too, Gregory."

Once at the elevator bank, he pressed the large antique button marked
with a flourished upward facing arrow. He could hear the iron safety gate
sliding open on the other side of the thick steel door before the elevator opened.

Stepping in, he was greeted by the building's aging elevator operator,
Charlie, who tipped his hat and greeted him. "Good evening, sir."

"Evening, Charlie."

Charlie pulled the gate closed, then pressed the smooth round button
marked "PH." As the elevator jerked into motion, the scents of spice and
rose dislodged from Bill's clothes. Zoë's scent had saturated the fabric of
his shirt, determined to follow him home.

Lifting his gaze, he watched the ticking floor counter: seventeen, eighteen, nineteen…feeling it represented the number of times Zoë had crept

into his mind since he'd left her house. He found it unsettling that even though they hadn't had sex, she'd somehow infiltrated his thoughts in a manner both unyielding and absolute. The counter struck twenty and after the elevator came to a halt, Charlie slid the safety gate open.

The elevator door opened while Bill pulled his keys from his pocket. He could hear Winston barking on the other side of the apartment door, his fat feet prancing back and forth while he waited for it to be unlocked.

Bill inched open the door and before he could stop him, Winston rushed into the elevator, put his paws on Charlie's narrow shoulders, and licked his wrinkled face.

Bill pulled on Winston's collar until he was back on all fours. "Sorry about that."

Charlie smiled and offered, "He's the highlight of my day, sir."

Bill led Winston out of the elevator and Charlie closed the gate behind them.

He shut the apartment door, walked into the living room, and sat in his favorite chair. Looking out over Central Park, the moon brilliant against the backdrop of the winter sky, he felt his thoughts pulled toward Zoë once more.

Winston placed a wet nose beneath Bill's dangling palm. Bill wished he could share his excitement with Winston, but he wanted it for himself—it was the first night in months he'd felt alive. He now knew what the glimmer in J.T.'s eyes had meant when he'd passed over a business card with Zoë's number written on the back.

Of their own volition, his thoughts rolled back in time.

"This woman is a very special friend of mine." Before Bill could pummel J.T. with questions, J.T. raised a hand and said, or rather demanded, "Just call her. She'll know what to do."

With that, J.T. had slapped his shoulder, smiled, and turned to leave. "Oh, and take a shower before you meet her—you look like shit."

Bill's focus was pulled back into the present by the sound of Winston growling while he chewed. He looked down to make sure it wasn't one of his dress shoes, which Winston loved to drag from the closet and devour, and his heart sank as he watched him gnawing on a cream-colored slipper. His first instinct was to rip it from between his paws, but when he realized it was the one thing Winston had left of her, he couldn't bring himself to follow through.

Feeling uncomfortable in his favorite chair, he stood and walked into the bedroom, then flipped on the light. Standing in front of the open closet, he examined his wife's clothes as if the fabrics might merge and form a ghostly version of her.

It was a closet that would make a marine proud—even her jeans were hung and pressed. She'd arranged her closet in a kind of gradient: black on the left, colors in the middle, white on the right. The tiny color section had its hangers spread farther apart than the rest of the closet, as if trying to appear larger and more important than it was. But there was no competition: black and white could overtake color's territory without effort.

Winston darted into the room with his head hanging low, then looked around and ran out. Bill thought it wise to follow suit and made his way back into the living room, feeling a boulder where his heart should be.

Sitting on the couch, he focused on his wife's purse on the coffee table. He hadn't touched it since they handed it to him at the hospital two months prior, the memory of which overtook his thoughts.

"Mr. St. James, we're sorry for your loss. Here are your wife's possessions."

Everything hurt in that moment: his eyes, his heart, his skin. He carried his wife's purse from the hospital as if it were a child cradled in his arms.

Now sitting on their dark wooden coffee table, the purse—with its buckled eyes, soft leather feet, and braided arms—was motherless. Leaning forward, he took the bag, put it in his lap, and stared at its organized interior.

While examining the contents of her purse, he braced himself, but not one tear fell. Their previous years together refused to be tarnished by grief, despite the last few months of lonely nights, casual I love yous, and sexless Sunday afternoons.

He forced himself to retrieve her cell phone and turn it on. After coming to life, the phone displayed an animated envelope and a message appeared on the screen: "15 New Messages. Click to Play."

Outside himself, he pressed the envelope icon and held the phone up to his ear as the metallic voice chimed, "First message, October seventh, one twenty-one a.m." His chest tightened.

"Hi. I heard about the case—congratulations. I'm sorry about our trip. I wasn't feeling well. I've left five messages—I gather you're angry. If you can get away for a few nights, I'll make it up to you. I miss you."

Echoing through his mind, the man's voice slowed time and made the room spin as the words "I miss you" slithered into Bill's ear. It was a voice he knew well.

Fury boiling in his veins, he shoved his wife's phone into his coat pocket, got up from the couch, and walked to the front door. Taking his phone from inside his suit jacket, he dialed.

"Hey."

Bill cleared his throat. "Beer?"

"Now?"

"Yeah. Now."

Looking down at his clenched fist, he watched his knuckles turn white. "Usual place? Thirty minutes?"

He unclenched his fist. "I'll be waiting."

7

CAFÉ TÊTE-À-TÊTE

Lula stood in front of the stove and looked out the window at the snowy December morning thinking how barren the house felt without Zoë in it. The snowflakes were the largest she'd seen, like pieces of falling cotton, and it seemed the mounting snowdrifts outside might swallow the tree-lined courtyard whole.

Lucille wound herself around Lula's leg and let out a squeaky meow while Lula's thoughts drifted to Mr. Black's instructions on the day she'd gone to meet Zoë: "I've arranged for her to buy the house and you're part of the deal."

Zoë was never to know whose house she'd purchased, nor was she to be privy to Lula's and Mr. Black's long history. What Zoë needed was a clean slate, a place to rebuild her life from the ashes of both her mother's death and Mr. Black's hasty departure. At Mr. Black's behest, Lula would serve as a co-builder of that new and life-sustaining platform. Her point of insertion into Zoë's life was to be that of a surrogate mother, a caretaker; she'd fill up the space of a house too vast for one so alone, and watch over Zoë as Mr. Black had instructed.

Lula recalled the day she had first met Zoë, in the foyer of an empty and lonesome 66 Jane Street.

"Are you Lula?"

Lula had found it hard to believe Zoë was only eighteen. Even then she was put together, yet beneath her snowy skin and red lipstick, Lula could sense traces of the pain Mr. Black's absence had left like colorless tattoos. Her presence had always been arresting, alluring. It was easy to see why Mr. Black had fallen in love with her, and in time, Lula grew to love her as well. Now she would do anything to protect her.

Pawing Lula's leg, Lucille let out a whiny meow. Lula turned off the burner beneath the simmering pot on the stove. "It's almost ready. Just sit tight."

Lucille bounded onto the countertop.

"Get down!" Lula poured the steaming mixture into a steel bowl and set it on the floor. "Let it cool, now."

After leaping off the counter, Lucille dove headfirst into the bowl, then squealed.

"What did I just say?"

Lucille looked up at Lula and twitched her tail as she licked her lips. Lula scolded her under her breath. "You never listen."

Hearing a loud ring coming from her purse, she walked over to the counter and retrieved her cell phone. "Is everything all right?"

"We need to meet."

"Leaving now. I'll be at Nan's in twenty."

As she hung up the phone, Lula's curiosity overwhelmed her. What was so important that they couldn't discuss it over the phone? Rushing to exit the kitchen, she almost tripped over Lucille, who was sitting in the hallway peering at her. "Stop lookin' at me like that!"

Lucille's eyes were wild as she licked bits of meaty breakfast from her chin. After a moment, she narrowed her gaze and trotted past Lula into the kitchen.

Lula walked down St. Mark's Place as the falling snow covered her dark coat. Reaching the restaurant, Lula caught the eye of a beautiful Asian woman—her friend and ally—watching her through the window.

Opening the door, she let the warm spicy air wash over her as she stepped inside. Walking over to her table, Lula noticed that although her friend was smiling, there was concern in her slate-colored eyes.

Lula lowered herself onto a swirl-backed wooden chair and removed her coat. The curiosity lodged in her bones intensified as the woman slid a square envelope across the table. Recognizing the style and stationery of the envelope, Lula felt her pulse race.

Lula:

There are no words to express my gratitude for your friendship, your kindness, your care of Hannah, and your care of Zoë. But things have progressed for the worse on all fronts and this will be my last request: You must keep silent.

It is imperative that you let things take their course, unaltered and without intervention. But take comfort in knowing that "in all chaos, some order exists."

In farewell,
Evan Black

Lula's heart sped up to a quick and rhythmic knock. "Is he bloody kidding? Thirty years, and this rubbish is his goodbye?"

The woman lowered her chin and countered, "It's not that simple—"

Lula interrupted, "Gigi, he can't expect me to stand by and do nothing."

Gigi ordered, "You must." Looking uncomfortable in her skin, she watched Lula closely. "I need to ask you something."

"Alright."

She lowered her voice, looking around before continuing. "How much do you know about Zoë's mother?"

"Why do you ask?"

"Zoë might be part of something larger than either of us yet understands."

Lula shot back, "Seems unlikely considering how isolated she is."

Gigi paused for a moment, then spoke. "But is she?"

The knocking of Lula's heart grew stronger, pounding now. "What exactly are you implying?"

Gigi's gaze sharpened. "That we're in the dark. In more ways than one."

Lula shifted in her chair. "Evan always said Zoë was the light among us."

Each sat without a word until Gigi broke the silence. "He also insists that you cannot, in any way, interfere or reveal to her what you know." She retrieved the envelope and forced a smile, her bottom lip not quite willing to follow along. "I know how much Zoë means to you." Placing the envelope in her purse, she urged, "Promise me you'll keep your distance."

Steel tears sat behind Lula's eyes like rusty ball bearings. "You believe she's in danger?"

Gigi leaned forward. "I think we all are."

8

REVEL REBEL

Zoë crossed her legs as she watched Dr. Lawson scribble in a small notepad. "Whatever do you write in there?"

He looked up at her over his black-rimmed glasses. "Does it bother you?"

"No. Well, it's a tad distracting. I sort of feel like you might be writing down all my secrets."

With a crooked grin, he lowered his pen. "Do you feel you've shared any of your secrets with me?"

Touché, you cagey bastard. "No, I suppose not."

After standing, he walked over to her, then handed his notepad to her. "I don't want any secrets between us."

She took the notepad, catching a few of the phrases he'd scribbled: "Eye contact? Distracted. Isolated. Unchallenged self-image."

Lifting her gaze, she focused back on Dr. Lawson, who now sat in his chair. Words leapt from her lips before she could stop them. "In my dreams, there's a presence."

He didn't respond and instead seemed to be waiting to see if anything more would squeeze itself from her locked psyche. When she remained silent, he queried, "What kind of presence?"

She wanted to tell him she was being hunted from within her mind…her soul. Yet all that left her lips was a flimsy half-truth. "I'm not entirely sure."

Dr. Lawson watched her for a moment, then pushed further. "Can you describe it?"

Feeling like the chair was squeezing her in its leathery fist, she forced herself to speak. "It's darkness. Personified."

He leaned forward. "Male?"

"Yes."

"If you had to guess, what would you say its intentions were?"

She felt a rush of heat flush her face. "To consume me."

"Does he speak to you?"

"No."

Resting his chin between his thumb and forefinger, he continued querying. "How does he manifest—what do you see?"

A flash of the black mist consuming the woman racked her mind. "There's no real body to speak of—but he is conscious and calculating."

"Does he ever reveal anything to you?"

Thinking about his question for a moment, she realized that in all the dreams in which he was present, he revealed, or rather caused, some sort of violent death. With this new revelation, she spoke. "Death, or perhaps, shadow."

Zoë knew that the Cherokee believe the shadow side exposes all; it's often referred to as "living death." Nothing can stay hidden when shadow and light combine within a soul. This made her wonder: if in her dreams, shadow had its representation, when would she experience the representation of light?

"Do you actively participate in the dreams?"

"Not really. I don't usually remember much."

An image of the black mist morphing into its gruesome semisolid form raced through her mind.

Dr. Lawson steadied his voice. "You don't remember, or you would rather not discuss it?"

She fidgeted with the bracelet on her wrist while avoiding Dr. Lawson's gaze.

"Ms. Hall—"

"Please, call me Zoë."

"Is it possible the dreams are related to your profession?"

Looking at him, she asserted, "I love what I do."

It took him quite some time to respond, as he appeared to be lost in his thoughts. "Last week you mentioned something about your grandfather being a reason for the line of work you've chosen."

"No. I chose. It had nothing to do with him."

Searching the weathered skin of Dr. Lawson's face, she pondered what he liked and what he'd ask of her if he were a client. Judging by the look of anticipation in his eyes, it was delving into a person's psyche that turned him on. It was the same for her. "More often than not, there's no sex with my clients. Most of them just want someone to listen, to care for them."

"Perhaps that's true, but—"

"We're not so different, you and me." Seeing that their time was up, she stood, walked toward him, and laid his notepad back in his lap. "'Discerning' is a better word."

He looked up at her, puzzled. "Pardon?"

She motioned to his notepad. "In your notes, you wrote 'isolated.' But 'discerning' is more accurate."

A knowing smile graced his lips as he spoke. "I'd like to encourage you to let your dreams happen, participate and immerse yourself. Exploration in, and of, dreams is the only way of crossing into your unconscious. I want you to keep a journal of your dreams and bring it to our next session."

She walked to the door, then turned toward him. "See you next week."

Without waiting for his response, she left the room and closed the door behind her.

9

INTO THE WOODS

Night wrapped itself around her as Zoë walked up the steps of 66 Jane Street, her mind still buzzing from her session with Dr. Lawson. Stamping off the cold and snow from her shoes, she unlocked the door and stepped into a darker than usual house. "Lula?"

Just then, she heard a door slamming upstairs. Walking toward the staircase, she called out, "Hello?" She climbed the stairs until she reached the hallway landing. Peering toward her bedroom, she noticed a bright silvery light radiating from beneath her door.

She made her way across the hall, and when she opened her bedroom door, Lucille slammed into the side of her calf, then tore down the stairs. "God dammit, Lucille!"

Zoë stood inside the doorway and watched the dying fire while trying to calm her racing heartbeat. Turning to close the door behind her, she spotted a small vine wrapped around the handle. In response, the hairs on the back of her neck stood on end.

She backed away from the door, then walked over to her wardrobe while removing her coat, scarf, and gloves. After opening the wardrobe's thick oaken doors, she took off her shoes, undressed, and hung up her clothes.

Standing naked in the dim room, she couldn't shake the sensation that she was being watched. There was something peculiar about the way the house felt on this night, and with winter's chill settling into her bones, she slipped into an oversized sweater.

She placed a large log on the fire and blew into the orangey-red coals beneath it until fresh flames brought the fire back to life. On this late afternoon turned dark winter's night, she would dig into the book Lula had given her, *A Tale of Two Cities*, a story both fitting and alluring. But with her mind growing hazy and her limbs heavy, despite her desire to stay awake, she couldn't keep her eyes open.

Crawling into bed, she let her weight settle into the softness of her mattress, the fatigue saturating her limbs so intense it felt as if she'd been drugged. While part of her mind fought the wave of coming sleep, the other was desperate to let it swallow her up.

Then, as if sinking into a lightless sea, she felt herself losing consciousness as darkness closed in on all sides.

I'm an array of moving pieces jetting through the blackness of pure empty space. It seems as if I've been traveling for hours, and I find myself anxious for this relentless forward motion to cease. Then, like hitting a wall, I feel myself crash into the ground. A charge runs through me and before I can process what's happening, I'm sitting upright with my eyes open.

Blood resumes its flow through my limbs, and I clench my fists to bear the pain. Taking a breath and letting my head fall back, I send my gaze upward to a canopy of trees towering overhead. The branches of the trees are knitted together, and with the moonlight shining down through the branches, the canopy looks like a finely woven fishing net.

The smell of burning cedar mixed with the distinct scent of musky damp firewood causes me to shift my focus in the direction of the scent. In seeing a small structure beyond a bank of trees, without understanding why, I walk toward it.

As if guiding me, the moonlight filtering through the trees sprinkles a patterned and ghostly path along the mossy forest floor. I follow the path, navigating small clumps of ferns and thick vegetation.

After a few minutes of walking, I see the moonlight-made path leads to a small round cabin constructed of logs that curve around the exterior and support a thatched roof. A stone chimney sends puffs of smoke billowing toward me in a low-hanging haze.

Cedar-scented smoke makes its way into my nostrils, stirring within me a dreamlike wistfulness. With every step, the forest around me seems more familiar, the cabin resembling the one where I spent my childhood summers. That forest with our tiny little cabin was my mother's favorite place, a magical sanctuary she and I would retreat to whenever we had the chance. That is, until I was eight.

During that summer, my mother had begun showing signs of illness and was often bound to her bed. To spend as much time with her as possible, my father had insisted he join us and bring my three half sisters along.

My father's triplet daughters, the Deadlings, or so I called them as a child, were carbon copies of one another. Alike in demeanor, speech, mannerisms, and cruelty, they made it their life's work to torture both my mother and me.

With my mother too weak to accompany me, I would walk through the forest alone, listening to the trees whisper, as she had taught me. It was a way, she'd said, to always know who you are. "Pay attention to the whispers so you won't have to listen to the screams," as the Cherokee saying goes.

In listening to the trees, I had hoped to hear their wisdom, their secret guidance as to how I could make my mother well. But I never heard the forest's voice without the interference of the triplets, who would hide amongst the trees making frightening sounds and jeering, "Foxy Loxy's gonna getcha. He's closer than you think. Can't you hear him gettin' closer…your blood he's gonna drink."

They would chant over and over like little witches taunting me from the brush. They called me Alice, saying, "You're not in Wonderland, idiot. Only stupid, ugly little girls talk to trees." I tried to shut them out, ignore them, but their vicious voices eroded my relationship with the forest until all that was left was a deadened, soundless void. I lost my innocence that summer. I'd never experienced that kind of hatred. Like wicked thieves, the Deadlings had stolen my peace.

Hearing something scurrying along the forest floor, I'm pulled from my thoughts. Lowering my focus, I watch the ground and see a white rabbit dart into my path, then stop a few feet in front of me. Sitting on its hind legs, the rabbit perks up its ears, twitches its nose, then stares at me for a moment before turning around and making its way toward the little round cabin. I smile, and in finding the rabbit both endearing and apropos, decide to follow it.

Moving forward, I keep my steps slow and steady. Every few feet, the rabbit cranes its neck as if checking my progress. Then, stopping in front of a high thicket to the right of the cabin, the rabbit takes one last look at me and hops into the underbrush.

After a series of vigorous rustling sounds, a high-pitched cry pierces the air and I duck behind a tree beside me. With the sound of the rabbit's distress still ringing in my ears, I peer around the tree and notice a pair of aqua eyes staring at me from inside the thicket.

My blood grows hotter as a feeling of magnetism courses through my bones. And although it makes little sense, I feel my body wants to move toward the thicket and get closer to the person—or thing—concealed inside it.

I hear the rabbit cry out once more, weaker this time, like a chirp. I can't bear to hear the sound again and am about to move toward it when someone calls out from the forest. "Zoran. Stop."

I look in the direction of the voice and see a woman emerge from a bank of trees and walk toward the thicket. Her tall, willowy frame floats along the forest floor, and as she passes through a beam of moonlight, I notice her hair is flaming sienna red. Once in front of the thicket, she bends down, reaches inside, and with some effort, retrieves the rabbit.

In a calculated manner, she stands, then turns around and stares in my precise direction. I'm concealed behind a large tree without any moonlight to give me away, yet she sees me with pinpoint accuracy.

Stroking the rabbit, she walks toward me. Behind her the thicket rustles, allowing me to catch sight of a piercing aqua-eyed stare for a second before whatever was hidden inside the brush vanishes.

The woman covers the distance between us at a superhuman rate and now stands before me. I am speechless. Something about her makes me feel she lives and breathes the forest—as if they are one. The very soil beneath her feet merges into the loosely woven robe she wears and the moonlight settles along the curves of her greenish-hued skin. Her long sienna hair, draped to one side, glides over her chest and down to her waist, mimicking a molten stream.

The rabbit is resting in the crook of her arm, and as if it were a small child, she strokes the side of its face. The poor creature looks to be at death's door, its body trembling, blood dripping down its face and its right eye wounded.

While keeping a fixed stare on me, the woman wipes blood from the rabbit's face and continues stroking its white fur. "Mahayla gave her life for you."

The woman's face takes on a sunken, deathlike quality as she flattens her palm and runs her hand over the rabbit's eyes. Cocking her head, she removes her hand, and when she does I see the rabbit convulse, then go limp. "No matter her reasons, she deserved better."

Images of the woman's death flood my mind's eye. Part of me doesn't understand the visceral twinge of guilt lodged in my gut. In my attempt to temper the uneasy feeling overwhelming me, I take a breath and push the images of her hellish demise from my thoughts.

"Come." She walks in the direction of the cabin, and for a moment I wonder if it's she who lives there.

Watching her cross the forest floor like an apparition, I notice the fingers of her right hand are wrapped around the rabbit's ears as it dangles from her grasp like a mangled toy. If I were of sound mind, I would run the other direction; but of their own volition, my legs are moving forward, and I follow her.

As she walks in front of me, the train of her robe catches bits of leaves and forest debris in a way that makes me feel the forest wishes to become part of her clothing. My gaze drifts up her body, and I watch the sensual sway of her hips, which appear to have caused an undulatory breeze to rock back and forth through the trees.

We're almost at the cabin, but before entering its grassy yard, she turns right and heads toward a clearing. I see her eyes flick toward the cabin's back door, and my instinct tells me she wants me nowhere near whoever lives inside.

The mossy forest floor merges into a vast bed of tiny clovers, which are soft beneath my feet. The scent in the air shifts from burning wood to that of a fresher grassy scent, like the smell before it rains.

I hear a strong male voice call out from behind us, "Ayalah—"

The woman turns toward the voice, and in brighter moonlight, I notice her eyes appear lavender in color. Whoever the man is, she respects and has an affinity for him, and it's clear to me he's somehow asked her to leave him alone with me. She bows her head, then moves past me and back into the forest.

I hear him walking toward me, the scent of pre-rain growing more intense by the second, but I can't seem to turn around. Being no stranger to the presence of a man, I find my reaction to him unnerving and foreign.

Now he is standing behind me; his breath is falling on my neck, and in response my skin raises and forms tiny bumps. Feeling his hand come to rest on my shoulder, I glance right and see that beneath the silvery moonlight his skin is ghostly white, like porcelain. He is light in the flesh.

"Zoë." His fingers put just enough pressure onto my skin to let me know he wishes me to turn and face him. But by the time I will myself to do so, I feel my knees give way and I collapse to the ground.

"Zoë!"

Someone was shaking her.

"Zoë!"

Her eyes flew open.

"Good God, are ya all right?"

Lula was standing above her. Looking to her right, she realized she was lying on the floor.

Lula helped her to her feet. "Let's get you under some cold water."

As Lula walked her into the bathroom, she could see that Lula was alarmed, but it wasn't until Zoë looked at herself in the mirror that she understood why: bits of moss and leaves were threaded throughout her hair. She didn't look at Lula as she disrobed and pushed the shower curtain aside. Without a word, Lula left the bathroom and shut the door.

Zoë let the water rain down on her as dirt and forest debris fell onto the porcelain below. Her gaze drifted to a tiny leaf floating toward the drain, which she swore was twisting and moving in objection to being washed away.

She washed her hair, soaped off a few last bits of dirt, then turned off the water and stepped out of the shower. Having grabbed a fresh towel, she burrowed into its clean, cottony comfort and dried off. Without the energy to dress, she turned out the light, left her bathroom, then dropped her towel and crawled into bed.

Body clean, mind numb, she retreated under silken covers and closed her eyes. As she neared the precipice of sleep, she swore the scent of pre-rain was drifting from her skin.

10

SLICE OF NIGHT

Lula sat in the shadowy dining room and sipped a glass of her favorite scotch, feeling heavyhearted and restless. Her loyalty to Mr. Black was unshakable, but his request that she not interfere in Zoë's current plight was proving to be the most difficult thing he'd ever asked her to do.

It wasn't like him to be cryptic, and despite the sincerity of his letter, she couldn't understand why his last words had given her so little information to go on. How was she supposed to trust instructions centered upon "in all chaos, some order exists," which to her was a careless way to let things unfold?

She drained her glass, poured another shot, and reminded herself that in all their years together, she'd never been given cause to question Mr. Black's judgment. He was a strategic and precise thinker, a man who did nothing without a reason. Yet it was impossible for her to see how the situation would end well, or even favorably.

A line from his letter kept floating through her thoughts like thread unraveling from a once-colorful tapestry: "This will be my last request."

She felt her chest grow tight. His was the most binding friendship she'd ever known, and the thought of learning to live without its support was more than she could bear.

A flash of light coming from the courtyard forced her from the heaviness of her thoughts. She shot from her chair, rushed to the large bay window, and scanned the snowy ground outside.

Everything was peaceful, dead quiet, and dark save for a thin silvery light coming from the corner of the courtyard. Incomprehensible as it seemed, it appeared the light was shining through a slice—or vertical rip—that was hanging in midair, as though the night was comprised of fabric that had been cut.

After a moment, a small, dark figure pushed the slice apart like two halves of a curtain and stepped into the courtyard. The blood in Lula's body ceased to circulate, and her limbs felt like cement as she watched a black-skinned skeletal creature creep toward the house with something in tow. It had an ominous yet graceful way of moving, a lithe demon closing in on unsuspecting prey. Whatever it was dragging left a thick trail through the snow, like the imprint of a mammoth snake.

A lifelong Catholic whose beliefs were often tested by the things she'd seen and heard in Mr. Black's employ, Lula had strayed rather far from the discipline of daily mass and vigilant prayer. Still, even with her faith in flux, there was no denying the fact that she'd just watched a child-sized devil slice through the fabric of space and time and birth itself into existence.

Lula reached for the small silver cross hanging around her neck and whispered a prayer her grandmother had taught her when she was little: "Evil shall not touch me, death shall not know me, and whatever darkness dare cross my path, I rebuke in the name of my Savior. Amen."

With the creature ever closer to the house, Lula backed away from the window and pressed herself against the dining room wall. She inched her way toward the arched entrance into the kitchen but stopped when she heard the back door open.

The sound of something scampering along the kitchen floor sent her pulse racing, and as she peered around the archway, she watched the creature dart into the kitchen's dining alcove dragging what appeared to be a small makeshift sack behind it.

Lula crouched down, entered the kitchen, and grabbed a large serrated knife from a wooden block next to the stove. Her instincts were screaming that a culinary knife couldn't protect her, but in that moment it was all she could think to do.

Sneaking across the kitchen, she could hear quick, shallow breathing, which gave her the impression that the intruder might be more afraid of her than she of it. Then, in the alcove, she saw it cowering inside the fireplace.

A stream of light coming in through the window allowed her to see that its facial features were human and that its body was a leathery black. It had long, gnarled fingers with sharp claws that scraped along the brick as it backed farther into the fireplace.

Until this moment, Lula had considered Luciferian mythology to be just that: a fable meant to keep the Shepherd's flock in check. A kind of invisible electric fence to keep the sheep from being tempted to stray. But the half-human standing before her had been touched by a very real evil, and whatever lifeblood had once inhabited its veins had been replaced by a putrid substance that sent a stench into the room like a low-hanging fog.

She almost felt a twinge of pity for the human-cross-demon that had infiltrated the house. As if in response to her thoughts, the creature let out a menacing hiss, then wrapped a few bony fingers around the top of its sack and crawled up the chimney.

Hearing something scurrying across the wood floor behind her, Lula whipped around just in time to see Lucille tear through the room and run out the back door. She raced to the door intent on chasing after her, but before she could take another step, Lucille sped across the courtyard and leapt into the suspended opening before disappearing in a silvery flash of light.

11

PANDORA'S BOX

Zoë awoke to the percussive chorus of Lula's walk:
HEEL toe, HEEL toe...

A knock on her door was imminent—within seconds, any moment now. There it was.

"You up?"

"Yes." Feeling groggy, she watched as Lula opened the door and walked into the room.

"Good."

Something was bothering Lula. She seemed distracted, and the usual lightness she carried had been replaced with a weighted sadness. "What's wrong?"

Lula sat on the bed next to Zoë's feet and patted her leg. "Not a thing."

"I don't believe you."

Holding Zoë's gaze, Lula changed the subject. "You sleep all right?"

Feeling more than hypocritical, Zoë urged, "Whatever it is, you can tell me."

Lula's thoughts seemed to be churning, and in that moment, Zoë knew Lula was forming a lie.

"I miss…home, I suppose."

Zoë responded, in the hopes of digging deeper, "In the twenty years I've known you, you've never once mentioned missing Glasgow."

Lula looked up. "Well, I do now." Standing, Lula seemed to force a smile. "Breakfast is nearly ready." With that, she walked from the room on the quietest feet Zoë had ever heard.

Zoë got out of bed and walked into the bathroom, wondering what was troubling Lula. In all their time together, she'd never seen her so downtrodden. Once in front of the bathroom sink, she washed her face, brushed her teeth, then grabbed her robe from the back of the bathroom door and headed downstairs. While making her way into the foyer, she passed the sitting room and noticed that her mother's ever-present lilac bouquet was missing from the end table.

She called out, "Lula? What happened to the flowers in the sitting room?"

Lula popped her head out from the kitchen. "I haven't touched them."

She stared at the empty vase, unable to shake the strange feeling welling up in her gut, as the vase was always filled with a memorial bouquet of lilacs, her mother's favorite flower. No matter the expense or season, it had never been flowerless—not once.

After stepping back into the kitchen, Lula thundered, "Breakfast's ready!"

Zoë continued down the foyer, then walked into the kitchen as Lula placed a steaming cup of coffee and a breakfast plate on the table. Zoë sat down while Lula poured a splash of cream into her coffee cup and absent-mindedly put the cream away in the china cupboard.

Unable to stand black coffee without a heavy dose of cream, Zoë retrieved the cream from the cupboard, then poured it into her cup.

Lula stood by the stove, talking to herself as she wrote out a shopping list. "Cheese, Windex, lavender hand soap…"

In earnest, the shopping list sounded more appetizing than the meal sitting in front of Zoë. Lula was an unrivaled cook, known for her unusual food preparation, but here were two runny eggs flanked by burnt sausage and soggy, over-buttered toast.

Always present at any meal was the butterscotch-colored princess herself, but the one time Zoë wanted her there to gobble up unwanted breakfast bits, Lucille was absent.

Zoë forced down one egg and a piece of toast before excusing herself. "I have to change. Thanks for breakfast."

Waving a plump, pen-laden hand in the air, Lula continued composing her list. "Downy, pillar candles, yams, butter…"

Zoë walked into the foyer, then climbed the stairs and crossed the hall toward her room. The hallway was ice cold and there was a strange scent emanating from her room, like a decay-noted perfume had soured the air.

Pushing her door open, she took a step into the room and froze at the sight of a tiny trail of lilac petals leading from the door to her bed. With a dose of hesitancy, she followed the trail of petals until she came to a raised floorboard in front of her bedside table.

The board was covered in deep scratches, like a wild animal had attempted to pull it from its grooves. Kneeling, she studied the carved claw marks, which all culminated on one edge of the board where a corner looked as though it had been gnawed off.

Hearing Lula's heavy feet clomping up the stairs, Zoë stood and ran to the bedroom door and locked it tight.

Lula hollered, "You gettin' ready?" The door handle shook. "Why is this door locked?"

Steadying her voice, Zoë answered, "I'm fine." Backing away from the door, she continued, "Just let me finish getting dressed, and I'll be right down."

She could feel the silence slithering through the keyhole until Lula spoke. "You're late for your meeting." Again, the door handle shook as Lula tested it one last time before giving up and walking back down the stairs.

Zoë walked back to the floorboard, expecting to find it nailed down, but when she attempted to lift the planked board, she could remove it with ease. Setting the board aside, she reached down to retrieve a small round metal box hidden beneath it.

Elaborate in its carvings, the box's top had a symbol made up of two dragons whose intertwining tails formed a braided pattern that connected two large circles. Beneath the dragon symbol, four inlaid lines met at the box's center and formed four quadrants, each containing a geometric marking.

Curious as to what the box contained, she examined every inch, looking for a way to open the lid. After finding the top of the box sealed, she studied the bottom and noticed an etched inscription: "In bocca al lupo."

She had seen the phrase before but couldn't remember where.

Lula called up from the landing below, "Zoë, you're late!"

Feeling a little irritated, she shouted, "I'm coming!"

Lula shouted back, "What's going on up there?"

Replacing the floorboard, she felt her mind churning with questions: Where had the box come from, who had put it there—and why? Like lightning to rod, her thoughts flashed back to where she'd seen the phrase before. She reached toward a small stack of books by her bed and sorted through it until she located a worn red book of her mother's filled with Cherokee poems and stories.

She opened the book to the inside cover, where her mother had handwritten an inscription:

Zoë:

Do as did Pandora, save for don't leave hope inside.
In bocca al lupo.

—Mother

Below her mother's inscription was a faded stamp from a bookshop. A memory of her mother drifted into her thoughts. A few days before she died she had shown Zoë the stamp on the inside cover of the book. "When there's no one else, he can do what I can't." They were the last words her mother had ever spoken to her.

12

SCREED

"I'm here to see Mr. Lewis."

"Yes, he's expecting you. Follow me."

Trailing behind the Barbie-built blonde bobbing in front of her, Zoë couldn't help eyeing the woman's frame, watching her cast a spell as she passed the offices of men trying not to look at her.

Throwing a blasé glance over her shoulder, the woman directed Zoë into a spacious corner office where J.T. welcomed her with a warm smile and outstretched arms, hugging her until she couldn't breathe.

"Please, sit."

"I'm sorry I'm late."

J.T.'s baritone voice broke through the air in an awkward, hyper chirp. "Coffee? Water?"

"No, I'm fine, thank you."

Instead of leaving, the blonde stood in the doorway and gave Zoë a thorough once-over. The contained silence caused J.T. to clear his throat while tapping his fingers on his desk.

The woman lowered her chin and sent a glacial gaze toward him. "Will that be all, Mr. Lewis?"

He stopped tapping his fingers. "Yes, Melinda, thank you."

"Don't forget you have a two o'clock downtown."

"Yep."

Unbelievable as it was, the woman continued standing in the doorway, and with her increasingly frosty disposition, she resembled a rigid sex Popsicle. Thawing enough to turn on her heel and leave the office, she mumbled something under her breath as she made her way down the hall.

J.T. focused on Zoë and smiled. "It's been a long time!"

The sun cast muted wintry light onto the right side of J.T.'s handsome face, and she swore he was wearing makeup beneath one eye. "J.T., are you all right?"

"Of course!"

She leaned in, the afternoon sun brightening enough for her to see the bluish bruise beneath his messy cover-up. "Melinda—she's your secretary?"

"She prefers 'assistant.'"

I'm sure she does. "She's very—"

"Protective. She means well."

With as much grace as could be mustered, she changed the subject. "How's business? Good I'd say, judging from the new office."

"Well, it's not an easy market right now. But I always find a way."

She glanced at a large photo on J.T.'s glass desk. "Is this your wife?"

Rotating the silver frame toward her, he answered, "Yes, that's Ava."

"She's gorgeous."

Warmth crept into his voice. "She is." J.T. fidgeted with his wedding ring. "I sent a friend your way. Bill St. James—"

"Thank you for that."

"And?"

"I don't discuss clients. Confidentiality and discretion are the cornerstones of my business."

Relaxing and behaving more like himself, J.T. flashed a dazzling smile and settled sideways into his leather chair. "It's good to see you."

In his silence, he was reaching out to her, but she wanted to keep things professional.

"So, you wanted to discuss my accounts?"

"Okay. Straight to business." He angled one of his many monitors toward her and continued. "See here, your accounts are doing well."

He clicked onto a different screen littered with pie charts and line graphs, all of which showed an uptick in her portfolio's value. Seeming to avoid eye contact, he spoke while returning the monitor back to its original position. "But more importantly, I'd like you to consider a rare investment opportunity."

The air in the room grew stagnant, providing enough of a change to inform her that their meeting was being driven by an underlying agenda.

"What is it?"

"It's a company called Limerick Technologies—" He shifted his gaze toward her, examining her as he continued. "Backed by Black Industries."

Feeling a bit like a cat trapped in a corner, she replied with a more defensive tone than she intended. "I'm not interested."

His expression grew serious. "I've known you almost twenty years—"

"Please don't make an issue where there isn't one."

"But it's an unprecedented opportunity. This company's something out of a science fiction novel. What they're working on would blow your mind—"

"I understand. I'm still not interested." He stared at her as she continued. "J.T., your counsel and expertise are irreplaceable."

He turned the monitor away from her. "You don't have to baby me."

She smiled. "Yes, I do."

J.T. softened as he put a warm hand on hers. He was a good man, strong and dependable, at least to her. A love-bound connection had always existed between them, and it felt like home sitting with him, their hands intertwined.

She felt a sense of deep longing sneak up and lodge itself behind her eyes. It was impossible to see J.T. without thinking about Evan, as the two memories were fused. Tension blanketed the office as she avoided his stare and inquired, "Do you still speak to Evan?"

He patted her hand. "I don't discuss clients. Confidentiality and discretion are the cornerstones of my business."

She met his gaze. "You have no mercy."

He watched her for a moment before speaking. "Evan's the past. Look at you, Zoë—you're beyond all that now." His words felt like molten glass pouring into her skull.

"I simply wondered if he's all right."

J.T. sat back in his chair and surveyed her. He had told her once that she was the only person he'd ever known who made him feel at ease; and in this, part of her wondered if he had organized their meeting for the sole purpose of soaking in the comfort she offered.

With a hint of reserve, she commented, "It was lovely seeing you."

J.T. squeezed her hand, then stood. "You too."

She leaned over his desk and whispered, "That shade of cover-up doesn't suit you and neither does adultery."

He smiled as he came out from behind his desk. "How do you do that?"

"Well, the signs weren't exactly subtle. Do you love her?"

He took her in his arms, their faces now inches apart. "Melinda? No."

She rubbed her thumb along his cheek. "Then it's not worth it."

She held his gaze and gave him the affection she knew he needed. Then, turning to walk out of his office, she felt his loneliness follow her through the door like an abandoned puppy.

"You said One Minetta Lane, right?"

She pulled her mother's red book from her purse and attempted to confirm the faded address below the stamp on the inside cover. "Yes. One—no, Eleven Minetta Lane."

The cabbie inched along the narrow street searching for the house number while she put the book back in her purse beside the box she'd found in her room.

With the inscription in her mother's book containing the same phrase from the box, she assumed the two objects were somehow related. It was her hope that whoever resided at 11 Minetta Lane—if indeed they still did—could shed light on how the box may be linked to her mother.

The taxi jerked to a halt. "Here. Eleven Minetta."

She paid the driver and exited the cab. Turning away from the street, she walked toward an unkempt grey-blue brownstone, then climbed up its shoddy concrete steps and rang the doorbell.

The top half of the door had an inset stained-glass panel and through it, she could see an old man making his way down a steep staircase. His stocky figure looked clownish through the thick colored glass as he stepped onto the landing and walked down the hall toward her.

Once in the foyer, he peered outside, then opened the door. The youthful beam in the old man's eyes caught her off guard as a flirtatious grin appeared on his wrinkled lips. "Been a long time since a pretty lady came to visit."

He took a puff from his pipe while Zoë inquired, "I'm looking for Sumel and Sons Bookshop. I'm sure it's no longer here, but I was hoping maybe—"

The man's knobby finger pointed to the window beside him where, although faded, the words she'd just spoken were painted in cracked bronze lettering.

"Are you Mr. Sumel?"

After exhaling a long stream of smoke, the old man replied, "Come in and have some hot cocoa."

She stared at him for a moment, then stepped inside and followed him down a low-lit hallway reeking of cinnamon and pipe tobacco. Every bookcase lining the hall was stuffed with books and when she passed by a sitting room on the left, she felt that the cozy, mismatched furnishings made it look like an old-world gnome inhabited the house.

She continued trailing behind him into the kitchen, where he began lighting several antique oil lamps that were mounted to the wall. He nodded his head toward a chair in front of a round wooden table. "Have a seat."

Having sat down, she studied the knickknacks covering the wall beside the table. There didn't seem to be an inch of wall space visible through what she would describe as a mounted trinket circus.

He shuffled across the floor, then took a steaming kettle from the stove and poured water into a mug. Pulling a tiny red bag from a tin on the counter, he emptied the bag's contents into the mug, then walked toward her. "Come."

"Aren't you having any?"

He stopped beside her chair, then patted her on the shoulder. "Mine's upstairs already." Leaning in a bit closer, he offered, "We'd better get started. You have many questions." With that, he scuffled out of the kitchen and down the hall.

After grabbing the mug of hot cocoa, she followed behind him while taking in the spicy scent of the mug's contents.

"Old recipe from Granny." He began climbing the staircase, which for him seemed a Herculean task.

"Mr. Sumel, I should introduce myself."

Winded, he spoke over his shoulder. "No need, child. Besides, a man doesn't complain when he's struck by a rose!"

Upon hearing the first stair creak beneath her feet like an angry troll, Zoë gripped the thick wooden banister for support, as it seemed the entire staircase was seconds from collapsing. Stepping up each subsequent stair, she was mindful not to knock over the tall stacks of books piled on them. She let her gaze drift upward toward the old-fashioned oil lanterns lining the wall, taking in the knickknacks that had been hung every few feet in a haphazard manner.

Reaching the top of the stairs, Mr. Sumel stopped to rest. Out of breath, he leaned on the banister, then turned to her. "Who needs a gym when you've got these stairs, eh?" He turned back around and moved down the hall into a small study.

She followed and entered the room as he wrestled himself into an armchair, relit his pipe, and propped his elbows on an oversized wooden desk. Looking around at the scattering of artifacts and baubles, she felt Mr. Sumel's eyes boring into her while he puffed on his pipe.

He motioned toward a small, rickety chair in front of his desk. "Make yourself at home."

Sitting, Zoë shifted her focus to the smoke-stained wall behind him, which was covered by a hand-drawn diagram of what looked like a massive electrical circuitry system.

Focusing on his desk, she took in the smattering of objects, one of which was a large, tarnished silver frame with a picture of a dark-haired young man.

Recognizing the mischievous smirk, she inquired, "Is this you?"

Mr. Sumel pulled his pipe from his mouth and winked at her. "Not bad, eh?"

She grinned. "I bet you were trouble."

A bit of phlegm cackled in his throat as he laughed. "Still am!"

Anxious to get the information she came for, she changed the subject. "Mr. Sumel, I have something I'd like to show you." She reached into her purse, retrieved her mother's book, and put it on the desk.

Upon seeing the book, he took a bent pair of half-moon spectacles from his desk, put them on, and flipped through it. Stopping in the middle, he pulled a dried lilac from in between the book's pages as an unmistakable expression of loss crept across his face.

The sight of the lifeless, scentless lilac made Zoë feel as if her heart was sinking into her stomach. To give them both a minute, she took a sip of the cinnamon-laced hot cocoa Mr. Sumel had made.

He glanced at her. "Good, isn't it?"

"Yes, actually."

After spinning the pressed lilac between his thumb and forefinger, he placed the dried flower back into the book and removed his glasses. "This is a very special book."

Putting down her mug, she interjected, "Read the inside cover."

After listening to him recite her mother's inscription, she took the box from her purse and set it on his desk. "Have you ever seen this before?"

Mr. Sumel's brow furrowed, his demeanor downshifting and leaving her feeling surprised that so little a man could take on such intensity. He picked up the box and examined its carved lid as he continued. "That was Pandora's mistake."

She queried, "What do you mean?"

Still scrutinizing the box's lid, Mr. Sumel replied, "Her fear of the box's shadows kept her from seeing what lay just beneath them: hope."

Mr. Sumel turned the box over and ran a knobby finger along the phrase engraved on the bottom.

Zoë pressed him. "Do you know how to open it?"

He set the box down on his desk and refocused on her. "'In the mouth of the wolf.'"

They watched one another for a moment before she broke the silence. "I don't understand."

Mr. Sumel seemed distracted as he leaned forward onto his elbows. "'In bocca al lupo' means 'In the mouth of the wolf.' It's there that you'll find the answers."

Wondering why he wasn't giving her a straight response, she felt annoyance flash through her along with a twinge of distrust. Hoping to settle her thoughts, she examined the schematic on the far wall.

She studied the diagram, noticing there was a gradient from left to right, evidence that the paper had aged year after year: the far left was a dingy, creamy brown; the middle, off-white with yellow edges; and the far right, shiny white. Finding the complex drawing fascinating, she questioned in earnest, "Did you draw that diagram yourself?"

Mr. Sumel swiveled his chair and glanced at the circuitry diagram behind him. "Yep. It's been a lifetime in the making." A visceral sense of pride emanated from him along with what she could only describe as impatience. Turning back toward her, he continued, "Not finished yet. But soon."

"What is it?"

The ever-present twinkle in his eye brightened. "Where electric current and the spark of God intersect. At least, in theory."

When first arriving, Zoë had assumed he was an eccentric and dawdling old bookseller. Now she surmised he was anything but.

Mr. Sumel opened his desk drawer, retrieved a small black-and-white photo, and placed it in front of her facedown. Looking at the back of the photo, she read the thin black handwriting in the corner: "Phinneas & Nilah at Wardenclyffe."

She turned the photo over: it was her mother and Mr. Sumel.

"'When there's no one else, he can do what I can't.'" Looking up at him, she continued, "She handed me this book, pointed to your shop's stamp, and said, 'When there's no one else, he can do what I can't.' It was the last thing she said to me before she died."

Mr. Sumel's eyes misted over. "There was no one in the world like her."

For reasons Zoë didn't understand, she felt that the room was too hot, the house too small, and all she could think about was getting outside into the winter air.

Puffing on his pipe, he focused his soft gaze on her, and when he did, her gut told her that he knew far more about her circumstances than he was willing to divulge.

After exhaling a thin line of smoke, he set down his pipe. "Zoë, you're going to need my help." The breath in her lungs turned cold as he continued. "And when you do, I'll be here."

13

WATCHMAKER

They sat in front of the fire, veiled in their respective cocoons. Bill was watching the flames dance atop a fresh set of logs inside the fireplace while Zoë recalled the look of loss in Mr. Sumel's eyes when he talked about her mother. She wondered why her mother had never mentioned such a close friend and confidant.

Bill shook his head. "I'm sorry, I've got a lot on my mind."

It was the same for her and in a way, she appreciated the fact that they could sit together in silence without the need for forced conversation. "We can sit as long as you like. There are no rules."

He smiled while watching the fire. "No rules?"

"Well, within reason," she quipped.

Turning to her, he seemed to have emerged from his cocoon. "Reason is subjective."

The playfulness of his tone was contagious as she, too, found herself breaking from her silo. "Gauging my boundaries?"

"Perhaps."

The intensity of his stare made her feel like he was peering at her very insides, a watchmaker examining each intricate gear as it spun. The longer he stared, the more transparent she felt. Lowering her chin, she challenged him. "There is one rule. The way you're looking at me right now—you can't do that."

Leaning forward, he put a warm hand on her thigh and looked into her eyes. "Okay, but just so you know, I'm a nonconformist."

She felt her skin flush. "Will I have trouble keeping you in line?"

He traced his finger around to the back of her knee. "Nope. I'm harmless."

She watched his finger drifting down her leg. "Somehow I doubt that."

With his arm extended and the cuff of his pressed shirt creeping upward, she could see a small black cross tattooed on the inside of his wrist. "Interesting place for a tattoo."

His finger stopped moving. "Better the mark of the creator than the mark of the beast." He seemed to withdraw back into the safety of his cocoon before continuing. "Can I ask you a personal question that's probably none of my business?"

Her pulse sped up. "Sure. But I can't promise I'll answer."

His gaze was pure and searching. "Do you believe in God?"

"No."

"An atheist?"

Her cocoon beckoned as she replied. "Yes."

Looking toward the fire, he leaned back into his chair. "I don't think God wants us to get too comfortable in life."

"Why do you say that?"

He turned his face toward her. "You disagree?"

Thinking about his question, she took a moment to respond. "In order to agree or disagree, I'd have to subscribe to the concept of God, which I don't."

It appeared to her that he was sinking into his thoughts. "Well, I do, and it seems that if I become too comfortable, He rips the rug out from underneath me. It's always been that way." She listened and waited for him to continue. "It's a sadistic sort of order to things, don't you think?"

Watching the honesty with which he awaited her response, she realized how crucial the topic was to his identity and systemic beliefs.

"What I think is that we are all responsible for our own lives." While continuing her thoughts, she felt her body stiffen. "And at the end of the day, the concept of God is conjecture anyway."

He appeared to be processing what she'd just said, like a mill wheel grinding down hard grain. "Do you truly believe that?"

"People need to believe there's something bigger than they are. It makes them feel safe."

Bill turned his gaze back toward the blazing flames. "I suppose there's a bit of truth in that. But don't you find it lonely?"

Gathering her words, she answered, "I don't believe in the concept of loneliness." His stare was now fixed on her as she finished her thought. "Companion or not, I don't think you're ever really alone."

His light eyes gleamed. "Why do I get the feeling I'll never know more about you than you want me to?"

She smiled and countered, "Because it's true."

He leaned forward in his chair. "You underestimate me."

Taking both of his hands, she guided him from his chair toward the bed. Once there, she laid him down, then positioned herself in front of him. Feeling his arm wrap around her waist, she melted into him and let the softness of his breath fall onto the back of her neck.

Intertwining her fingers with his, she closed her eyes and swore that his heart was beating inside her chest.

Tick, tock, tick, tock…

14

CRADLE TO TOMB

t feels like I'm a million pieces moving through darkness. There is newfound freedom as I travel and a sense that the molecules making up my misty form could split apart at any moment in search of their own patterns of flight.

I revel in the sensation of my many pieces gliding as one, but then hit what feels like a rock-solid wall. Suspended midair, my pieces compress until I'm whole again; and once the weight of my body is unified, I free-fall until I hit the ground and my eyes fly open.

With the wind knocked from my lungs, I'm lying flat on my back in a splayed position like a stunned bird. Fighting to take in a full breath, I dig my fingers into the soil to feel the earth beneath me while I wait for my blurred vision to sharpen. The soil feels like velvet and the air is filled with a floral fragrance that coaxes my sight back into vivid clarity. I inhale and feel my lungs expand with a fresh rush of air.

Easing myself into a sitting position, I take in the forest glade around me, then stare up at the cedar trees flanking the clearing like soldiers. This place is haunting in its serenity, and although I'm sure it's due to the impact

I've just experienced, I swear there are soft female voices floating around me like invisible fireflies.

Struggling to my feet, I stand for a moment and wait for the sensation of pins and needles to leave my legs. While my body comes back to life, I hear the blood rushing through my veins, fueling the muscles that will soon allow me to take a step forward.

The voices are saturating my mind, growing louder and focusing the origin of their sound into a single point behind me. As if commanded to do so, I turn and see a blown-out stone structure at the edge of the clearing. Realizing it's the same circular cathedral from my previous dream, I see the woman's execrable death emblazoned in my mind. With all the mental strength I possess, I bury the images and walk toward the cathedral's entrance.

The damage to the structure is monumental. The stained-glass ceiling is obliterated, the wall closest to me blown wide open, and the gates within, twisted piles of iron. In seeing the cathedral's grandeur reduced to wreckage, I feel my heart grow heavy. It occurs to me that the structure is a metaphor aligned with my father's memory; therefore, it makes a crude sort of sense that its stone is now rubble, just as his bones are dust.

With the voices still whispering all around me, I step over what's left of one of the walls and find that most of the stone floor has disintegrated into little more than chalky sand, which has fallen into a stark-white marble room below.

Peering into the room, I notice it's filled with white marble tombs that form a perfect circle. As if driven by the voices, I'm desperate to get a closer look at the tombs, and find myself moving along the edge of the blown-out foundation.

After navigating shards of glass, bent iron bolts, and splintered wood, I come upon a ladder made of iron rods embedded into the wall of the tomb. Bending down, I maneuver myself onto the ladder before descending into the crypt-like room. Once on the last rung, I place my foot onto the sand-covered marble floor, and when I do, the voices cease.

Moonlight floods downward from an indigo sky, painting the white crypt in violet light. The room captures the light and holds it captive like the very walls are drinking in the moon's glowing strands. Sending my gaze sweeping around the room, I notice one portion of the wall across from me has a small archway that looks to be an entrance into the tomb from underground.

Continuing to scan my surroundings, I focus on the unlit glass lanterns hanging along the walls, each a different shade of stained glass. The air smells of fresh flowers, but just beneath the notes of sweet perfume lingers the subtle yet distinct smell of death.

Walking around the room, I study the tombs and notice that lying on top of each one is a marble statue portraying its inhabitant. I count the Roman numerals carved into the sides of each individual tomb—twelve in all—until I come to an empty space in the circle where the thirteenth should be.

Next to the empty space, the twelfth tomb is covered in fresh flowers and wreaths. I brush away a thin layer of sand, then push aside several white roses from the statue's face, recognizing the woman's angelic features. Running my finger along her cheek, I'm disturbed by how realistic the statue seems. Like she is still alive and slumbering, her long hair flowing down the side of the tomb and wrapping around the letters of an engraved name: Mahayla. Beneath her name in smaller cursive lettering is the phrase "The Guardian of Winter's Rose."

While continuing to walk along the tombs, I observe that all the statues are of women, each of them carved with delicate care and skill. Every tomb bears an inscription, the first being "The Guardian of Spring's Seed," the second, "The Guardian of Summer's Seed." I keep moving around the circle to the fifth tomb, which reads "The Guardian of Spring's Thorn"; the ninth is identified as "The Guardian of Spring's Rose."

The inscriptions sink into the tissues of my mind as I ponder their meaning—the progression of seed to rose, the exquisiteness of the bloodred rose equipped with a flesh-piercing thorn—we women are a metaphor of the rose incarnate. As I run my hand over the smooth marble of one of the tombs' statues, reverence rises within me. The women are speaking, sending pieces of themselves into the room and covering me in the complex splendor of their souls. My body is responding to them, and what should be an eerie, death-filled crypt is for me a room filled with life. I feel I belong amongst them, as if together we form an inexplicable and binding sisterhood.

Now having returned to the empty space where the thirteenth tomb should be, I feel the air take on a damp chill that hovers around me like a rogue storm cloud. With my back to the center of the room, I stare into the arched underground entrance and am certain I'm being watched.

My muscles tense and the blood in my veins grows hotter while my bones become magnetized and charged with the desire to move toward the entrance. Then, as though they are materializing from the darkness, I see a pair of aqua eyes watching me from the shadows just inside the arched entryway.

The blood in my body rushes forward, pushing into my skin and begging to break free, while my heart thumps in my chest as if my blood is wild and swelling to twice its normal quantity. I meet its stare, take a breath, then attempt to intuit everything I can: I'm certain it's male, and feel it's in violent contrast to the sanctity of the women around us. There is a brutal, dangerous element in its eyes, like an animal filled with insatiable hunger and ferocity.

Yet unlike the smoke-filled presence from previous dreams, the entity before me feels more protector than predator. I'm about to take a step toward it when I hear someone speaking behind me.

"You complete the circle."

Turning away from the arched entrance, I face the center of the room.

Like fabric that has been ripped, a tear hangs in the air about six feet from me. A breeze drifts through the opening, causing either side of the slice to sway like curtains on a window through which a streak of silvery light shines.

As a man emerges from the tear and walks toward me, I'm unable to breathe. The black robe he wears clings to his strong body like a second skin and drags behind him, leaving a wide, serpentine trail in the sand-covered floor.

My bones are still magnetized, and I know the entity concealed at the arched entrance behind me is watching. I'm not sure why this knowledge gives me comfort, but it does; and in response, I'm able to take in a full breath.

The man is examining me like I'm a priceless work of art of which he's come to confirm authenticity, his piercing blue eyes inspecting each of my features before he fixates on the right side of my face.

Leaning forward, he studies the skin on my cheek, and for a moment I wonder if he's looking for the birthmark that once was there. Standing beneath his scrutinizing stare, I feel how calculating and cold he is, and were this not a dream, I'd seek to put swift and permanent distance between us.

Pulling away from me, he offers, "They speak to you." His gaze sweeps along the tombs surrounding us. "It's because you are one of them." The sharpness of his jawline matches his cold demeanor, and my dislike of him increases by the second.

He's about to speak again but pauses, then leans to the right and peers into the arched entry behind me. A knowing smile creeps across his full lips as he takes a step forward and whispers in my ear, "He is a deceiver." His hand is on my waist, and I feel his smooth skin against my cheek as he pulls me closer and continues, "And he cannot protect you."

His other hand moves up my arm, then slips along my shoulder and comes to rest on the side of my neck. It's unfathomable that I'm making no attempt to escape, but I feel anesthetized by him. Something in his eyes won't allow me to back away, and the longer I stare at him, the more muddled my thoughts become.

As if I'm standing before a fire, I feel heat radiating from his body while behind me the intensity of the aqua-eyed presence reaches a fever pitch. My magnetized bones are vibrating with such fervor they're creating sound in my ears until a melodic hum bustles in my head and melts into words: "Look away from him."

The man in front of me leans forward, kisses the side of my face, and before I can push him away, his mouth is on mine. His kiss is smothering me in raw lust, an experience both frightening and electrifying. My hands are on his chest and I'm shoving him as hard as I can, but his body is like steel.

Pain shoots through my lip like a shock. He's bitten me. Hard. I can taste my own blood and as he pulls away, he presses his lips together and forces my blood into his mouth. Closing his eyes, he revels in the taste, and my instincts tell me that now that his appetite has been whet, he'll want more.

Opening his eyes, he focuses on me and I swear his features have become distorted, as if the face of a demon is pulsing through the canvas of his smooth skin. "Now you cannot hide from us."

Behind him, thick black smoke spills in through the tear while the scent of burning sugar rams up my nostrils. My bones recharge and I hear the voice inside me again, stronger this time—a warning.

"*Run.*"

I race toward the ladder and climb. I'm at the top when my foot slips from the rung and I fall backward onto the ground with a skull-cracking crash. My temples are pounding, I can't keep my eyes open, and although I'm fighting with every sinew, I'm unable to stop myself from losing consciousness.

The scent of cinnamon and clove stirs my senses, but as I try to move, I feel a flash of pain all the way down my spine.

A gentle voice slips into my ears. "Take your time."

The sound of a fire crackling brings me closer to a conscious state until I'm able to open my eyes. My sight is hazy, but even still, I know I'm not at home in my own bed; and with that realization, I feel my body tense.

With my vision coming into focus, I let my gaze settle on the wall to my left, which is covered floor to ceiling with wooden shelves housing thousands upon thousands of colored jars and bottles. I scan the labels and contents of the glass containers: dried fire grass, willow root, silk tree sap. On the lower shelves, the contents of the jars edge toward the bizarre: crows' feet, water spider venom, moon sparrow wings.

Feeling a warm hand on my face, I turn my head away from the wall and see a beautiful woman sitting next to me. She watches me as though she's seen me before, her pale-blue eyes kind and emanating a depth of wisdom that indicates she's lived far more life than her appearance would suggest. The features of her face are delicate, her skin smooth, and although my mind may be playing tricks on me, I could swear that in the dim firelight her skin appears not brown, but jet black.

She shifts her focus to a table by the bed, then takes a damp cloth from a bowl and dabs my forehead. With her leaning over me, I watch a copper medallion around her neck swing forward and come to rest just below my collarbone. The strong scent of lavender drifts from her thick black hair, which is pulled back and fastened loosely at the base of her neck.

The open and flowing top she wears slips off her shoulder, revealing a set of crude scars where her breasts should be. Switching the cloth to her other hand, she reaches over me and dabs it along my hairline, and as she does I see another deep scar that runs from beneath her armpit down to her waist.

While putting the cloth back into the bowl on the table, she has turned the other side of her ribcage toward me, and I notice that it, too, has a long vertical scar from her armpit to her waist. She smiles while commenting, "No one is without battle scars. Some are just more obvious."

I want to apologize for staring, but she continues before I have the chance to speak. "Daegan will be along shortly."

As she rises from the bed, I take in the curves of her figure through the thin fabric of her long, billowy skirt. I watch her walk away and leave through a door to the right of the bed, and after hearing the door click shut, I study my surroundings.

I'm in a small one-room cottage, which appears to have materialized from the pages of a Grimms' fairy tale. Shifting my gaze upward, I examine the thick wooden beams supporting the vaulted roof, then send my focus to the walls, which are lit by several hanging glass lanterns.

The furniture is sparse—just a bed, side table, and small woven rug. As the fire lets out a loud pop, I look to the oversized fireplace beyond the foot of my bed. A log toppling from its perch hits the fire grate and breaks into tiny flaming pieces, sending a small plume of smoke drifting past a mural above the mantel.

The mural is a tile mosaic of a dragon, and the reflection of the firelight on its smooth tiles gives the dragon an element of life. It's an image I know well from a Cherokee story read to me as a child, a tale of a fearsome and relentless warrior who made it his mission to eradicate the white man from Cherokee lands. The warrior showed no mercy to those he slaughtered; and in this, he was given the nickname the Dragon. It was a story my mother referenced often to illustrate how the fires of hatred consume a person's soul.

The details of the mural are identical to those in my mother's book, even the way the black and white scales blend together to make the dragon appear black at times and white at others. Leaning against the bed frame, I continue watching the fire as it sends bits of smoky breath up toward the mural. I hear my mother's stories floating around in my thoughts like she is right beside me; and although the character of the Cherokee warrior was negative in the story, I always loved the image of the dragon, in part because I identify with its struggle.

Scanning the rest of the cottage, I notice someone standing in a dark corner to the right of the fireplace. Without a word, a large male figure emerges from the shadows; and as he moves toward me with his stark-white skin, tower-like build, and spiked white hair, I feel weightless, as though his presence has forced the density of gravity from the room.

Emanating from him like a vapor is the scent of pre-rain, which rushes toward me and seeps into my skin like liquid light. Now at my bedside, he takes me in with a pointed stare, his irises a bright emerald green that merges into darker hazel at the edges. The longer I stare into his eyes, the more relaxed I become.

Sitting on the bed and facing me with the firelight behind him, it looks like his spiky white hair is comprised of flames. And as he studies every inch of my face, I have the strong feeling he's unnerved by my presence.

While he continues examining me, I watch how the firelight hits the angles of his cheekbones, his skin poreless—almost porcelain—with the faintest hint of a white-haired five o'clock shadow. At his temples are sky-blue tattoos that appear alive as they swirl and coil in on themselves like miniature snakes.

The entire room fills with his sinewy thought, which creates a spider-like web around us. When he places an index finger on the inside of my wrist, I hear his booming heartbeat in my ears and feel a gentle pressure in the back of my head. Images flip through my mind until the scene of the woman's death is resurrected from my memory. Her death replays in my mind's eye, and as if he, too, sees the memory inside my thoughts, his sturdy build deflates and his heartbeat fades to near silence.

For his sake, I attempt to close my thoughts and encircle my mind with an invisible barrier. In response, he releases his finger from my wrist. As he takes my shoulders in his strong hands, I find that his touch brings with it the sensation that each of my cells is being cleansed, wrung out, and rewired. When he lays me down, I've little will to protest and instead let him turn me over and inspect the sides of my neck and upper back.

Pulling down the blanket and revealing my naked skin, he rolls me onto my side. I feel his gaze sweeping over my bare skin like he's searching for something, but for the life of me I can't imagine what. After having looked at every inch of my body, he pulls the thick blanket back over me and sits, pensive, at my bedside. While focusing on his broad shoulders, I see the weight he holds there like an invisible mass of debris.

As an afterthought, he reaches out and tucks the blanket under my chin. Then he leans toward me and exhales a sweet breath in the center of my forehead. The breath seeps into my mind until my thoughts become empty and I feel myself sink into deep, spongy sleep.

15

LIE 'N' WAIT

Straining to open her eyes, Zoë felt something soft brushing against her chin while a thunderous vibration rocked her chest. Taking in a deep breath, she exhaled what felt like liquid air as her vision cleared.

Lucille's furry face was inches from hers, and instead of the usual you-mean-nothing-to-me sideways stare, Lucille stretched a tender foot forward and pawed her face. Continuing to purr, Lucille closed her eyes and kneaded Zoë's chest. Inexplicably, Zoë felt comforted by Lucille's presence.

A dying candle on the bedside table reflected off the window that framed the darkness of the indigo-black night. A fire sputtered and spat its last smoky breaths as Zoë settled into her covers, feeling grateful to be awake and in her own bed.

Despite herself, she reached out and began petting the top of Lucille's rump while her heart beat in time with the steady rhythm of Lucille's purr. Upon hearing Lula's bedroom door creak open down the hall, Lucille leapt from Zoë's chest, bounded to the floor, and slipped under the bed.

A quiet knock drifted into the room as the door's flourished antique handle dipped a shadowy eye toward the floor. Lula stepped in on un-characteristically light feet. "You all right?" Walking across the room and sitting next to her, Lula placed a motherly hand on Zoë's cheek. "You've slept nearly twenty hours."

Trying to hide her unease, Zoë replied, "I must have needed it."

Lula looked toward the floor. "Why don't you cancel tonight?"

"I'm fine."

Zoë had a strange feeling that Lula was more than just concerned, as she had a bit of panic in her voice. "What about taking a break? Out of the city, perhaps—"

Zoë interrupted. "I don't need a break."

Lula examined her with an accountant's precision. "You don't seem like yourself." Placing a plump hand on her cheek, she continued, "Please consider getting away. The old cabin, perhaps? I know the forest soothes you—"

As the house phone rang, Lula gave her one last pleading look, then left the room to answer the clanging phone in the hallway.

Now awake and present in her body, the dream faded, but he didn't. The porcelain man remained emblazoned in her mind and she could still feel his hands on her skin. An intense scraping sound interrupted her thoughts and drew her gaze to the right, where Lucille had snuck from underneath the bed and was now up on her hind legs shredding the back of a velvet chair. Zoë hurled a small pillow across the room, missing Lucille by inches as she flew back underneath the bed.

Lula entered the room with a resounding huff and settled herself onto the bed. "The Prince of Darkness is going to be early." She placed a gentle hand on Zoë's shoulder. "You'd tell me if something was wrong, right?"

Zoë swallowed hard. "Of course."

Lula bent forward and kissed the top of her head, placing a loving and waxy seal on the lie she knew Zoë had just told her. She got up and walked to the wardrobe, opened it, then took out a vintage peacock-blue corset and laid it on the back of the chaise lounge. "Up an' at 'em."

Zoë ambled out of bed, then walked into the bathroom, and without even turning on the light, washed her face. Part of her still couldn't believe she had slept for twenty hours. What must Lula have thought? Burying her face into the softness of a downy white towel, she took a breath and attempted to steady her thoughts.

Walking back into the bedroom, she made her way to Lula, who was standing by the bed with her clothes. She gripped the bedpost hard while Lula wrapped the corset around her waiting frame. With the sturdy metal beginning to shape and form her torso, Zoë closed her eyes and reveled in the comfort the corset offered: it would hold her in and keep her together.

After a few tugs of heavy cinching, Lula tied off the last of the laces and turned Zoë around, her voice colliding with the blanched air. "You're a vision. Give us a smile."

Zoë forced a smile, then watched Lula zip from the room.

Wishing she'd been able to convince Zoë to leave the house, Lula paced in the foyer, fingering a small vine she'd pulled from Zoë's door handle. Whatever was going on in the house was intensifying, not to mention the fact that a mini-demon had taken up residence within the fireplace and walls.

As was her habit with all things, Lula paralleled the creature to its mythological counterpart, Eurynomos, a carrion feeder inhabiting Hades' Underworld who sucked the meat from the bodies of the dead until nothing remained but the polished ivory of de-fleshed bones. Concerned that her immersion into her mythological stories was polluting reality, Lula wondered if the presence was real and if she had indeed witnessed it scrambling up into the fireplace like a thief in the night.

But only a moment into challenging her own mind, her gut resounded back that what she'd seen was real; and explainable or not, it was a problem needing a swift and permanent solution. Mired in thought, she wondered. What business did Hades' death-eater have in a house filled with the living?

Again, she thought of Mr. Black's letter: "Take comfort in knowing that 'In all chaos, some order exists.'" She spoke quietly to herself. "That's not a comfort when my hands are bloody tied."

Lula stopped pacing and brightened for a moment as she spied a few butterscotch hairs littering her immaculate floor. Lucille was back. She didn't have a moment to process Lucille's return before her thoughts were stamped out by the sound of Mr. Llewellyn mid-conversation as he walked up the front steps.

Mr. Llewellyn's voice shot out while Lula snuck to the door and placed an ear against its thick wood. "Get to the point." Frozen silence crept beneath the door until his voice found her again. "For a man at the top of your field, I expected a more creative approach to my situation."

She could feel his frustration pushing through the door as he fired back, "No. I understand. Nothing, in your professional opinion, can be done." Mr. Llewellyn's voice dripped with acid as he continued. "That won't be necessary. I'll find someone more competent."

After a moment, the doorbell chimed. Lula waited, then opened the door. "Evening, Mr. Llewellyn. Please, come in."

His steel stare swept over her as he walked toward the living room without a word.

"Right, then. I'll just let Zoë know you've arrived."

Sidestepping from the foyer, Lula hurried up the stairs, crossed the hallway, then stopped outside Zoë's room and watched her through the slivered opening of the bedroom door. Sitting in her chair studying herself in the mirror, legs crossed and lapis robe spilling to the floor, Zoë was picturesque.

When Zoë was younger, she'd once said, "I may never be beautiful, Lula, and I don't care. I just want my life to have meaning." But she was beautiful. She was an artist's lady, a breathing image, and her life, in many ways, meant everything.

Seeming to sense Lula's lingering stare, Zoë called out, "Is he here?"

Lula pushed open the door and stepped into the bedroom. "Yes. A bit of warning, though. He's not in the best of moods."

Zoë's body stiffened as she turned, storm-gazed. "Send him up."

16

BOUND

He was so fucking furious from the conversation with his doctor that the soles of his feet were throbbing. Every step up the staircase brought him closer to the undetonated explosion waiting beneath his steel-bound exterior.

Reaching the top of the stairs, he let the scent of Zoë's perfume drift into his consciousness, hoping its sweetness would offer a temporary reprieve from the ferocity and bitterness inside him. But as the doctor's words slithered through his mind—"Medically, there's nothing more we can do"—her floral perfume lingered in his nostrils a moment longer, then collided with his rancorous thoughts and turned stale. In his entire life, he'd never given up on what he wanted, nor had he ever accepted no as a final answer. And in this, he knew he'd have to find an alternative, another avenue to pursue.

He stood outside her bedroom door and attempted to regain his composure while reminding himself that the last time they'd been together, there had been significant progress. She was the closest he'd come to an alternative, and at times, he hated her for it. He felt one shouldn't put their happiness in the hands of another, but where Zoë was concerned, he didn't have a choice. What she offered was an abstract form of liberation.

Looking down at the bright-red shopping bag in his hand, he stared at the corset peeking out from the impeccably folded tissue paper inside and tightened his grip around the bag's handle. He'd chosen the corset for its hard leather exterior and white satin lining, both of which represented Zoë to perfection.

He shifted his focus to the fiery light coming from beneath her door and watched the orangey glow lighting up the tips of his shined shoes. Fitting, he thought, seeing how she was his trial by fire, his trek across a threshold of hot and unforgiving coals.

He loosened his grip and traded his shallow breaths for deeper, more controlled intakes of air; when his lungs expanded, he felt his back ache in response. Yet the pain was welcome because he needed her brutality again tonight—the urge was so potent that he loosened his belt buckle beneath his closed suit jacket in preparation.

He opened her bedroom door, and when it swung open, he saw her standing by the bed draped in a silk robe he'd purchased for her several months prior. She was beautiful, but in a way that spoke to a bygone era. One far from the modern, rail-thin, overly bleached plasticky types who often sought his affections. Studying her, he noticed the look in her eyes was cold, yet the features of her face were relaxed and inviting. It fascinated him that she had the ability to both entice and rebuke a person with a single glance.

While walking toward her, he surmised that her mood was no more settled than his. Something was on her mind, and for a moment he felt a flash of anger rise through him at the notion that her attention might be in any way divided.

Now in front of her, he set the bag down, removed the corset, and placed it on the bed. She eyed him before turning around and gripping one of the four carved bedposts. He removed her robe, then watched it fall to the floor and gather around her stilettoes.

The collar of his shirt felt tight as his eyes swept up her legs, past her waist, and to the pale skin of her upper back. Her hands were raised above her head and clutching the bedpost in a way that made her look like she was bound at the wrists and suspended from the canopy bed's frame. Never having seen her in a position of such physical vulnerability, he was surprised at the effect it had on him, and he felt his skin flush with heat.

He untied the laces of the corset she was wearing, then reached around her waist and unclasped the hooks in the front one by one until it slipped from her body and fell to the floor. Taking the leather corset from the bed, he put it around her waist and hooked each clasp as though he were pounding nails into the lid of a coffin.

Once all the clasps were secure, he brought his hands around to the back of the corset and pulled outward on the crisscross of each lace until the corset's firm leather cut into the skin under her arms. He moved downward and tightened the laces at her waist, yanking so hard the muscles in her back tensed.

Hearing her attempt to take a deep breath, he wrenched the laces taut, held them outward, and cut off her ability to inhale. Her waist was now infinitesimal and the sight of it was pushing him to the point of losing control.

The cruelty he craved from her had been turned outward, and he found himself wanting to play her role instead. Jerking the laces again, he watched the muscles in her neck and back become rigid as she tried to take in the slightest bit of air.

But he couldn't let her breathe; he wanted her to feel the pain of being alive but unable to suck in the life-giving oxygen around her. Then, if just in metaphor, she'd understand the cruel and weighted inequity of the circumstances he'd been forced to live with every day.

Part of his mind was commanding him to stop, but the harder he bound her waist, the more powerful he felt. It was like a drug, seeing her struggling to breathe, and knowing she might pass out only seemed to fuel his ruthlessness.

She was clawing at the front of the corset, desperate to free herself, and he could feel her wrath as she fought against his unyielding grip. There was a frenzy rising inside him, a perverse pleasure that left him desperate to see how far she would let him go.

Having been at the feet of her mercilessness, he felt that if he could keep her bound a little longer, she'd soon find, as he had, that on the other side of agony is bliss. Pure, unsurpassed bliss…

Somehow she ripped open a few of the steel closures at the front of the corset, whipped around, and hit him so hard he almost fell to the ground. Blood leaked into his mouth and the sight of her so furious further provoked him.

There was one thing he knew that would send her over the edge, and before she could stop him, he kissed her. Her mouth was hot and wet, and the taste of her lips drove him mad. Pulling away from him, she shoved him backward and hit him again—this time so hard he felt a sting all the way down his spine.

The look in her eyes was pure, unadulterated rage, and he knew he'd pay for what he'd done. But feeling the surge of sexual aggression inside him, the insatiable need to release all his pent-up hunger, was worth whatever vengeance she'd exact; because for the first time in years, he wanted to be alive.

17

FABLE TO FIRE

She unbound herself from her corset, threw it to the floor, and fell into a chair, forcing a gulp of air into her aching lungs. As her skin made contact with the velvet chair, she felt relieved to be naked—and free.

They had never explored reversing their roles, and having had a taste of the true nature inside him, Zoë wouldn't hesitate to express the full range of her wrath when next they met. Yet although she was incensed, she had to admit she'd never felt him so aroused, so close. For it was pain, whether given or received, that gave him pleasure. And without hesitation or mercy, she would make him bleed.

Her thoughts were interrupted by the sound of her phone buzzing on the vanity. She walked across the room, picked it up, and read the waiting text. "We newd to talkj. tonight. Urengt. -p.s."

She typed back, "Who is this?"

Minutes crawled by until her phone vibrated. "Nilah's friend"

She texted, "Mr. Sumel?"

After another lengthy pause, her phone buzzed. "please. Come...tongiht"

Curious as to what could be so urgent, she confirmed, "Be there as soon as I can."

She walked to her wardrobe and dressed in jeans and a sweater. Crossing to the vanity, she threw her hair in a ponytail, grabbed a pair of boots, and headed toward her bedroom door.

After opening it and stepping into the hallway, she slipped across the hall and crept down the stairs. But once at the last step, she almost tripped over Lucille, who sat at the base of the stairs in total darkness.

Regaining her balance, she leaned against the wall and put on her boots while Lucille twitched her fat tail back and forth in wide sweeps across the floor, her eyes seeming to glow in the dark and her whiskers sticking straight out like severed fishing line.

Walking on light feet across the foyer, she grabbed her coat from the closet and made her way to the door. Lucille chased after her and let out a whiny meow as Zoë opened the front door and stepped out into the cold.

Struggling to put on her coat in the bustling wind, she descended the steps and turned to head down the sidewalk. As she passed the living-room window, she saw Lucille sitting on the windowsill glaring at her.

Focusing on the street, she kept walking and let light from the moon surround her like an old friend. She recalled her mother saying that the moon cleanses the soul, and beneath its incandescent light, Zoë would often find her mother praying to Great Spirit, "Watch over my Little Dragon. Keep her spirit strong and her heart pure."

Zoë twisted the bracelet on her wrist and ran her thumb over the small stone at its center while examining the flood of moonlight shining down and bathing the street's leafless trees in radiant light.

I'm strong, Mother, but my heart is not pure.

She felt a sharp chill in her bones like a brutal jab from winter's knife. After reaching the street corner, she was about to hail a cab when she realized the street was devoid of traffic. Looking around, she found it odd there wasn't a soul in sight on what was supposed to be a bustling and well-traveled street; it was as though the entire neighborhood was no more than a painting frozen in time.

Appearing from thin air, a lone cab came down the street toward her. She held up her hand to call the taxi over, then stepped down off the curb and onto the icy pavement. After the taxi stopped beside her, she watched a man exit the other side of the cab and walk across the street. Keeping her focus on him, she ducked into the cab, noticing his stride was precise and measured, as if he had calculated the exact number of steps it would take to reach the curb.

The collar of his long black overcoat was turned up and his fedora was tipped to one side. Catching a glimpse of his black and white wingtip shoes as he stepped up onto the curb, it seemed to her he had materialized from a noir film.

The driver inquired, "Where to, lady?"

"Eleven Minetta Lane."

The taxi pulled away from the curb while she continued watching the man through the back window.

After only a few steps, he stopped, turned, and stood in the shadow of a building on the corner. The brim of his hat was tipped downward, and although she couldn't see his face, she could feel him watching her. Somewhere in the back of her mind, she couldn't shake the feeling that they'd met before.

Zoë rang the dingy doorbell at 11 Minetta Lane, and after what felt like ages she saw Mr. Sumel walking down the hallway with a candle in hand.

Opening the door, he flashed a warm smile. "Thank you for coming." He hobbled down the hallway toward the kitchen before disappearing into the darkness.

She stepped into the foyer, then turned to close the front door and felt her body stiffen. Across the street, hat brim pulled down over his face, was the man with the wingtip shoes. Slamming the door, she whipped around and called out, "Mr. Sumel!"

Turning back toward the front door, she peered across the street but found the man had gone.

"Mr. Sumel?"

He bellowed back, "In the kitchen."

With her back now to the door, Zoë pulled out her cell phone and used the light to navigate the hallway. While walking past one of the stuffed bookcases, she noticed a large black book inching itself off the shelf. She stopped in front of the bookcase, then reached out and caught it before it fell to the floor.

Looking back toward the empty space where the book had been, she found herself face-to-face with a beady-eyed, furry white rodent. "Jesus Christ!"

Mr. Sumel appeared next to her with a cup of cocoa. "That's Ziggy." After handing her the mug, Mr. Sumel adjusted his half-moon spectacles. "Ready?"

"For what?" she quipped.

Mr. Sumel took Ziggy from the bookshelf and rubbed the top of his head. "Did she scare you, little fella?" Tucking Ziggy under his arm, he turned from the hallway and began his labored ascent up the creaking stairs.

Putting the book back on the shelf, she read the title stamped into the book's spine: *Nikola Tesla: Colorado Springs Notes, 1899–1900*. She continued down the hall and followed Mr. Sumel up the stairs. "Why don't you have any electricity?" While waiting for him to reply, she studied Ziggy and realized he was a guinea pig, albeit the fattest one she had ever seen.

"I do. It just doesn't work very well."

Once at the top of the stairs, Mr. Sumel stopped for a moment and turned to look at her. "Those stairs are a killer!"

She followed him down the hall into his lantern-lit study. Placing her mug on the desk, she sat and watched as he lit his pipe and reveled in the first puff. Ziggy waddled to the center of the desk and stared at her.

"Mr. Sumel…"

He smiled and sent a cloud of smoke billowing into the room. "Please, call me Phinneas."

"Your text—"

"Yes, sorry about that. I don't type very well. Bum hand," he explained. As he held up his knotted hand, she could see that his ring and pinky fingers were pressed into his palm like petrified wood.

"I don't remember giving you my mobile number."

Squinting, he spoke. "You didn't."

Ziggy walked to the edge of the desk, then launched himself into her lap. Mr. Sumel winked. "He likes you."

Although reluctant, she ran her hand along Ziggy's back, which caused him to flatten out like a pancake. "So how did you get my number?"

Mr. Sumel lowered his chin. "Well, I'll tell you." He leaned forward. "I'm smarter than I look."

With a dose of annoyance, she changed the subject. "Your text sounded urgent."

He retrieved a large black and white shopping bag from the floor and set it on his desk. She read the silver lettering on the side: NAUGHTY NOIR.

Noticing her focusing on the bag, he offered, "Not too proud to steal the neighbor's recycling. Never know when you'll need a good sturdy shopping bag." His chair let out a creaking sound as he leaned back and continued. "I need a favor." Taking a puff of his pipe, he watched her, then exhaled. "I need you to get something of your mother's. I believe one of your half sisters may have it."

She felt her muscles tense.

"It's a small painting of a meadow."

Quite certain he was mistaken, she countered, "I have all my mother's things."

He pulled his pipe from his mouth. "You don't have this." Before she could contest, he offered, "Besides, I'd never ask a favor without giving something in return."

He slid the shopping bag across the desk toward her, which she took and set on the floor. While she stared at the antique lettering of NOIR on the bag, an image of the man with the wingtip shoes crashed into her thoughts. "Mr. Sumel, I think someone followed me here."

He gummed his pipe. "Well, for one, I'm sure someone did, and for two, I'd be lying if I said I wasn't concerned for your safety."

Ziggy squirmed as she placed him back on the desk. "What do you mean?"

Mr. Sumel leaned forward, put his elbows on the desk, and began petting Ziggy. "I had a visit from a man the other day. A very odd fellow."

She nudged him. "And?"

"He wanted information about you."

Zoë felt adrenaline racing through her system. "What kind of information?"

Without answering her, Mr. Sumel set down his pipe.

She prodded him further. "What aren't you telling me?"

He smiled and shook his head. "Just like your mother."

A measured ache shot up from her heart and lodged itself inside her throat like a piece of splintered wood.

"I see so much of her in you. You have her fire." He stopped petting Ziggy and eyed her. "I suppose you get it from both sides, actually."

She shifted in her chair and forced herself to speak. "Mr. Sumel, what information did the man want about me?"

He picked up his pipe. "He thinks you're…unique."

She refuted, "He'll be disappointed. I'm actually quite ordinary."

Mr. Sumel watched her for a moment before continuing. "And not only has he told me how to confirm his suspicions, he'll pay handsomely to have me prove it."

"Prove what?"

Mr. Sumel paused. "Give me your hand." He pulled a safety pin from his desk drawer and reached across the desk. "Bear with me here."

Laden with reluctance, she leaned forward and put her hand on top of his rough palm. Quick as lightning, he pricked her finger and squeezed several drops of blood onto the center of his desk.

Taking an antique lighter from a small tray, he positioned its strike head above the drops of her blood. He struck the flint and lowered the flame until it leapt from the flint and hovered above her blood. Zoë felt her heart begin pounding in her chest, and in response, the flame suspended above her blood shot upward several feet.

Mr. Sumel looked up at her, his eyes filled with astonishment as he spoke. "I just needed you to understand—you're anything but ordinary."

18

'NIGHT, LOVE

Zoë awoke to an explosive clap of thunder followed by the sound of sleet pelting the large bay windows of her bedroom. Realizing she'd had a night of dreamless sleep, she breathed a sigh of relief, turned on her side, and took in the warmth of the fresh fire.

Shifting her gaze to the clouds looming outside her window, she thought about how much she loved days like this, curled up with a storm raging outside. But the burgeoning lightness was shoved aside by the image of the flame hovering above her blood, a flame that responded to her mood, her emotions—an event she'd never have believed if she hadn't seen it with her own eyes.

Seeking refuge from her thoughts, she let her focus drift to the tattered sketchbook on her bedside table and felt her heart growing heavy. After having taken it from the bag Mr. Sumel gave her the night prior, she'd peeked inside and read the inscription her mother had written to him on the inside cover: "For my friend, the Watcher. Love, Nilah." Part of her had wanted to study the sketches inside the book, but she hadn't been able to force herself past the first page, as being that close to her mother was too much weight to carry.

Shifting her gaze away from the book and toward the window, Zoë thought of her mother's inscription to Mr. Sumel and how she'd called him the Watcher. Such a name made it seem her mother had not only trusted him, but also relied on him—both of which Zoë was having difficulty accepting.

Once out of bed, Zoë made her way across the room to her vanity, then sat, opened her laptop, and typed "Phinneas Sumel" into the search box.

Results For Phinneas Sumel: 42

The first item caught her eye: "Heralded Inventor Phinneas Sumel Disgraced After Ethics Scandal." She clicked on the article. Her screen flashed neon blue, then black before the page reloaded.

Results For Phinneas Sumel: No Results Found

She attempted her search several more times, all to the same end before putting in "Sumel & Sons."

Results For Sumel & Sons: 1

She clicked on "Sumel & Sons Antique Books" and was taken to a simple landing page that read "Established in 1924 by Felix M. Sumel, Sumel & Sons houses a unique inventory of the world's rarest antiquarian books."

She closed her laptop and resumed watching the storm, reminding herself that her mother trusted him, so by proxy, she should as well.

Mr. Sumel said he would make contact when he knew more about the man who was seeking information on her, but in the meantime she'd agreed to the insurmountable task of contacting the Deadlings. She could still hear their voices—Evie, Gracie, and Fiona—whispering, "Ugly little savage…"

Her cell phone vibrated next to her. She looked down as two new text messages appeared. The first one was from J.T. "Coffee? i come to ur house…15 min?"

Finding his text odd, she typed, "You okay?"

While waiting for a reply, she checked the other text, which was from Bill. "Hello. Can we make it 8:30?" Bill was the only client to whom she'd ever given her cell phone number. He'd asked her for it as a way to set up appointments, and although that was Lula's task, she couldn't bring herself to tell him no.

The phone buzzed with J.T.'s response. "Details later. need to meet."

She texted him back. "Rather not meet here. See you @ Rose Café."

She then typed a reply to Bill. "8:30 is fine."

A clap of thunder boomed like cannon fire outside the window, and she swore the residual electricity in the air was rattling her bones. She crossed to her wardrobe, dressed, put on her boots, and walked down the stairs into the foyer. Grabbing her coat and scarf from the closet, she bundled up and headed toward the door.

Stopping to grab an umbrella, she saw a note taped to the door: "Errands. Left you a bite in the fridge. —Lula"

She opened the door and left the house, then walked down the steps as a gust of wet, cold wind swept down the street and almost knocked her to the ground.

The sleet was turning hard, like icy knives raining down from the sky; as it hit her face, she felt her cheeks sting. Straining to open her umbrella, she ran for cover under a construction scaffold down the street.

She ducked under the scaffold and saw a small dark-haired girl swirling her finger in a slushy puddle. The girl's mother was next to her and fumbling through her purse as the little girl looked at Zoë. As if sucked into a vignetted flashback, she was the little girl's age and a younger version of her own voice rang in her ears. "Mamma, why does it rain?"

"To cleanse our shadows."

"Oh."

Though her mother smiled on the outside, Zoë knew even then that cancer was rotting away her insides. Gentle words floated from her mother's lips. "Who loves you?"

"You do."

Her mother placed a soft finger to the tip of Zoë's nose. "How much?"

"More than this world," she answered.

Her mother knelt as she pulled the two sides of Zoë's coat together. "A thousand worlds aren't enough to hold my love for you. Now, button that coat or people will think you're a motherless child."

Her heart had ached in that moment as she realized her mother's love would soon be gone. Fighting tears, she'd stared at the ground, hoping her mother wouldn't see how upset she'd become. But knowing Zoë as well as she did, her mother lifted her chin and looked into her eyes. "Little Dragon, I'll be with you always."

A rolling crack of thunder overhead transported Zoë back into the present. She watched with envy as the little girl and her mother darted from underneath the scaffold and ran across the street hand in hand.

I am and will always be a motherless child.

Finally opening her umbrella and walking out into the rain, she rounded the corner and made her way to the Rose Café. Once in front of the door, she could see J.T. sitting at a table in the back, looking nothing less than woeful, and in response, she felt a knot forming in her stomach. Continuing to stand outside the door, she watched him wringing his hands together in a manner that made her feel he'd soon wear through his skin.

Steadying herself, she entered the café, and when J.T. looked up at her, he brightened. At the table, she was greeted by his kind smile and a kiss on the cheek. "Took the liberty, hope that's okay."

Sitting down, she glanced at a steaming latte.

"I know it's your favorite—made with whole milk." The tone of his voice was riddled with nervousness as he spoke. "And…merry Christmas."

After removing her scarf, she set it in her lap. "Thank you, but Christmas is weeks away." Staring at the waning bruise beneath his eye, she inquired, "J.T., what's going on?"

"I've known you a long time. I…" He trailed off and looked down at the table. She'd never seen him so flustered. "I…"

Still wringing his hands together and watching the steam rise from her cup, his lips seemed to be glued shut.

"J.T., what is it?"

He looked up at her and spoke. "I felt I should be the one to tell you."

"Sorry, I don't understand."

Leaning forward, he took her hand. "He's gone, Zoë."

She couldn't breathe. Instead, she sat still, like a statue.

His words reverberated in her ears and caused her now-twisting and bloody guts to rise in her throat like a horde of tentacled madmen who wanted nothing more than to strangle the messenger sitting before her.

J.T.'s warm hand was still on hers. "He left everything to you."

She didn't want any more of Evan's money. She'd give it all away just to know he was in the world somewhere—alive.

J.T. pulled an envelope from his coat pocket and set it on the table, the writing on the front crooked and shaky like that of an old man's. As if in a trance, she found her voice sounding foreign as it left her lips. "He was the last of them."

"The last of who?"

"My guardians."

J.T.'s posture hardened as he instructed her, "You'll need to see his lawyer. She's the executor of the estate."

Shock had set in now and she was feeling lightheaded. "Yes, send me the information."

"The accounts he has with me are being put in your name." J.T. squeezed her hand as if to infuse her with solid strength.

She stared at the envelope on the table, refusing to touch it, as contact with its pearled face meant admitting his passing was real.

"Are you going to be okay?"

All three of them were gone: she was motherless, fatherless—and now Evan, too. "I have to go."

"Let me help you home." He reached across the table and rubbed her shoulder.

Zoë stood and wrapped her scarf around her neck like the noose she wished it to be. "I'm all right. Thank you for coming in person."

Tracing his thumb along her cheek, he offered, "I'm here if you need me." Gathering her in his arms, he kissed the top of her head.

"I know, thank you."

As he held her, she could sense what he wanted to say, but she prayed he wouldn't. She knew he loved her but couldn't stand to hear him say it, at least not now.

"Promise you'll call me if you need anything."

She pulled away from him and forced a smile. "I will."

Seeming to understand she couldn't do it on her own, he took the envelope from the table and slipped it into her purse. Squeezing his hand, she walked from the café into the icy rain.

Rounding the corner onto Jane Street, she felt her bones throbbing as if her bits and pieces didn't quite fit together anymore—her skeleton was now just a creaky and shoddy structure failing to support the pale skin of her adult silhouette.

The tentacled madmen inside her squirmed and thrashed as though wanting to break free from their fleshy cage. Nothing felt right and her mind was a jumbled pile of thoughts, memories, and voices: his laugh, his kiss, his love…

By the time she reached the steps to her house, she was ceasing to function, and used the last of her energy to haul herself up the stairs and through the front door. Mourning Evan's death in kind, the house felt lifeless and cold, which only served to further unsettle the fury-filled guts inside her.

Forcing her leaded legs up the stairs, Zoë tried to bury her thoughts. But as she crossed the hallway into her bedroom and closed the door, she knew nothing could subdue the ache lodged in her heart. She stripped down to her underwear and crawled into bed while outside the thunder rolled and the sleet beat her window until it sounded like it might shatter into a thousand pieces.

Rolling onto her side, she curled her knees up into her chest and let the memories of him play in her mind. Then, like an image coming to life, she swore she could feel his arms around her, his breath on her neck, his whisper in her ear as exhaustion overtook her.

What I want is dreamless, motionless sleep, but instead, I'm stuck between the parallel lines of dreaming and waking. I feel like a doll that's been torn apart, and as I hover in empty space, pieces of my soft stuffing drift around me like an array of cottony snow.

My mind's eye fills with a full and vivid memory of Evan: I'm watching him sleep, it's a warm summer night, and he's lying on his side facing me. He's naked save a small corner of the sheet that's draped over his hip and upper thigh. Studying his smooth skin in the moonlight, I trace a line from his neck down to his shoulders and onto his upper arm with my finger like I'm drawing him into life.

There is a natural curl to his dark hair, which he hates and I love. Most of all, I adore how it falls to one side when he sleeps, like a wave has frozen in place on its way in to shore. He's affectionate when awake but even more so in slumber. He can't go a minute without some part of his body touching mine, and if I inch away, I feel his hand find my waist and pull me toward him.

The rhythm of his breathing is slow and steady, which echoes the way he does most things in his life. With our bodies intertwined, both of us are overheated yet neither seems to care; and in a kind of liquid unison, I feel a bead of sweat roll down my neck as I watch a twin drop slip down the side of his face.

There are gentle lines around his eyes and distinguished-looking flecks of grey in his weekend-whiskered face. Next to his sun-touched skin, my skin is pale and nubile in a way that calls the vast difference in our ages to light, but I care little for such trivialities. He is perfect for me, and I can't imagine ever fitting into the curve of another man's soul the way I fit into his.

A feeling of deep, guttural loss grips me from the inside out and pushes me over the cliff of my memory until it feels like I'm in an unending free-fall. I fight the descent knowing that what I need now is stillness to gather my tattered pieces and stitch them back together.

I'm desperate to restuff myself, to push my cloudy fibers and mangled bits into a smooth-sewn and seamless exterior. For beneath that doll-like skin of ivory muslin, everything will be new again and perhaps then I can learn to live in a world without him.

Without warning, my head slams into something hard and my temples begin to throb. Warm liquid drips down my face, and when it enters my mouth, I taste the iron-laden spice of my own blood. Like a light being snuffed out, my thoughts grow dark on all sides, and I embrace the emptiness overtaking my mind.

19

FALLEN

Zoë opened her eyes and waited for the details of her surroundings to come into focus. Her forehead was aching and sending pulses of pain down the side of her neck while the lingering memory of Evan stayed in the back of her thoughts like a ghost in the shadows.

Turning her head to the right, she took in the moonlight beaming in through the window and saw someone in a dark corner of the room.

"How worried should I be?"

She watched Bill cross the room and sit on the bed next to her.

Trying to shake off disorientation, she spoke the first words that came to mind. "Is Lula here?"

"I don't think so," he replied.

Distracted by her pounding headache, Zoë attempted to sort through the confusion muddling her thoughts. "How did you get in?"

"The front door was open."

She couldn't remember getting home from seeing J.T., let alone whether or not she'd locked the front door. Embarrassment was ambling along the edges of her thoughts, and the intensity of his stare made her feel he could see right through her. "You didn't wake me."

His focus moved downward toward her chest. "I tried. I stopped the bleeding. Was about to call someone—"

She looked down at her bloodied bra and felt her pulse race. "I just need a minute."

After standing, she went into the bathroom, turned on the light, and stared at herself in disbelief. There was a cut at her hairline, and she could see where Bill had wiped some of the bloodstains from her face and neck. She washed her face, then removed her bra, cleaned the remaining blood from her neck, and threw on a robe.

Bill's voice drifted in from the bedroom. "You were out cold."

She stood in the bathroom and listened to her heartbeat pounding in her ears while she attempted to compose herself. There was no feasible explanation she could offer him that would quell his concern, seeing as she didn't herself understand what had happened.

She stepped from the bathroom and stood in the doorway, meeting his steady gaze while tension worked its way through the features of his face.

"If I asked you what happened, would you tell me the truth?"

She sat next to him on the bed and uttered the one thing she could think to say. "I fell."

He watched her for a moment, then countered, "For argument's sake, let's just say you *didn't* fall."

"Bill—"

"Let me finish," he insisted.

She felt her heartbeat slow as she waited for him to continue.

"I'd be angry if I thought someone hurt you. I'm surprised at how angry that would make me."

"I promise you, I fell," she reassured him.

Like Evan, Bill's eyes were kind, and in the short time she'd been awake, she had almost forgotten that a piece of her soul was gone. Yet after a moment of looking at him, she realized a piece of his was, too, and she wanted to know why.

A single question pushed to the surface of her mind, stealing sound from her vocal cords and leaping from her throat like a sly thief. "Are you married?"

His eyes registered a flash of hesitation before he replied, "I was." Searching her, he continued, "She died."

She placed her hand on his. "I'm sorry."

"When it happened, she was with another man."

Zoë ran her thumb across the top of his hand and waited for him to continue.

"But if I'm honest…I knew." He shifted his focus to the floor as though the heavy wooden planks beneath his feet would keep him separate from the ache threatening to unearth itself. "There are times I think I'll never find peace."

His words were resonating inside her with such force, she felt like her guts were winding in on themselves. "I believe you will."

Raising his head, he refocused on her. "Maybe. Or perhaps I'll learn to live without it."

She took her hand from his. "I could live without peace."

In earnest, he inquired, "What couldn't you live without?"

Twisting the bracelet on her wrist, she answered, "It sounds trite, but— hope." The guts inside her stopped moving, then tightened into a compact coil as she continued. "'The miserable have no other medicine, but only hope.'"

On cue, he added, "*Measure for Measure.*"

Warmth washed over her. "It was one of my father's favorite plays."

"A teacher?"

"An actor." Her father's round, rosy-cheeked face floated through her thoughts. "He was a player in a circus of other people's words."

Bill reached forward and brushed a stray hair from her cheek. "I love seeing you like this."

She couldn't imagine what he meant, considering the fact that she was disheveled and unshowered. "Like what?"

He traced his thumb across her lips. "Undone."

She felt his hand come to rest at the side of her neck as he continued taking her in. "I was never with anyone else while I was married. I haven't been since she died. You're beautiful, and I want to, but I'm—"

She reached forward, took him by the shoulders, and laid him down beside her until they were face-to-face, hands clasped and legs intertwined. His words—"You're beautiful"—lingered in her ears.

Her father used to tell her, "You're not pretty, Zoë, but you're smart." Most of her life, regardless of men's affections, she had believed it. Words spoken over a child are powerful and have the ability to plant seeds that are impossible to keep from taking root.

But Evan, ever the skilled and tender gardener, had planted a counter-seed, one that had since outgrown her father's weed-like assertion and bloomed into something bearing an unusual—albeit thorned—beauty.

Bill closed his eyes, then pulled her closer. And for the first time since Evan's death, she felt her guts, the tentacle madmen inside her, uncoil themselves and settle into anesthetized slumber.

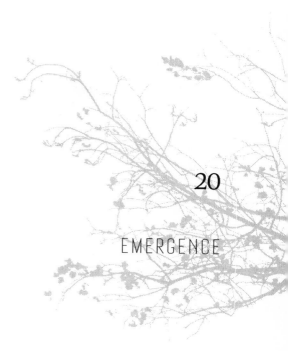

20

EMERGENCE

The sound of thunder booming outside stirred her from a deep and dreamless sleep. As she opened her eyes, a bright flash lit up her bedroom like a thousand high-wattage bulbs.

Rolling onto her side, Zoë could smell the scent of Bill's cologne drifting from the pillow. The intensity with which she felt his absence was unnerving, and even more disconcerting was the fact that he had left money on her bedside table.

Lula's heavy feet tromped across the hallway like tireless soldiers before she knocked on, then opened, the door. "Miss me?"

Zoë propped herself onto her elbows and looked at the clock. "It's almost midnight."

Lucille trotted across the room and sat at Lula's feet while Lula spoke. "I texted you that I'd be late. Didn't you get it?"

Turning on the small lamp on her bedside table, she picked up her phone and saw the text from Lula along with a message from Mr. Sumel: "call me —ps"

After walking across the room with Lucille in tow, Lula stood at the foot of the bed. "What in God's name happened to your head?"

Pushing herself into a sitting position, Zoë answered, "I tripped and fell against the bedside table."

Lula crossed her arms. "You tripped."

It was clear Lula was about to press her further, but Zoë didn't dare utter a word about the day's events: not her dream, not Evan. "I'm going to try to go back to sleep."

Leaning forward, Lula questioned, "You sure you're all right?"

Zoë attempted to sound sincere as she assured her, "I'm good. Just tired."

"'Night, then." Lula gave Zoë an affectionate pat on the top of her foot, then walked toward the bedroom door with Lucille sauntering along behind her.

"'Night, Lula."

Giving Zoë one last glance before turning into the hallway, Lula closed the door.

Zoë placed her phone back on the bedside table next to her mother's sketchbook, then ran her hand along the book's soft leather spine. Picking it up and studying a series of leather straps attached at the center of the spine, she followed their path with her fingers as they wrapped around the book several times and met in a tidy knot that rested on the front cover. Compelled against her will, she untied the knot and opened it.

The book's paper was unusual, like tracing paper except thicker and semitransparent. When she placed her hand beneath each page, she could see the charcoal pencil lines of her mother's drawings. The sketches were comprised of natural elements—trees, flowers, landscapes, and the like—but toward the back of the book, the sketches became more defined in their complexity. They conveyed sentimental storytelling, as if her mother were speaking through the weighted lines, shading, and artfully constructed details of her drawings.

Reaching the last page of the book, Zoë stared at a sketched image and felt her pulse race. Moving the page closer to the lamplight, she could see it was a drawing of the same lines and symbols on the lid of the box she'd found beneath her floor.

Like the box, the sketch had lines dividing a circle into four sections, each marked by an elemental symbol. Yet the sketch had labels for each of the symbols: air, earth, fire, and water. At the bottom of the page in her mother's handwriting was a quote with corresponding Roman numerals:

In the blink of the dragons' eyes, around the sun Mother Earth does fly: L-III, R-IV, L-II, R-IV.

Feeling out of her body, she got up from her bed and walked across the room to the vanity, where, opening its drawer, she retrieved the box and moved toward the bed.

Sitting back down, she examined the box and studied her mother's writing a second time. "As Mother Earth rounds her sun…" Wondering if they were instructions, she tried the lid to see if it would rotate, but it wouldn't budge.

Looking closer at the dragon symbol on top of the box, she noticed that both the dragons' eyes were raised, and when she ran her thumbs over them, they depressed and clicked into place. Again she tried to turn the lid, and this time she could rotate it with ease. Steadying her hand, she turned it to the left as instructed by the first letter and Roman numeral in her mother's inscription: L-III. Hearing three successive clicks matching the numeral's value, she did the same to the right, left, and right once more until she felt the lid release.

Opening the box, she found the inside fitted with a copper bowl. Etched into the interior were the same elemental markings she'd seen on her mother's drawing, and at the base of the bowl was a sharp spade-shaped point protruding upward.

Setting the lid down beside her, she noticed a soil-filled vial fastened to the lid's underside with a piece of thick twine. She removed the vial and unwound a piece of parchment paper that was wrapped around it, then read the calligraphy-like handwriting:

Mother Earth shall bathe in rainwater and set her winds upon
the ashes. Sister moon shall breathe the winter air as her veins
fill with blood.

She read the words a second time and in so doing felt that certain words
were darkening before her eyes: earth, rainwater, ashes, air, blood. It was
clear the passage was a veiled set of instructions.

Now burning with curiosity, she couldn't keep herself from opening the
vial and pouring its soil into the copper bowl. She moved to the window,
opened it, then held the box outside and watched icy rainwater gather at
the bottom of the box's copper basin.

She closed the window, went to the fireplace, and knelt in front of it.
Setting the box on the floor, she leaned forward, then gathered ash from
beneath the fire grate and put it in the copper bowl. She exhaled and let her
breath drift into the bowl while with a measure of reluctance, she pressed
her finger against the bowl's spade point until blood dripped down onto
the contents below.

Pulling her hand from the box, she got up, grabbed a tissue from her
vanity, then secured it around her finger. Kneeling back down in front of
the box, she watched as the contents in the bowl began a chemical reaction.

As if a flame was blazing below the copper basin and heating its contents,
the ingredients were liquefying and beginning to boil. Smoke was rising
from the box, and when she inhaled, the inside of her nose stung and a
sweet, spicy taste coated her tongue.

She felt dizzy and at the feet of a potent high, her mind viscous and filling with the strange notion that the walls around her were breathing. There
was no denying that her senses were heightened, more refined. When she
took in a deep breath, her nose filled with a million comingling scents: the
hard wood of her floors, the perfumes on her vanity, the fresh linens on
her bed—but a scent more powerful than all the others emanated from
her fireplace, pungent like rotting, unwashed flesh.

Then she caught a blur of movement in the fireplace, as though the
dark brick was taking shape and forming into a black, sinewy creature that

emerged from the shadows. With its gnarled hand reaching out, a long, razor-sharp claw scraped along the brick as it maneuvered itself past the fire grate. Zoë knew what she was seeing had to be a hallucination, which would explain why she sat dead-still as it pushed its head from the fireplace and sized her up with pure black eyes.

The skin on its face looked like black leather, and its features were a jumbled mash of skeletal, demonic, and human traits. There was no hair on its head and although its ears appeared human, they looked to have been burned off at the tops.

Her eyes swept along its thin, wiry body, which, other than its clawed hands and black skin, looked close to human. It was staring at her, its tiny white pupils widening as it cocked its head in a way that made her feel it recognized her.

Crouching down, the creature unfurled its long fingers and let something roll from its palm onto the floor. She could hear its breathing intensify as it watched the small object come to rest in front of her. Leaning forward, she picked it up and realized it was a bone that had been lacquered in what looked like blood before being fired and sealed with a clear, shiny substance. Despite feeling unsettled, she continued examining the bone, having little doubt that it was human.

The sound of Lula's door opening sent the creature bolting back into the fireplace. Zoë could hear its shallow, frantic breathing as it stood inside the stone frame watching her, and upon hearing Lula pass by the bedroom door, it backed farther into the shadows.

As it scrambled up the brick, she could hear its claws scraping the inside of the chimney like nails on a chalkboard. It sounded like the creature was climbing toward the roof, and as it struggled up and out of the chimney's slim top, dirt, soot, and brick fragments came crashing down into the fireplace.

After a moment, she heard a clawing sound on the outside wall of her bedroom. Like a trick of the eye, the creature moved past her window, and when Zoë ran to peer outside, she watched it leap from the side of the house and onto the snowy ground. Leaving a trail of small child-like prints as it sprinted toward a thin stream of silvery light in the corner of the court-yard, the creature bounded through a rip in the night air and disappeared.

21

CLOSER

Zoë stood in the lobby of Dr. Lawson's office feeling dazed as his tiny, tidy, and too-tolerant receptionist smiled at her.

"You all right, dear?"

Zoë took a step toward the woman's sleek desk. "Yes, sorry. I'm here for my appointment."

The woman motioned to the couch. "Have a seat. He'll be out shortly."

Zoë crossed the lobby and sat down, wrapped in thought as the smell of the white leather couch infiltrated her senses.

As on the previous night, her senses felt heightened and her hearing was so sensitive that the clicks of the receptionist's typing sounded like miniature hammers on thin wood. Layered on top of the pounding in her ears was the hissing of blood rushing through her veins, pushing through her body like a raging river.

There was no denying that she felt off, different, or perhaps still altered, and not being in firm control over her physical and mental state sent a twinge of agitation along the bottom of her feet until she felt like she wanted to kick something.

Hearing her phone vibrate in her purse, she retrieved it, checked the screen, and hit ignore, feeling guilty for sending Mr. Sumel to voicemail. She still couldn't believe that in their last meeting he had insisted she contact the Deadlings. At his behest, she'd emailed Evie, the least spiteful of the three, hoping the encounter would be fruitful.

Clenching her toes inside her shoes, she felt full-fledged anger at the thought of the hell the Deadlings had put her through.

"Ms. Hall?" Dr. Lawson was a few feet away from her, smiling. She stood, then followed him across the lobby and down the skinny hallway toward his office.

Once at his door, she walked inside the room, feeling like her presence was in violent combat with the serenity of his domain. The coziness of his office warranted a sensible sweater and jeans, yet she had chosen the armored comfort of a long black leather skirt, six-inch stilettos, and bloodred lipstick.

She slipped past the well-worn chair reserved for clients and sat in his boxy, male chair. Leaning back and inhaling, she wished his chair would eat her up, spit out the rotting parts, and regurgitate her calm and dreamless.

Dr. Lawson took a notebook from his desk, then walked across the room and sat down. Despite her mood, she couldn't help noticing that he was clean-shaven on this day, and in response she eyed him like a math problem on a chalkboard. The sum of all parts equals what...

"Any progress with your dreams?"

Tension crawled up her spine. "How do you mean?"

After jotting down a few black-inked notes, he looked up at her. "The immersion I mentioned. Making the dreams active, lucid. If you let the experience take over, you may learn a great deal about what we need to work on."

While looking out the window to her right, she pressed her back into his hard chair, hoping to squash the anxiety now scuttling up toward the base of her neck. "I'm not quite there yet."

"How's the journaling going?" he pressed.

She refocused on him. "Journaling?"

The faintest hint of a smile inched along his lips. "Your last session, I wanted you to begin keeping a journal." She shifted in her chair as he continued. "Often what terrifies us the most can teach us the most."

You sound like a fucking Hallmark card.

He put his notebook down on the table beside him. "Ms. Hall, are you truly here for my help?"

"Yes. I think so," she replied, then cleared her throat.

He leaned forward. "I'm here for you. You know that, right?"

"Yes." She pulled her purse closer to her body.

"I want us to move forward, I do. I'm just not sure how far we can go without your willingness to participate."

Silence floated between them until, without even thinking, she pulled the envelope J.T. had given her from her purse and handed it to him.

While taking it from her, he never took his eyes from hers. After watching her sit down, he leaned back, took a letter from the envelope, and read aloud:

Zoë:

Not a day goes by when I don't regret leaving you. Please know that it wasn't by choice and I would have died long ago without your care. With Hannah gone, all that I have is yours. It always was.

I love you.
—Evan

He refolded the letter, put it back into the envelope, and looked up at her. "I think I am unlucky."

"How do you mean?" he inquired, removing his glasses.

Words were spilling from her lips before she could stop them. "His daughter, Hannah, was so beautiful, you can't imagine. We were on our bikes racing—one minute she was laughing, the next she was dead in my lap."

"How old were you?"

"Fifteen."

An image of Hannah in her lap—her golden-spun hair knotted with clumps of blood, bits of bone and brains—plagued her thoughts. The moment was so fresh and vivid that it was making her nauseous. "She hit the ground and her skull was open—everything just out and on me." The image in her mind's eye traded places with one of Evan at Hannah's memorial service. She could see him sitting on his own and unable to take his eyes from Hannah's white coffin.

"He was alone. I took care of him…for her. A few months later, I made meatloaf, her recipe. It was awful, sickening. I cried over that meatloaf like it was Hannah. He gathered me up off the floor, like a father, but—" She gripped the side of the chair. "I'd never even kissed anyone. It just happened."

The weight of Dr. Lawson's probing stare, coupled with his veiled yet ever-present sympathy, was making her feel claustrophobic. "I don't mean to be impolite, but I need to stop."

He leaned forward and handed her the envelope. "Of course."

"Thank you." She rose from her chair, then took the envelope and put it back in her purse.

"Write, Zoë. Things are safer on paper."

She shook his hand, then let her fingers rest inside his palm before walking past him.

Opening the door, she made her way into the narrow hallway and felt her heart lighten. Although expressed in inky scribble, Evan's letter confirmed that he hadn't lied about having to leave. For a split second, she could almost feel him beside her.

22

NIGHT FALL

With the onset of nightfall, the icy chill penetrated her coat and gnawed at Zoë's flesh. Wanting to escape both the cold and the trailing memory of Evan's letter, she hurried up the stairs to her house while reading an incoming text message. "call me –ps."

Forcing herself to do so, she pressed the icon next to Mr. Sumel's text, then lifted the phone to her ear. After several rings, he picked up, but rather than a proper greeting, all she could hear was heavy shuffling in the background.

"I hate this damn phone. Hello?!"

"Mr. Sumel?"

"Who's this?" he demanded.

"It's Zoë. You asked me to call," she said, trying to veil her aggravation.

"Oh. Hi! Can you come by?"

"Uh—"

Silence hung on the phone line like an electrocuted bird until his gruff voice pushed its way through the phone. "I've had another visit from that strange fellow."

"Can you be more specific?" Her heart thumped in her chest.

"Not over the phone. My house?"

Despite wanting to decline, she agreed. "All right."

"Any progress on the painting?"

She exhaled, making sure it was audible. "Working on it."

"Okay, then. When can you come?" he asked, sounding like a giddy schoolboy.

"I'll text you."

"Cocoa'll be ready!"

Hanging up her phone, she unlocked the front door, stepped in, and let the warmth of her house swallow her up. Lucille sat in the middle of the hall twitching her tail as Lula popped her head out from the kitchen. "Dinner?"

"Not hungry, but thank you." She made her way up the staircase and crossed the hallway into her bedroom.

The warmth of the blazing fire wrapped around her like a blanket and soothed the chill that had burrowed into her skin. She set down her purse, removed her coat, then sat at her vanity and watched a flurry of snow falling, the large pieces of snow tumbling down outside making her feel as if she were in the center of a snow globe, isolated in a glass bubble and surrounded by the heavy liquid of her thoughts.

Her focus was pulled by the sound of several incoming emails on her phone. Picking it up, she saw there were two new messages: one from J.T. with the name of Evan's estate attorney, the other from Evie. Shocked that Evie had responded, she clicked the email and read.

Zoë:

I received your email this morning. I did have such a painting, which was left to me by our father. I wasn't aware it had sentimental significance to you.

The above, however, is moot, I'm afraid, as the painting turned out to be of great value. I thought it was a cheap garage sale item but after finding a receipt from a similar painting

Father sold, I contacted Willoughby's and arranged for the painting to be put up for sale.

It was left to me in Father's will so there is nothing left for us to discuss. Happy holidays to you.

—Evie J. Hall

Witch.

It had to be a lie. There was no way her father would sell one of the paintings, let alone leave something of her mother's to a Deadling. They were his daughters and he had always been protective of them, but he was well aware of their faults. Regardless of how mentally absent he'd been in his last days, she didn't believe for a second he'd rob her of the right to have anything her mother had left behind for her.

She felt saturated. Defeated. Drained.

After rising from the vanity chair, she walked to her bed and stripped down to her underwear. Before she'd even commanded her body to do so, she was already beneath the covers and drifting toward what she hoped would be dreamless sleep.

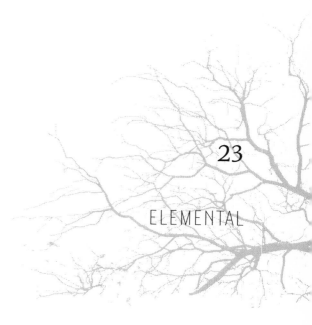

23

ELEMENTAL

am floating, a drifter in my own thoughts, and I can't get my bearings. I feel blood pulsing through my unresponsive limbs, pounding against my skin like an impatient child. Everything in me wants to wake and be present in my body, yet I continue in a state of unrelenting travel.

The only thing I feel outside myself is the sensation of liquid fabric. When I spread out my hands, I swear the air responds with a gentle wave of movement that undulates around my entire body. Until I start falling.

Without warning, I hit the ground and my eyes fly open. It takes me a moment to come back into oneness with my thoughts, and I feel the receptors firing in my brain as if its two hemispheres are trying to synchronize with one another.

The air around me is weighty with moisture, and my skin feels swollen, like I'm being waterlogged from the inside out. Above me the sky darkens and fills with ominous clouds, heaving as though the heavens will open at any minute. Hearing the low roaring of thunder rumbling overhead, I watch the sky's furious foreboding while thick droplets of rain splash onto my skin.

Scrambling to my feet, I find myself standing on a narrow cobblestone path that ends at a small thatch-roofed cottage. With the rain's intensity ever increasing, I run down the path. Once at the cottage, I stand in front of its bright-red door, which is rounded at the top and covered in a fresh coat of lacquer. Juxtaposed with the pristine painted door are primitive iron hinges that bear the marks of the tool that pounded them into their imprecise shapes.

Before I have a moment to form my next thought, the door clicks open and although only a sliver of the cottage's interior is visible, it's enough for me to see someone walking away from the door and toward the back of the room.

Feeling hesitant, I push the creaking door with the tips of my fingers until it swings open and reveals the interior of a room I've been in before. Glancing left, I see the mosaic-tiled black and white dragon above the fireplace, the firelight below changing the dragon's scales into bursts of miniature flame.

While entering, my focus is pulled from the mural to the far corner of the room. He is there, watching me, his porcelain-like skin shadowed in the dim firelight. I sense agitation in his demeanor, which is compounded by the unmistakable urgency in his eyes.

I find his stare unnerving, and for some reason I have the feeling he's been waiting for me for quite a while. Walking from the corner of the room, he removes his long coat and, once face-to-face with me, wraps it around my shoulders.

His spiky white hair looks like shards of ice beneath the moon and as a few drops of sweat roll down the side of his face, the sky-blue tattoos at his temples tumble in an unbalanced circle like tiny strings coiling, then releasing themselves.

In reaching toward me to pull the coat closed and fasten it at my waist, he has reminded me that I'm almost naked. In a hasty effort to protect my modesty, he secures the clasp—too tight—beneath my chin. We watch one another, the emerald irises of his eyes hypnotic, until I feel lightheaded. A crack booms outside, so loud it rattles the cottage windows, and when we shift our collective focus toward the far window, a blinding flash of light illuminates the room.

Thunder rumbles overhead before another blast of lightning crashes outside. I bring my gaze back toward him and realize my fingers are wrapped around his upper arms, yet I don't remember reaching for him. My head is pounding and my ears are filled with the sound of two heartbeats: his and mine.

His is like a great bass drum, a steady rhythmic thump that forces my heartbeat to synchronize. I release my fingers from his arms and the sound of his heartbeat vanishes. Like miniature snakes, his tattoos grow wild at the sides of his temples, churning and looping against themselves.

With his stare locked on the right side of my face, he takes my chin and turns my cheek toward the firelight. "You have a mark."

I feel the tone of his voice in every cell of my body. He is expecting a response and for the life of me, I can't get my vocal cords to function. So I say nothing.

The warmth of the fire coupled with his heavy woven coat is causing me to sweat—it's either that or the weight of his finely tuned stare. Ridiculous is the word that comes to mind as I continue pondering whether or not to engage in a conversation with a character in my dream; I'm puzzled as to my emotional state and, for the time being, still mute.

My toes clench the floor and resistance roots my feet into their spot. I can't figure out what the hell is going on inside my own mind, as it seems two parts of me are colliding: one wanting to respond, the other refusing to do so. I feel him soften toward me as he senses my confusion, the tension in his face relaxing while Dr. Lawson's voice plays in my head. "Make your dreams active, lucid."

"Have you had the mark since birth?" He is staring at my right cheek where an eggplant-colored mark once was, and although it has been removed, when I'm flushed you can see its faint, pinkish traces.

Thoughts roll around my brain like storm clouds, memories of different moments in my life—one being of the Deadlings painting their cheeks with dark red lipstick to mimic my birthmark.

"I need to know if you were born with it."

I force sound from my taut vocal cords. "Yes."

The rain outside eases, and I unbutton the coat to my waist and feel the stifling heat of my body release. Kindness fills his eyes as he brushes a few beads of sweat from my hairline. It's difficult to ignore the electricity of his fingertips, and I'd be lying to myself if I didn't admit his touch affects me.

"If I asked you to trust me, could you?"

This question short-circuits my brain, until I find enough compliancy and truth to respond—considering that, in essence, I'm responding to myself. "I don't know."

He lowers his head and I can see that his tattoos have slowed and are tumbling in balanced circles, which gives me the feeling he finds my answer reasonable.

"Would you be willing to suspend your disbelief long enough to try?"

Now I feel like I'm playing chess with myself. I'm not sure how to intellectualize this, let alone reply to a question from inside my own dream. Again I will myself to speak. "I suppose so."

He appears to be contemplating my reply while staring at the bracelet on my wrist. Then, after what feels like a lengthy and empty silence, he speaks. "I'd like to ask you to come with me."

Standing beneath a thick forest canopy, I find the thin streams of indigo light slipping through the trees haunting—like beams of sunlight diving deep into an ocean the color of a liquid bruise. Watching the last trickling drops of the subsiding storm, I shift my focus toward the edge of a meadow a few feet away and am struck by its perfect, circular cutout shape.

Dewy grass glistens beneath the moon's moody light, giving the small clearing a magical feel, and coupled with the patches of wildflowers carpeting the grass, the meadow radiates a serene storybook quality. The trees surrounding the meadow have stout, misshapen trunks that support giant sprawling branches, some of which form a maze of wooden limbs with low-hanging offshoots that look like leafy hands clawing toward the grass.

Yet the feeling of the meadow and adjacent trees seems to clash: one is innocent and vibrant, the other rough and foreboding.

Shifting my gaze, I look at the man standing beside me, the tattoos at his temples swirling in tight, resolute circles. His skin seems to be made of stone, like a white canvas upon which the moon can paint its melancholy light. I follow the line of his stare and begin resonating with the filter through which he sees the meadow in front of us; there is no doubt this meadow is a sacred place, a woodland altar to which all must bring an offering. It's difficult to ignore my connection to it, as I understand it needs me somehow, as if it were a living and conscious person. I feel the forest holding its breath, waiting for me...

I want to get closer and am about to walk from the dense tree cover to the meadow's edge when his hand wraps around my waist—a silent request for me not to leave his side.

He turns his head to the left as a voice calls out, "Daegan, the other Delphics will be here shortly and—"

A man steps toward us from the shadows, and when his eyes lock with mine, the remainder of his sentence ceases to form. The youth of his face and his robust build belie the wisdom emanating from his stare, the depth and darkness of his eyes telling the tale of a man who has seen many years of the best and worst life has to offer. He moves into a thin stream of moonlight and it cuts across his angular face. In seeing that he is of Native American descent, I feel grounded by his presence.

Nodding his head, he introduces himself. "Balfore." Seeming to sense that I won't respond, he addresses the pale man at my side. "Everything is ready." With his body rotated away from me, I see two large, holstered swords on his back. My thoughts grow quiet, which allows their conversation to enter my consciousness.

"Once they're here, we can begin."

I'm listening to the conversation between the two men, thinking that they look, sound, and feel real, and it's interesting that they have given themselves names: Daegan and Balfore. Or perhaps I have given them names.

I'm having difficulty immersing myself as I'd resolved to do, my aptitude to follow Dr. Lawson's directive declining. I feel a desire to detach from this experience and wonder if "suspending my disbelief" is plausible for me. My roiling musings are interrupted by the sound of footsteps to my right. I see two women walking in our direction, moving in a smooth yet determined manner. I've encountered both women before in previous dreams, and as they arrive in front of us, each takes a moment to nod her head.

The brutal, threaded scars of the midnight-skinned woman's chest are no less shocking now than when first I saw them, and despite her mutilation, she radiates a penetrating warmth. Colliding midair with her openness is the reticent yet earthy presence of the sienna-haired woman at her side, a woman I've deemed nature incarnate and one that I sense is both wild and mercurial. The woven gown she wears is made up of thick twine that floats along the curves of her body like a second skin. A faint scent of musty soil drifts from her, and when it hits my nostrils, I find its muskiness intoxicating.

A voice comes from my left—the porcelain man…Daegan's voice. "Ayalah, is Zoran coming?"

The sienna-haired woman nods.

Daegan looks to the midnight-skinned woman. "Prayna, you'll take the North." He speaks again. "Ayalah, the South. Balfore, the West."

All obey without question and move off in different directions.

The train of Ayalah's gown catches bits of vines, leaves, and wooded debris as she walks away, and although her gaze is focused on the forest in front of her, I feel her full attention on me. I watch her move into the forest, feeling certain she either doesn't like me or doesn't trust me.

Daegan takes my hand and leads me to a twisted, knotted tree at the meadow's edge. With my fingertips now touching his palm, the sound of his steady, rhythmic pulse fills my entire body. My heartbeat slows to fall in line with his, from a hummingbird's pace to that of a lion's.

Tiny golden lights fill the spaces in between the trees, and as we near them I realize they're fireflies. As the forest fills with their fiery glow that flickers between dull and bright, the night feels magical and my thoughts float to a few lines from *A Midsummer Night's Dream*. I see Father in my mind's eye crouching next to a chair and reciting Puck's lines as though our living room were an enchanted forest:

> If we shadows have offended,
> Think but this, and all is mended;
> That you have but slumbered here
> Whilst these visions did appear.

We reach the knotted tree and Daegan lets go of my hand, the silence inside my head deafening without the sound of his heartbeat coursing through me. Moving closer to the tree, he puts his pale fingers on its coarse bark and feels his way around the trunk.

I notice the lower-lying branches of the tree have fiery red leaves and long thick thorns that jut downward; several of the tree's branches hang out over the meadow and sweep along its plush green grass. Standing here in this woodland womb, I feel the forest is waiting to exhale, pregnant with a full and anticipatory breath.

Across the meadow, I see the Native American man—Balfore—watching me, and along with him, the two women are fixated on me as well. Including Daegan, who is behind me, each of them is positioned in front of an unusual-looking tree, all of which appear to be at exact compass points along the round meadow's edge.

Daegan pulls a thick thorn from a branch above me and, without a word, holds my right index finger. Even with his heartbeat pounding in my ears again, mine remains at a hummingbird's pace, and before I can protest, he gives me a quick jab that causes blood to form on my fingertip.

He looks outward toward the meadow, and in response to his glance, the other three turn to face their respective trees. I'm still watching them when Daegan turns me toward the fiery-leafed tree at our backs.

I'm so caught off guard by the way he's holding me, with all the fingers of his left hand gripping my hip, that I let him press my index finger into a small opening in the tree's bark. There is a gentle sucking sensation against the flesh of my finger as the tree takes blood from me, and I feel it flowing from my body as my ears fill with an intense rushing sound.

Carried by the river of my racing blood is a permeating euphoria, a flood of intoxication that warms me from the inside out; and from within my altered state, I'm aware that my mind is steeped in the understanding that I am part of all things. My body feels as though the seeds of life are sprouting from my bones, and my feet are aching like they might split apart and root into the ground at any moment.

From inside myself, I see my vascular system, but instead of red tissue, I perceive fleshy walls of deep green. Playing inside my mind is an animated illustration that shows my veins splaying outward, shooting through the forest, and connecting to every living thing around me.

With my balance faltering, I lean back and feel Daegan's strong chest against my back. My knees are weak and my vision is doubled as though I can view things in multiple dimensions: there is what I see with my raw sight and what I see with my mind's eye. I study the tree in front of me and see its trunk, but if I push my raw sight into another place in my mind, I'm able to examine the tree from the inside out: heartwood, root systems, leaves…

Daegan pulls my finger from the tree and guides me a few steps backward. The rushing sound has left my ears, but my feet are still throbbing and my finger is numb. My dimensional vision has merged back into normal sight and aside from lightheadedness, I feel myself again.

As the moments pass, I inhabit my body in full and am able to stand upright without Daegan's assistance. The one difference I sense is the undeniable physical connection I have to the forest around me—it's as if I've been seeded, planted, and grown from the very soil beneath my feet.

My thoughts drift to a Cherokee story about the creation of the first woman. She was planted by Great Spirit next to the sleeping primordial man and soon grew over the man's heart before coming into being: she was and would always be the seed of the earth. My mother told that story with such passion and wisdom, and although it was far-fetched to me when I was a child, it's tangible to me now.

A faint sizzling sound interrupts my thoughts. The smell of burning wood is in the air and ashes fall from above while the leaves of the red-leafed tree disintegrate as though they're burning from the inside out. I watch a leaf above me become an ashen skeleton of veins before it dissolves and floats downward like jagged snow.

The scorching sound intensifies while the bark of the tree turns stark white like it's being consumed by an invisible fire, leaving a caked, flour-like substance behind. Daegan pulls me away from the tree as its bark and remaining leaves dissolve to the ground in a pile of pale, powdery soot.

The tree is bare now, yet far from frail or lifeless, and although its smooth, honey-colored underskin is all that remains, the tree's thick limbs continue reaching toward the moon in an evocative demonstration of resilience.

Feeling Daegan leave my side, I turn away from the tree and watch him make his way toward the meadow's edge. After a moment, I follow and arrive beside him. He's looking out into the meadow, surveying the trees under the care of Ayalah, Prayna, and Balfore. The tattoos at his temples flow in perfect, balanced circles. I follow his sightline to our left and settle my gaze on Ayalah, who, like the others, is facing the center of the meadow.

Ayalah steps away from her tree, which has also been stripped of its foliage and bark. A mound of earth surrounds it and a fine dust lingers in the air around the trunk as if the tree is continuing to shed its disintegrating parts.

Across the meadow from Ayalah, Prayna walks from her tree, which is leafless save for a few pieces of what look like bits of cotton floating away from its smooth branches. I watch a few cotton-cloud pieces trail behind her as they fall from her hair and clothing.

Opposite me, Balfore walks from a willow tree, its leaves in full bloom and dripping a thick, syrupy substance into the grass below. The willow tree has a hint of phosphorescence, and beneath the moon's bluish underwater light, it's a vibrant minty green.

The three of them move toward me carrying something in the palms of their right hands, their approach ritualistic in both precision and concentration. Balfore's eyes are closed as he walks, his lips moving as though he's mouthing a silent prayer.

Daegan lifts his right hand, revealing a small square of muslin with ash from the fiery tree at its center. The others step across the meadow's edge into the forest and without a word, the three of them form a circle around me.

I feel my heartbeat speed up. They look to be in a trance, each with their right hand extended, palm up, and holding a square of muslin. Daegan is standing in front of me, and as he steps forward, he completes and closes the circle around me.

In a ceremonial manner, they pass their squares clockwise in a complete circle before handing their original muslin to the person on their right. As Daegan passes his into Prayna's hand, I watch pale ash float to the ground.

Prayna speaks in a steady, quiet voice. "Mother Earth, Father Sky..."

Upon hearing her voice, my consciousness slips, like falling back in time. Prayna is still speaking, but I am no longer listening. Beyond my control, my eyes are closing and my mind is going backward into my childhood.

I'm eleven and my mother and I are at our cabin in the woods, sitting outside beneath the stars. She is streaking my face with ash, asking our ancestors to bestow upon me their great wisdom, and I feel entranced by her words. My eyes are closed, and although I'm seeing my mother and wholly inside the memory of her, I feel the present moment on the outskirts of my thoughts.

Past and present are happening in parallel, like a dance between two moments in time. I see my mother's face and hear her voice, yet also hear a whisper from the present: "Element of fire, be a lamp unto her feet..."

I feel hands on me, fingers bathed in a chalky substance making a mark on my forehead. The vision of my mother is clear and vivid: her black hair long, thick, and billowing down around her shoulders like raven-colored waves. Her eyes are closed, her palms to the sky, and beneath the moonlight her smooth skin shines.

The scent of lilac drifts from her wrists as it does from mine, a way for us to call upon "Great Spirit." I'm so enraptured in the memory that the words being spoken in the present are like distant thunder.

"Element of air, be of her breath..."

Two fingers stroke my throat like butterflies on silk.

The memory playing in my mind grows more realistic, like I'm stepping inside a movie instead of watching it, and just as I did as a child, I feel the presence of my ancestors. I sense the safety and protection of being part of something grander than myself, even though I don't comprehend the role I play in it. My mother is still speaking, but her words are muffled by a female voice in the present.

"Element of earth, be her grounding..."

Two fingers trail my cheekbones while the smell of fresh soil fills my nostrils.

Then the memory changes and takes on a life of its own as my mother's deep, earthen eyes open and lock on me. She is more serious than I have ever seen her, and I feel the memory transforming into a forewarning, her voice strong, inhuman, like a thousand voices at once. "Starve them both, and it is you they will consume."

Like a dreadful nightmare, her eyes turn fiery red with pinpoint black pupils. A jolt goes through me, my eyes fly open, and I'm yanked back into the present with such force that it feels like my legs can no longer hold my weight.

Looking around me and noticing everyone but Daegan has gone, I wonder how much time has passed—if minutes have in fact been hours.

"Element of water, be of her spirit..."

Daegan touches a pale finger to my lips. A sweet floral taste floods my tongue, and I feel anesthetized. His face is inches from mine and his heartbeat pounds in my ears: strong, steady, and unyielding. I study the silken surface of his poreless skin, the pronounced bow of his upper lip, his unusual emerald-green irises, and find I'm having difficulty coming back into my body.

But in hearing movement behind us, my senses flood with the intense awareness that we're being watched. Adrenaline rushes into my system, and I'm sobered, in my body, and clearheaded.

Daegan breaks our stare and with his hand on the small of my back, leads me along the forest's edge. "For now, I must leave you in the care of another." He ushers me into the meadow but doesn't follow. I'm about to inquire as to why when he turns around and disappears into the darkness of the forest.

After a moment, thousands of fireflies line the meadow. I watch as their light illuminates the space between where the forest ends and the meadow begins. They are calming and their presence serene, yet I can't stop my mind from tumbling back into the nightmarish vision of my mother's fiery red eyes, nor can I stop her voice from replaying in my thoughts: "Starve them both, and it is you they will consume."

Staring out into the moonlit meadow, I catch a glimpse of something moving near the forest's edge and feel my pulse race as its shape becomes clearer. I now know what, or rather whom, my mother's warning was referring to because I'm watching it slip through the tree line and walk toward me.

24

GIRL WHO CRIED WOLF

take a few steps backward. The hunger in his aqua eyes is wild and uncontrollable, and although he moves in a slow and methodical manner, I sense his presence rushing toward me like part of him intends to devour me. I retreat another few steps knowing any attempt to distance myself is futile. Considering his size and stride, he can overtake me in no time at all.

With the black of his fur so dark it appears night's twin is moving in my direction, he is a living, breathing expression of the story my mother used to tell me about feeding the black and white wolves. It has always been my strategy to starve them both, and I am defiant on this issue. Since childhood, I have refused to acknowledge, let alone decide, which side of myself to feed. By standing silent between them, indifferent and out of reach, I've never had to face either one. But I'm within their reach now, or at least within reach of one of them, and I wish I were indifferent, yet to say so would be a lie. The truth is, I find him captivating.

I realize I've seen him in past dreams, albeit shrouded in darkness, never knowing who he was. My bones vibrate like they did then, as if he can control the electric current running through my body, intensifying then calming the vibration with his will. He's in front of me now, and the blood in my veins is growing hotter, pushing against my skin as if magnetized and seeking escape, my bones vibrating with such force it blurs my vision.

The cells in my body feel like they are on fire, burning because he's directed them to ignite. I'm gripped with a rising fear that he may harm me; the look in his eyes is one of craving and untamed thirst. Yet I can't stop myself from raising my hand and reaching out to touch the fur on his neck.

With my fingers grazing his fur, searing pain shoots through my hand and the tips of my fingers throb as though they've been submerged in fire. I've never physically felt like I do now, the heat in my veins, the connection I have to him. My bones vibrate to the point it feels they may shatter, and an intense humming sound has begun in my ears.

The sound in my ears has motion, like the particles and waves are attempting to organize themselves and become something more.

"We must never touch."

I've heard what he's said, but the tips of my fingers are still resting on his fur, and despite the pain, I can't remove them. Brazen in my desire, I force my fingertips forward until I can feel the heat of his skin, and the resulting pain shoots up through my arms and into my shoulder before lodging into my spine.

The warning he's given is founded in truth, seeing as another minute of this pain would be unbearable. But I've crossed into him now, and the burning in my fingers numbs just enough for me to become one with the blood-saturated pieces that make up his soul. Beneath the physical responses to being near him, at the base of our connection, inside the darkest chamber of his emotions, I feel a profound loneliness that overtakes everything else. There is an empty space inside him where a sacred and complete love once existed. I can see it in my mind's eye, a gut-ripping sorrow.

I pull my hand away and notice that underneath the primal thirst in his eyes is shame. I sense he is unnerved by my ability to see inside him, but if I go deeper, I feel he wants to be exposed.

Breaking our stare, he walks to the center of the meadow, and with his departure my blood begins to cool. I feel him calling me, wanting me to come with him, but before I command my legs to do so, they're already moving. Once I'm at his side, my blood heats up and pushes against my skin as if wanting to synchronize with the blood pumping through his veins.

We are standing above a small, flat, circular stone with black cursive writing around the edges, and at the center of the stone, as though sprouting from rock-bound soil, is a white marble rose. The rose appears to have been carved by loving hands—an artist's mystical masterpiece—each of its curled petals uneven and wild. The longer I stare at the rose's splayed grandeur, the more I get the feeling it has a personality of its own; it radiates a devout, feminine nature that is divine in both sensuality and appeal.

It's a strange experience to be looking at a marble flower yet sensing a sentient being, and when I lean forward, I notice a dark syrupy liquid inside the rose's stone interior. The liquid's scent is intoxicating, floral with a hint of what I'd swear is blood.

He takes a step toward the rose. "Read the inscription."

I shift my focus from the rose to the circular stone at its base. The writing is small, so I take a step forward and lean over to read the fine script:

THE STONE WILL REVEAL ALL THAT IS AND HAS BEEN.
WITH BLOOD IN THE ROSE, ETERNAL NIGHT BEGINS.

Standing, I fight through the thickness of my thoughts. I'm struggling because I have questions and want to know more, form a relationship with, speak to…him. This is a difficult development for me, to invest myself in what I know to be an imagined world.

My vocal cords feel warm, heated, perhaps due to the heightened temperature of my blood; I want to speak, but I'm suppressing my own voice. I'm unsure about making this decision—to engage with him, to have a conversation. It's what Dr. Lawson asked of me, yet I'm beyond adhering to that request at this point, and before I can come to any kind of resolution, he interrupts my thoughts.

"Your blood has mixed with that of the forest and flows through Loryian, the heart of the realms."

My mind tries to stay present and focused on whatever I'm supposed to gain from this experience, seeing as I'm lost in this dream and feel the characters in my imagination are more in command than I am. Resistance floods my hands and feet as though I'm battling for the right to take back my own consciousness.

His gaze is firm and his demeanor serious as he speaks. "If you wish to know more, kneel before the rose."

I elect to set aside my reserve, if temporarily, as I will indeed learn something about myself by allowing this experience to play out. With just enough curiosity to fuel the effort, I kneel and settle my gaze on the liquid at the rose's center, which now boils and releases a thin white stream of wispy smoke. The stone at the rose's base warms beneath my skin and electricity flows through my bones until there is no doubt that I'm altered, as I can no longer remember who I am or what I'm doing.

I feel my body sway in response to my failing equilibrium, and I'm aware that I'm about to pass out, or at least lose what I know to be consciousness within this dream. Then, like a tunnel of light opening, my vision brightens on all sides until I'm unable to form comprehensive thought.

My eyes are closed, my mind groggy. Feeling the warmth of a fire against my face, I hope to open my eyes and be in my own bed. The scent of pre-rain fills my nostrils along with the strong aroma of pine, and as my senses awaken, I become aware of damp wood crackling and hissing as it burns.

I'm lying on my side and can feel soft fur against my skin, but when I attempt to move my legs, I realize I'm wrapped like a cocoon. Seeking to free myself from my fur-cased prison, I open my eyes and wait for them to focus.

Once my vision has cleared, I see a fire burning in a large fireplace a few feet from me. A copper fire grate is illuminated by the flames, casting a long shadow toward me like a flaming ghost. My position is such that I am able to take in the black marble floor of the room, which merges into dark stone walls that support a vaulted wooden ceiling above me. A large iron chandelier is suspended from the ceiling, its candles unlit save for a few dwindling waxen nubs. To me, the room feels as though it belongs in a medieval or Edwardian castle.

My focus is pulled back to the fireplace by a loud pop that echoes throughout the cavernous room like a gunshot. I pull my gaze from the ceiling, letting it settle on the wall above the fireplace, which is lined with colorful forest-themed tapestries that come to life as firelight hits them from below. With the sudden sense I'm not alone, I look behind me.

Daegan is there, like a king, sitting in a carved wooden chair. Dressed in black, he would be invisible in the shadowy light if not for his pale skin and spiky white hair. Staring at me while the tattoos at his temples churn in unbalanced circles, his body is relaxed and his head is tilted, resting on his index finger and thumb. Seeing him, molded into his chair, I wonder how long he's been watching me.

I sit up and feel a wave of nausea grip my stomach. Throwing a hand over my mouth, I do everything possible to keep from vomiting. In seconds, he is at my side with a hand on my back and I hear his heartbeat thundering in my ears.

"You have to give your body time to adjust." He moves my hair to one side and strokes my back. "Breathe."

I inhale into the warmth of his hand and feel my nausea subside. Memories and thoughts pour into my consciousness: I'm seeing words, scenes, diagrams, and symbols as though recalling a memory from someone else's mind; and while I watch the collage of imagery rippling through my thoughts, what unnerves me most is that I don't feel like myself. The "Zoë" in me seems like a distant and fictitious form, a life lived in another time and place.

Primal instinct taking over, I feel panicked; I would do anything to wake up at home. Even Daegan's touch is not enough to soothe the claustrophobia developing within my own mind. I'm desperate to be freed from this dream, this delusion. But I can't stop the visions playing through my thoughts, nor can I deny the impact of the things I'm seeing.

Somehow, having been infused with the knowledge of the world I'm in—whether dream or nightmare—I understand its structure and its needs. The knowledge being imparted to me is profound, rising from deep within me, a suppressed secret or knowing that surfaces because I no longer have the will to hold it down in a locked, faraway place.

There is one image that keeps emerging: a flower with twelve petals or segments surrounding a pulsating, multilayered sphere. Appearing as a diagram or blueprint, it's alive and conscious. While floating in dark space, it speaks to me—this three-dimensional blueprint—telling me who or what it is, calling its segments realms.

At the center of the realms, the sphere is playing images like a TV screen: newsclips, movie scenes, childhood memories, and every few minutes, a bold image of the numeral XIII. I hear voices coming from the sphere that fade in and out like a static radio station, while the sphere appears to be playing all the world's footage—whether a part of my life or outside of it.

Another wave of nausea courses through me as the blueprint spins and flips over, revealing its underside. One of the segments turns inky black and emanates a sickly sweet sugary scent as massive iron gates cordon off each segment one by one, crashing down like boulders. I somehow know I'm in control of these gates, and I try to stop them from slamming through my mind. With every ounce of my strength, I command the blueprint to disappear until, sweating and out of breath, I force my mind into blank, imageless white space.

Daegan's voice rings in my ears. "When a Guardian first unites with the realms, it causes disorientation."

The fabric of his shirt is thin, leaving nothing to the imagination: his body is perfect, and I'm affected by it. I look into his eyes, the emerald green of his irises shining in the firelight as he continues. "But there are no barriers now."

One part of my consciousness rationalizes that his statement makes sense. It is, after all, my dream, so of course what he says could be a version of truth. Yet the other part of my consciousness fights with me, as though this alterative dreamscape reality is separate and somehow urgent in importance. I'm supposed to listen—it *needs* me to listen.

Our faces are inches apart and his hand is still on my back as he continues. "In the end, it will all come down to what you can accept."

I hear his steady heartbeat in my ears and in this moment, I trust him. I know he intends me no harm, but I can't help feeling that where I'm concerned, he's conflicted. He helps me lie back down, then positions himself beside me.

I close my eyes and hear myself speak, almost begging. "I need to go home."

Unwavering, he offers, "You are home."

25

MIRRORBALL

I open my eyes and take in the dying fire. Fading embers rest atop the claw-shaped fire grate, sending trailing waves of ghostlike, greyish smoke up into the flue. With the fire's warmth waning, I feel a chill making its way along my skin like an icy cloak being laid on top of me.

Rolling from my side onto my back, I look toward the rear of the room and find Daegan's chair vacant. The frame of his kingly chair is made up of carved wooden animals, one animal flowing into the next: a raven's wings merging into that of a dragon's, the dragon's tail merging into the body of a snake, the snake's head biting the tail of a wolf...

"*She* is our greatest threat."

Sitting up, I turn my head toward the front of the room, trying to determine where the cross female voice is coming from, when I notice a faint vertical stream of light leaking through a seam in an inset panel door beside the fireplace. The voice reduces to a murmur before being joined by other bits of muffled conversation; without hesitating, I'm standing and moving across the room.

The marble floor is unforgiving and cold, and for a moment I feel like I'm walking on black ice, which only serves to further the chill encasing my skin. As I reach the fireplace, I realize it's large enough for me to stand in; and while studying the stateliness of the flourish-carved marble mantel, I feel, even at my considerable height, like a miniature doll in a giant's house.

"Her very presence has not only awakened Lukaes, it's altered the state of the realms." The unhushable female voice drifts toward me like a harsh wind. "They're weakening so quickly, it's now possible to tear through them."

I maneuver myself in front of the door's seam as the voice again pierces my ears. "This isn't conjecture. We know it's happening…in Draknam and here in Loryian."

Ever so carefully, I push the door inward a few inches until I have a full view of one of the most spectacular rooms I've ever encountered. Every inch of the walls and ceiling is covered with mirrors. There are thousands upon thousands in every design, shape, cut, and framing option imaginable.

Mirrored sconces at the center of each wall bounce candlelight around the room as though sunlight were shining through a prism. With the light culminating in the center of the room above a round wooden table, I shift my focus to Daegan, who is seated with the others I met near the meadow.

Looking pensive, each one appears to be ruminating inside the opaque tufts of their own personal storm cloud. Ayalah pushes her chair away from the table, stands and paces from one side of the room to the other, her sienna-colored hair catching the light and reflecting in all the mirrors around her as though she has a thousand flaming heads. Her sharp voice punctures the heavy air in the room. "We can't trust her."

Even from where I'm standing, I see her disdain for me like an arrow hurtling toward the sliver through which I now observe her. I'd be lying if I didn't admit that the sting of its poisoned tip is radiating all the way down to my toes.

The dark-skinned woman, Prayna, responds. "I think she'll surprise us."

Balfore speaks while looking at Daegan, who is quiet and staring at the wood of the table as if it was a well-worn book. "I'm not in to-tal agreement with Ayalah, but I do admit that she's unprepared for her responsibilities. With Eternal Night upon us, we have precious little time to get her prepared."

My mind is processing Balfore's words, and as I settle into his stoic and grounded presence, I feel my thoughts drift into an evaluation of sorts. He's a good man, one I can trust, and sensorially, one I find familiar.

I snap from my reflectiveness as a rival thought—a realization—dips into my consciousness: he, *they*, are all me. I would not consider myself a scholar by any means, but I do know enough about psychological theory to understand that characters in a dream are often facets of the dreamer, pieces of themselves pushing up through the crusted soil of the unconscious like screaming zombies from a grave in order to unleash their voices, their ails. Yet in my case, to what end I cannot say...

Ayalah cuts in. "By 'prepared,' you mean the Leveling—something a person from the Thirteenth has never been through and that could very well fracture her mind?"

Unruffled, Prayna counters, "We need to focus on Lukaes's awakening. Even though he's been exiled to Draknam, he's still one of the four Asdans and even without a body, he's powerful—"

Ayalah interjects. "And in so being, he knows what we need to do with her and how we'll do it."

Appearing deaf to Ayalah's concerns, Balfore looks toward Daegan, and as he does, I see how much the two men revere one another. "Daegan, he was your friend. He knows you. By involving Zoë in Mahayla's death, he intends to cloud your feelings toward her."

Prayna chimes in while shifting her gaze to Daegan. "Yes, but we know Mahayla's death wasn't her fault."

The liquid silence that has befallen the room is visceral. I sense they're struggling to believe I am not, in one way or another, a destroyer—someone who stole their angel from them, a bringer of her definitive and unavoidable end—and in this, I feel like the ultimate outsider.

But then again, that is who I am: an outsider. These mirrorball talking heads who speak their truths from inside my own mind—some turning vicious while laying their grievances before me like dead animals on an altar—are, after all, correct in their assessment. I have always been on the outskirts, skimming along the edge of societal normalcy like a tight-rope walker, terrified that I may fall, yet intoxicated by the risk of taking one more step along a rope that could slip out from beneath my feet at any moment.

Were Jung or Freud here with me, sipping tea and analyzing the weavings of my overactive imagination—or unconscious mind, as it were—to what conclusion would they come? That I am indeed selfish, lacking account-ability for my obligations, and incapable of something the talking heads call "the Leveling"? Do I need to be "leveled," and has my architecture degraded such that it must be razed?

"I realize the risk, but perhaps we should consider invoking the Elders," Prayna suggests in earnest.

Ayalah fires back. "Releasing that kind of force now could risk a total collapse of the realms."

"If the force can be contained, it could strengthen the realms and buy us time," Prayna ripostes.

"Besides, the Scribe would never provide the blood we'd need for an invocation. It's solely our responsibility to ensure the Thirteenth Guardian is in place."

I feel a twinge of anger creep up from the bottom of my feet and inch along my heating veins like a fiery snake. Growing tired of being scruti-nized by the sharp, mirrored pieces of my own mind, I will my body to wake, even though I realize it's certifiable to be affected by what are—in essence—characters of my own creation.

Ayalah finishes. "To do that, we need to focus on her—and our—most immediate threat, Lukaes. With the Book of Elders and her blood, he'll be able to permanently take solid form."

Ayalah's holier-than-thou attitude and self-righteousness serve to irk me further. Her highbrow stare and lifted chin make me want to gouge out her eyes and were she within my reach, I might just do it.

"But that goes both ways. It can also banish him from solid form for good," Prayna offers.

Balfore weighs in. "As far as we know, the Book was lost after—"

Daegan interrupts, and when he does, I notice him shooting a knowing glance at Prayna. "I'm not sure that's true. But we have more important things before us now."

"Such as?" Ayalah demands.

All of them send a fixed stare toward Ayalah.

Daegan answers. "Zoran. Their connection will test them both. If I'm to fail in any capacity, it will be in managing their connection."

Zoran, my midnight-tainted beast and apparent weakness. Somehow, I take refuge in knowing that I'm his as well. That may be why my body responds to him the way it does: with hot blood, magnetized bones, and an ache so torturous I'm willing to submerge my skin in fire just to be nearer to him—or seeing as I'm his creator, nearer to myself?

Daegan looks at each of them. "The challenge will be in letting things unfold without interference. She coexists in two worlds now, and it will take patience from all of us to ensure they don't prematurely collide."

Daegan appears to have wrangled the wills of everyone except Ayalah, who has stopped pacing but is immovable in her position that I am all but a lost cause. Watching her fume at the mere mention of me, let alone Daegan's request that she employ patience, I realize who she embodies and why I have conjured her like a rotting corpse from the graveyard of my childhood: She is the Deadlings all rolled into one—venomous, beautiful, fork-tongued, and in every way a formidable adversary.

I find it interesting that I've chosen to merge her image with the arcane presence and qualities of the forest and its seraph of sorts, Mother Nature. Her sensual figure, raw sexuality, and perfect breasts all suggest she is the ultimate representation of nature's need to procreate, bloom, and nourish. But from her breasts flows sour milk; there is a bitter seed inside her growing into a cancerous weed around her heart, and as her conjurer and mirrored reflection, I must face the fact that that weed may be growing inside me as well.

Everyone stands while Daegan makes his way toward the door. His rapid approach breaks me from the recesses of my thoughts and sends me racing across the room just in time to drop down into my makeshift, fur-covered bed.

I'm on my side with my back to him, facing his chair and feigning a calm version of sleep. The scent of pre-rain rushes toward me along with the weighted, saturated thickness of his thoughts, and the closer he comes, the more I'm sure my presence unnerves him, that I've uprooted him somehow.

I hear him sit in his chair and feel his stare sinking into every inch of my skin like water seeping into woven cloth. He's watching me sleep, knowing that beneath my locked eyelids, I'm wild-awake and sending invisible tentacles toward him in the hopes of hijacking the viscous channel of thoughts flowing between us.

Pushing myself further into our connection, I understand how he sees me. I'm a trespasser, a "have-to," and a thief who stole Mahayla from him. Yet on an opposing front, I'm his responsibility, his charge; whatever it is that I represent to the world around him trumps all else, and should the need arise, he will protect me with reverent fierceness.

My body relaxes against my will, as if he's also peering inside my thoughts and in so doing has anesthetized me to lower my resistance. I counter by diving deeper into him. His being is cavernous, like an ocean, jewel-blue, teeming with life, harboring hidden underwater landscapes yet to be explored and with more capacity to feel than any other man I've experienced.

There is a veil in front of what I sense to be a voracious sexual appetite, one that was reserved for a true and binding love, and one he would only give in to with her. She was everything to him: his Venus, his pivot point; and what he struggles with most is that I'm the mortal instrument—albeit unintentional—who helped reduce her to ash and inflict the festering wound that is decaying parts of his resolute sovereignty.

With my arms and shoulders exposed and my thoughts pulling back from the depths of his mind, I feel the biting chill return as my skin forms tiny bumps that rise and spread across my body like nubbed icicles. I hear him get up from his chair, then walk across the room before the sound of heavy logs being tossed onto the fire grate breaks the silence between us like cannon fire on a quiet winter's night.

With lighter steps than those that had carried him to the fireplace, I hear him walk toward me and stop. I needn't open my eyes to know he's standing above me, and when he kneels to pull the blanket up and over my exposed flesh, I wish he'd lie down beside me.

But it's a childish notion, for he is only a figment of my imagination, a version of me that echoes the selfless caretaker I must play to the men I choose. My broken toy soldiers, my life's work, my soul. He brushes a stray hair from my cheek, then returns to the comfort of his chair and resumes watching me as though he fears I may vanish from the room like a vapor.

I'm tired now, exhausted from wading in the ocean of him, and without the will to stay awake, I drift into darkness.

26

VEXED IN THE CITY

Lula stood over a sleeping Zoë trying to curb her concern, as she'd slept an entire day—and then some. Zoë had thrown off her covers and surrounded herself with a bevy of pillows as though forming a protective barrier. Although Lula had checked on her a few times, it appeared she hadn't moved, which begged the question: Why were the bottoms of her feet black with what looked like soot, or dirt?

Leaving Zoë's room and continuing down the dark hallway, steaming cup of cinnamon tea in hand, Lula felt a knot forming in the pit of her stomach. Once back in her room, she glanced at the clock: 3:33 a.m. There was no way around it. Yet again, a full night's sleep would elude her.

Turning on the lamp at her bedside, she set down her tea, got into bed, and propped herself up against several large pillows. Ever since her meeting with Gigi and Mr. Black's subsequent death, insomnia had been a nightly occurrence.

Lucille was curling up at the end of the bed, unaware that Lula was in a state of exhaustion and frustration. Lula buried her bustling thoughts, took a book from her bedside table, and opened it, hoping reading would help her pass the time until morning.

She had been reading an engrossing book on the history of Greek mythology and felt losing herself in its pages was far better than allowing her mind to sift through the complicated details of her circumstances. The current chapter was on Greek goddesses, which had always resonated with Lula, both on levels within herself as well as traits she experienced in Zoë.

Along with her degree in Celtic studies and a love of all things Druid, Lula's interest in mythology ran deep, a sort of obsession, mostly because of its insightfulness on life. With such a stifling Catholic upbringing, she enjoyed the guiltless freedom mythology offered. To her relief, God was now just an archetype, an artisan-like mythic figure responsible for fashioning its own universe.

As was often the case, Lula's mind was running away from her. She refocused her thoughts on the open book in her lap and began to read:

> To Athena the warrior—her oldest manifestation—belong the epithets Promachos ("one who fights in the foremost ranks") and Alalcomeneis ("one who repulses the enemy"). She is the protectress of towns and the guardian of acropolises.
>
> Athena may have instigated war and chaos, but as Carl Jung famously said, "In all chaos, there is a cosmos, in all disorder a secret order." Possibly, Athena's wisdom was in which war she chose to fight.

Lula stopped reading, her mind ablaze after reading the word *chaos*.

She hurried out of bed and headed for her closet. She flipped on the light switch, then stepped onto an oaken chest toward the back wall. Balancing on the chest's sagging wood, she riffled through a pile of musty sweaters on the shelf above it. Her reach was shorter than it had been when she'd hidden the envelope and as a result, her bones groaned and resisted while her fingers flitted along the shelf.

"Got it."

She retrieved a large pocket envelope and almost tumbled to the floor as she stepped down from the chest. Lucille was now awake and sitting in the doorway of the closet, firing off a silent protest with her pointed stare.

Moving past Lucille, Lula sat at the small desk by her window. Brushing dust from a worn envelope, she read its handwritten inscription. "In all chaos, some order exists."

She peeled back the deteriorated, yellowed tape and opened it. A rush of stale cologne drifted upward, carrying with it the memory of Mr. Black. He had given Lula the sealed packet for safekeeping twenty years prior and out of respect for his request, she'd never opened it.

When Gigi gave her Mr. Black's last note in the coffee shop a few days ago, Lula hadn't made the connection. She'd been too distracted by Mr. Black's approaching death as well as Gigi's insistence that she not interfere in Zoë's life.

The hint had been in the note's last sentence. "But take comfort in knowing that 'in all chaos, some order exists.'" She realized now that he was giving her instructions.

Lucille leapt up onto the desk and sat across from Lula as she pulled a stack of jumbled papers from the envelope, many of them covered in handwritten notes. She glanced at each piece of paper looking for clues as to what Mr. Black had meant for her to find.

Lula scanned several pages before one titled "Recipes" caught her eye. The page had two labels, "Slowing Ascension" and "Speeding Ascension," and below each label was a list of foul-sounding herbs she'd never heard of.

She continued through the stack of papers until she came upon a faded typewritten page titled "Black Family." Her heartbeat quickened. This particular piece of paper was creased and looked as though it had been through a thousand cycles in a washing machine.

The page had two separate columns, one marked Wolf Clan and the other Blackwood. Below each heading was a list of names, several of which had boxes drawn around them.

Toward the bottom of the page in the center, a third column of names began, each name connected with a line to a boxed name in one of the original columns. The more Lula stared at the connected boxes, the clearer it became that she was looking at a family tree. She felt as though her room had shrunk to half its size.

One piece of paper that was sticking out from the stack on her desk had her name written at the top in bright-red ink. She unburied the page and read the only words typed on it:

Find Phinneas Sumel

27

NOCTURNE

Zoë bolted upright and stared into the narrowed eyes of Lucille, who was at the edge of the bed biting Zoë's toes. Lucille dug her claws into Zoë's ankle, readying herself for another brutal bite, but before she could sink her teeth in, Zoë shoved her off the bed.

Lucille skidded across the hardwood floor like a stuffed toy and smacked into the vanity table. After struggling to get on all four legs, she arranged herself in a regal sitting position beneath the vanity. Half of Lucille's face was hidden in shadow, but there was no mistaking the agitation in her eyes, the tip of her tail twitching up and down like she was contemplating a secondary mode of attack.

Stepping out of bed, Zoë ignored her throbbing toe and made her way to the fireplace. Kneeling, she retrieved a large piece of wood from a metal basket and threw it on the dying fire, which sent Lucille tearing across the room and out the door.

Zoë focused on the flames and watched them shoot higher while that night's dream intertwined with her thoughts. More prominent than all the images swirling inside her mind was the feeling of Daegan's pale hands on her skin and the searching, aqua eyes of the wolf. They waited at the edge of her conscious state, bordering the hemispheres of her brain like banished companions. Neither of them had lost their intensity upon waking—if anything, she felt an unfamiliar yearning to be near them.

Speeding like a freight train and crashing into her thoughts was the rigid, single-minded realist within her. It was simple psychology: her dreams were a means of sorting through the unconscious; vivid stories that mirrored her past experiences, and nothing more.

She made her way toward her bed, then crawled in and tucked the covers beneath her chin. Her mind continued flipping between the two characters from her dream, each of them triggering separate sets of reactions inside her: one carrying the symbolism of her mother, who had always been fascinated by wolves, the other bringing the lightness of a sensual connection she hadn't allowed herself to feel in many years.

Pleasure in some ways had become a tool for her, a method to unlock the psyche of a client, a way to free them and discover the true reason they had sought her care. But there were strict rules in place when it came to clients—commandments, really. She must never permit herself to become vulnerable or attached. It was possible she had forgotten what it felt like to lose control or to consent to someone possessing her body; she couldn't recall the last time she'd felt uninhibited and unbound.

In her dreams, she was traveling through the landscapes of her mind, defining and expanding the boundaries of her self-possessed territory. Such nocturnal explorations had revealed the two halves within her: the wolf, her primal nature; and the pale man, her purity. It was difficult to say with whom she felt more aligned, and even with the attraction to the pale man feeling stronger, were she to delve into the core of her longings, it was the wolf she'd choose.

Reason being, the primitive, pained, and searching loneliness in his eyes had captured a piece of her. Although he wasn't real, something about the feel of his fur beneath her fingertips enticed her. Knowing he could end her life with one swift motion, sensing the beast just below the surface…

168 | THE LEVELING

Both of them, the halves of her—one human and the other animal—were parts of a once-unified picture. One in which the pieces didn't quite fit together now, an irreconcilable mingling of scattered fragments that had once made up her whole and pristine likeness.

But that was the art of life, she supposed. The portraits people presented to the world were seldom, if ever, accurate; and instead of being repaired or reexamined, they were renewed over the years by layer upon layer of thicker and more vibrant paint.

Regardless, beneath the fresh, frescoed exterior people portrayed, there was an underlying darkness. She had experienced it many times with the men who came to her; it was like a shadowed copy, a second man within them she needed to soothe and entice into the light.

It had never occurred to Zoë that she shared in their plight. Conceivably, she had exalted her status as being above such duality, and perhaps in order to understand herself better, she needed to be taken, bitten, and devoured by the wolf inside her own mind.

A watery image of his face appeared in her mind's eye as the presence of space and time around her became a tunnel through which she was being guided; her movement was frantic, different than with other dreams, too fast and as if she were being pulled by a force stronger than anything she could fight.

With the aqua of his eyes hypnotic in a way that tricked her consciousness into giving up any remaining resistance, she understood that she was being summoned, called to join him, and with that realization, she willed her mind to let him take her.

28

W. I. L. D.

A gentle breeze glides over me as something brushes against my face, carrying with it a strong minty scent that lures me toward a wakeful state. My eyes open, and moonlight is all I can register with my muted sight. The moon seems larger than it should be, like a bluish, milky circle hovering above me, and although my perception that it has somehow overtaken the night sky isn't logical, for the life of me I can't force my thoughts into whole and rational concepts.

In what feels like a bolt of electricity being plugged into my spine, my sight sharpens. I'm present, conscious, and staring into the aqua eyes of my midnight-twinned beast, and when I sit up, he puts distance between us by retreating several steps.

As before, I want to touch him, feel his fur beneath my fingertips, hear his voice resonating from the center of my body. I remind myself that he isn't real, but the pull I have toward him is so strong I feel myself responding sexually.

A flash of embarrassment rises up and through me, and I'm not sure how to compartmentalize or structure my physical response to being near him. The most perplexing thing is that when I look in his eyes, I feel his yearning as though he were human. Before me stands a wolf; yet were I to close my eyes and trust my intuition, I would sense the presence of a man.

He has moved to the middle of the meadow, near the marble rose, and while watching him, I feel the same soft, sweeping sensation against my back as I had on my face earlier.

Behind me, I watch the heavy, drooping branches of a willow tree sway back and forth as its velvety leaves sweep against my skin. A slight breeze moves through the meadow, but not enough, in my estimation, to cause the willow's branches to touch me. I have the feeling they're reaching for me of their own volition, as the tree feels alive and conscious.

The leaves rustle and deliver another waft of minty sweetness, but the tree's perfume fails to mask the scent of what I know to be musty cemetery soil. I'm well acquainted with the smell, and as odd as the notion seems, I find comfort in its stale, deathlike fragrance.

As a child, I went to a Cherokee burial ground where below a giant willow tree lay the body of my great-grandmother. I remember sitting beside the tree and being able to feel her living presence underneath me. I feel that now, as if there are buried souls living within the dense fabric of earthen soil beneath the tree.

Blood is pushing up against my skin, and without looking, I know Zoran is walking in my direction. I turn my head back to the meadow and watch him move closer while my bones vibrate and my skin grows hot.

I feel the power of his voice travel up the base of my spine. "All that has been buried within you will be exhumed."

Eyes locked on mine, he peers into my very soul, and within the intensity of the connection, I sense he knows me better than I know myself. There is an umbilical-like bond forming between us and for reasons I can't pinpoint, I'm quite certain he, too, will be forced to disentomb that which is hidden within him.

Breaking eye contact, Zoran turns away from me and walks across the meadow. Without willing myself to do so, I'm on my feet and following him. We cross the threshold of the meadow and make our way into the dense forest, which is lit by the giant, misty blue moon above.

The enormity of his presence holds me captive, and I feel my bones vibrating in response to being near him. Heat emanating from my body collides with the cool night air, and as we move deeper into the forest, I feel the air temperature drop several degrees.

Up ahead, nestled between two mammoth, gnarled oak trees is a stone tomb-like structure overgrown with ivy vines. Thin beams of moonlight seep through the tree canopy and illuminate an entryway that leads into the tomb, and the closer we get to what I assume to be a crypt, the more restless I become.

I'm transfixed by the peculiar crypt and realize that I recognize it. It's identical to a tomb I visited in New Orleans when I was a child. My mother and I were walking through St. Louis Cemetery when we came upon the stone tomb of Marie Laveau. Mother told me about Marie's history, a renowned Voodoo priestess, and although Marie was half African, Mother said Marie had Choctaw blood.

Something about that tomb or the woman inside it troubled my mother, and I could see the unease etched into her face like ink on fragile parchment. I watched her take in the details of the tomb. "Great Spirit gives us much power, but there are those who bow to the demons of a darker craft."

I'd never seen my mother incensed, but she was livid that day. She stared down that tomb as though she would wrestle Marie Laveau into a second form of death. Before leaving the cemetery, Mother put her hands on my shoulders and spoke to what I felt was my very soul. "The knowledge of our people is a sacred flame and should never be used in this way. Dark magic is a path to the Underworld, and once on it, one is lost."

My mother's earthen eyes were flooded with concern, and she watched me for a long time before taking her hands from my shoulders. There were moments during my childhood when I felt she was injecting a part of herself into me—and that moment was one of them.

I'm pulled back into the present by the low and penetrating sound of distant whispers drifting from inside the crypt. Now standing just outside the tomb, both of us are listening with an equal amount of distress when, without a word, Zoran walks through the tomb's entrance and disappears into darkness.

Hesitant, I step onto the stone floor of the structure and move forward. There's a faint glow ahead of me, and after my eyes adjust to the dark, I see him descending a set of broad stone stairs. Midway down the staircase, a waft of warm, musty air wraps around my body as the whispers grow louder, their tonal quality shifting into an arrangement of ghosted voices. I continue down the rest of the stairs into a dome-shaped room constructed of small, round, black stones.

The structure is supported by the root systems of the oak trees flanking the tomb's entrance aboveground, the roots serving as a kind of living mortar holding the room's stones in place. Torches lining the wall hiss and crackle as I pass by.

My bones vibrate when Zoran's voice resonates through the room. "Come."

He walks into a narrow torchlit corridor at the far end of the room. I follow behind him, uneasy and anxious as the vibration in my bones is replaced with a feeling of despair that starts at my feet and inches up my legs like an unwelcome insect. The chorus of voices intensifies, and I'm certain it's not unified sound but a cacophony of distraught cries.

It's difficult to take in a full breath, and with every step my legs feel heavier. I inhale and force my mind to focus: I'm positive this underground passage is a representation of the depths of my mind, the proverbial Underworld of my psyche.

The Cherokee believe the Underworld exists below the Tree of Life and that the tree's heavenly light is the sole source of goodness within its shadowy depths. I welcome the thought of such illumination, anything to eradicate the crushing loneliness of this place. The voices grow louder, oozing from the walls, and it appears that death lingers just beyond them; even the flames of the mounted torches burn with its decaying greyish hue.

A few feet in front of us, the corridor's floors merge into smooth, carved stone that slants downward toward a large room. Zoran stops walking and stares into the room like he's taking a moment to prepare himself. The voices cease as though they've been silenced by his presence, and with the corridor now quiet, the heaviness in my legs subsides. He moves forward, and in what feels like an involuntary need to be at his side, I do the same.

We enter the empty room and I find myself awestruck, as it looks like a grand hall fit for royalty. Round black-and-white checkered tiles cover the floor, and upon closer inspection I notice there is a large inlaid marble symbol at the floor's center, the same triangular mark as one of the symbols on the box I found in my room.

Colorful murals decorate the walls and hanging from the gilded vaulted ceiling are massive iron chandeliers with lit candles. Although the room is dim, the lack of light does little to diminish the pure grandeur of the hall.

One of the frescoes next to me depicts a life-sized medieval town market scene complete with people bustling about their work, buying items from shops and riding in horse-drawn carriages. In response to my attention, the scene appears to move, like the paint is coming to life, and I wonder if my eyes are playing tricks on me because it looks like there are translucent, ghostly bodies floating in front of the mural.

One of them comes toward me, staring with hollow goldish-colored eyes while its body darkens like ink being poured into water. Studying the being before me, I have the feeling it was created by vacuuming out the insides of a human being until only a wraithlike version of its once robust self remained.

Several more of them begin floating around me, and although I see them in my peripheral vision, I can also sense them. They're circling me like grubby little children, and with them this close, I can't breathe. Feeling a spot of cool air at my back, I turn toward the center of the room and freeze. They're everywhere, hanging in the air like murdered relics. I can't even see the walls of the hall, there are so many of them.

I turn toward Zoran. "What are they?"

His presence is heavy, as if the sight of them has weighted down his spirit. "Shadows. They're the spirits of those who've been Excised."

I can only imagine what he means by "Excised," but before I can inquire, a Shadow to the right of us begins mumbling, and when he takes a step toward it, the Shadow calms. While watching him with them, I understand that Zoran is their shepherd, their keeper.

The look in his eyes shifts to that of shame, and I can't imagine what he's done to elicit the amount of regret emanating from him. For a moment, I forget the absurdity of communicating with a character in my dream and find myself wanting to know him—fix him. "Were these people?"

He shifts his gaze toward me. "Before the Great Battle, they were, yes. They're the result of my recklessness."

The hairs on the back of my neck stand on end. "You did this to them?"

He's about to respond when a ghoulish little Shadow comes toward me and whispers, "I want to fuck you."

I stare into the Shadow's hollow eyes, and despite its obvious vulgarity, I keep thinking how childlike it seems. It's as though a person still exists inside the Shadow but is fractured and unable to function properly.

"What will happen to them?"

More Shadows circle us like moths to a flame.

"Their Shadows will stay here with me. Their physical remnants, their Drogues, were exiled to Draknam."

Outside myself, I inquire, "Why?"

He continues in a matter-of-fact tone I find disconnected from the obvious distress the subject causes him. "Drogues only live a short time after Excision and when near death, they become unstable."

A dainty doll-looking Shadow floats toward me, speaking in a fragile voice. "I am pretty. I must be pretty. Am I pretty? I am good. I must be good. Am I good?"

My heart breaks; I look into Zoran's eyes and know his does as well. "They're like children."

"In many ways, they are. But they're smarter and more dangerous than they appear. If they wished it so, nothing would survive them."

The Shadows stop circling and form a claustrophobic, constrictive circle around us.

"Why did you bring me here?"

"It's part of your Leveling."

I flinch at hearing that term again. I didn't like it when I heard them talking about it in the mirrored room, and I like it even less now after having experienced part of its meaning.

He opines. "They reveal a person's capacity for darkness."

Surrounded by thousands of ghostlike bodies, I feel my "capacity for darkness" must be immense, an observation my mind negates while Zoran continues, "One of them will expose your greatest weakness."

"Zoran?" A woman's voice calls out and the Shadows scatter like frightened birds, disappearing into the wall.

Zoran turns toward me. "Go!"

I run toward the corridor at the corner of the room and, once inside, flatten myself against one of the walls. Across the room and within my sightline, a door opens and a woman enters the room like a white squall as I inch myself sideways up the corridor's incline.

She is focused on Zoran, her tall, razor-thin frame making her look like a knife ready for attack. Pale, with severe, short black hair, she almost floats, the hem of her snow-white dress hovering along the floor.

Zoran's voice fills the room. "Arvada—"

The woman's sharp facial features grow taut as her dark eyes sweep the room. "You're not permitted to be alone here with her. You know that." Weighty silence hangs in the air as she continues. "Please tell me you haven't begun without me." I needn't be in the room to know she is livid, and her tone of voice confirms my deduction. "You're already on shaky ground, and for this, I can make things more difficult for you."

Taking a large step sideways until both are out of my sightline, I make my way up the steep incline, sensing I should put as much distance between the woman and myself as possible. As I reach the end of the corridor, the torches' flames dim to the point of being extinguished.

The muggy air around me is suffocating. Truth be told, I find this place disturbing, and I can't get the Shadows out of my thoughts: their gaunt faces, their hollow eyes, their soulless presence. Like a wave of their darkness has followed me out of the hall, the torches behind me go out, causing me to run to the stairs leading out of the tomb.

My foot is on the first step but after hearing quick and shallow breathing behind me, I stop. With a spot of cool air hovering near my right ear, I feel a gentle tap on my arm as an inky-black Shadow creeps around my shoulder, its mouth forming a misshapen, gummy smile. "Little Dragon."

"What did you say?"

The Shadow's hollow eyes take me in for a moment before it floats across the room and is swallowed up into the blackness of the corridor. Unable to control myself, I race after it, but as I reach the entrance, Zoran appears.

I step forward and am face-to-face with him as the Shadow's tiny voice slithers through my brain. "Little Dragon…"

With him blocking my path, my blood boils. "Get out of my way."

He takes a step toward me. "No."

I can't breathe and in this peculiar moment, I hate him. With my temper flared, I feel I could rip him apart with my bare hands.

"The Shadow has revealed what we need to know."

As Zoran passes by me and heads up the staircase, I contemplate the idea of defying him and running after the Shadow. But perhaps this is the test: it's a kind of trick, one meant to trigger what I know to be the darkest place inside me, a place I never allow myself to go because to do so would mean admitting that it exists. Shunning the challenge of reentering my own internal shadow-filled room, I turn away from the tunnel and walk up the staircase, feeling defeated and confused.

Reaching the top of the stairs, I take in the fresh scent of the forest and am grateful to be leaving the musty underground crypt behind. Walking along the cold stone floor, I reach the edge of the tomb's structure and stand next to Zoran.

"We'll now be led to your Primer."

I'm about to inquire as to what he means by "Primer" when I notice the forest floor pulsing, coming alive, and that's when I see them: palm-size, jet black, and formidable. Spiders. Thousands upon thousands of spiders.

My skin is crawling. There is nothing more repugnant to me than spiders, and I don't know what to do. I'm terrified to the point that rational thought and physical response are both implausible.

I used to stomp on spiders as a child, stepping on them until their guts squished out. Mother caught me once and sat me down, explaining that it was a spider that carried fire embers through the water on her back. She told me Cherokees believe that without the spider's courage, man would not have fire. I always listened to my mother, but on this subject, I was deaf. I've never met a spider that I haven't stomped to death.

The spiders form lines in front of me like soldiers awaiting orders, their rows so precise it's unsettling. Every one of them is watching me, and I have the feeling they're frightfully intelligent.

Stepping down from the stone ledge, I walk forward while the spiders part and make a path for me as though I am their exalted queen. Making my way through them and toward the meadow, I think of something my father once said: "Liberation comes when you begin to love what you once hated."

Whether spiders or something far more apropos, if his words are true, on many levels, my liberation seems unattainable.

29

WARRIOR'S CURSE

We stop at the edge of the forest behind the legion of spiders as they spread out along the forest floor and line up at the bases of the trees like scouts surveying the landscape beyond the forest.

Standing at the top of a steep rolling hill and staring downward, I'd be lying if I said I wasn't in awe of the walled circular city that lies below us—it's magnificent and feels like I've stepped back in time. The medieval city is quite large with four distinct quadrants that surround a colossal stone gazebo at the city's center. I get the feeling each section has its own personality or identity, evidenced by the varied types of architecture and lighting used within each one.

The wall surrounding the city is formidable, high, and thick, with large glass lanterns that hang every few feet and turreted towers at the four cardinal points. Lamplighters walk along the walls' stone ledges, and as they light the stained-glass lanterns, glowing multicolored light spills out into the surrounding night.

I glance at Zoran, whose gaze falls upon the city with an unmistakable air of longing, and based on the vigilance with which he scans a darkened portion of the city to our left, I'd guess he's either not supposed to be here or not sure if it's safe for us to advance.

Zoran's stare is still locked on the city as he follows the spiders along the tree line using the forest for cover. I trail behind him until we reach a patch of trees across from the city's dimmest quadrant.

The forest forms a second wall around the city, flanking it in the same circular shape, and as the spiders begin maneuvering toward the wall through the trees' thick underbrush, it's evident they're ensuring we're not seen.

We're moving down toward the darkest part of the wall when the spiders slow their approach as Zoran lowers his head and walks in a predatory crawl. His ears are perked, the hair on his back is on end, and with him on such high alert, I pull in closer behind him as my adrenaline kicks in.

The underbrush has been replaced by a blanket of ivy that has spread from the forest and overtaken the tower nestled within the wall. We're across from the tower, and as I follow Zoran's searching stare up toward its turreted top, I see a lit candle pass three times across the inside of an arched window.

After looking in both directions, we make our way from beneath the trees toward the base of the tower, and as we do, the spiders line up along the forest's edge behind us. Faint light drifts down from a lone lantern on the wall, its iron base bent and leaning toward the ground. When I follow the lantern's beam of light downward, my gaze settles on thousands of skulls embedded in the stone blocks of the wall.

The skulls have been dipped in copper, which makes their misshapen, bony structures more grotesque. Even without skin and muscle to portray facial expressions, the skulls embody the hellish deaths that consumed their human forms. They're mere talismans now, watching from the wall and guarding against whatever undead creatures made them.

I shift my focus to Zoran, who is fixated on the skulls with the look of penetrating shame and regret I noticed in the tomb. Based on the change in his demeanor and the sadness flooding the space around him, I wonder if these skulls are somehow related to the same horror that gave birth to the subhuman ghosts he calls Shadows.

Hearing footsteps, I turn my head and see a group of spiders leading a woman toward us along the outside of the wall. She is staying close to the wall to remain concealed by its dark silhouette, and I sense she's taken a grave risk in venturing beyond the city.

When she reaches us, I can't take my eyes from her, and considering the way she's looking at me, she's in a similar state. There are differences in our appearance, but by and large we resemble one another, and as if she's a person-turned-spirit, she has slipped past all my defenses and made me care for her in a matter of seconds.

The deep color of her draped robe makes her skin appear milky white and the subtle trace of honey-laced perfume drifting from her skin does little to mask the muskiness of the man she's recently been with. It's a scent I'd know anywhere and were I to wager a guess, I'd bet she's bedded far more than one man on this—or on any other—night.

Seeing a deep scar across her cheek and lip, I wonder if her trade once led her into the den of a monster. Yet even with the vicious mark, she's celestial, like a broken, dark-haired angel, and I'm sure men pay a king's ransom to be near her.

Judging by the sensuality oozing from every inch of her, I'm resolute in the knowledge that she's supreme in the art of giving pleasure; and in this, we form our sisterhood. We are artists, and although I surmise she wields her brush for different reasons, in the end, both of our strokes result in a living painting few would have the courage, or patience, to create.

She breaks from our stare, understanding that we are beyond introductions, and instead turns to Zoran as she caresses the fur on his neck. "Are you all right?" She takes him in with large brown eyes while letting her fingers trail along his chest.

Zoran looks to be at peace, as she seems to offer comfort that he can find nowhere else, and in the way they look at each other I sense a woven trust between them. But their connection feels pure and untainted by desire. Their love seems more familial, or perhaps theirs is a friendship based on many years of moving through the trials of life at one another's side.

"Can I see it?"

Adhering to his request, she pulls back the sleeve of her robe and reveals two interlocking circles carved into her skin. I stare at the blood leaking from what looks like a blade-created tattoo as Zoran speaks. "The Scribe has chosen well."

She hardens her gaze and studies him long enough for me to feel that she's unsure what he's spoken is the truth. Appearing to change the subject, Zoran confirms, "You've been with Griksvold." By the tone of his voice, it's apparent he feels betrayed in some way.

"The closer I keep him, the more I can help," she asserts. Reaching around his neck, she presses herself against his chest and whispers, "And with Griksvold having told the Luminaries who she is, it's only a matter of time."

Zoran backs away from her. "He can't find out you're her Primer."

"He won't."

"Sola, you need to leave the city."

Sola takes a step toward him. "I'm not afraid. Perhaps I should be, but I'm not. For all his wickedness, he cares for me and speaks freely in my presence. Think of the opportunities that affords us—*all* of us."

Having removed a small bottle from the pocket of her robe, she hands it to me. Reluctant, I retrieve the bottle from her, feeling a bit like Alice in Wonderland confronted with a similar mysterious glass-encased liquid labeled DRINK ME. Were I to drink whatever bright-red liquid the bottle contains, would I shrink into a miniature version of myself as did Alice?

Sensing my hesitation, Sola smiles and does her best to quell my concern. "It's harmless. But it matters."

I look to Zoran, who is in apparent agreement that I should consume said mystery potion. Having committed to this dream, or rather to tumbling down the proverbial rabbit hole, I uncork the bottle and drink down what tastes like sour red wine mixed with what I'd swear was blood.

The thick substance coats my tongue and throat, and when it hits my stomach I feel lightheaded. I'm about to inquire what was in the bottle when I see Zoran lift his head like he's caught a familiar scent. He looks to our right while behind us, ousted from their positions, the spiders break from the forest's edge and rush forward en masse.

Turning back toward Sola with his eyes wild and the hair on his neck on end, Zoran demands, "Did he see you leave?"

Sola's face registers a streak of dread. "No. He was dead asleep."

"He's here." Zoran scans the length of the wall, his muscles tensing.

Sola races toward me and wraps her arm around my waist. "I'll take her."

I've moved all of two steps when a sharp ripping sound cuts through the air. It could be the moonlight playing tricks, but it seems the night scene in front of me is opening like a curtain being pulled aside. I don't have a moment to process what I'm seeing before someone reaches through the opening, grabs my shoulders, and yanks me inside, away from Sola.

Sola screams as the tear closes and I'm forced into a vast mist-filled corridor. It seems I'm standing in a sliver of space that exists between the bands of time, a kind of walkway separating two worlds. Stabbing pain is shooting up my left leg and when I look down, I see one of the spiders clinging to my thigh. Then a man wraps strong arms around my waist and drags me backward with brute force until I'm pulled from the cloudy corridor through what feels like a weighted curtain.

Now on a stone path and with his grip loosening, I whip around and stare into the piercing blue eyes of the man from the tomb of the marble women. He wears the same black robe from our previous encounter, and I find the raw sexuality emanating from him frightening.

There is no disputing how uncomfortable I feel. I must find a way out of this place and back to the dreamscape I've come to know as Loryian. If it weren't for the distraction of the spider making its way to the back of my leg, I would try to run, yet for reasons I don't understand, I stand still and allow it to continue down to my calf.

The man stands in front of me like a dog guarding its prey, and as I look to my right I notice the path ends just in front of the blown-out cathedral. I turn my head the other direction and see nothing save the haunting trees along the path, their jet-black, leathery bark shining beneath the moonlight as though dipped in oil, every branch crooked, like broken bones beneath smooth skin. Other than the bluish moonlight, there is no color—everything is monochrome and drained of life like the landscape has been sucked dry by a bloodthirsty incubus.

As he takes a step closer, the tree branches around us twist and drip a tar-like sap onto the blackened, sand-covered ground below. My instincts tell me to run and hide in the darkness of the surrounding forest, but the rational part of my brain knows that my single chance for escape is to get to the blown-out cathedral.

Abrupt and violent, the man grabs my shoulders and puts his mouth on my neck. He licks up and down my jugular vein until I'm paralyzed by a potent injection of both disgust and fear. With a hand on the side of my neck, he covers the front of my throat with one last swipe of his tongue before pulling away and looking at me. "You're almost there. I can taste it." Behind him, branches undulate beneath the moon like the knotted hands of a conjuring witch. "He'll come for them one by one until you have no one left and then, when it's time, he'll come for you."

His words go straight into me like a blade. I know to whom he's referring, and I feel his pure malevolence to my core. I manage to back away from the man but can't seem to find enough strength to run.

Feeling sharp fangs pierce my calf, I flinch. He sees my leg move and is now staring at the blood running toward my ankle as though he's ready to drop to his knees and let it flow into his mouth, holy water to a wicked priest.

The spider leaps from my leg and charges him, and before it reaches the hem of his robe, its body erupts into a ball of violet flame, causing me to step backward as his robe ignites. Fire races up his body as he lets out a bloodcurdling scream and drops to the ground, rolling and thrashing. With the man engulfed in flames, the spider darts past me and into the forest.

I see its glowing light through the darkness and follow as it weaves between tight clusters of trees, seeming to know where it's going. The spider is hurried and I'm struggling to keep up, but when the scent of burning sugar creeps over my shoulder and rams up my nostrils, I force myself to run faster.

Like the dwindling light of a dying fire, the spider's flame dims to almost nothing. In hearing it making metallic clicking sounds, I know it's attempting to give auditory direction, but with the density of the surrounding trees, the sound bounces around the forest. Unable to see anything in front of me, I stop running and listen.

With effort, I hear scurrying along the forest floor, and as I'm about to take a step I feel something sharp dig into the top of my foot. After a few metallic clicks, the spider's bright flame lights up in front of me.

The spider takes off into the forest and turns to the right around a bank of trees. I follow, then round the trees and trail the spider into a circular clearing filled with small round rocks that form a spoked wheel. The bluish moonlight gives the stone formation a graveyard quality, and I can't imagine what we're doing here, nor can I understand why the spider has stopped inside the wheel. For a moment I question my judgment and wonder if I should bolt back into the forest on my own.

My thoughts are halted when I see a thick black mist spilling into the clearing from all sides. It skulks along the ground like a calculating predator and surrounds us. But when the mist reaches the outer ring of the stone wheel, it stops, hovering outside the rocky perimeter as if unable to cross over.

The mist amasses on the opposite side of the wheel and to my horror morphs into an immense male figure. The fear overwhelming my body is pushing me backward out of the safety of the wheel, yet I simply cannot stop myself from putting distance between me and the most primeval form of darkness I have ever encountered. I feel his soullessness throughout every cell, as though I'm being consumed by the black blood I sense running through his veins.

Now out of the wheel and edging into the forest, my back makes contact with something solid. Whatever I'm standing against is so large, I assume it's a wall of some kind. Cautious, I reach behind me to figure out what's blocking my path, but instead of stone, I feel cold, smooth scales.

Hearing a deep exhale, I turn my head and swear the night itself is breathing. I know something is there, as I'm touching its scaled skin. But whatever it is blends into the darkness to the point that I can't see where night's blackness ends and *it* begins.

As it turns toward me, my pulse races. It's the warrior torn from the pages of my mother's book. The living legend of the man who eradicated the white man from the Cherokee lands and whose nickname echoed the destruction of his hatred. Yet it's not a man before me, but the warrior's counterpart: I'm face-to-face with the warrior's cursed form, with his alter ego come to life. Black as night with a hard-plated chest of stark white, he stares at me and the emerald irises of his eyes contract.

Shifting his enormous body, he sits straight up and takes out several tree branches as he maneuvers himself to full height. His python-sized arm wraps around my waist, pressing me against his chest. Drum to blood, my ears fill with the sound of a familiar booming heartbeat and I feel the spider latch onto my foot as we launch from the forest floor.

30

THE SCALE OF THINGS

aegan is shivering, naked, and in excruciating pain. If I hadn't seen him change form, I'd never have believed it, but like the warrior from my mother's story, he is two in the body of one.

Although it's almost invisible to the naked eye, I see a thin white vapor appear, then retract back into his pale skin, like he's having difficulty remaining in his current form. I'm attempting to help him across the black marble floor toward the fireplace, but with every step I feel his body contracting in agony. His breath is shallow and labored, and I'm not sure if the change is making him ill or pushing him to the verge of death.

Once we've reached the fur rug, I feel his knees give way and do my best to lower him down. Curling into a ball at my feet, his body trembles while his muscles clench and he lets out a muffled cry. There are no blankets in the room, the fire is unlit, and it's so cold I can see my breath. I walk to the fireplace and see a few red embers still smoldering amongst the ashes. One by one, I take logs from a basket and place them onto the embers. Leaning down, I blow a few times, attempting to bring the fire back to life, and after a moment, the dry bark of the logs catches fire and sends several loud popping sounds into the room.

Behind me Daegan lets out another stifled moan, and in response I stand and go to him. I'm not sure how to ease his pain so I lie behind him and wrap my body around his to keep him warm. He tenses when he feels me against him, and with his steady heartbeat filling my ears, I feel my own heartbeat slow until it comes into time with his.

The fire is blazing now, casting orangey light into the room as it edges away the cold. I hear him trying to speak through his pain, but he can only do so after several strenuous breaths. "Upstairs. My clothes…"

I stand, move toward the corner of the room, then climb a set of uneven stairs. Once at the top, I carefully make my way along an open walkway before coming to a crooked doorway that leads into a simple room with candlelit lanterns.

A rustic four-poster bed is nestled in the far corner; on top of it sits a lone pillow propped against a rough wooden headboard. Across from the bed is a worn chair flanked by a small side table piled with books, and the more I stare at the chair's fraying velvet, the more I feel that this room is where he takes refuge from the world.

I walk through a narrow doorframe into a connecting lantern-lit room lined with floor-to-ceiling bookcases on the left and shelves of clothing on the right.

I scan the books lining the crude wooden bibliothèques; almost every book appears to be hundreds of years old—some tattered to the point that they're missing bindings and held together by pieces of twine.

In the center of the room is an antique slant-topped writing desk upon which are a torn-out page and a blank piece of paper with a small note at the top. I move toward the desk and study the page, which is of considerable age and covered in scribbled black writing that starts in the center and spirals outward in tight looping circles like a long, word-made worm.

Next to the torn page, on the sheet of paper, is a phrase written in hurried handwriting: "Book of Elders? SSJS?"

"Did you find them?"

Startled, I turn around and do my best not to draw attention to the fact that Daegan is walking toward me stark naked.

Once in the room, he retrieves a pair of pants and a shirt, but when he attempts to put them on, he is stopped by a wave of pain. I take his clothes from him, wrap my arm around his waist, and help him into the bedroom. "What's happening to you?"

After sitting him on the bed, I kneel and attempt to help him dress as he answers, "Convergence. A kind of expansion resulting in an equally taxing contraction…"

I hear his airway constrict as his voice trails off and a flash of his massive alternate form floods my mind's eye. Looking up at his face, I see his exhaustion and discomfort and am about to help him when he takes his clothes and dresses on his own.

My mind churns as I inquire, "How is it possible that you—"

Daegan responds before I can finish my sentence. "I'm a Satient."

With the inside of his wrist visible, I notice a time-faded scar in the shape of two interlocking circles identical to the carved mark Sola bore. Intent on shifting my focus from the scar, he stands and pulls me up from my knees. Once he's walked into the adjoining room, he takes a long cloak from the clothing shelves, then returns.

Having wrapped the cloak around my shoulders, he fastens a thick iron clasp at my neck and warns me, "Although he's important, you need to be careful with Zoran."

He puts his hand on my shoulder for support while, thunder to sky, I feel his heartbeat booming throughout my body.

He seems unfazed by the fact that I've failed to respond and continues. "You also need to be more cautious when in the Thirteenth."

"What do you mean, the Thirteenth?"

His tattoos circle in on themselves like corkscrews. "The realm you call home."

I don't know how to process what he's just said, nor am I sure what such a concept means in the context of exploring my own psyche. But then, it makes a strange kind of sense that I would choose to give myself a separate yet neighboring domain to this darkly pertinent dreamscape realm I've heard referred to as Loryian.

Placing a gentle hand on my shoulder, he offers, "You must be discerning with those you let close to you now."

"Including you?" I banter.

Rather than retort, he puts his hand on the small of my back and leads me out of the room.

31

TESLA'S GYRE

Phinneas bolted upright and wiped several beads of sweat from his temples. The house was buzzing as if the air had been replaced with pure electricity. Wrangling his knobby legs from beneath the covers, he got out of bed and made his way to the door. Ziggy plopped to the floor and scurried toward Phinneas, who picked him up, tucked him beneath his arm, then walked into the upstairs hallway.

Getting down the stairs was more difficult with each passing day, and on this night they seemed to go on forever. Doing his best to force his old bones to cooperate, Phinneas reached the downstairs landing and turned toward the blinding cobalt-colored light shining from the basement.

Working his way down the basement staircase, he shielded his eyes from the storm of blue light below. Making contact with the cold concrete floor, he moved toward the source of light in the corner of the basement, which dimmed as if comforted by his presence.

Setting Ziggy down on a small desk, Phinneas sat in front of an old keyboard and monitor. He let his gaze follow the hodgepodge of clipped wires from the fuse box to the back of the computer, then to a 1950s bubblegum machine he'd converted into what looked like a crude, makeshift lightbulb.

Bits of candied gum shells still littered the inside of the glass, which was half covered with twisted copper wire. A ball of light bobbed around inside, its glow faint and muted with neon-blue tentacles streaking out from its center. When Phinneas put his knobby hand on the glass, the tentacles grew brighter and thicker as if agitated.

Next to him, the computer booted up, and in response Ziggy backed away from the monitor and almost fell off the desk. The old dinosaur of a monitor flickered before a blinking green cursor appeared and the glowing light inside the glass dimmed to virtually nothing.

After a moment, letters appeared on the monitor, their blocky type slow and deliberate. Both Phinneas and Ziggy stared in disbelief as the message was completed:

> *coil corrupt*
> *current unstable*
> *give her nilah's journal*

The glowing light next to him faded. Panicked, Phinneas leaned toward the glass, feeling helpless while a feeble tentacle lost its grip against the inside and vanished into thin air.

Moving back to the computer, he typed a few letters, knowing better but unable to help himself:

> *i miss you*

The blinking cursor grew dim, then the monitor shut down like an old television until its last bit of light disappeared into a tiny circle at the screen's center.

Phinneas picked up Ziggy, put him in his pocket, and made his way toward the basement staircase. The ache in his joints and the rumbling outside told him that a storm was coming, a billowing of elements that would change his environment in both the literal and figurative. And as he made his way up the stairs, a low, disconcerting buzz followed him like every electrical wire in the house was hissing.

32

IRON & BLOOD

Petting the soft, rust-colored coat of the large dog sitting at my feet, I feel at home in the old Blacksmith's shop. Tufts of white hair are visible on the dog's chin and his eyes are clouded over as if the years have left layer upon layer of dusty film behind.

Shifting my focus to the Blacksmith, I can tell by his demeanor and playful smile that he must have had a way with women in his day. Even though his shoulders droop and his back harbors a large rounded bump as if a small half-cut boulder is resting below his skin, I've no doubt he was once strapping and handsome.

Studying the lines and valleys on his face as one might a map of rough terrain they're attempting to navigate, I inspect every groove, pencil-thin line, and blotched age spot like they're a secret alphabet embedded within thick and time-warped paper.

Glancing around the Blacksmith's well-kept shop, I take in the shelf-lined walls and buckets of iron scrap stacked in the corner. Returning my gaze back to him and Daegan, who are sitting with me at a small wooden table, I notice both staring into a shot-glass-sized copper cup filled with my blood.

I find it strange that next to the cup is another of identical size whose contents appear to be a dark, syrupy substance that almost looks like tar. What's more, I could swear the ever-so-faint scent of burning sugar drifts up from the cup like an invisible, candied snake.

The Blacksmith dips a small iron rod into my blood and watches with fascination as it melts into the cup like ice coming into contact with hot water. Daegan seems disturbed by what he's just seen, the tattoos at his temples now churning in unbalanced circles.

The Blacksmith pulls a pair of spectacles from a center pocket of his heavy leather apron. They have two standard lenses, as would any pair of glasses, but there are eight extra colored lenses, four on either side of the frame that fan outward like a peacock's tail feathers.

While staring at my blood, he alternates the colored lenses over each eye, one by one: orange, purple, red, blue, green, then yellow. Cautious, as if he's afraid of what he'll see, he pulls down a cloudy white lens and leans closer to the cup, troubled by whatever has been revealed through its hazy glass. He swaps it for a black one and when he does, his body tenses while he flips the dark lens up and down a few times as if hoping it will yield a different result.

Daegan looks past me toward a crooked doorframe at the back of the shop. "Do you mind waiting in my room upstairs?"

My focus is locked on the Blacksmith, who appears to be lost in his thoughts as he continues flipping the lens while staring at my blood. But when I stand and am ready to walk across the room, he removes his glasses and sends a concerned gaze my direction.

Turning from the two men and sensing their eagerness to be alone, I walk toward the door with my unflinching and loyal canine companion trotting along behind me. His wet nose nudges my palm and I give him an affectionate, light scratch, which causes him to wag his tail with such excitement he almost topples over.

I pass through the doorframe and make my way up a tight spiral staircase while straining to hear Daegan and the Blacksmith's hushed conversation.

"The foundations of the base cardinal elements are present, which makes her the same as past Guardians. Where her blood differs is in the presence of three pillars of Asdan matter."

"That's not possible—"

The Blacksmith's voice is coated with unease as he interrupts. "Well, there's the pillar we already knew about—which was concerning enough— and now we have the recent consumption of both dark matter and aether."

Daegan is silent for several moments before querying, "Are they stable?"

The Blacksmith responds, "Barely. She'll have to subsume the cardinal elements then the final pillar of matter from you in very short order."

Daegan interjects. "Infusing a fourth along with the elements could—"

"It's a problem, for sure, but the matter you possess is crucial if she's to have any chance of surviving."

The eerie silence blanketing the room causes me to continue up the stairs, and as I do, the dog bumps his nose against my calf as if signaling for me to quicken my ascent. I'm at the top of the stairs when I hear Daegan walking across the room.

"We can't forge the new gates until we know more about how her blood will react—it's too dangerous."

The Blacksmith counters. "But without the gates—"

"I know who might have the information we need. I'll be back shortly."

With that, I hear the front door open, then close.

I step up onto the last stair and cross a narrow hallway into a large wood-paneled room while the dog saunters in behind me, then plops down and curls up in the center of the floor. A waft of cold air leaking through the large paned windows across the room sends chills along my skin. Although a fire burns in the small fireplace next to me, it isn't enough to keep the cold from settling into my bones.

Standing in front of the fireplace, I let the fire's warmth seep into my skin while reading a few titles from the stack of books on the mantel. Judging by the deep creases in their bindings, each of them has been read so often Daegan must know them by heart.

Shifting my gaze to a large mirror hanging over the mantel, I study the room through its reflection and wonder if this cozy den-like space is Daegan's hideaway—a place he can downshift into the life and time of an ordinary man—his quiet retreat in the heart of a city, in the home of a companion with whom he has a deep and trusted friendship. After watching the two of them together, I feel the Blacksmith is a father figure to him, a kind of mentor or scholarly parallel who helps fill in the blank spaces life's mysteries and hardships have left unfilled.

Lowering my sightline back toward the mantel, one of the books catches my eye: *Tropic of Cancer* by Henry Miller. Without thinking, I pick it up, open it, and find an earmarked page and know which passage had captured Daegan's attention.

> For some reason or other, man looks for the miracle, and to accomplish it, he will wade through blood. He will debauch himself with ideas, he will reduce himself to a shadow if for only one second of his life he can close his eyes to the hideousness of reality.
>
> Everything is endured—disgrace, humiliation, poverty, war, crime, ennui—in the belief that overnight something will occur, a miracle, which will render his life tolerable...

Anaïs Nin is one of my favorite writers, so it's no coincidence that I should find her lover's, Henry Miller's, book sitting before me. I feel his words all the way through me as though I have consumed their ink-laden letters. I'm about to continue reading when I hear a deep male voice coming from behind me.

"I'm surprised he sent you up here alone."

I put the book down, then turn around while a man emerges from a shadowy corner of the room. When he walks toward me, his cloak shifts enough for me to notice a large sheathed knife attached to his belt. My instincts tell me I've no need to be afraid of him, yet there's a latent threatening quality that floats around him like a waiting storm.

He's in front of me now, and with him so close, I'm confronted by the overpowering scent of burning cedar drifting from the thick black fabric of his cloak. It's apparent he wants to speak, but instead we both stand in silence and take one another in as if we're two parted friends who've been reunited.

A stray piece of his greying hair slips from the confines of its leather tie and comes to rest by the corner of his almost black eyes. I study his fair skin, which is unevenly weathered as if age had only elected to leave its mark in certain places.

Bits of pine needles are caught in the fabric of his cloak and judging by his tall, tree-trunk frame and the woodsman-like air he exudes, I surmise he knows the forest better than he knows himself, or anyone else, for that matter.

After a moment he speaks, and when he does, I detect a note of apprehension coloring his voice. "I take it they're still experimenting with our blood?"

I realize the foul-looking dark blood next to mine must have been his, which in looking at him is hard to fathom.

He continues while staring at a drop of blackish blood seeping from the top of his index finger. "Your bloodline carries the light; mine, the dark. I think they're hoping you can help me."

He takes my knife-pricked finger, somehow knowing it's still oozing blood, and holds it up next to his before pressing our fingers together. When he does, the oil-slick black veins on his hands turn a faint bluish grey.

Within seconds of our blood mixing, his veins return to normal and the dormant storm I sensed when he walked toward me earlier is replaced by a tranquil peace that radiates from him like warmth from the sun. He closes his eyes as though having shed a great weightiness from his spirit, and when he pulls our fingers apart and refocuses on me, the gratitude he feels is visceral.

"Freedom is still freedom, even if only temporary."

We both focus on the veins in his hand, which now appear like tiny velvet-black worms are crawling through them. The looming storm is returning and when I look in his eyes, I feel myself wanting to help him, to give him another infusion so as to relieve the burden I sense threatening to crush his spirit.

While still holding my hand, he speaks. "We can help one another."

Unsure of what he means or in what manner he assumes I need his help, I elect to stay mute in the hopes that he will elaborate. He watches me, seeming to understand that I won't respond, then continues. "You won't get through your Leveling without me."

I flinch upon hearing this word again. Why, in these dreams, have I given such importance to this concept of deconstruction? What good can come from tearing down everything that makes me *me?*

I hear the spiral staircase stairs creaking outside the room as the Blacksmith calls out, "Brought you some tea."

The sound of rattling china rings from the hallway. He enters the room on rickety legs, holding a wooden tray on top of which sits a small teapot and a dainty cup complete with matching saucer.

After setting the tray down on a side table, the Blacksmith eyes the man. "Nikolai, I thought you'd left."

Nikolai doesn't have a moment to respond before we hear the sound of breaking glass coming from downstairs. The dog shoots to his feet, his tail like an arrow, and barks while the Blacksmith rushes forward and ushers us across the room toward the far wall. "Quick!"

Reaching the wall, the Blacksmith pushes on a small round peg, which causes a hidden door to pop open. Nikolai and I duck inside and once all the way in, I feel him pull me toward him while the Blacksmith closes the door.

I hear heavy footsteps bounding up the staircase like an army of irate militiamen while through the thin spaces in the wooden slats of the door, I see the Blacksmith sit in a chair next to the fire and attempt to calm his vicious, growling dog.

Three beefed-up men burst into the room, thug-like and charging the air with a penetrating hatred that ignites my fear like fuel to flame. I'm terrified, and as capable as I sense Nikolai's skills for survival are, I'm certain he's no match for the seething madmen beyond the closet door.

The largest of them, knife in hand like a merciless Butcher, is leaning down over the Blacksmith and eyeing him like a stuffed toy he's contemplating shredding. "Where is she?"

With an impressive amount of composure, the Blacksmith responds, "I honestly don't know."

The man puts the tip of his knife to the Blacksmith's heart and when he does, the dog lunges toward him. To my horror, the man grabs the top of the dog's head and slits his throat in what is one of the cruelest displays I've ever seen. The man is indeed a Butcher and my stomach lurches as I watch the dog hit the floor, his blood spilling out from the gaping wound in his neck.

The other two men snicker and grunt while they walk around the room looking at every window, corner, and crevice as if they might find evidence of me there. Both men pass by the closet door, and as they do Nikolai holds me against his chest.

The Butcher's voice sounds like tires on gravel and when he speaks it grates my bones. "Last chance, little man. Where is she?"

The Blacksmith's stance is defiant, his face hard as he stares down the giant before him. "Haven't a clue."

Enraged, the man shoves the tea tray to the floor, lays the Blacksmith's hand flat on the table, and lops off one of his knobby fingers. The Blacksmith lets out a stifled cry and pulls his hand to his chest while the man sneers, "Next time it'll be more than a finger."

While looking out the window, one of the men calls out, "Griksvold, we have to go."

The Butcher, Griksvold, slams his hand against the side table. "When I get my hands on that fucking cunt."

After taking one last look around the room, the man leads the others into the hallway and down the stairs.

Hearing the front door slam downstairs, Nikolai opens the closet and listens to ensure the men are gone. The house is stone dead silent, like the marrow has been sucked from its wooden skeleton.

Seeing the Blacksmith nodding off, his head drooping to one side, Nikolai races across the creaky old floors. "Jakob."

Reaching his chair and kneeling, Nikolai taps the side of the Blacksmith's face. "You have to stay awake." The Blacksmith fails to respond and resembles a rag doll as he slumps into the chair.

Joining Nikolai, I kneel in front of the Blacksmith with my knees to the right of the dog's lifeless body. I can't help but look in the dog's cloudy brown eyes, which are open and filled with a searching look, like his soul is still inside the room and using his eyes to connect with and cling to some form of life.

Shifting my focus toward the Blacksmith, I feel nauseated as I examine the copious amounts of blood on the side table. Even more disturbing is the sight of his severed finger teetering on the table's edge with its cleaved bone and serrated flesh.

Nikolai removes his cloak and rips off the sleeve of his shirt, which he uses as a makeshift tourniquet. Turning toward me, he speaks. "I need your blood."

Without waiting for my response, he unsheathes the knife from his belt and shallowly slices the top of my finger. Blood leaps to the surface along with a vapor that drifts up from the cut like a stream of thin liquid cellophane.

Nikolai stares at the tiny wisps snaking up from my skin with equal parts fascination and unease. He puts my finger to the exposed bone of what's left of the Blacksmith's finger, and when I feel its slimy sharpness, my mind shuts down like a dying battery.

Whether it's coming into contact with severed bone, or the fact that the vapor appears to be rushing from my open cut and wrapping around the man's finger like a transparent bandage, what I'm experiencing is more than my body can accept. Collapsing, I fall sideways against the soft fur of the dog's bloody corpse.

Nikolai reaches for me, his arms strong yet gentle as he pulls me up toward him while still forcing my skin against the sharp bone of the Blacksmith's finger. Darkness is closing in on all sides and the last thing I see is the look of shock on Daegan's face as he rushes into the room. Then everything goes black.

33

THE COLLECTOR

Zoë awoke on the floor with a furry round rump inches from her face as Lucille's fat marmalade tail swished across her nose. Lucille gave her a backward glance, then sauntered across the room before leaping up onto the windowsill.

With dawn peeking through the window, Zoë watched a small beam of dull morning sun illuminate enough of her hand to reveal that it was covered in blood, the sight of which forced her into a state of momentary panic.

Having struggled to her feet, she walked into the bathroom, grabbed a towel, and tried to wipe the blood from her skin, but it refused to be removed, as though the Blacksmith's dream-spirit was fighting her attempt to erase his memory. She turned on the faucet, put a corner of the towel beneath the running water, then scrubbed her hand clean.

Feeling nonplussed, she walked into her bedroom and stood beside Lucille, who was perched on the windowsill watching snow floating by. Lilting flakes swept by her window with effortless grace and for a moment she envied their lightness. Her mind felt heavy, her body foreign, and there was a slight buzz at the base of her heels like an electric current was trapped inside them. She wanted to walk, run—anything to stamp out the restlessness.

What she needed was to press herself into normalcy for a few hours, to get out, in the hopes of shedding the feeling of being an alien in her own life. Once she'd crossed to the armoire, she dressed, put on a pair of boots, and not even sure where she was going, left her room.

Slipping across the hallway and down the stairs, Zoë felt the house had succumbed to winter's gloom. Quickening her descent, she reached the bottom of the stairs and rushed to the hall closet to put on her coat.

Venturing outside, she let the morning air pull her down the steps with bitter arctic fingers. When she stepped from the last stair, she felt the sidewalk's sturdy concrete meet her with a solid, weighted currency nothing else seemed to offer.

As she began walking, she noticed there were downed branches littering the street, and a streetlight at the corner hung precariously by one wire. Several small trees lining the sidewalk were damaged and others had been uprooted and were lying on the ground like discarded bark-covered corpses.

Once at the end of the street, she rounded the corner and entered the Rose Café through its painted, beat-up doorway. The café was lit with candles that had been placed in haphazard fashion throughout its wooden interior.

A thin, large-chested woman came through a set of beaded curtains at the back of the café. Her eyes were kind and her unpainted face beautiful in its plainness. "Sorry, we're not open. The storm cut the power."

Zoë tried to conceal her disappointment.

"Wait one sec." The young woman's lips widened into a smile as she turned around and disappeared through the beads.

Looking around the café, Zoë settled her gaze on the wall next to her, where a lone candle's flickering glow shed light on an enormous mural of a tabby cat labeled "La Rose Sauvage." The cat's tail was wrapped around a worn book standing on end, its ivory fangs clenching a red rose dripping blood…

Strands of thick beads rattled as the woman returned and placed a paper cup in front of her. "Gas still works. Made it from the French press for myself, but—"

"You don't have to do that."

"I'll make another. No biggie."

Zoë reached for her wallet, which sat next to the letter J.T. had given her from Evan as the woman spoke.

"No need. It's on the house."

"Thank you, really." Taking the cup from the woman, Zoë inquired, "Anything in the neighborhood open this early?"

The woman squinted and wrinkled her nose. "Not really. Maybe Sinclair's Antiques down the street? Definitely an interesting place to kill some time."

Zoë thanked her, then left the café and walked outside, savoring the unfolding moment as her first sip of hot coffee met the cold of her lips in polar combat.

Continuing down the street away from her house, steps slow and mouth hot, Zoë felt the caffeine focusing her rest-deprived brain. She decided to follow the woman's advice, seeing as she didn't want to go home; she needed a few more minutes in the land of the wakeful as an alien in fleshy disguise.

Nearing the street's corner, she found herself in front of a quaint shop with a large bay window next to the front door that read:

Sinclair's Antiques:
A true collector knows there is no such thing as garbage.
—Delano Sinclair

Peering inside, her focus was pulled toward a florid antique desk littered with silver candelabras, a ratty stuffed white rabbit missing one eye, and a triangular opal-faced pocket watch that had four ticking hands rather than two. To the right of the desk, a grandfather clock chimed, its high-pitched bell juxtaposed to the clock's giant size. It was 7:30.

Leaning against the clock was a small letter-sized painting of a shadowy grey brick building on a black background. A small fuzzy white rodent was making its way up the stairs toward the building's front door, and a bloodred crescent moon hanging in the canvas's upper right-hand corner cast a ray of gloomy light toward a window at the top of the building.

Zoë felt haunting loneliness drifting from the painting as though it were alive, sentient.

"Early bird gets the worm, so they say!" A glossy voice wrapped around her like tight silk. "Beautiful, isn't it?"

Looking left, Zoë met the steady gaze of a young man standing outside the shop's door.

"Come in!"

She tried not to stare at him, but with his long blond hair, Victorian shirt, waistcoat, black velvet slacks, and tapered shoes, he looked like a queen's companion lost in a foreign court. He opened the shop's front door and led her inside while speaking over his shoulder. "Wait here."

He made his way through stacks of books, piled furniture, and leaning artwork to retrieve the painting she'd been eyeing.

She inquired, "How long has this store been here?"

The man moved the myriad items jailing the painting in its place. "My family's had this shop since the beginning of time—feel free to take a look around."

After a moment, she walked past the register toward the back of the candlelit shop. "I've never noticed it before."

The back wall was lined floor to ceiling with old books and records. A Victrola sat in the corner next to a large empty birdcage.

"My grandfather believed everything that came into our shop was seeking the perfect home and that, inevitably, when the time was right, owner and possession would unite."

Turning, she watched him make his way toward her with a look of triumph in his eyes. "Got it."

As he held the painting up to the candlelight, she noticed two parallel copper strips fastened to the right side of the canvas's border.

He walked to the sales counter behind her, set down the painting, and retrieved a small piece of paper from an envelope beside the register. "A woman brought this in last week. It was tightly wrapped, looked like it hadn't been opened in ages. I only unwrapped it a few days ago."

She hesitated before inquiring, "How much do you want for it?"

He flashed a commercial-perfect smile. "That's not how it works here. Everything is traded."

"I don't understand."

He shifted his long legs and leaned against the counter. "Under normal circumstances, you'd trade something of equal value, but not in your case."

She questioned him while wondering how he could afford to keep his shop open without a proper income. "I'm still not sure I follow."

He handed her the small card he'd taken from the envelope, which she took and read to herself:

> Beauty's in the eye of the beholder,
> And desire makes the heart grow bolder.
> The painting's yours to have and hold,
> The price is meeting its owner of old.

She set the card down on the counter as he spoke. "I have to admit, I thought she was crazy, but here you are."

Studying the laminated sticker on the painting's side, she inquired, "Did you know the woman who brought this in?"

A whirl of black wings barreled toward them as the largest raven she'd ever seen landed on the counter with an elegant thump. The bird looked her up and down, its strange cobalt-colored eyes starry bright in the dim light.

"Meet Henry. I'm Delano, by the way."

She shook his hand. "Zoë."

Delano's glossy voice crept into the air as a candle behind him burned out and sent a wispy band of smoke toward him. "I thought it was strange, but the woman gave me that card and said the painting would choose a new owner. And so it has."

The smoky ribbon rounded Delano's shoulder, then hung in the air between them. "She didn't leave any contact information?"

He held her gaze while petting Henry. "Nope."

"So, a woman walked in, gave you this painting and a card, then left?" she pressed.

"Yep."

Henry cocked his head and stared at Zoë as she inquired, "What did she look like?"

Delano seemed to have developed a paralyzing dryness in his mouth as arid silence billowed between them. "If you agree to the meeting, take the painting. I'll handle the rest."

She didn't know what to do, as her overwhelming desire to have the painting overshadowed everything else. "If I were to agree, how do you know I'd keep my word?"

Delano's excitement rushed toward her carried by his weightless and charming smile. "Is that a yes, then?"

Zoë and Lula sat on the edge of the bed staring at the painting, which radiated moody, pigmented silence.

Lula crinkled her nose and tilted her head. "Kind of dreary, isn't it?"

Zoë smiled and offered, "It's beautiful in an Edgar Allan Poe kind of way."

Lula walked closer to the painting, then leaned over and examined it while quipping back, "Complete with a bloody raven as well."

Zoë stood and joined her. "Where?"

Lula motioned toward a small tree next to the sidewalk in front of the brick building where an all but undetectable raven sat perched on a tree's leafless branches. While staring at it, Zoë had the peculiar sensation that the raven was somehow gazing back at her.

Lula confirmed, "In the hallway, then? Are you sure?"

"Yep, right outside my door."

Lula took a hammer and picture nail from a small bag sitting on the vanity top, then scooped up the painting and walked into the hallway. After a few deliberate strokes of her hammer, she made sure the nail was in place, then secured the painting to the wall.

She walked back into the bedroom while Zoë stood in the hallway inspecting the painting's misshapen, bloodred crescent moon—a reminder of the mark she once bore and how Evan used to kiss her stained cheek, calling it a "human stain," saying it was the price an angel must pay to leave heaven. Odd that he had been the one to finance the mark's removal. So it was that the crimson of her cheek had migrated into the fleshy resettlement of her always painted bloodred lips.

Lula called out, "The bed's got an extra comforter since tonight's supposed to be unreasonably cold. Or so they're predicting."

Leaving the hallway then getting into bed, Zoë watched Lula lay several large logs onto the fire. Neither of them spoke, as they were both mesmerized by the orangey-red glow spilling into the room from the mouth of the fireplace like breath from a dragon.

Lula walked over to the bed and patted the top of Zoë's foot. "You didn't eat dinner."

Nestling beneath her covers and feeling her limbs growing heavier, Zoë replied, "Honestly, I'd rather sleep."

Lula gave Zoë's toes an affectionate squeeze and then turned off the lights, left the room, and closed the door behind her.

Thoughts swirled around Zoë's mind while an image of the painting's melancholy landscape swept across her consciousness like it was reaching out from the hallway and speaking through its bruise-hued scene. It felt as if the painting were delivering an avid reminder that the price for its possession was the meeting of a stranger, a fee-come-promise she regretted having made.

The painting then overtook her mind's eye, its thick, pigmented strokes undulating throughout the canvas as though phantom-filled and seeking escape. Engorged and almost bulging from the shadowed night sky, the blood moon pulsed out of time like an arrhythmic and dying heart.

With her skin turning cold, Zoë pushed deeper beneath the covers as the painting's ominous presence was overlaid by the faces of those she'd encountered that day: the woman at the Rose Café, Delano, and Henry, the raven.

Heavy and stonelike, she began sinking—sleep was unavoidable, and when her thoughts surrendered to a murky abyss of pure lightlessness, she felt a thousand ash-dusted fingers pulling her into the coming darkness.

34

LUMINARIES

orcing my eyes open, I take in the surrounding moon-lit forest, which in the haze of my half-consciousness seems foreign to me, like the setting of a children's dark-woven fairy tale. Turning onto my back, I take in a needed breath and stare at the sea of intertwining branches overhead, a canopy that feels alive and alert, like the trees are reaching out to one another to form a bark-made net.

Hearing voices to my left, I see Nikolai and the beautiful dark-haired woman, Sola, both blanketed in thick, pervading tension.

"Griksvold, do you let him—"

Even though they're quite far from me, I see the look of disgust on Nikolai's face as Sola interrupts him. "I'm yours, and you know that."

Running his thumb along her cheek, he demands, "Then why?"

She takes his hand in hers. "What he knows is invaluable."

His body stiffens as he prods. "And Zoran?" At the mere mention of Zoran's name, I sense the visceral hatred Nikolai has for him.

"He's my friend. I owe him my life."

Moving closer to her, Nikolai traces his lips along the deep scar on Sola's cheek until their mouths meet.

Pulling away, she urges, "You need to get her inside the cabin."

"Where will you go?"

Omnipresent darkness coats the forest like a blackened leather veil until she answers, "If I'm gone much longer, he'll look for me."

As if her words have given birth to reality, the sound of men's voices along with a succession of rabid, guttural barks echoes through the trees.

Her face fills with terror. "Trackers."

Both rush toward me, and before I've commanded my body to move, I'm standing.

Nikolai grabs my arms, his dark eyes filled with alarm. "Can you run?" I nod and he turns to Sola. "Go!"

Sola locks eyes with me, then makes her way into the forest to our left. Nikolai grabs my hand and we run toward a round, thatch-roofed cabin I've seen before, and the closer we get, the more relieved I feel.

I glance at Nikolai and despite the look of determination on his face, I know he's afraid. Both the barking and the men's voices have ceased, and the only sound is that of Nikolai and me running through the thin underbrush. Then out of nowhere, a man grabs my waist and ratchets me backward against his chest.

Nikolai whips around, unsheathes the knife on his belt, and springs toward me as several rough-looking men with their accompanying hellhounds emerge from the forest and surround us. The largest of the men lunges at Nikolai from behind and, with one blow to the back of his head, sends him toppling to the ground while the massive hounds stand beside Nikolai, snarling.

I struggle against the man holding me with all my strength, but it's useless. It feels like I'm being restrained by a man made of cement-covered steel, and in knowing there is little I can do to free myself, I plead with my own consciousness to wake.

The man who struck Nikolai turns his hard stare in my direction and when he does, I recognize him as the Butcher who cut off the Blacksmith's finger. The muscles in his arms tense and with his glare unforgiving and ruthless, he strides toward me like a raging bull.

Now face-to-face with me, the Butcher's scent of sweat, smoke, and unclean skin envelopes me in a toxic cloud. A vision of him attacking the Blacksmith rips through my mind's eye until my vehement revulsion for him rushes into my clenched toes.

He scowls at me and while he does, I notice a tattoo of an L with a falling drop of blood carved into the side of his neck. With a burst of anger, he grabs my face and twists it from one side to the other as if trying to decide in which manner he intends to torment me.

His gruff voice pierces the air. "Some say you're a savior. I say you're a savage."

Like accusers around a cursed witch, the other men surround me and their vile, angry faces form a wall on all sides, one of them so close his acid breath seems to melt away my skin.

The Butcher places his hand around my neck and squeezes until my eyes bulge. "We Luminaries are the breakers of will—we're here to break yours. Bleed darkness, swallow light."

My airway is cut off and I'm being pressed against one of the men behind me as the rest of them continue clawing at my body.

The Butcher taunts, "I wonder how many of us it'll take."

Their hands are everywhere. Through the frantic barrage of searching fingers and crammed bodies, one of them spits in my face.

A gust of wind whips toward us as the branches overhead rustle and send leaves spilling to the ground. There's a sense of helplessness emanating from the forest, like every tree belongs to a band of immobilized soldiers desperate to have use of their limbs so as to aid me in some way.

The Butcher squeezes my neck harder as he threatens, "By the time Lukaes comes, we'll have you begging to submit."

Hearing that name, my blood grows hot like I'm being cooked from the inside out. Dream or no dream, I fear I'll soon take my last breath, and the dread gripping my thoughts is worse than the feeling of the men tearing off my clothes.

With my life passing before my eyes, a film begins playing in my mind: I see my mother's face, her smile, hear her laugh, then feel Evan's kiss and think of how his touch was gentle, never forced.

The men around me are breathless and aroused, the Butcher yanking my hair with a violent tug. The smell of sweat and musty skin swirls around my swelling brain while hungry fingers grab at my bare skin. Then the Butcher snatches one of my exposed breasts and shoves it into his mouth before inflicting a ferocious bite, the pain excruciating to the point that I'm nauseated.

The film in my mind plays too fast, like the projector has malfunctioned, and sends a cannon of images through my mind until I hear the Deadlings screaming that I'm a savage for being the daughter of a Cherokee. I see them all dead, everyone I loved and everyone who loved me: visions of Hannah and her crushed skull, Evan, my mother's cancer-ravaged body…

One of the men behind me wraps his arm around my waist and presses his penis between my legs and my blood begins to boil. I squeeze my thighs together in the hopes of keeping him out, but he is close to entering me. Feeling my stomach muscles bear down, I'm unable to stop my body from being overtaken by a panicked revolt.

The man bites my neck and I hear his voice in my ear. "Maybe we should try two at once?"

My blood is a raging river of lava pushing through my veins as my throat floods with bile. I'm so hot inside I can't breathe, and I swear there is a viscous vapor leaking from my skin as if I'm on the brink of exploding.

Staring at me like he wants to cleave me in two, the Butcher tilts his head to one side and shoves what feels like his entire fist inside me. "It's me who's going to break you."

The pain is mind-numbing. I feel every ring on his fingers scraping the flesh inside me. A stream of blood begins running down my inner thighs, and when I smell the stench of burning sugar in the air, I start screaming.

The film in my mind rips apart and flies from my throat in a flock of undigested fury while the other men, now frenzied, unfasten their pants. Something erupts within me and I feel a shockwave leave my body.

The men are jettisoned away from me as if they've been hit by an atomic bomb, some of them crashing into trees, the Butcher soaring so high into the air he shoots up and through the canopy of branches overhead.

Feeling my body beginning to cool, I realize I'm still screaming and take a moment to silence my glass-shattering screech as the Butcher crashes back through the canopy and lands a few feet from me with a bloodied and lifeless thud.

From what I see, I assume the men are dead; the telltale scent of burning sugar has been replaced by that of the forest's wintry breath. Yet within this window of what I'm sure is a temporary reprieve, all I want to do is escape. I run toward Nikolai and drop to my knees, trying to wake him. Feeling his pulse, I know he's still alive, but no matter what I do, he remains unresponsive.

Without knowing what else to do, I lock my hands beneath his arms and drag him toward the cabin. The heat in my veins has been replaced with adrenaline, and the renewed strength allows me to get him across the forest floor.

After a few minutes, my arms begin aching from carrying Nikolai's dead weight. I stop at the thicket just outside the cabin's entrance where I spot the formidable hounds splayed stomach first on the ground as if their skeletons have been pulverized into liquefied bone.

Laying Nikolai down, I kneel beside him and attempt to wake him again. He stirs and lets out a belabored moan before opening his eyes and locking his gaze on me. Fighting to regain consciousness, he speaks. "He won't stop until you submit."

Hearing someone running toward us, I stand on my unstable legs. Heart pounding, blood racing, I'm straining to see through the trees, readying myself for whomever may emerge from the forest.

My stomach hardens in response to another flood of adrenaline, but I'm relieved to see that it's Daegan who appears from the darkness of the forest. Behind him a small army of spiders fans out around us like shiny black watchmen, and for once I find the sound of their steely legs scurrying along the ground comforting.

Daegan walks toward me and as he does, I notice the expression on his face turns to one of concern as he focuses on my chest. Looking down, I realize my bruised and bloodied breast is exposed, and cover myself. His gaze diverts long enough to survey the bodies littering the forest floor around us.

Tender in his touch, he puts his arms around my shoulders and pulls me into his chest, his steady, booming heartbeat filling my ears until I feel my body relax.

I recoil at the sensation of being touched and can't bear having hands on me now. Even with the kindness in Prayna's eyes and the comfort Daegan's bedroom offers, my mind and body are in lockdown.

Prayna's mouth is tight as she dabs a minty-scented salve on the marks left by the men. I don't watch and instead look up toward the ceiling, refusing to acknowledge any evidence of them. She's moving down my body, and I know the worst is yet to come as I feel her hands pull the blanket down below my waist.

"I need to—"

In refusal, my legs press together and I realize how much pain I'm in. It feels as though they've invaded my womb and scraped out all the parts that make me a woman.

My mind flips back to the Butcher and I feel my thoughts tumble into the memory of him shoving his hand inside me. My eyes close and I hold my breath, willing myself to forget until like a plated prison door, my memories slam shut. With this, my leg muscles loosen, but I keep my eyes closed while her soft fingers raise the fabric of my robe and put the salve between my legs.

The resulting sting shoots up my spine like pieces of glass, and I feel the splintered shards get stuck in my throat. It's as though I'm trying to swallow the rising shards rather than letting them fly from my lips, electing to keep the brokenness within, like a glass eater.

I open my eyes and see that she is watching me. With the midnight color of her skin serving to accentuate her threaded scars and barbarically inflicted wounds, I can't help feeling ashamed by my discomfort when I stop to imagine what must have happened to her. She is unabashed in her appearance and lets me study every inch of her healed—yet still barbarous—cuts through her thin dress.

"Men can only break you if you let them."

Her voice resonates in my thoughts as my focus falls upon the concave scars where her breasts should be. Although I've seen her scars before, the sight of them on this night crashes into my consciousness. I want to ask her who did this but am silenced by the shattered glass in my throat.

She takes my face in her hands, her kind eyes giving me a sense of peace. I feel she cares for me in a way I don't understand. There is a conversation happening behind her gaze, one in which I'm a silent participant. I know she's experienced horrific things and that her body has been defiled in ways I will never comprehend, yet she is somehow intact and able to sit before me, offering a maternal comfort I haven't felt since I was a child.

In thinking about the night's events, part of me wonders if I've used my one true bliss—sex—as a weapon against myself, concocting the violence of this dream because I somehow needed it. For other than losing those I've loved, my guardians, I suffer for nothing, I bleed for nothing, and have remained isolated in a world controlled and constructed by me and me alone. Has this unchecked queenly reign driven my mind to seek retribution? Is my own psyche attempting to "Level" me so that I may be a more committed and willing participant in the life it wishes us to live?

Prayna lays me down, calming my internal melee as my mind ceases to form cohesive thought, my limbs relaxing until I feel glass-dusted air leave my lungs.

35

WHAT SEURAT KNEW

Zoë awoke with a start and waited for her sharpening sight to focus on Lucille, who was standing on her rib cage looking down with saucer-like eyes. She placed Lucille on the bed and eased herself into a sitting position, feeling like she inhabited a foreign body: her heart beating out of rhythm, her mind numb, and any thoughts wanting to take form stopped by a brick wall. It felt like her mind was bifurcating and separating itself from a nightmare that was real enough to shake the very foundation of her existence.

A thin stream of warmth drifting from the fireplace swirled, undulated, and wrapped around her like an invisible blanket, counteracting the dark afternoon's wintry wind seeping through the old bay windows. Looking around the room, Zoë took in an oxygen-saturated breath, then forced her aching bones into motion. With care, she lowered her legs until her feet touched the sturdy hardwood of her bedroom floor.

Sitting at the edge of the bed, she felt the room spin as if her mind was fighting the sensation of being upright. The touch of vertigo reminded her that she wasn't in full control of her faculties, and in so knowing, she wondered how long she'd been asleep.

Once her equilibrium settled, she stood and walked to the vanity where her phone was blinking with unretrieved messages. She picked up her phone and was surprised to find that it was less than twenty-four hours from her last waking moments at home.

She scanned the waiting texts: a confirmation for that evening's appointment with Bill and a text from J.T. making sure she was okay. About to put the phone down, she stopped upon seeing a voicemail icon appear on her screen.

She pressed the icon and listened while a calm yet determined female voice leapt into her ear. "Ms. Hall, this is Evan Black's attorney, Giulianna Xu. We should meet as soon as possible. Please call me at your earliest convenience. I'm sorry for your loss."

The woman's voice lingered in Zoë's thoughts as she sat at the vanity and pulled Evan's letter from her purse. Letting it lie in her lap, she stroked the letters on the outside of the envelope where Evan had handwritten her name. Part of her felt time rewind; she could feel, smell, and taste him.

Her phone vibrated with an incoming text from Mr. Sumel, a garbled reminder that he needed to see her and asking if she could come at four o'clock. Noticing that it was 3:33 p.m., she stood and undressed, then froze when the firelight cast an ominous shadow on the rabid, animal-like bites scored into her breast. Forcing her to relive the encounter, the brutal marks resurrected a vision of the Butcher, whose gruff, corroded voice pressed into her ear. "You're a savage…"

Pushing his image from her swelling mind, she put on a sweater and jeans while the scent of lavender drifted from her fresh laundered clothes— Lula's signature touch while doing laundry, five drops of pure essential oil. "Calms your feisty Irish blood," she would say, and under usual circumstances, Lula was right. But not on a dark day such as this. Not when Zoë felt like a foreigner in her own skin and not when her dreams had punctured through to her waking life, a thought that forced two questions to the forefront of her mind: Was her sanity a delusion, or was her savagery self-inflicted?

Seeking the open chill of the winter afternoon, she left her bedroom, made her way down the stairs to the foyer, and grabbed her coat. Lucille was planted at the front door like a furry orange soldier, her eyes half-mast as her fat tail twitched from side to side. Putting on her coat, Zoë walked toward the front door and tried to open it. Lucille wouldn't budge.

"Move."

The cat looked up, her ears now pinned back to the top of her head. Undeterred, Zoë yanked the knob until Lucille's fat rump inched along the wood floor enough for her to squeeze through the door.

Striding out into the heavy falling snow, Zoë surveyed the street, which was empty and pastoral in its pristine quiet. Once down the stairs and at the curb, she hailed a cab and stepped in.

"Eleven Minetta Lane, please."

Her phone vibrated in her hand and without even looking, she knew it was Lula. Picking up the call, she greeted her. "Hi."

"You up?"

"Yep."

"Listen, I'm at the market shopping—dinner?"

"Sure."

Lula pressed. "You all right?"

"I'm good."

"Okay. Seven?"

"Perfect," Zoë confirmed.

After ending the call with Lula, she pressed Giulianna Xu's number from the recent call list. The phone rang until a bright, too-joyful voice chirped into her ear.

"Black Industries, how may I direct your call?"

"Giulianna Xu, please."

"May I tell her who's calling?"

"Zoë Hall."

A pregnant pause ballooned into awkward silence until the woman transferred the call.

The phone clicked as a matter-of-fact voice darted into the phone. "Ms. Hall, thank you for calling."

"I received your message—"

"Yes, it's important that we meet. Does Monday work for you?"

"What time?"

"Noon at the Twenty-One Club?"

Zoë hesitated for a moment, then agreed. "That's fine."

"I look forward to meeting you."

"You as well."

After hanging up, she put the phone in her coat pocket, feeling anxiety burrowing into her bones.

She was standing at Mr. Sumel's, about to ring the buzzer, when he opened the door and beckoned her into the dim house.

"Come in!"

Ziggy was sitting on his shoulder, peering at Zoë with black beady eyes as a kettle whistling from the kitchen sent Mr. Sumel shuffling down the hallway.

"Making hot cocoa. Had a feeling you'd need it!"

She followed behind him while watching Ziggy, who let out a wicked sneeze, lose his balance and almost tumble from Mr. Sumel's shoulder. She reached forward and pushed Ziggy's immense rump back up to his shoulder-top perch.

Feeling impatient, Zoë asked, "You sounded urgent on the phone?"

"Yes, that fellow came again."

Mr. Sumel tinkered around the kitchen, putting bits of just about everything into a mug before pouring in hot water from the kettle.

"Who is he?"

Without responding to her question, Mr. Sumel broke a piece of chocolate off a block, then dropped it in the mug and handed it to her. "Made some improvements to Granny's recipe." Raising his eyebrows, he waited for her to taste it, which she did with a dose of reluctance. But to her surprise, it was quite pleasant. His face lit up as he remarked, "Not bad, eh?"

Leaving the kitchen, he hobbled down the hallway and made his way up the rickety stairway. Zoë followed and after a few more sips of cocoa she felt her mind and body coming back into some semblance of synchronistic unity.

At the top of the stairs, he spoke over his shoulder. "You enjoy the sketchbook I gave you?"

Reaching the office, she sat while Mr. Sumel eased himself into his chair. "Did my mother give it to you?"

Ziggy crawled onto the desk from Mr. Sumel's shoulder and stared at her as he responded, "Not exactly, no."

"Then how did you get it?"

He savored a sip of his cocoa, then replied, "I took it." A mischievous smile formed on his lips as his face softened. "I used to sneak in and see her at the hospital. Wasn't easy because your father was there every minute he could be, always reading to her."

His words hit her ears with a resounding thud as images of her father sitting next to her mother's almost lifeless body infiltrated her mind.

"There was a nurse, tall, with the strangest eyes." Mr. Sumel appeared lost in the recesses of his thoughts for a moment. "Anyway, I think that nurse and your father were in cahoots, trying to keep me away, taking shifts like guards."

"Why wouldn't my father have wanted you there?"

"Well, that's a tricky one to answer."

"Why?"

He looked at her and squinted. "Let's just say it's a tale for another visit and another cup of cocoa."

A flash of aggravation traveled through her as Mr. Sumel continued.

"Your mother was prone to strange dreams, visions and the like. During the last months, she used writing and painting as a way to express them."

Setting down her mug of cocoa on his desk, she refuted, "Mother didn't paint."

"Your mother was an incredible artist," he countered.

Zoë fidgeted with the bracelet on her wrist, staring at the engraved "L.D." in the scarlet stone. "Yes, but she made jewelry."

"Made that, did she?" Perplexed, he inquired, "Your father didn't share much with you after she died, did he?"

"No, we rarely spoke. He would just sit in his leather chair reading. Died there, actually."

"What happened to you after he passed?"

Zoë pushed down the lump forming in her throat. "A family friend became my legal guardian…"

And my world.

Mr. Sumel reached for her hand. "Your father loved you very much." Holding her gaze before leaning back in his chair, he took a lingering sip from his mug. "I digress. You asked about the sketchbook—well, one night I snuck in, brought her some cocoa, sat with her. She could hardly speak with all the tubes and whatnot, but she managed to whisper that she wanted me to bring her a box she'd been keeping at my house. But before I could get it to her, she passed. So, I kept it."

"What was in the box?"

"Some of her artwork, along with the sketchbook, a few journals, and some other loose sketches."

The word *journals* lingered in her ears. "Do you still have the journals?"

"I do."

"May I ask why you waited to tell me about them?"

After setting down his mug, he stroked Ziggy, who flattened his body like a pancake. "It wasn't the right time. Now it is." He reached down by his feet and handed her a brown paper bag with the words Nan's Noodle House printed on the side in bright-red lettering.

Putting the bag in her lap, she fought the urge to reach across the table and tear Mr. Sumel apart. Every line on his face seemed to be tracing its way to the bull's-eye of his smiling lips, a place her fist wanted to plant itself as a way of punishing him for the unpardonable crime of keeping her from the solace of her mother's words.

With her heart beating out of tempo like a rhythmless band, she forced herself to take a deep breath. Turning toward the window and watching the snow falling in fat, cottony pieces, she found its serenity juxtaposed to the sudden unrest she felt inside. There wasn't a fiber of her being that could settle or find a place to nuzzle itself for warmth and safety.

"Did your mother ever speak to you about a book? Something that would've been passed down from her Clan Elders?"

Caught off guard, Zoë turned back toward him and shifted in her chair. "Not that I recall. She had a few handwritten remedies from my great-great-grandmother, but they were written on loose paper. They weren't in a book."

Although disappointed by her answer, Mr. Sumel spoke in a gentle, fatherly tone. "Well, in any case, I need you to be careful. At least until I find out more information on the man who came to see me."

"What do you think he wants?"

He watched her and his eyes flooded with kindness. In that moment, his familial tenderness provided a place for a few of her unsettled pieces to nestle themselves. "I'm still working on that."

Before she could press him further, Mr. Sumel reached across the desk and patted her hand. "You're so much like her."

Breaking eye contact with him, Zoë stared at the paper bag in her lap while Ziggy crawled inside the sleeve of her coat and rested his nose on her forearm. Feeling claustrophobic and overheated in his tiny office, she asserted, "Mr. Sumel, I need to get going."

She took Ziggy from inside her sleeve and placed him on the desk, then retrieved the bag, stood, and made her way toward the hallway.

Just inside the doorframe, she turned to him and uttered the only words that were willing to rise to the surface of her consciousness. "For whatever it's worth, I'm glad she had you."

His eyes misted over as he shifted forward in his chair. "Let me walk you—"

"I can see myself out."

She made her way down the stairs, the flaming lanterns flickering as she passed. Once at the base of the stairs, she walked down the hallway, opened the front door, and stepped out into the snowy night.

The city was awash in cushioned whiteness, and with the sidewalk donning a soft layer of downy snow, there wasn't a sound to be heard on the tucked-away street. A streetlamp popped and went dark as she passed beneath it while bits of her conversation with Mr. Sumel replayed in her mind.

Walking toward McDougal Street, she stared up at the full December moon peeking through a cluster of parting clouds. The Cherokee called it the Snow Moon, a time when families were busy storing up goods for the next season. In the event a family couldn't, Zoë's mother would share her Christmas bounty even though her own family had so little. "No one should be without a Clan," she would say.

Seeing a lone cab inching its way down the street, Zoë raised her hand and called the taxi over. The cab pulled up to the side of the curb and when she opened the door to step inside, a single snowflake floated down from the sky and landed on her sleeve as though the Snow Moon wished to infuse her with a piece of itself.

She got into the cab and closed the door. "Sixty-six Jane Street."

As the cab pulled away from the corner, she opened the bag and retrieved a small journal and rectangular letter-sized object wrapped in newspaper, which she placed on the seat beside her.

The journal was bound in light brown leather and felt heavy against her legs as if weighted down by her mother's unread words. Opening the journal, she let her mother's graceful handwriting seep into her very soul.

> *You have just left my side, my dearest daughter, and although you are gone, I still feel the warmth of your body against mine.*
>
> *I marvel at how fast you're growing, a seed sprouting beneath the brilliance of the sun. But I fear that at the Gardener's hand you may become a flower growing faster than the soil can keep up, your tender leaves unfurling before nutrients can ensure their strength.*
>
> *I'm settled by the knowing that there is warrior spirit in you, a blessed strength—but take heed, for it could be a curse should it not remain balanced.*
>
> *Although you consider it a burden, I am proud you carry*

the warrior's mark, in plain sight, on the canvas of your face so your opponents may know Great Spirit has bestowed upon you special gifts.

As you grow, my child, remember that beauty is defined by a soul's depth and that strength of spirit is where the truest form of grace converges into a river of hope.

Little can stop the progression of the great beast that eats my insides, but I will always be at your side, whether of the flesh or of the spirit. I will float in the river and await your arrival.

Until tomorrow,
Mother

A smile crept across Zoë's lips and a quiet sensation made its way through her. A piece of her mother's soul lay in her hands, words written only for her in the hopes of preserving their private and timeless connection.

The cab turned onto Jane Street and stopped in front of her house as she put the newspaper-wrapped object back in the paper bag. She paid the cabbie and got out of the taxi, holding the journal against her chest. So near to her mother's words, her heartbeat came back into rhythm, not due to the electrical pulse of the automatic but rather to the flicker of spirit—the spark of light in the darkness.

After walking up the steps, Zoë entered the house as her mother's words hovered in her mind: "The Gardener…" She had meant Evan. Always thinking she was better at hiding things from her mother than she was, she realized her relationship with Evan had been no exception.

Entering the foyer and removing her coat, she recalled Mr. Sumel saying there were "a few journals," which made her question why he'd only given her one.

She pulled her phone from her purse and texted him: "Do you have other journals?"

She hung up her coat and headed up the stairs toward her bedroom as Lula called after her. "Almost ready! Wash up and come down!"

The smell of Lula's delectable, if unusual, cooking permeated Zoë's very skin. It was food for the soul. A few more unrested pieces fell into place as she filled her lungs with spicy air.

Lucille sat at the top of the staircase letting out a whiny hello before darting down into the hallway and out of sight. Zoë reached the top step, crossed the hall, and opened her bedroom door, and a waft of warm air rushed toward her from the fireplace.

She walked across the room to her vanity, then sat down and put her purse and the paper bag on the floor next to her. Lula's Wagnerian voice bellowed up the stairs, "Dinner's ready!"

After clipping her hair back, Zoë leaned down and took the newspaper-wrapped object from the bag. Unwrapping it, she found a small painting, facedown, inside with a laminated sticker in the upper left-hand corner of its frame: WILLOUGHBY'S AUCTION HOUSE—LOT 182.

Upon seeing the sticker, and based on Evie's email, she surmised that this was the same painting Mr. Sumel had asked her to get from the Deadlings. Yet in her email, Evie had stated that it had sold for a great deal of money at auction, which left her wondering how in the hell Mr. Sumel got his hands on it.

Turning the painting over, she felt her blood racing. A scene was illustrated in painstaking detail, making it impossible to deny her connection to the landscape: it was the moon-bathed meadow with the white marble rose at its center, exactly as it had been when Zoran met her there…in her dream.

The bottom right-hand corner of the painting harbored a familiar flowing signature—her mother's.

Lula was at the base of the stairs, calling out, "Don't make me come up there!"

Zoë called down, "Be down in a minute."

The more she studied the painting, the more elements began to appear. It was like an optical illusion, letters rising up from the bath of paint concealing them.

"Miss Zoë, get your butt down here!"

Taking the newspaper wrapping, she was about to cover the painting when a black-and-white picture of a man in a dark suit at the center of the page caught her eye. Leaning in closer, she realized the man was standing in front of her house. The caption below the photo read, "L. Lloyd Black, founder of Black Industries and grandfather of the late Evan Black, in front of his home at 66 Jane Street. Circa 1940."

She shifted her gaze to the article's title: "A Legacy Lost: What Will Become of Black Industries?"

"Zoë, what's goin' on up there?"

Zoë's phone vibrated in her purse. She retrieved it while answering Lula, "I'm coming!"

She read a text from Mr. Sumel: "there were twoi journals. –ps: wrapping paper can be interesting readign, no?"

Annoyed, she fired back, "Can I have the other journal?"

She stared at the picture of Evan's grandfather standing in front of her house as Mr. Sumel's response appeared on her phone. "in due time"

Lula bellowed up the stairs, "Am I eatin' alone or what?"

The heaviness of Lula's exasperation mixed with the smell of spicy food floated up from the kitchen in a thick haze as Zoë texted J.T. "Did you know the broker for my house or was it a referral?"

Putting down her phone, she slipped into the hallway and down the stairs. Stepping from the last stair into the foyer, she let her bare feet linger on the hardwood floor, wondering what connection the Black family had to her house.

36

MADMEN

Zoë could still taste the flavors of Lula's artful cooking. The night's meal was a favorite: balsamic roasted vegetables with spicy cranberry-mint salsa and an avocado salad, all washed down with a habanero-chili-infused martini.

After putting on her dress, she sat at her vanity and stared at the newspaper article with the picture of Evan's grandfather standing in front of her house. For a moment, it felt like the very floorboards beneath her feet were stained with Evan's memory, their oaken sturdiness a supporting foundation, just as he had once been.

Sidestepping his memory, she zipped up her dress and felt dinner's spicy juices stinging her mind, as though the tightness of the fabric left the liquids in her body without any retreat save for the cushion of space between her brain and skull.

Putting the newspaper article aside, she applied crimson lipstick, the deep-rouged red making her pale skin reflect the peppery blood circulating inside her veins. Just as the doorbell rang, she watched her pupils dilate.

Pressing her toes against the floor, she felt the floorboards beneath her feet growing cold as Evan's memory was edged out by the potency of Bill's presence. Although he was outside, waiting, she could feel him like he was standing right beside her.

Lula's heavy steps clomped along the downstairs hallway as she went to let Bill inside, and after a brief pause Zoë heard muffled voices and the sound of the front door closing. Bill was walking up the staircase with a steady, rhythmic step that sweetened the fiery juices in her brain. To her, he approached with great care, every motion and action meant to disarm the defenses stopping their two respective forces from coalescing.

Seeking refuge from the intensity of his presence, Zoë fixated on the vanity's mahogany top, examining every grain in the antique wood along with the marks and discolorations that showed its use. In the upper right-hand corner, there was a faint set of tiny initials she'd never noticed before: "g.r.b." Seeing as the vanity had come with the house, she now wondered with whom she shared the vanity's beveled mirror. Even the sound of the door opening couldn't pull her focus until she felt strong hands gripping her shoulders.

Through the mirror, she studied him, noticing that the cold outside had given his fair skin and full lips a rosy flush. With the firelight lighting up the dark auburn hair at his temples, Bill's face seemed distorted in the old mirror, like his skin didn't quite fit the hills and valleys of his face. When their gazes locked, a single strand of sorrow threaded through his eyes.

Shifting his focus down her body, his face relaxed as he tilted his head. "You're stunning."

Placing her hand on his, Zoë smiled as her phone buzzed on the vanity top. She glanced at the text: "Broker was referral from Evan. Why?"

Mind swirling, she dipped inside her thoughts as Bill inquired, "Everything all right?"

Refocusing on him, she replied, "Of course."

She stood and ushered him to one of the chairs in front of the fireplace. He sat, leaned back, and stared into the fire's flames as she continued. "It was J.T."

Bill's eyes turned cold at the mere mention of J.T.'s name, his entire body going stiff as he unbuttoned the collar of his shirt.

"You okay?" she asked.

He stood and walked toward a bookcase on the far side of the room, and although he had vacated the chair, he'd left fragments of himself behind.

Perusing the books on the shelf, he spoke, "My father used to say you can learn all you need to know about a person by the way they eat and the books they read. I've actually found it to be quite true."

She pressed. "Is something going on between you and J.T.?" Bill was silent, his legs rooted to the floor as she expounded. "J.T.'s a good man. But I'm aware of his flaws."

Bill's gaze shot across the room like a bullet. "I wasn't." His face grew hard and she could see his mind churning as he went on. "It's a defining moment in a man's life when he realizes he can trust no one. I never wanted to be that type of man."

"You're not." Watching him, she could feel how raw his emotions were as he explained.

"J.T. knew about them. The whole time. Saw them, ate with them, drank with them. He actually spent time with my wife and…I can't even say it out loud."

He walked back across the room and returned to the chair in front of the fire.

"Have you confronted him?"

"Of course. He caved, immediately. Said the man was his biggest client, 'the foundation of his business.' I'm not proud, but I hit him. Probably the most juvenile thing I've ever done."

It now made sense why J.T. had a waning bruise around his eye when she last saw him.

Bill's words fired toward her. "The worst of it is, I knew him." He leaned forward. "What's strange is that I'm more angry with J.T. than I am with my own wife. The situation with her—it takes two. I have to accept some responsibility. But nothing can excuse his actions."

"You think you were to blame for her affair?"

"I think the signs were there and I ignored them." He shifted his focus to the fire. "I just wish I could talk with her. The fact that she's gone makes this exponentially more difficult."

She, too, stared into the fire and in so doing thought of Evan and knew, for different reasons, exactly how Bill felt.

"What are you thinking about?"

She wanted to respond, but instead pressed her heels into the floor and could almost feel Evan's presence seeping up through the soles of her feet. Bill's voice yanked her back into the room.

"Who was he?"

Before answering, she softened her gaze and looked at him. "It was a long time ago."

Able to see right through her, he countered, "Maybe. But you're obviously still affected by him."

"All that matters is I know what it feels like to have loose ends."

Sitting back in his chair, Bill watched her for what felt like an eternity before speaking. "I get it. You have to keep me separate."

The spice in her blood ignited; a lightbulb across the room popped and went dark.

Leaning forward, he put his hand on her face. "But I'd be lying if I said I wasn't curious."

With his thumb tracing her cheek, she felt her equilibrium falter until she began shutting him out. Whether motivated by habit or fear, she wasn't able to stop herself. Hoping she sounded more assured than she felt, she offered, "I'm here to explore what *you* need."

His stare was penetrating, and the scent of his cologne mixing with the spice in her blood felt like fuel on an already raging fire. "If you said out loud only a fraction of the things behind your eyes, it would be a very interesting conversation."

"Is that what you want? Conversation?" she quipped.

A spark lit up behind his stare. "You're clearly more than just a sexual outlet."

Feeling the interwoven connection between them strengthening, she wished he only wanted sex, as it would simplify things. Unwilling to continue the conversation, she leaned forward and let her lips graze his neck—once in contact with her mouth, his flesh grew hot. Guiding his hands around her waist, she laid his fingers on the zipper of her dress, which he unzipped and let fall to the floor.

After pulling her up from her chair, he backed her toward the bed while she removed his suit jacket and unbuttoned his shirt. The scent of him drove her mad: clean, sweet, and laced with faded cologne.

His hands were strong and searching, and the longer he touched her, the more time slowed. With his lips hovering above hers, he took down the straps of her slip and with his mouth open, watched it glide down her body.

Closing her eyes, she pulled him toward her until she felt he was her very skin. She wanted to consume him. The backs of her thighs touched the bed and as he laid her down, her lips found his bare chest and devoured its flesh while the sweet smell of him sweltered and saturated her skin.

Taking his face in her hands, she tilted her head and brought their mouths closer while his finger traced the line of her collarbone, then came to rest at the top of her breast. Letting her head fall back, she lingered in the sensation of him pulling down her bra.

Though her eyes were closed, she felt the air vacate the room. When she opened them and looked at him, he was staring at her right breast, his face flushed as he ran a shaky finger over the vicious bite marks encircling her nipple.

In that moment, she wanted to die. In the heat of desire, she'd failed to shield him from the collision of her two worlds: her wound, a temporary branding from a dream that was now a living nightmare.

The sight of her breast was shocking in the firelight. Bruising had set in and the hellish teeth marks seemed to deepen in color by the minute. The Butcher's face impaled her mind as she was thrust into the memory of him violating her most intimate parts.

Bill continued brushing his fingertips across the marks as if he couldn't believe they were real. "Who—"

"It's not what you think."

In seeing him so upset, never in her life had she so wished her tongue would twist together a believable lie.

Covering her breast with his hand, he looked at her. "Then what…"

Knowing he was unerringly perceptive, she elected to tell him the truth, just not the circumstance. "I was attacked."

"By a client?"

"No."

He sat up and locked eyes with her. "Please, do not lie to me."

Meeting his gaze, she responded, "I'd rather not talk about it."

"Were you raped?"

In a manner, she had been, but there was little value in making it known. "No." With his gaze sharpening, she could see he didn't believe her. "Bill, I realize I'm asking a lot of you, but I'd rather not talk about this. I promise you, I'm all right."

Distraught at the sight of her branded skin, he continued tracing it with his finger. "This was not a client."

"No." She could sense him pushing down his springing questions one by one.

"I want to believe you."

With guilt skimming along the edges of her mind, she asserted, "I wouldn't lie to you."

He stared at her for a long time before the tension in his face released. Then the softest kiss she'd ever felt graced the bite marks on her breast, as though his gentleness might counteract the brutality of each teethed imprint. Watching him kiss her, she felt her world rotate several degrees into an upside-down position while he inched his way toward her lips.

Pulling away, she slid down his body and knelt before him, feeling the oaken wood beneath her knees provide a welcome grounding.

"Not like this—" He tried to stop her, but she was determined. One of them had to give over, and it needed to be him.

✧ ✧ ✧

Bill opened the door and let the icy night blanket him as he left Zoë's house in a state of full and visceral consumption. Walking down the stairs, his legs felt weak. He didn't want to leave. He felt better with her by his side.

As he reached the street corner and hailed a cab, a smile edged along his lips. Even without having had sex, the beast inside him lay full and passed out in a coma of ravaged flesh.

Letting swirling thoughts float around his brain, he watched snow tumble downward from an uncommonly dark night until the beast inside him stirred, igniting a barrage of questions that nagged him with sharp, unrelenting teeth.

Why was a newspaper article on Black Industries on her vanity? Did she know Evan Black? He wondered where Zoë had been when he had awoken. He'd felt her beside him only an hour before, then she seemed to have vanished—where had she gone? And why would she do anything to avoid his kiss when he felt it was what she wanted?

The pangs of husband's remorse that he'd expected to experience were absent, and in their place was a safe, crafted harbor. Any attempt he made to analyze Zoë, or their situation, was pointless. They fit. They made sense in an unexpected yet undisputable fashion, and for the first time in years, he felt a sense of peace.

His bliss soon imploded at the thought of the bite marks on her breast; it was like his own flesh had been pierced. The sincerity in her explanation had been convincing but he couldn't shake the feeling that her story was either inaccurate or incomplete.

A vision of her attack played in his mind, his imagination piecing together the circumstances under which her injuries might have been inflicted. With the brutal images shredding through his thoughts, he felt the patient and deep-rooted man he knew himself to be trade places with a ruthless and frenzied madman.

37

EXODUS

'm naked and lying alone in Daegan's bed wrapped in a blanket made of the softest cloth I've ever felt. It seems one with my skin, its fabric a cross-weave of silk and fur-like velvet. As I turn onto my side, I swear the threads being warmed by the heat of my body are releasing the scent of blooming roses.

Reveling in the blanket's perfumed embrace, I stare at a lone candle atop a flourished copper holder on the bedside table. My mind slips back in time and the lingering, sweet taste of Bill floods my mouth. I can still feel the way his hands threaded through my hair when he gave in to the urgency with which I consumed him, and were I with him now, I'd again gratify the hunger he rouses within me.

I remind myself to compartmentalize him, for he is a man like any other, one to whom I play a given role until together we can travel the road to his truest form of self-expression, whether emotional or sexual. It is, and so it will remain: my care will propel him to the tipping point where his suffering ends and a new life begins. Once upon that interconnecting path, he'll forge forward and I'll retreat to my path-side castle and attend to the needs of my next chosen journeyman.

My thoughts are interrupted by the sound of a female voice floating up from the room below, and even though the door to Daegan's room is ajar, I must strain to hear it.

"With Asdan matter in her blood, her Leveling will be violent."

I'm on my feet with the blanket wrapped around me, making my way toward the door. I reach for the wooden handle and open the door enough to see out over the narrow walkway's banister and down into the black marble room below.

Daegan sits in his kingly chair in front of the raging fire while Prayna stands a few feet from him, her skin so dark she almost blends into the midnight-colored marble walls around her.

Through the crack in the door, I watch Daegan and can feel his mind churning.

"We need more time to understand the new variables in play."

Prayna shifts her focus toward him. "We don't have that luxury. Eternal Night is set, and Lukaes is getting bolder."

Daegan weighs in. "Six nights shy of twelve—what do you think our chances actually are?"

Prayna takes a step toward him. "In the end, it will come down to how well her mind weathers what's happening. From her perspective, we don't even exist."

Daegan's voice is laced with tension as he opines, "That's why I had hoped to keep her and Nikolai apart. At least for now."

"Quite honestly, him telling her could help us—"

Daegan interrupts. "His condition worsens, and without knowing how that will influence his behavior, I don't want her knowing who he is."

"Then that leaves us with Zoran."

Daegan pulls his gaze from the fire and looks up at Prayna. "It's a risk, but if Zoran tells her the truth, it might be the only thing that gets her closer to accepting."

"Maybe, but we can't lie to ourselves. Just because she accepts doesn't mean we're out of harm's way. Irreparable damage has already been done."

Breaking their stare, Daegan looks back toward the fireplace, and while watching them, I feel like an outsider in my own fabricated world. A feeling of betrayal gnaws the wooden buttresses supporting the walls of my consciousness as I witness characters of my own creation deciding what they will and will not disclose to me, their maker. It's an experience I find disconcerting.

Daegan's tone is reflective as he asserts, "She should be able to repair the damage."

"Were she to accept now. But if we wait much longer, not even she can restore the realms." After watching him for a moment, Prayna probes deeper. "Something else is bothering you."

Even in the presence of his assuredness, I can hear the concern in Daegan's voice. "The dark matter. We have no idea how it will affect her. Our lives are quite literally in her hands, and it's difficult to be confronted with that kind of powerlessness."

As Prayna speaks, her gaze is unyielding. "Cassian has the greatest knowledge of dark matter. Perhaps we should—"

"We've not heard word from Cassian since last spring. He's been away far too long for us to know how being in Draknam might've changed him."

"Are you suggesting he's lost to us?" Daegan's silence permeates the room while Prayna continues, "He saved my life and he risked his life to get close to Lukaes. He gave up everything. He is and will always be one of us…" Her voice trails off as she turns away from Daegan.

"When this is over, we'll find a way to bring him home. You have my word." Daegan puts a tender hand on hers. "I need you to stay with her."

Prayna turns toward him. "Where are you going?"

Walking to the back of the room, Daegan speaks over his shoulder. "To see Zoran."

"Are you sure about this?"

"Yes."

After watching him leave, Prayna makes her way toward the wooden stairs leading to Daegan's bedroom.

I rush across the room and get back into bed, noticing that my stomach is sour, tossing and turning as though I've just swallowed poison. Nausea floods my system like all the fluids in my body are seeking escape. Intense cramping grips my insides—pain like I've never experienced—and I'd do anything to make it stop. I want to be flipped inside out, sterilized, and the desire to give in to the process is overwhelming, like my body is stuck beneath a layer of thick sludge, and with the promise of becoming unpolluted, it refuses to bear one more moment of grungy, pain-filled darkness.

Blood rushes from my nose as the cramps in my stomach worsen. My blood is too hot and feels like thick lava as it pushes through my burning veins. I'm so overheated it seems a raging fire is engulfing my feet, legs, pelvis, and spine—I taste blood in my mouth. I'm gagging.

Prayna bursts into the room and races toward the bed. Forcing me to sit up, she puts one of my arms around her shoulders and pulls me up and onto my shaking legs. We make our way out of the room, then along the open walkway until she all but drags me into an adjacent stone room.

My nose is gushing blood and my stomach is heaving. I'm seconds from vomiting. The fluids inside me are seeking exit, and the pressure building in my veins makes me feel as though I might explode. With my legs collapsing and my vision faltering, she lays me down on a wooden grate. The air smells damp and drops of cold water are dripping onto my face. Then I hear a grinding sound, stone on stone, before a steady current of water streams down on me from above.

My body is in full revolt now and I'm starting to vomit. Everything is leaving my system, and if I weren't in such a state of mental shock, I'd be mortified by the prospect of soiling myself in front of another human being. Unfazed, Prayna pulls me into a sitting position until my back is against her chest and she's holding me upright.

The scent of my own waste swirls in the air and even the fresh water pouring down on us isn't enough to drown the stench. I feel on the verge of death as every drop of blood inside me leaks from my nose, my ears, my eyes, my rectum, my womb. Parts of my mind are starting to shut down and all I can focus on is Prayna's arms holding me in place.

She's drowning with me in what smells like a thousand years of death, selfless in her support of my almost lifeless frame. I can't imagine how horrific the scene is, what she must be witnessing, and for some reason I feel ashamed.

I vomit one last time and feel my bladder give in to the pressure of my contracting stomach muscles, and I can't help feeling this will have to be over soon, seeing as there is nothing left inside me. Then it stops.

Prayna's arms tighten around me while the sound of water splashing onto rock fills my ears. There is an echoic quality to the way the water hits the surfaces around us, as though we're in a small cave, and the strong smell of my encroaching death has been replaced by the musty scent of wet moss and damp stone.

Prayna gathers me up closer and, kissing the top of my head, rocks me like I am a small child. Her lips carry with them an essence of clarity, and in response my mind comes into focus until I understand what the night's events represent. This experience is metaphoric, a purging of the untended wounds and fears of a stunted childhood. I know what Prayna's motherly touch embodies and whether it's real or imagined, I intend to give in to it for a little while longer.

PART TWO

Who looks outside dreams;

who looks inside awakes.

—*Carl Jung*

38

GARDEN AT MIDNIGHT

"Fresh air will do you good."

Standing outside the cottage, I watch the mural of the mosaic-tiled dragon disappear as Daegan closes the red lacquered door behind us. We step onto a winding cobblestone path lined with swarms of glowing fireflies.

Sea-hued moonlight spilling through the tall trees flanking the path makes the rough stone look like a prism-lit ocean floor. With each step I take after what seems like days of heavy slumber, I'm awake and merging back into a body I can only describe as foreign. My system has been renewed somehow, each of my body's organs restarting and relearning how to function.

Daegan's thick, woven cloak hangs heavily from my shoulders, as if the weight of him were contained in the twists and crosses of its threads, and as I walk, it floats above my skin and flirts with the chills rising in my flesh. The scent of pre-rain drifting from the collar travels through the passages of my sinuses like speed-laced perfume, and as it does, I'm affected by the heightened state of my senses.

While continuing along the path beneath the night's oceanic light, I'm struck by the serenity of this place. Rounding a tight corner, we step from the path into a mountaintop garden high above the forest. It appears the top of the mountain has been sheared off to create a level surface on which is built a kind of palace-worthy oasis.

Standing at the edge of the path with Daegan at my side, I gaze across the garden toward a medieval castle that looks out of place on its mountaintop perch. The structure's light-grey stone glows beneath the bluish moonlight and its grand entrance is marked by a wooden arch covered in vines that creep from the top of the arc onto the rough walls to form a leafy tapestry.

I marvel for a moment at its architectural sophistication—it looks like Hamlet's castle was stolen from Shakespeare's page and brought to life. As though informed by the state of Hamlet's fractured mind, most of the windows are dark and lifeless and part of the castle is in disrepair. Only the rooms at the far left side are lit, and the lush canopied trees surrounding the castle on either side seem to be supporting it somehow, as if holding up a wounded comrade who is too fragile and fevered to stand on his own.

A few tall flowers lean toward me and rest against the side of my hand. It feels they wish to remind me they exist, or perhaps seek the warmth of my skin as shelter from the snow they sense may fall at any moment. Daegan takes a few steps forward, and I'm about to follow when I see what looks like a small cluster of birds rocketing across the garden toward us.

In the blink of an eye, they're in front of me, all eight of them just larger than hummingbirds and hovering in a perfect horizontal line. They appear to be of the same species, yet each has a different color and style of crest. Before I can study them further, three drop out and depart, leaving the white, black, and red birds behind.

"Hold out your hands."

I do as I'm told, and the white and red birds land in each palm while the black bird stays suspended at eye level. I feel the bird is studying me, its head cocking to one side just as it convulses and drops to the ground at my feet like an electric current stopped its heart.

Shifting my focus to Daegan, I feel he's troubled by what's happened. I'm about to inquire as to the black bird's fate when, as if its feathers are emitting a physicalized aura, the white bird becomes encased in a cloudy sphere and the red bird is engulfed in flames. Then both birds launch from my palms, leaving their manifested auras behind.

I watch the small spherical cloud churning in one palm, then shift my focus to the other, which harbors a single blood-colored flame.

"The moon sparrows are part of your Leveling."

Again, that cringeworthy word creeps into my ears and lodges inside my consciousness as Daegan continues. "They show us your favored element along with the element that will pose the greatest challenge."

"Meaning?"

"You most favor aether. Your greatest challenge is fire."

Although unsure of what aether is or implies, I'm not at all surprised that fire is my challenge. With my mother having told me as much, I find it apropos that in this case, dream imitates life. A sense of pliability rises through me, and for the first time since Dr. Lawson advised me to immerse myself, I feel willing to do so—even if only temporarily.

"What exactly is aether?"

The tattoos at Daegan's temples rotate in slow, unbalanced circles. "The Elders call it the Breath of Creation. I've always considered it the fabric of space and time. But to be honest, what we know about it is more theory than practice."

With curiosity getting the better of me, I query, "What did the black bird represent?"

Daegan is silent for a moment and when he does respond, I sense he isn't telling me everything. "Dark matter. In its blackest form, it counters life."

Unwilling to divulge anything further, he puts his fingers around my wrist and raises it until the small cloudy sphere is at my eye level. When he does, I notice the element becomes rogue, swirling around in circles like a miniature storm. With Daegan's heartbeat pulsing in my ears and my mind having been given permission to engage, my inquisitiveness takes command of my voice.

"What are your elements?"

Shifting his focus to the hand still cradling the dwindling flame, he replies, "Traditionally, only Guardians have elemental abilities. But due to the nature of my Satient form, I have one. Fire."

Returning his gaze to the little cloud hovering in my other hand, he unsheathes the knife attached to his belt and puts a deep slice in my palm. I feel no pain and when blood begins leaking from the wound, it looks more like amber-colored sap than blood.

"Now, close your eyes and recall one of your fondest memories."

I follow his instructions, fearing I won't be able to conjure a memory that falls into the requested category. But rather than my concerns being realized, a lighthearted and unexpected vignette begins playing in my mind.

I'm about seven years old and my father, who is in an uncharacteristically jovial mood, is motoring us out into the middle of a fog-covered lake in the dawn hours of a crisp fall morning. The small aluminum boat is rustic at best, with two makeshift wooden bench seats and an outboard motor that screams rather than hums.

My mother has bundled me in layer upon layer of clothing knowing that I can rarely, if ever, regulate my own body temperature. I'm almost always cold, whereas my father sits at the back of the boat in a T-shirt, jeans, and what I call his duck shoes, which are in reality a ratty old pair of orange and brown waterproof ankle boots.

One hand on the outboard's steering stick and the other braced against the side of the boat, he's charging through the fog like a Viking king on the way to battle. With a wooden box in my lap containing two thermoses— one of soup, the other of black coffee—a Styrofoam container of worms, a beat-up tackle box, and two cheese sandwiches, I feel like the Viking king's trusted right hand, chosen to guard his irreplaceable treasures. And unwilling to part with such an important role, I bury my fear that the dense fog will cause us to crash into a boat, buoy, or, God forbid, the shore.

He bellows in his thick Irish accent, "None of this packaged rubbish. Real men catch their own fish!" He pats my back hard enough to nearly knock me from my seat. "Your da's a real man, eh?"

Securing my box of treasures, I plant my feet against the bottom of the boat and press harder into my seat, all the while forcing a smile.

After a few more minutes of roaring, fog-blanketed travel, my father slows the boat, motors us into a serene alcove, then kills the engine, and when he does, I delight in the quiet sound of the water lapping against the side of the boat.

Leaning forward, he untucks two fishing poles from the inside of the boat's frame, one unforgiving and over-rigged with sea-weight fishing line, the other elegant and rigged with line meant for lake fish. We're like those rods, he and I—they're our inanimate counterparts in every way.

He takes my pole and threads the fishing line through each loop, his fat fingers just able to do the job, while I sit and watch his flame-red hair tousling in the slight morning breeze. His hair is too long, his whiskers hard and sharp, and I can smell last night's whiskey on his breath; but I don't care because it's him and me now without a Deadling in sight, and I wouldn't trade this moment for the world.

Once he's done threading my pole, he takes the box from my lap, sets it on the bottom of the boat, then sits and pats his knee. "Today's the day!"

I move toward him and sit. He hands me my pole, takes the end of the fishing line—complete with barbed hook—and holds it up while focusing on me with his stormy blue eyes. "Baitin' the hook's an art."

Reaching down into the wooden box, he fumbles around and retrieves the Styrofoam container. "Pop off the top."

I do as I'm told, then stare into the writhing soup of earthworms and feel my stomach lurch as he commands, "Choose a big fat one. A good 'n juicy one."

I wouldn't dare disappoint him or behave like anything but the boy he wishes me to be, so I snatch the fattest worm I can find and yank it from the cup as he puts the hook in my hand.

"Now, you just run 'im through. Kind of thread it, like you're mendin' socks."

What he's proposing is *nothing* like mending socks, but I don't argue and instead plunge the hook into the worm while its guts squirt out. In, out, in, out—I pretend the worm is a slimy woolen sock, and when I'm done, the poor thing looks like a bloodied bit of intestine.

He slaps my back, then holds a plump finger in the air. "Now…the cast. Also an art."

Moving me from his knee so I'm sitting beside him on the seat, he positions the pole in my hands then puts his arms around me. Like a conductor, he swings the rod back and forth a few times before, together, we cast the line. The reel spins and whizzes as the hook-threaded worm sails through the air and lands in the water with an effervescent pop. I watch the ripples fan out from where the line went in, the boat rocking us as my father and I sit, his arms around me, and wait for a fish to bite.

My back is against his chest, the air is cold, but he is warm, and I can't imagine being anywhere else, as it's the closest I've ever been to him and the only time I've felt like he loves me.

"Open your eyes." Daegan's voice severs me from my memory and transports me back into the present.

I look toward him and follow his gaze to my palm, where the cloudy sphere hovering above my hand grows smaller and transitions from opaque to semitransparent before seeping into my skin and disappearing. My palm is healed, even though on the same hand, the cut Nikolai gave me the night the Blacksmith was attacked remains.

Daegan moves behind me, reaches around my waist, and takes my other flame-filled hand in his. Along with his heartbeat, I hear what sounds like a live electric wire sending bursts of high-voltage current through me.

The current transfers into my veins, then focuses into my arms, and in reaction the flame hovering above my palm lengthens as Daegan tilts my hands and puts my palms together.

"Now think of what angers you most."

With only the slightest impetus, an image of the Deadlings floods my mind, and in response, a ball of fire engulfs both our hands and spreads to below our elbows. Evidenced by the fact that our flame-filled skin remains unburned, some part of me knows this is a dream. But I don't want to let go of this feeling, as the unbridled power coursing through me is euphoric, and I feel in this moment that we are fire, unified and blazing.

"Go deeper into your emotions, but separate your mind and focus on keeping the flames from spreading."

Even though I'm intent on doing what Daegan has asked, I tumble back in time until I'm standing in a hallway watching the Deadlings as they congregate outside my mother's room. She is very sick, days from what I know will be a permanent admission to the hospital. While peeking through her door, they muffle their laughter as they mimic her death, rolling their eyes back in their heads, grabbing their necks, sticking out their tongues, and making choking sounds while they clutch at each other.

Fury floods my system, and try as I might, I can't free my mind from the memory's grip. As a counter, I try recalling the images of fishing with my father, but it's useless. I'm locked in the recesses of my emotions and am held prisoner by the unrelenting hatred I have for the Deadlings.

Fueled by my ire, the fire flares upward and races up our arms, almost engulfing my face. With the flames raging, Daegan's hands grow icy cold against mine, his white skin edging toward a bluish grey until the fire dwindles to nothing.

Turning me toward him, he assures me, "Fire is the hardest to master. It takes time."

Putting his hand on the small of my back, Daegan leads me into the garden and I study the flower beds that have been planted to form a garden maze, one in which we could wander amongst the flowers, twisting and turning along the different paths, for hours.

Finding this dream heavy with symbolism and metaphor, I inquire, "The eight sparrows represent eight elements?"

With his tattoos lilting in balanced circles, he responds, "Not exactly. All Guardians must master the cardinal four elements. But you also have three pillars of matter—soon to be four—which is why your Leveling has become violent."

Despite myself, I'm interested enough to dig deeper, and with this realization, I elect to mine as much information from him as possible. "What exactly is 'Leveling'?"

"It's the process by which everything is reduced to its base."

"For what purpose?"

Reaching to touch a tall, jubilant flower leaning into our path, he answers. "A Guardian cannot accept their place until they've experienced the primal spectrum of both their light and their dark. They must strip themselves bare until only their raw being remains."

"And how do they do that?"

I detect levity in his voice as he responds, "They surrender to the process. Willingly."

"Are you asking me to surrender to being stripped bare?"

Letting his hand glide along a row of flowers, he counters, "Well, I find it difficult to imagine you surrendering under any circumstances. Yet you do—with them."

I know he's referring to men, and for a split second, I feel my privacy has been invaded until I'm reminded that he's a facet of my own mind.

"You do submit to them, don't you?"

I take a moment, then correct him. "Not in the way you mean, no."

Appearing sincere in his intent to understand the topic at hand, he queries, "But in one form or another, isn't it always sexual in nature?"

I'm confident his question isn't meant to be intrusive, but I'm starting to become uncomfortable. "When a man reaches a certain point of pain in his life, an intolerable disconnection from whom he thought he was or wanted to be, he'll find his way to my door."

Daegan appears to be reflecting on what I've expressed. "Is it enough for you?"

I process his question before seeking additional clarity. "The role I play in their lives, or the sex?"

"Both."

Although I find it challenging, I push myself toward the most candid response possible. "It's what I know, and there's comfort in that."

Walking alongside him in silence, I look out over the flower beds, unable to suppress the incontrovertible feeling that graves lie beneath them. I surmise that this velvet-petaled Valhalla is a burial ground, a place where souls have been put to rest in a crested sanctuary, where human flesh and bone can become sprout-ready earth. For reasons I can't explain, I'm quite certain all those who are buried here died bloody and gruesome deaths.

"Soldiers are buried here."

Guiding us out of the maze and toward a low stone retaining wall lined with small turrets, some of which are overgrown with bits of moss and wildflowers, he walks beside me, seeming to be affected by what I've said. "You could call them that, yes."

What I don't express to him is that I'd know death anywhere; I always have. It speaks to me, and whether it's whispering or shrieking, I've never been able to silence its voice. As if the dead are now sucking the life from the garden around us, I'm hit with the musty odor of rotting plants. When I survey the landscape, which is wilting, I notice the flowers and shrubs look to have been subjected to a sudden drought.

Once we're at the wall, I place my hands on the cold stone. With a skyscraper-like view, I examine the circular city at the forest's center below, which is getting brighter as though thousands of lanterns inside it are being lit at once. Soft light spills into building-lined streets and illuminates a procession of people that is moving outward from the heart of the city toward a larger crowd congregated at its walled border. Although I've seen it before, from my current view the city looks as though it's been built to resemble a wheel, with main roads as spokes and the wall a rock-sturdy rim.

The city wall teems with people from whom the faintest sound of chanting rises through the night air like a winged prayer that permeates the garden around us. The voices grow louder just before immense flames shoot up like fiery sky-bound pillars from two of four mounted towers at the cardinal points of the city. Violet-white flames blaze upward with such vigor that I can hear them sizzling from where I'm standing, and with the intense light, I'm able to see the massive cauldrons housing the fires mounted on the top of the towers.

"Why have the fires been lit?"

Daegan's tattoos flow in large, open circles. "They mark the halfway point of Eternal Night. The twin flames are meant to merge the souls, or Sehlms, of the new Guardian with the Guardian past." I'd be lying if I said I didn't feel a sense of loss emanating from him. "Each Guardian represents a different season, and when their season comes to an end, their flesh returns to the soil, but their essence remains intertwined with the realms. It is that essence that the fires call forth to help ease the new Guardian's Leveling."

In my mind's eye, I see her, Mahayla, staring at me through the bars as she did on the night I watched her being consumed, her death emblazoned on the canvas of my consciousness.

I speak in a quiet tone, seeing as even within the confines of a dream, my guilt feels real. "I couldn't help her."

Turning to look at me, Daegan's face softens as he responds. "A season ends at a Guardian's will. She chose."

He breaks eye contact with me and looks out over the city. But if there's one thing I know, it's a man in pain, and he is, in this moment, lodged within his ache like an armored warrior trapped in quicksand.

With less grace than intended, I change the subject. "When will the other two fires be lit?"

He dislodges from his struggle long enough to reply. "The third will be lit during the final hour of Eternal Night, and the fourth when the Guardian has accepted."

"What happens if a Guardian doesn't accept?"

Shifting his focus to me, I notice his pupils have dilated to the point that they're almost nonexistent. When he turns his body toward me, I feel on edge.

"The realms without a Guardian are like a body without a heart. Eventually, without the other, both perish."

The severity of his stare is not lost on me, and even though I'm losing my will to engage, I question him. "And you assume I am that heart."

"It's not about what I assume. It is so. That's why Mahayla's choice has left us in a challenging situation."

"How so?"

I watch his body tense. "Her essence was destroyed, which means the realms are without a connection to a Guardian. With every night that passes, they deteriorate further."

I feel myself shutting down and hardening toward the concept of being a savior. It's one thing to explore the inner workings of my own mind, and another to indulge in any manner of self-deification. I don't have any interest and don't see the point in it continuing to be explored.

Then, like my mind is fighting for the right to test my resolve, Daegan goes on. "We've never had a Guardian from the Thirteenth, and were it up to me, you'd already have left."

He is steadfast in his honesty, for to him, this is indeed a matter of life and death. In this, I decide to engage enough to find out why, as after all, he *is* me.

"You'd expect me to give up everything I know and love?"

Daegan processes my question while his tattoos tumble in unbalanced circles. "When you say 'love,' what—or whom—do you mean?"

My mind is racing, and I'm finding it ever more difficult to stay open. "I have a good life. There are people I love."

"Yet you are the greatest threat to the survival of both those things."

I'd like to dismiss the notion that I could be the cause of such a morose scenario, but the flowers wilting near the wall in front of me seem to be supporting his statement. While I watch their white petals melt and curl like over-burnt candles, Daegan continues.

"All I'm asking is that you consider the facts."

Pulling my gaze from the dying flowers, I refocus on him as he motions to our surroundings.

"Some part of you has to know this is your truth."

My stomach twists into a tiny, single knot. "I think it would be foolish of me to consider this as anything other than an exercise in self-examination."

"How can you refute the concrete signs of our existence?" The fierceness in his eyes only serves to push me closer toward shutting down further. "That cut on your finger won't be healed by the time you wake up. Will you just ignore it?"

Having tired of navigating the labyrinth of my own subconscious, I ask the last question that comes to mind. "What is it that you want from me?"

Daegan doesn't respond, and I can't tell if he doesn't know what to say or if I've offended him in some way. After watching me for quite some time, he offers, "I want you to believe."

My heartbeat thumps in my chest while my thoughts churn, and as though we're connected, which by proxy we are, his tattoos whip in tight, unbalanced circles. I'm trying to understand what this dream dialogue means and how I can use it to unlock my own psyche, but he has asked too much of me, or rather, I've asked too much of myself.

I believe in what is tangible, real. I don't believe in an omnipotent God, nor do I subscribe to New Agers touting books about "spiritual awakenings." I can't listen to gurus insisting a person is incomplete without a thousand-dollar past-life regression, and I refuse to wait around for the second coming of Jesus. To me, the Rapture is when I'm doing what I do best, which, however unholy, is my version of heaven. So all of it, everything that equates to the intangible, goes in the same bucket: nonsense.

"Then you're wasting your time on me."

With my mind shut down and my willingness to participate nil, I harden my stare and watch while a hint of sadness sweeps across Daegan's face, and as it does, I'm certain I've let him down; or perhaps I've let myself down.

Sounding defeated and even angered, he leads me away from the wall. "Let's get you back to the cottage."

Without another word, we make our way toward the stone path while passing row upon row of rotting flowers. When I pass by, they wilt toward the ground as if I am a flesh-covered form of lethal poison.

39

WHITE KNIGHT, BLACK HORSE

oë's eyes flew open as though a burst of electricity had
shocked her to life. She read the neon numbers on the
clock by her bed: 3:33 a.m. Although it felt like her dream spanned several
days, she'd only been asleep for a few hours and she could still smell Bill's
cologne lingering in the air.

Feeling overheated to the point of sweating, she threw back the covers
and swung her legs over the edge of the bed as a bead of sweat rolled down
her neck and settled in the small basin at the center of her collarbone.

The scent of rain drifted from her skin, making it seem as if Daegan
was still with her, like part of him had slipped through the weakening
barrier between dream and reality. Cold air seeping through the old glass
windowpanes floated toward her, mixing Bill's scent with that of Daegan's,
and once intermingled, their scents grew sour as though resentful of having been combined.

She put her feet down on the smooth wood floor and walked to the
window, the old floors moaning and creaking beneath her feet. Peering
outside the frosty glass, she felt soothed by the snow-covered city until

her thoughts were thrust aside by an innate need to feel the cool night air on her skin. After walking to the wardrobe, she dressed, as the impulse to release the heat inside her was almost unbearable. Once she'd slipped on her boots, Zoë left the room and made her way down the stairs.

Her conversation with Daegan replayed in her mind; his questions about the men in her life—the broken soldiers she'd given pieces of herself to repair—made her wonder if her exchanges with men were as inequitable as he'd implied. Feeling her skin flush with hot blood, she couldn't stop one of her soldiers, Bill, from surfacing in her mind's eye until she felt like he was on the street outside waiting. She could feel him against her, his hands strong and his lips close to hers—too close.

Having stepped from the last stair, she grabbed her coat and purse, then made her way down the foyer, opened the front door, and let the winter wind embrace her in its icy arms. Taking a deep breath, she walked down the steps and onto Jane Street, where the sound of her shoes on the sidewalk brought her thoughts into a steadier rhythm.

Pressing herself into the balanced time of each step, she let her mind find a more concise pattern. In response, she felt the churning of her thoughts merge into single-file marching lines that made their way along the paths of her brain.

With her consciousness in an organized state, she understood that her urge to escape the house was due to the current state of her life, which was unbearable in its isolation. With her dreams now bleeding into the waking world, or rather, with her saneness in question, she was afraid to be around anyone. For the sake of self-preservation, save for a few exceptions, she'd elected to keep her own counsel.

The truth was, she didn't mind being alone, seeing as she had been most of her life, but it had always been her choice. The need for her present isolation felt forced, imposed, and she resented it, because up until now, she'd only had to manage two separate lives asleep next to one another:

Her life | Her men

Yet like a tidal wave, a third life was threatening to crash into shore and displace the other two:

Her life | Her men | HER DREAMS

Zoë stopped at the end of her street and noticed that the neighborhood was empty, desolate, a winter-white wonderland that seemed to have lost its inhabitants—all but her, anyway. Standing alone and awash in falling snow, she wasn't sure what to do next; the proposition of turning around and going back inside pushed an excess of heat into her blood, but the idea of wandering around the city in the middle of the night offered even less appeal.

A car pulled up beside her, and she focused on the cab while it parked at the curb. The man inside was paying the driver, and even though Zoë couldn't see him, there was a sense of darkness surrounding his presence. Her instincts demanded she walk away, but instead she moved closer, as though her body were under the command of a force outside the directives of her own mind. For reasons unknown even to her, she had to see him. So like moth to flame, she stood outside the door, intent on meeting him face-to-face.

When she heard the door open, she watched him exit, and upon spotting his fedora, long overcoat, and wingtip shoes, she recognized him. Keeping his head down, he stepped away from the cab, and as he passed by her, his body brushed against hers hard enough to pull the strap of her purse off her shoulder.

Refusing to make eye contact and using both the wash of snow and the brim of his hat as concealment, he walked away, leaving her with a feeling of unease. After wrestling and reasoning with herself not to follow, she got into the cab and gave the only address that came to mind.

"Eleven Minetta Lane."

The taxi pulled away from the curb and the darkness the man had left in its back seat floated outside the swell of heat still radiating from her skin. Looking out the back window, she watched him walking down the street, and while studying his tall build and strong, confident stride, she sensed him wanting to turn back around and come to her. The more she let herself feel him, the clearer things became: it wasn't darkness he'd left behind, but desperation, and in that moment, she knew with absolute certainty they would meet again.

Snow swirled in thick, clustered flakes, a wall of blurred white as Zoë turned away from the back window, almost glad to be encapsulated in the taxi as it navigated the flash storm. Watching the heavy flakes churn, she felt like the sky had dispatched tiny white warriors to block her from seeing the man, or at the very least, thinking about him. Her mother used to say that Great Spirit would call upon Father Sky to aid those in need. "Snow covers our wounds and gives them a quiet place to heal."

Almost against her will, she focused on her finger, as though her unconscious mind was forcing her to acknowledge the cut from Nikolai's knife—a wound that seemed to sting in response to being seen, laying open as if refusing to let the two sides of her skin come together and erase its existence.

She attempted to separate from her thoughts, but images played in her mind like a splice-edited movie. The scenes were hard-lined and choppy, like they were filmed with different cameras in multiple locations, and each frame filled with nauseatingly disjointed motion.

The memories of her recent dreams and waking life were cascading through her mind, the images racing like the movie was stuck on fast-forward while bits of mangled conversations raged in her head, as if the audio of the movie had gone haywire and was out of sync with its visual counterpart. She heard her father's voice but saw Evan's face; Daegan's words merged with a vision of Zoran in the meadow; the lament of the Shadows calling from underground was intermixed with a picture of the Deadlings, cruel and brimming with spite. Nothing made sense. It was a tangled mess of cinematic data in her head.

Then, as if the editor of the movie had siphoned the color from the film, there was a single black frame, a blank box of time, silent and vacuous. The wind wailed outside the taxi window, and a final image of Zoran crashed through the black space like lightning on a dark night. His face filled the entire frame in Zoë's mind, his aqua eyes vivid and urgent as the wind battered the cab's steel body back and forth as though he had sent its howling force. The image of Zoran's face then pulled back, zooming outward into a larger picture of him standing in the meadow with his eyes locked on her.

The taxi stopped moving and the meter made a ticking sound, then displayed her final fare. Turning toward her, the cabbie spoke.

"You okay in the storm?"

The man's eyes were deep brown, wide and round like her mother's, causing a memory of her mother's face to overlay the picture of Zoran. In that moment, what the cabbie failed to understand was that she needed the storm. It would wash her clean, bury her under its purity and cool the hot blood in her veins.

"I'll be fine. Thank you." She smiled and, after paying the fare, exited the cab.

Standing on the street, she closed her eyes and took in a deep breath, feeling like Father Sky was a friend to her, sending down his cottony warriors to battle her rogue thoughts. Yet holding a firm frame in her mind was the image of Zoran. While walking toward Mr. Sumel's house, she continued focusing on Zoran's face, recalling her father, who was of Celtic heritage, telling her about a Druid belief that the gods often used dreams to communicate, sometimes conjuring animal spirits as messengers to lead a person toward their truth; it made her wonder what missive Zoran carried and what truth his presence was meant to reveal.

With each step she took up the stairs, she watched Zoran's face fade from her mind's eye. Once at the front door, all that remained in the scope of her vision was an oil lamp burning softly in the hallway inside Mr. Sumel's house.

When she pressed the dirty white doorbell, she noticed that it rang with only half its usual chime; the other half sounded like a drunken church soprano. After waiting, she decided to try the doorknob and was relieved to find it unlocked.

She opened the front door a crack and poked her head inside, and was greeted by the pungent scents of cinnamon and what smelled like burning electrical wires. Once she'd stepped into the house, she closed the wind-beaten door and called out, "Mr. Sumel?"

Looking around the faintly lit house, she spotted a narrow door ajar at the end of the hallway before the kitchen's entrance. As she moved from the entryway, a flash of blinding neon-blue light shot toward her, then dimmed.

Inching down the hallway, she was keeping a firm focus on the light flickering through the door's sliver of an opening when, while passing one of the many bookcases, she was startled by a furry rump backing out from between two books.

"Jesus, Ziggy."

Reaching a back foot toward her, Ziggy attempted to perch on her shoulder, but instead of taking him from the bookcase, she kept walking.

Reaching the door, she opened it, then peered down an enclosed set of narrow stairs leading into a basement where bright tentacle-like flashes of neon light were reflecting off concrete walls.

"Mr. Sumel?"

The light dimmed and she could feel the air in the room flatten.

"The door was open, I—"

Mr. Sumel called up, "Zoë? That you?"

"Yes."

Mr. Sumel's hearty chuckle crackled with phlegm as he appeared at the bottom of the stairs, then began climbing them.

"Twice in one day, huh?"

"I'm sorry. I hope I didn't wake you."

Smiling, he assuaged her. "Nah, I'm a night owl." Although only halfway up the stairs, he was puffing like an old steamboat and his voice was winded. "Came back for more cocoa, did ya?"

It had been a knee-jerk reaction, coming to his house, and unsure of what had brought her there, Zoë said the first thing that came to mind. "I couldn't sleep."

Once at the top of the stairs, he patted her on the shoulder. "Follow me."

After leading her into the kitchen, he lit a few more oil lamps and put a kettle on the stove while she sat at a round wooden table and stared at the wall, which was covered floor to ceiling with odd trinkets. Still in her coat and with the cooling effect of the winter snow having dissipated, her blood was heating up as her thoughts tumbled backward to the image of her mother's painting of the meadow.

With her thoughts taking over her voice, she inquired, "The painting you gave me—where did you get it?"

Mr. Sumel kept his back to her while pouring a powdery concoction into two large green mugs. "Internet is an amazing thing. Just takes some know-how."

Annoyed by his evasiveness, she countered, "You don't have electricity."

The kettle whistled as he turned off the burner and poured steaming water into each mug. "Like I said, I do—it's just not reliable."

He shuffled over, mugs in hand, and sat down across from her while she continued questioning him. "And the article on Black Industries?"

"Just some interesting history. Powerful family with a fascinating past."

A piece of his hair was sticking straight out to the side, pointing toward the front door like a bossy finger, and she was half tempted to follow it, but she pressed him further. "What do you know about them?"

His stare narrowed as he blew into his steaming mug. "Not much."

Distracted by the knickknacks on the wall behind him, she scanned the myriad objects before spotting a single bare spot with a large faded outline of a cross.

Following Zoë's focus, he turned to see what had captured her attention. "Ah." Turning back around, he locked eyes with her. "On a wall filled with odds and ends, some are more ends than odds."

"What was it that ended?"

He sipped his cocoa. "Idealism, I suppose. I prefer the philosophical."

"Left the Good Shepherd's flock for Plato's Academy?" she bantered.

"Never was a very good sheep."

She asserted, "Just an inversion of philosophies, really."

Mr. Sumel smiled and leaned forward. "How so?"

"God—one is all. Plato—all is one."

"Actually, that wasn't originally Plato's idea," he said, holding up a knotted finger.

"No. It was Parmenides.'"

Looking like the most excited man in the universe, Mr. Sumel leaned back in his chair and gazed at her.

Still thinking about her mother's painting, she sought answers only he could offer. "You said my mother had dreams. Did she ever tell you what they were about?"

"Yes."

A large thud coming from the hallway caused her to lean to the left just as Ziggy shook himself off and waddled toward them.

"The dreams began when she was young."

"Did she ever talk about how they affected her?"

As he put down his mug with a shaking, gnarled hand, she noticed that his fingers were blackish-grey and scarred, like he'd been repeatedly burned.

"The dreams were very real, lucid. I'd say they affected her profoundly."

The wind howled outside and slammed against the kitchen windows like an irascible intruder as Zoë challenged him. "If you knew how to get the painting, why did you ask me to get it for you?"

"Actually, I asked you to get it for *you*."

She sipped her spicy cinnamon cocoa, which hit her tongue with a sizzle. "You know, a straight bullet hits a target a lot quicker than a curved one."

"Not when your gun's as old as mine!" Laughing, Mr. Sumel picked Ziggy up off the floor and set him on the table. With one stroke from Mr. Sumel's knobby fingers, Ziggy flattened out like a pancake.

"Why did you want me to have the painting?"

"Your mother wanted you to have it."

"She told you she wanted me to have it?"

"You could say that, yes."

"Are there more paintings?" she prodded.

Mr. Sumel's gaze sharpened. "I believe so, yes."

"Do you know where they are?"

"I do, but getting them will be nearly impossible for me." The heavy lines around his eyes softened, and before she could press him, he concluded the matter. "You needn't worry. They'll find you."

Both focused on one another and sipped their cocoa in silence. Mr. Sumel stroked a heavy-eyed Ziggy, who lay splayed on the table like a miniature dead animal skin. "Puts him right to sleep."

Without warning, an insuppressible question leapt from her lips. "Were you lovers?"

"Not of the body, no." Mr. Sumel smoothed back a few strands of his silvery hair. "Not in my deck of cards."

Certain that she wasn't going to glean any additional information from her current line of questioning, she elected not to inquire further. Although she was grateful for Mr. Sumel's company, she was starting to feel the weight of exhaustion, her mind seeking refuge from itself.

"Thank you for taking me in at four in the morning."

Mr. Sumel leaned forward and put his hand on hers. "Any time, my dear."

They sat looking at one another until she stood and made her way down the narrow hallway with Mr. Sumel shuffling along behind her. At the front door, she turned and hugged him, an unplanned gesture, yet one that allowed a few more of her unsettled pieces to take shelter in the kindness emanating from him.

Pulling away, she opened the door and stepped out into the snowy night.

40

ONE HALF OF LIGHT

t wasn't quite dawn by the time Zoë arrived home from Mr. Sumel's house. Slumber begged her to succumb to its shadowy caress, and truth be told, she felt she could sleep an endless cycle of days and nights, for dreamless, blackened peace was all she craved…

Removing her boots and letting them topple sideways onto the floor, she turned toward the vanity mirror and switched on a small lamp. Maybe it was the grey light coming through the window or a result of having been outside, but her skin was translucent pale, with a ghostly quality that made her reflection unfamiliar.

She pulled her gaze from the mirror and looked down at the newspaper covering her mother's painting of the partial meadow. After moving the paper aside, she traced the dips and valleys of the painting as though her mother's ashes were mixed with its vivid, pigmented colors.

Shifting her finger downward, she noticed an ivy vine in the painting's bottom right-hand corner wrapped around a bare foot and ankle, suggesting that the vine was attached to a person walking off to the right. It seemed odd that her mother would put such detail into the subject's foot and ankle yet not paint the full body of the person they were attached to.

Examining the painting, she noticed a set of copper strips along both the left and right side of the canvas's border as well as a sticker on the back that read WILLOUGHBY'S AUCTION HOUSE—LOT 182.

Remembering that she'd seen a similar set of copper strips, Zoë almost tripped over the pair of boots next to her chair as she rushed into the hallway outside her bedroom. Hanging on the wall was the painting she had taken from Mr. Sinclair's shop, which she removed and took into her bedroom.

Sitting back down, she studied the right side of the dark painting's canvas, finding that, as with her mother's painting, the frame had a set of copper strips and a laminated sticker on the back that read WILLOUGHBY'S AUCTION HOUSE—LOT 008.

Setting the dark canvas flat on the vanity top, she reacquainted herself with the painting's scenery: a blackened night with a brownstone in the forefront that had been painted in varying shades of grey, a raven hidden in a tar-colored tree, a dingy white rodent making its way up a set of concrete stairs toward the brownstone's front door, and a bloodred crescent moon in the upper right-hand corner.

Based on the matching sets of copper strips, she assumed the paintings were related even if the scenes didn't seem connected in any way. So, taking the painting of the partial meadow given to her by Mr. Sumel, she pressed it against the right side of the darker painting from Mr. Sinclair's shop and found that the strips were in perfect alignment.

After making contact with the painting of the meadow, the darker painting's monochrome imagery changed, the white rodent growing whiter while the faded numbers on the brownstone became more pronounced. Leaning in closer, she read the brightening numbers above the doorway, and as the details of the brownstone became clearer, there was no question that it was her house.

Looking to the right, she watched the painted scene of the partial meadow growing brighter and more alive while she took in every inch of the painting's details: the willow tree, the lush green grass, the marble rose at the meadow's center. Even though the meadow was incomplete, everything was identical to how it had looked in the dream when she first encountered Zoran.

The more she analyzed the landscape, the clearer it became that there were faint letters indented in the canvas. Pulling the lamp closer, then opening her vanity drawer, Zoë fumbled for a pen and piece of paper, then wrote each of the letters one by one.

Finishing as much of the transcription as she could, she stared at the letters, which formed a series of broken sentences:

> A ring 'round the rose
> A crimson
> By the night of twelve
> Or all that was will

The air in her lungs turned stale as she tried to make sense of the unfinished poem, which was indecipherable without what she assumed was a missing third painting. She wondered what message her mother was trying to convey and why she had gone to such lengths to conceal it. Unable to do anything further without the absent third painting, she got up and undressed.

She opened the armoire, put away her clothes, and threw on a pair of pajamas before taking her mother's journal and falling into the softness of her bed. Letting the down of the comforter wrap around her, she sank into its feathery refuge and hoped her mother's words would quell the unrest inside her. Calmed by the feeling of the journal's thick ivory pages, she began reading where she'd left off:

> *My nurse has arrived. I see shadow in his eyes (I have named him HalfLight) and ask Great Spirit to bestow pardon upon him, though he's the* ᎬᎾᏎ ᏀᏍ ᎠᏊᎢ ᎠᏋᎠᏒ ᎠᏋᎭᎠ.
> *I see the way HalfLight looks at you when you visit and witness the power you wield, even though so young a flower, dangerous*

because you don't believe it is within you. I've heard your father say, "You're not pretty, but you're smart," and though your father is a good man, he doesn't know what I do—what you will become.

I am losing my battle with the beast inside me: HalfLight has doubled my medicine. But I am safe. My good friend watches out for me from corners and hallways and smuggles herbs and powders for my teas. I grind them secretly in the bathroom—a sly apothecary!

You will meet him one day, my good friend, the Watcher. It's because of him I've avoided the beast's fatal bite for this long.

I find comfort writing to you, knowing there will be words between us even when I'm unable to utter them. HalfLight has come for my nightly check. Reluctantly, I'll leave you for now, but take solace in knowing you will be close to me always.

Until tomorrow,
—Mother

She dog-eared the page she'd just read, intent on researching the meaning of the passage's Cherokee script and her mother's description of the man she called HalfLight, then put the journal on her bedside table and nestled deeper beneath the covers.

The weight of her limbs pulled her toward sleep like thousands of unrelenting hands until blackness filled her mind, a blank frame of nothingness flickering through her thoughts as she felt herself fall into the shadowy arms of unconsciousness.

41

BLACKOUT

Snow is molded around me like I'm lying in an icy coffin. The cold jolts me awake, and as I open my eyes, I feel a hand come down over my mouth.

"Don't make a sound."

With my vision coming into focus, I look up at Sola, who is leaning over me. When she removes her hand from my mouth and helps me into a sitting position, I notice the terror in her eyes.

"Can you stand?"

In response to my nod, she helps me to my feet. I shift my focus to the snow-covered landscape around us, which looks bloodied beneath the moon's moody watercolor light, the daggered icicles hanging from the trees' branches enhancing the forest's murderous sensibility.

We're standing outside a small moonlight-flooded clearing, shrouded in the darkness of a thick line of trees that make up its fence-like border. Hearing someone approaching from the right, I turn my head as Prayna rounds one of the clumps of pine trees and takes a few last steps toward us.

"They're coming. We've no time to move."

Prayna takes one look at me, then removes her black cloak and wraps it around my naked frame. Both Sola and Prayna are clothed in heavy robe-like gowns in varying shades of white. Prayna's jet-black skin is juxtaposed to the brilliance of her gown, and as I notice her gaze shift, I follow her sightline into the clearing in front of us, where the man from the tomb of the marble women is leading a procession of townspeople—all clad in colored ceremonial-looking attire—into the snowy glade like prisoners on a death march.

The man's face, head, and neck are burned to the point that his only identifiable attribute is the form-fitting black robe he wears. His nose and lips have all but melted away, leaving him defaced and more flesh-covered skeleton than man. He's a nightmarish sight to behold, and despite the obvious wickedness that dwells within him, I feel a tinge of remorse in knowing that I helped cause his disfigurement.

Once at the opposite edge of the clearing, he stops and turns toward the single-file line of people behind him who appear to be in a sleepwalk-like trance. A thin stream of smoke seeps in from the forest behind him, billows around his ankles, then races up his body and slams into the open cavities that were once his nostrils.

To my left, Sola lets out a quiet yet audible gasp as the three of us watch him puncture the neck of the first woman in line with a blade-like finger-nail. There is no reaction from her, no resistance. Instead, she stands and stares at the ground as bright-red blood leaks from her wound.

The man wraps her in an embrace, one of his bony hands deeply inter-twined in her hair as he opens what's left of his mouth and drinks from her until she goes limp. I'm sick to my stomach watching such a vile creature drain the life from this beautiful and innocent woman, and as he drops her to the ground and moves on to the young girl behind her, it's all I can do not to rush from the shadows and rip him apart with my bare hands.

Sola whispers, "Water spider venom."

Casting a sideways glance at Prayna, Sola seems to be grappling with the same questions plaguing me: Why aren't they screaming, running, fight-ing back?

Prayna focuses on her. "Has to be. He wouldn't be able to control this many on his own."

Sola's gaze narrows. "The water at the temple well."

Seeming to be of one mind with her, Prayna finishes Sola's thought. "To present an offering to the new Guardian, each of them would have had to drink from it."

Sola remarks, "I've no doubt Griksvold's part of this. But I'll find out for certain."

"Continuing to involve yourself in this is too great a risk—"

Sola interrupts as her eyes glass over. "It's already done." She reaches for my hand as I attempt to hide my dismay that the Butcher, Griksvold, survived the night of my attack.

After a moment, we shift our focus back toward the clearing and watch the robed man take in another body of immobilized prey. As he does, the scent of burning sugar rushes toward us and a stream of smoke jets from his nostrils and materializes into a transparent, smoke-filled, light greyish male figure.

The figure's smoky form evolves into a body covered in gummy, cellophane-thin skin through which I can see a pulsing system of veins carrying bright-red blood to his organs, limbs, and extremities. Like a developing fetus, he gestates inside the forest's frozen womb.

In front of the figure, the black-robed man punctures the necks of those in line; he follows behind and bleeds out the remaining catatonic victims. With each one he drains, his bones and vascular system grow more pronounced and his skin becomes opaque.

"We've underestimated him."

Sola presses. "How?"

Prayna watches him drain the last few victims. "Using Ronan as a conduit, Lukaes is able to take in blood."

Prayna's face is still, her eyes fixated on the man, Lukaes, and I have a terrible feeling rooting around in my gut as she continues.

"'First blood feeds the body. Then souls feed the flesh.' He's draining them, then he'll Excise them in order to fully form."

With a modicum of hope in her voice, Sola speaks. "But it's impermanent."

"Right, but if he can consume enough Sehlms, he'll be able to sustain a body longer."

"Meaning?"

Still watching Lukaes, Prayna whispers, "Time in solid form means regaining his abilities, and that could lead him to the Book."

"I thought it was destroyed."

"It's in the hands of its rightful owner, where it belongs. And he must never have access to the secrets it contains."

Sola and I shift our collective focus to Prayna and while studying her, I sense something deeper weighing on her mind, but before I can inquire, a glass-shattering scream crashes toward us.

All three of us turn toward the clearing where Lukaes is circling his gummy finger over a young woman's heart like a venomous serpent enfolding its prey. She continues to cry out, convulses, then arches backward like her spine has jack-knifed in half.

Drawing his fingers outward, I watch in horror as he snatches a dark, translucent copy of the woman's body from the confines of her own skin. Just when the last piece of its shadowy silhouette leaves her body, she stops screaming and a distorted ebony version of her likeness, her Shadow, glides toward Lukaes and hovers around him in a comatose circle.

Shifting my focus back to the woman's body, I watch a tiny sphere floating upward from her chest, bathing the snow in an eerie violet glow. Lukaes wraps his hands around it and shoves it into his mouth. The glowing sphere travels down his throat, then floats inside his chest cavity like a jellyfish in a gummy, grey sea. As it does, the translucence of his skin turns a lighter, more solid grey, while the necrotic mounds of flesh masquerading as his eyes form whites with the faintest hint of dark irises.

With his increasing solidity, the air around him becomes acidic. I can almost feel it eroding my skin, as if his pores are emitting poison, while his usual scent of burning sugar changes to that of something more human—skin mixed with strong notes of sweat.

Behind him, now only a shell, the woman's body shrivels as if liquids are being sucked from inside her flesh. Her skin becomes sunken and skeletal and her fingers curl in on themselves in gnarled kinks as sharp claws emerge from her blackening fingers. She is unrecognizable, the life in her gone, her body that of a hairless goblin-like figure—a creature resembling the one I've seen in the darkened fireplace in my own bedroom.

Both the Shadow and the creature amble toward the robed man like children to their keeper while Lukaes moves down the line repeating the same hellish ritual. Watching such blasphemous disregard for human life repulses me; I find it crushing to witness and feel it changing the very structure of my soul. The temperature of my blood rises and my flesh grows hotter by the minute, but when Prayna takes my arm and I turn to look at her, I feel my entire body cool.

"Once he's fully formed, he'll know I'm here."

"How?" Sola interjects.

Letting go of my arm, Prayna turns solemn as grimness grips her features. "He's had me. We've traded blood." Prayna sends her gaze toward the barbaric scars below the fabric of her dress. "We altered his form, so he made sure I suffered in kind."

Prayna lowers her head and removes a long, braided leather necklace from around her neck. She runs her fingers along the handwoven leather until she reaches the copper compass-like medallion to which it's attached. Stroking its etched surface as if preparing to part from an old friend, she hands the necklace to Sola.

"Tell Daegan I gave this to you."

"Prayna, he'll never accept me as a Delphic."

Undeterred, Prayna insists, "It's not for him to decide."

Prayna reaches beneath her dress and unsheathes a small but lethal-looking knife from a leather strap around her thigh and hands it to Sola. "As soon as you're able, head due west. You'll reach Laksha by morning."

Prayna looks toward me and runs her fingers along my cheek. "Darkness shall light the way."

Her words sink into my skin as though they're fragmented parts returning to the body that will inevitably make them whole. Then, like an apparition in the night, she disappears around the tree next to her, as if vanishing into thin air.

Both Sola and I shift our focus back to the clearing where the robed man, Ronan, is shuttling gnarled-handed black creatures through a tear in the landscape as though funneling them through a massive curtain. Fanning outward and away from Ronan, the shadowy remnants of those murdered float out of the glade and into the forest's blackness like ink returning to its harboring well.

Sola and I retreat farther into the darkness of the trees upon seeing Lukaes moving toward the clearing's edge. He's close to us, his body almost human and covered in black tattoos that are writhing and squirming inside his skin. Not even the canvas of his face is without the serpentine presence of hundreds of moving symbols, pinwheeled lines, and what appear to be blocks of writing. And with him this close, I'm aware of the sheer size of his gladiator frame.

Now alone in the clearing, Lukaes tilts his head back like he's attempting to catch a scent in the air. For a moment, he closes his eyes and the corners of his taut mouth bow into a self-satisfied and sinister grin.

After opening his eyes, his glance falls to the bloodied snow covering the clearing's once-pristine ground. "If you've come to save them, you're too late."

Sola clutches my arm and my heart pounds in my chest. As is she, I'm terrified he knows we're here and am quite paralyzed by the fear gripping my body until I see Prayna enter the clearing across from us. Watching her walk toward him, my fear trades places with anguish.

Moving toward her, his voice is like acid corroding iron. "We have unfinished business, you and I."

Now standing in front of him, Prayna meets his stare; he grabs the back of her neck and pulls her closer to him. I feel my muscles clench as I watch him take in her scent, his lips tracing the side of her face, her forehead, her hair…

"You've always been sweeter forced than most are willing."

Prayna's body tenses against him and in knowing that he's not only tortured, but also violated her, I can't keep my rising temperature in check. Sensing my mounting ire, Sola, who is behind me, puts her hands on my waist as if to stabilize a great building swaying in an emergent storm.

The tattoos on Lukaes's body are wild now, churning and thrashing like every bit of ink is seeking escape. I notice that a large block of text covering the side of his rib cage down to his hip is moving left to right like an electronic banner within a fixed frame.

"I'll have her as I did you."

I need not even question to whom he's referring, for deep inside the marrow of my bones, I know he means me, and with this realization, I feel my blood growing even hotter.

"I am always watching her—waiting for the moment when I can break her will. As well you know, one way or another, she will submit."

Prayna's expression changes enough for me to know that his assertion scares her, and in so knowing, I, too, feel fear mixing with my heated blood.

Clenching her hair, he jerks her head backward. "Where is the book?"

Prayna shoots back, "It was destroyed."

Yanking her head back farther until she's choking, Lukaes seethes, "You lie." Growing stone-still, he forces the tattoos on his body to stop moving. Each of them becomes stationary save the writing on his side, which continues moving left to right within its boxed frame.

"That Book and I have traded flesh. I know it survives." The exertion of rendering his tattoos motionless appears to be taking its toll on his body, which decreases in muscle mass and opacity. Infuriated by his loss of solidity, he takes a sharp fingernail, punctures Prayna's neck, and siphons blood from her.

While he does, his muscles and skin become engorged and once again, his tattoos thrash, frenzied by the fresh infusion. In seeing him suck the life from her, I feel my own blood—now like a river of liquid dynamite—teetering on the brink of detonation as Sola slips her arms around my waist.

Lukaes pulls away from Prayna and she sways backward, her pristine white dress stained by the stream of blood leaking from her neck. Holding her upper back, he keeps her suspended mid-fall as he tears away the front of her dress and traces the barbarous scars on her chest. "The other one's already paid with her life—now it's your turn."

He circles his finger over her heart. Prayna's bloodcurdling scream pierces the bitter air around us and in reaction, I attempt to free myself from the confines of Sola's embrace.

Sola tightens her arms around me. "Zoë, you can't."

While Lukaes rips a translucent copy of Prayna's likeness from her body, I see a look of pure bliss on his face. Killing, cleaving souls from their hosts and fracturing the living, is his heaven. Rooted in his chosen vice, he delights in wrenching free Prayna's Shadow, but the more effort it takes, the harder it is for him to maintain his robust human form.

Prayna's body shrivels, then shrinks into an unrecognizable, gnarled-handed creature while her Shadow floats in place like a child lost in an icy wilderness. A small glowing sphere, her soul, hovers just outside Lukaes's gummy grasp, and in seeing him close his fist around it—around *her*—I can take no more and feel my blood ignite.

Warrior to battle, I snatch the small knife from Sola's hand, break from her grasp, and rush from the tree line as though infused with the strength of a thousand mutinous men. Lukaes is mere feet from me, his hands clutching Prayna's soul, and in knowing how close he is to consuming her, I dip into madness. I will gut him throat to groin before I'll let him take her.

Murderous in both thought and action, I'll accept nothing less than his blood on my hands. At full gait and fueled by the melted marrow that resides in my vibrating bones, I feel the blood in my veins pushing up and forward, ready to burst from my skin. I'm steadying my grip on the knife, intent on plunging it into his weakening grey body, when I hear fierce growling. From the corner of my eye, I catch sight of a blurred black mass hurtling toward me from the left.

Wanting nothing to stand between me and Lukaes's demise, I refocus and force the knife toward his torso, feeling it dive into soft flesh as I'm struck to the ground with the force of a speeding car. The wind is knocked from my lungs and the skin on my hand is throbbing, yet all I can think about is whether I've delivered Lukaes to death's door.

Lying in the cold snow, I feel my bones stop vibrating and the heat in my body abating as Sola cries out, "No!"

I turn my head toward her voice and find myself face-to-face with Zoran's lifeless aqua eyes. Adrenaline floods my system and I sit up, confused as to what's happened. Sola and I are now alone in the clearing save for a bleeding Zoran, who lies between us.

Thick blood engulfs the underside of my thigh, and when I follow the crimson trail to its source, I see my knife protruding from Zoran's stomach. Looking back toward Sola, who weeps as she cradles Zoran's head in her lap, I feel my mind grow wild with thought as I try to resurrect the scene prior to being thrown to the ground.

Questions are pinballing around my brain, the most pressing of them being why Zoran would force me away from Lukaes, when my thoughts are interrupted by a sharp pain on my cheek. Touching my face, I feel something writhing beneath the surface, like a tiny, tattooed snake is trapped within the invisible borders of where my birthmark used to be.

"It's the mark of the soul you took."

Sola leans forward and studies the squirming tattoo. It's a ghastly sensation that makes me feel as though I've been infected with an unwanted pest that has burrowed beneath my skin.

"Despite the risks, you must reverse what you've done. He is worthy of life, and without him, we will all suffer."

Sola watches the side of my face in silence while I run my hand along Zoran's fur. With his body growing cold and sinking into the snow, I feel the tattoo on my cheek flip and lash until, with little internal debate, I inquire, "What do I need to do?"

Sola reaches for my index finger, which still has the cut from Nikolai's knife. "Lie down next to him."

The undersides of my legs are soaked in Zoran's blood. The snow beneath them is turning into a bruised, soupy slush, and as Sola helps me inch closer to Zoran's body, I feel the softness of his fur flush against my right leg when she lowers me down beside him.

Turning my head, I stare into his eyes and swear for a split second I see life in them. Watching the shadowed pinpoint of his pupils, I hope for movement, a twitch or flicker indicating he's hovering at death's threshold, refusing to pass over it.

"Close your eyes."

After doing as she's instructed, I see a radiant image of her and Zoran together in my mind's eye. Her thoughts are naked and exposed to me with a rawness of emotion I'm unaccustomed to feeling within the borders of my own thoughts. What I sense from her is loss, an inexplicable and heart-crushing ache coupled with an unending love for him—the bond between them palpable, like a wide sea of complex currents swirling around the islands of what I sense to be loyalty and friendship.

I'm pulled from my thoughts by something sharp ripping across my finger and the tattoo on my cheek throbs. I feel Sola lower my hand and place my finger against the rough skin of Zoran's tongue. His sharp teeth rest on top of my finger as a wave of exhaustion washes over me.

I'm leaving my body. My mind is altered; I could swear a soft, thirsty mouth is drinking from me like I'm a skin-sheathed barrel of wine and my finger is its spout. In response, the blood in my veins grows hot, rushes to-ward my shoulder, then shoots down my arm like my system is committed to expelling the blood inside me. Deep within my thoughts, a black frame appears, a colorless canvas upon which Zoran's watercolor face emerges.

I watch as his eyes widen, their liquid aqua spilling outward and seeping into every inch of my mind's eye. I feel weak, drained, and unable to stay awake any longer. Then my mind dips into the sea of unconsciousness until I'm submerged.

42

REALITY BITES

Coming back into her body, Zoë felt like her eyelids were glued together as a dull ache at the base of her neck traveled down her spine and made its way toward her legs. Each of her joints felt askew, like her skeleton had been taken apart and reassembled, and lodged in her muscles were what seemed like shards of ice radiating a pervasive chill throughout her body.

Her cheek was pressed against something hard and cold. The breath passing through her lips was like winter wind over a snowdrift, and as she released a long glacial exhale from her lungs, she coaxed her heavy lids to open.

Lying on her stomach with her head to one side, she stared into her darkened parlor and struggled to bring her mind into focus. She rolled over and edged herself into a sitting position, noticing she was beside one of the closed French doors leading to the courtyard.

Still trying to bring her consciousness into clarity, she watched a few round flakes floating from the sky like crystalized dandelions. The snow's backdrop was a deep-sea-colored night sky with a large moon that stung her eyes with its mystic glow. Letting her gaze drift downward, she could just make out a set of footprints leading from the back corner of the courtyard to the tiled outdoor landing.

Feeling her finger throb, she shifted her focus to her hand, which was resting on her thigh and covered in a thin layer of blood. Deft and clipped came the images of what she'd witnessed: men, women, and children ripped apart at the hands of a semi-solid demon who had become solid; Prayna slaughtered, mutilated body and soul, with her ill-fated beast lying lifeless beside her. The canvas of her mind's eye filled with Zoran's image, and the weight of his presence sent a wave of pain from her finger into her hand and up through her arm. The draw toward him from the blurred dream of their bloody union was visceral, and although she sat in the confines of her house, she could still feel his soft mouth drinking the liquid life from her veins.

Like a hologram catching the light, her mind continued switching back and forth between Zoran's image and her own polar physical state until warmth matriculated from deep within her chest, down her torso, and into her legs. Waiting for heated blood to bring her back to life, she stared into the room with a welcome yet temporary blankness of thought.

Tapering her gaze, she caught sight of two small red objects that were almost hidden in the fringe of the rug in front of her. Zoë struggled to her feet and walked a few steps to retrieve them.

She bent down to pick up two small bones; upon closer inspection, she realized they were identical to the one that was given to her by the creature from her fireplace. Tracing their shiny red lacquer surfaces, she felt disquiet seep into her blood as though the bones were leaching angst-laden venom.

Seeking refuge from her thoughts, she walked into the kitchen and retrieved an embroidered white hand towel, the softness of the fine cloth against her hand doing little to soothe the sensation of unease that continued to spread throughout her blood. Once back in the parlor, with the bones in one hand and the towel in the other, she bent down and wiped away any trace of her presence before locking the French doors and making her way into the foyer.

While walking up the staircase toward her bedroom, she stared at the once-white towel in her hand, noticing it was now a pinkish watercolor mixture of the snow's purity and the brutality of her dreams. And although she was guiltless of any real offense, she felt like a murderess holding the bloodied towel that had erased any evidence of her dream-true crime.

After making her way across the hall, she entered her bedroom and took a few steps toward the vanity before catching a glimpse of Lucille sitting motionless on the windowsill, her tail hanging straight down like a fur-covered arrow.

Zoë opened the drawer and placed the two bones next to the one she'd received several nights prior, and when they rolled together against the drawer's wooden front, she felt a chill rise through her flesh as she realized the bones formed a finger.

She attempted to calm her racing thoughts while the anxiety-laced toxin the bones had transferred into her blood metastasized into her cells, tissues, and brain. With both her soiled body and the skeletal finger in her line of sight, her consciousness plunged into a compromised state until she could no longer suppress the questions she'd been holding down for weeks: Could she trust her mind to decipher what was—and wasn't—real?

Ever the seer of two sides, her mind leapt to its own defense with a counterargument compelling enough to allay the restlessness inside her: hers were "lucid dreams," as Dr. Lawson had described. They were consumptive in their experience, playing themselves out in two worlds like a scripted film, yet metaphoric in what they revealed. In essence, whether Zoë was awake or asleep, illusion was her new reality; and so it would remain until she could unravel the mysteries of her own psyche.

Lucille hopped down from the windowsill, trotted across the room, and brushed against Zoë's leg. Thankful for the distraction, Zoë closed the vanity drawer and picked her up—a gesture Lucille had never permitted until now.

Although Lucille was cradled in her arms, neither she nor Zoë seemed to know what to do in the presence of a momentary truce. Lucille wasn't purring, nor was she relaxed, so Zoë remained still and held her like a stuffed animal.

After a moment, she reached out to pet Lucille's chin, but when Lucille spotted the slice down Zoë's finger, her entire body went stiff and she leaned forward to smell the dried blood cemented on Zoë's skin. Lucille licked the cut, her rough tongue pressing into its deep groove and extracting any remaining blood, as though she and Zoë were coconspirators, each doing her part to cover up that night's peculiar and ruthless events.

Once the cut was spotless, Lucille looked up at her with saucer-sized eyes before bounding from her arms and shooting back up onto the windowsill. Zoë stared at the moon shining on Lucille's back, giving her orange fur the appearance of icy-blue fire. The glacier-like hue radiating from Lucille's body had a hypnotic effect and pushed Zoë deeper into longing for a more solid reality. What she needed was to be washed clean, to feel the warm rain of a soothing shower that would separate her from the crusted layers of her thoughts.

Walking into her bathroom, she undressed, pulled back the shower curtain, and turned on the water. With the room in a state of semidarkness, she took solace in the pervading dimness as though not seeing herself in the mirror would allow her mind the luxury of ignorance.

Naked and free, she stepped beneath the water and let it fall against her back as a slivered beam of light shone down through the small round window in the shower. On any other night, the moon was a trusted friend, but on one such as this, it was an intruder, spotlighting the water flowing toward the drain and carrying with it traces of a blood-infused nightmare.

Having grabbed a bar of rose-scented soap, she scrubbed until her skin was flushed and raw. Turning her face into the water, she let it beat down on her forehead as if its purifying stream could somehow rinse Zoran from her senses: his lifeless eyes, the feeling of him drinking from her...

Calm found her mind long enough for her to take in a deep breath, but the silvery moonlight and misty steam joining midair seemed to form a hazy version of Zoran that infiltrated her field of vision like a specter in the shadows. Turning off the water, she stepped from the shower and dried off, feeling frustrated that she'd been unable to untangle him from her threaded thoughts.

Attempting to untwine him from her mind, she walked into her bedroom and sat on the bed before letting her head hit the softness of the pillow. Turning on her side, she let her focus drift to the journal lying on the bed next to her, and in that moment, she felt his presence swallowed whole by the void her mother's death had left.

Running her fingers along the cover of the leather-bound journal, she found it soft beneath her touch and took comfort in the hope that even if her current world was a mirrored illusion, her mother's words were real.

Opening to the page where she'd left off earlier, she burrowed beneath her bedding and soaked up the page's inky script.

> *HalfLight has been oddly absent, off his usual vigilant guard, which has allowed my friend the Watcher, my favorite "unauthorized visitor," a few stolen moments at my side. Today he has brought with him a glorious mug of cocoa (a welcome reprieve from HalfLight's constant medicating)!*
>
> *We stuff ourselves with jovial memories. I haven't laughed in so long. I feel new again as my health returns briefly, held in that moment of chocolate-scented bliss.*
>
> *We talk of you, dear daughter...I fear the parting I know lurks on padded feet, hungry and relentless with desire. I have no choice but to leave you in the Gardener's care; though his is imperfect soil, it is rich enough to ensure your growth.*
>
> *You visit far less now, but I understand. The hungry beast devours us both: my flesh, your heart. I know you cannot bear to watch my body withering. But we are joined, only inches from one another, and so shall it be, even after the pierce of midnight's clawed foot.*
>
> *Until tomorrow,*
> *—Mother*

With the void filled and her heart swelling in her chest, she reread the closing, "Until tomorrow," wishing that somehow the words were true. Hearing Lula's slippered feet shuffling down the hall, she closed the journal and shut her eyes to feign restful sleep.

The door to her bedroom opened as Lula attempted a stone-footed version of tiptoeing across the creaking wood floors. Lula pulled a few logs from the metal basket beside the fireplace, tossed them onto the grate, then stoked the fire until the warmth of fresh flames blazed into the room.

Feeling Lula ease herself onto the bed beside her, Zoë let the scent of Oil of Olay infiltrate her senses like a tranquility-inducing perfume. Lula's plump hand brushed her cheek, lingering over the place where the stain of her youth, her birthmark, had been.

Beneath Lula's motherly touch, Zoë lost track of how much time passed, seeing as the only thing registering was the comfort she felt. Nearing the edge of sleep, she heard Lula whisper, as though to herself, "The Celts say people live in each other's shadow. I'll gladly live in yours."

43

SHADOW CATCHER

Although I know I'm dreaming, the memory of my father is so real it seems like time has fallen backward and lodged within a preserved pocket of my childhood. He sits by the fire in his favorite wingback chair, whiskey in hand, spinning yarns about how we're descended from a long line of ancient Celtic Druids while I listen, perched on an oversized footstool in front of him.

Teetering on the edge of total inebriation, he makes little sense, but it's entertaining nonetheless, and in this dream-suspended moment, I feel close to him, like I matter.

"Your great-great-grandfather was a Seer, in communion with the spirits who spoke to him through visions he wrote down in mistletoe ink." Leaning forward, he takes my chin between his fat thumb and forefinger. "You see, too, don't you?"

The firelight makes his greying red hair look as though it's comprised of flames, and the gin blossoms on his nose and cheeks seem like tiny rivers of lava fanning out toward the edges of his face.

Knowing he has asked me a question to which I'm not sure he knows the answer, I respond in a relative whisper, afraid to speak lest it ruin this fleeting union between us. "Yes."

His light eyes blaze and to me he is larger than life, like a fire god who is scarcely contained inside his fragile human flesh. When he removes his fingers from my chin, the heat of his touch stays buried under my skin like a fiery imprint.

His whiskey-laden breath envelops my senses as he leans forward and inquires, "And what do you see?"

Almost inaudibly, I answer, "Everything."

There is a faint flirtation of love in his eyes—as though he's committed to owning the fatherly role he'd rather leave unclaimed—and as he gazes at me, both of us know that what I've spoken is the truth. I realize it is I who cause the ever-present distance between us. Neither because I'm a rebellious child, nor because I don't love him, but rather because I see him and he cannot hide.

With his demeanor toward me shifting, my father eyes me as one would an unwanted insect. "You're like a spider cloaked in the shadows. You see because you cannot be seen." He narrows his gaze. "My spider. That's what you are."

Sitting back in his chair, his stare turns cold as his skin loses its flush and turns pale. I watch the image of my father fade into the darkness of my mind as I'm yanked back into the present by the sound of a familiar female voice.

"Breathe, Zoë."

I suck in a life-infusing gulp of frosty air while a woman's arms wrap around me. I feel her pulling my back against the warmth of her chest, and with the honey-laced scent of rose drifting from her skin, I know it's Sola who cradles me against her.

Having forced my eyes open, I wait for my Vaseline-covered vision to focus and once my sight has cleared, I see Zoran standing in front of me. In response, my bones become magnetized and my blood pushes up against my skin, seeking to further fill his veins.

Somehow he appears larger than he was before, the muscles in his chest more defined and his fur shinning, like it's covered in oil. Surrounded by a barrier of snow-covered pine trees, sitting in between him and Sola, I feel like we are the only three souls remaining in this gelid, diamond-dusted realm.

As if wishing to be counted amongst the souls remaining and born from the canvas of my thoughts, I see a small, glowing sphere emerge from the spiny arms of one of the pine trees and drift toward me like a fractured violet star.

In the sphere's equalizing presence, my bones demagnetize and my mind slips into what feels like a sliver between space and time. While I watch it approach, I see myself reaching toward it in my mind's eye. I've not moved a muscle, yet inside my thoughts I'm merging with the sphere, which has now fanned out into a thin membrane of light that sinks into my skin like rain into parched earth.

I'm warm from head to toe, my body heat defying the bitter night as I feel the sphere's light spreading throughout every vein, tissue, and cell. Such peace I've never possessed, and I haven't one burden that can remain lodged within my consciousness.

Images flash inside my mind, snippets of memories flickering like candlelight on a dark wall: I see a girl, tall and lithe with long hair that flows down her back like spun moonless sky. Her dress is thin, and when the sun shines from behind her, it illuminates the silhouette of her adolescent frame. She is giddy, beautiful, and free, and her laughter fills my thoughts like a lingering song as she twirls, throws her head back, and dances like an Arthurian maiden in a meadow.

A handwoven crown of flowers sits atop her hair, and as she spins faster, it slips from her head in a strange and forced slow motion until it hits the grass with a silent, flower-flattening crash. The grass around the fallen crown begins dying, drying out, and turning brown like it's being sucked of color and life until everything turns into a shadowy, storm-ridden haze.

Through the darkness, I hear her scream and blurred images of her giving birth appear in my mind's eye. She is a young woman now, and blood soils her long gown as she bears down with all her strength and gives a final push; from beneath her dress I hear not one, but multiple infants crying.

From across the room, an elderly woman questions the new mother, and although her face is hidden in shadow, I sense her stern demeanor. "To secure their lives, the Book requires a trade."

"Whatever it wants, I'll willingly give."

My point of view shifts so that I am looking through the young woman's eyes at her bloodied nightgown and watching the skin of her babies turning from dark night to charcoal grey, then stark white as if they have been all but drained of life.

The vision goes black, warmth leaves my body, and I'm thrown back into the arms of the winter's night. I close my eyes, desperate to step back into what I surmise are Prayna's memories, but when I reopen them, I find myself face-to-face with a hollow-eyed Shadow and its counterpart, the starry sphere.

Sola pulls me tighter against her as a diminutive voice leaves the Shadow's transparent lips. "Did you save them? Are they here? Where is Cullen?"

My heart sinks deeper into my chest like it's being swallowed from the outside in. I know the Shadow is referring to the infants I heard crying in the vision, but without a male in the scene I'm unsure how the person she calls Cullen is connected.

Watching the Shadow and sphere hover in front of me, I've no doubt they're what's left of Prayna. I've somehow been infused with her memories, and the longer I stare at her ghost and its companion soul, the harder it is to bear the finality of the circumstances I wish I could've prevented but now cannot change.

The Shadow reaches for me and I take it in my arms without hesitating as Zoran steps into my peripheral vision.

"Zoë, listen to me."

While Zoran continues, Sola distances herself from me, then stands off to my right as I remain seated on my snow-cushioned perch.

"New Shadows are exceptionally dangerous. Very few can connect with them."

Before Zoran can finish his sentence, the Shadow throws its translucent, inky arms around my neck, looking frantic as it whispers, "The end is near. Darkness falls. She will leave and never return. The end is near. Darkness falls. She will leave and never return…" The Shadow clings to me while it watches its soul drift upward like an unanchored buoy until it finds moored safety in Sola's open palm.

I feel the unbearable weight of the soulless Shadow's fear and despondency like a boulder compressing my skeleton. Concerned, Zoran takes a step toward me, and in response, the Shadow shoots a menacing glance at him and sends a low, malevolent growl in his direction.

Zoran backs away, instructing me, "No matter what happens, you must stay calm."

I feel the Shadow tighten its cold, inky arms around my neck, and when I place a comforting hand on its back, my forearms fill with a painful current, like my hands are wire-deep in a shorting electrical socket. Looking down, I find it difficult to understand what I'm seeing, as the Shadow is quivering and pixelating like it's fighting to stay in one piece.

Zoran's words ring in my ears, and after taking a deep breath, I visualize a tranquil sea in my mind's eye until, arms loosening and eyes brightening, the Shadow looks up at me like a child gazing upon a loving mother. Studying the Shadow's face, I take in every detail of its inky-black, translucent exterior as it stares back, examining me with a similar avid fascination.

Soul still in hand, Sola urges, "We need to go."

I stand, stroking the Shadow's back, and although getting my frozen legs to cooperate is a struggle, the Shadow stays relaxed and content in my arms.

Once on my feet, I look to Zoran and Sola, who both turn away from me and peer into the surrounding forest. Following their lines of sight, I see a horde of phantom bodies drifting toward us through the trees, and as I watch their lifeless, gummy feet dragging through the snow, scraping tracks that lead in from all sides, I'm certain that the one thing they want without limit is me.

The Shadow releases my neck, turns its back to me, then presses against my torso in a protective posture, its stance toward the others, its brethren, not at all welcoming. Rather, it's fierce and defensive as it lets out a low-pitched growl.

The other Shadows emit the same ominous, almost demonic sound as the Shadow pressed against me quivers, pixelating and sending painful electric waves into my abdomen. In retaliatory fashion, the incoming Shadows take on the same semi-pixelated, agitated form, and grow louder in what morphs into a saber-rattling wail.

Zoran and Sola exchange a glance that leaves me feeling like neither of them is sure what to do. The more fearful I feel, the more erratic the Shadows' behavior becomes, and like metal to magnet, they surround me, squeezing into a tighter circle in order to touch me.

Over the swarm of tangled translucent bodies and hungry stares, I lock eyes with Zoran. The infusion of dark strength his presence provides forces me toward a more serene state of mind, causing the electrical current coming from the Shadow in my arms to ease. As a result, the fanatical focus of the others lifts enough for me to take in a courage-inducing breath. Once my mind has regained composure, the Shadows fall silent, their airy fingers searching me with the curiosity of emboldened children.

Zoran instructs, "Walk forward. Slowly."

I'm about to take a step when my heart begins to race, causing the Shadows to strike up a panicked form of chatter.

Sola urges, "Zoë, you have to stay calm—"

Before she can finish her sentence, I take a small but resolute step, and like a circular parade, the Shadows continue surrounding me, appearing excited at the prospect of following anywhere I choose to lead them. Now in my deified capacity and with a small burst of bravery, I take a larger step forward while Zoran leads and Sola edges around behind the forming line of Shadows.

As we walk through the snow-covered trees, the Shadow against me wraps its arms around my neck, almost fearful that we may soon be forced to part. In a gesture of reassurance, I place my hand on its back and follow Zoran through the crystalline forest with my ghostly brood in tow.

Embraced by the serenity of the indigo night, I feel a temporary reprieve from the heaviness of the Shadows and am thankful for the beauty of the moonlight's kaleidoscopic projection onto the snowy ground. With my worry-ridden mental space now free, my thoughts roll back into the memory-merged scene given to me by Prayna's soul. While replaying the film of her babies' skin morphing from moonless black to alabaster, I wonder what, if anything, her soul was attempting to convey.

I ponder whether the memories were a smattering of random visions or images doubling as deliberate crumbs I'm meant to follow toward a larger and more comprehensive picture. Whatever the purpose of the visions, I'm certain of one thing: even in her splintered form, Prayna longs for her children. They are her joy, her heart, her soul.

A swift and barbaric play-by-play of Prayna's demise sweeps across my consciousness and I feel the ache of her murder until I cannot quell the wrath rising within me. All my mind will now replay is the wishful scene of me plunging a knife into Lukaes's guts as the life in his malformed, globular eyes trades places with death's blank stare.

A deep, jarring male voice pushes into my mind. "Zoë!"

I'm yanked back from my murderous fantasy and greeted by the manic, ill-tempered, wailing Shadows that are circling me. My skeleton feels like it's on the verge of being crushed; the weight of the Shadows' frenzied state is bone-breaking. Aware that they're capable of killing me, I wrestle my thoughts toward any semblance of internal harmony I can muster.

Resurrecting the image of Prayna as a young girl, I watch her twirl beneath the blazing sun as her silken hair fans out like strands of ebony thread, her bright smile beaming with the unburdened purity of youth. Imagining her like this, elated and carefree, I feel the wrath give way to a mental stillness that allows the Shadows to cease their predatory circling.

Zoran watches me for a moment before turning back around and continuing forward, and the Shadows fall behind me in an organized fashion. I'm not sure what has possessed them to create such a precise line, but they float along, two by two like train cars running along a secured track, and the only Shadow still misbehaving is the one in my arms. But when I pull it closer, it grows docile and cradles itself against my chest.

In front of me, Zoran steps through the dense foliage at the forest's edge and crosses onto the snow-covered meadow. His enormous prints have left padded depressions for me to walk in, offering comfort with every step and allowing me to feel the heat of my life-giving blood racing within his veins.

Glancing behind me, I see Sola walking off to the left of the last two Shadows in the line, and as I watch her carrying Prayna's hovering soul, I find her bewitching, like a sorceress holding the spark of creation in her palm. It occurs to me that when in her proximity, I'm a cooler form of fire, a blue flame that contains within it a steady and focused will to err on the side of a more controlled burn. There is no denying our connection, and part of me wonders if it's the invisible channel between us that's keeping the Shadows in their portable, soldierly construct.

I shift my gaze to the marble rose at the meadow's center and notice the blood-centered rose looks somber sticking out from the miniature snowdrift gathered around its stony stem. As I move away from it, I swear the scent of its spicy perfume is pursuing me, a fiery demand that our past union not be forgotten.

As Zoran steps from the meadow into the forest and walks toward two immense oak trees, my body tenses; I know the tomb nestled between them leads to the desolate haunting Underworld I'd do anything to avoid reentering.

With my resistance full-blown, I send a ripple through the line of Shadows and lift my mind toward lighter thoughts in order to soothe them. As though on cue, snowflakes begin lilting from above, falling onto my skin with a welcome and cooling softness.

Now at the meadow's edge, again I step into the cushion of Zoran's prints, following them one by one into the forest until I arrive at the arched entrance to the tomb. Zoran stands inside the archway, part of his face hidden in darkness. A restless lament drifting from the tomb's entrance washes over the line of Shadows and causes them to stir.

I've bonded enough with them to feel their collective thoughts—or rather, fears—and in seeking a smooth transition, I feel compelled to speak on their behalf.

"They'll enter in their own time—and only with me."

The look on Zoran's face registers an all-out refusal to do as I've proposed, but when Sola steps from the forest floor and walks past him into the tomb, it seems he has little choice but to comply.

After watching Zoran walk down the stairs, I feel my heart speed up, seeing as I'm now alone with the Shadows. When I rotate toward them, I feel the Shadow grow cool against my skin.

They stare at me with a strange sort of adoration, which I find a confusing experience considering that behind their eyes, I sense unremitting volatility. I decide to experiment and give them a gentle smile, and to my amazement, they do the same, each of them brightening.

I step beneath the tomb's moss-covered archway, noticing that the voices coming from below have dulled to a mere whisper. In the absence of the mournful lament, I'm able to coax the Shadows into the tomb behind me.

Descending the stairs, I take each stone step in single, minute increments to keep the Shadows balanced, forcing my heartbeat to thump at a constant, metronome-like pace. Once my foot leaves the last stair, I lead the ghostly procession through the root-lined room and into the tunnel while focusing on keeping my pulse in time.

Challenging my attempts to maintain poise, the Shadow in my arms flips between warm and cool like a malfunctioning electric blanket as I navigate the tunnel's sharp turn and force myself to put one foot in front of the other, knowing I'm only minutes away from settling the Shadows into their final resting place.

After rounding the corner, I lean back to compensate for the steep decline of the tunnel floor, which causes the Shadows to whisper like frightened children behind me. Intrigued by the cacophony of murmurs, the Shadows residing inside the hall hover around the doorway and peer out at their approaching brethren.

The same tall, razor-thin woman I'd seen when previously in the hall parts the horde of Shadows at the entrance and sizes me up in a manner denoting palpable disapproval. In defiance, I avoid eye contact with her, as her presence is like that of an ear-splitting high note strong enough to shatter glass and I find my dislike of her incontrovertible.

Beneath her condemning glower, I feel a rush of anger surge through me. Seeming to mirror my thoughts, the Shadows behind me begin growling, and particularly vicious is the Shadow in my arms, which lunges forward to attack the woman.

In the hopes of subduing the tension, I shift my thoughts away from her and adjust my frame of mind. Refocusing on the hall's entrance, I continue walking, stroking the back of the still-growling Shadow in my arms.

I'm a few feet away, and without even seeing Zoran, I feel my bones vibrating, magnetizing at the mere hint of his nearness. My lips part long enough for a sweet and musty bit of air to enter my lungs while the Shadows behind me grow silent, like they're intoxicated by the potency of Zoran's effect on me. In this, I'm thankful for the passivity of their demeanor, as it keeps them from noticing the fact that we're passing through the entrance and into the vast hall.

The Shadows in the hall move backward and part to reveal Zoran, who walks toward me. At the far end of the room, I see the knife-like woman slip out through a door nestled inside one of the hall's painted panels. Once the door closes behind her, I feel the shrill dissonance of her presence vacate the room.

The Shadows from both sides of the hall move inward as Zoran's and my respective broods intermingle like dark chemicals in a gilded vial. We watch them mix, weaving in and out of one another as though trading skins, but the Shadow in my arms refuses to release my neck. At my attempt to pull it away from my chest, it sends a shockwave of electric current through my hands.

A small Shadow leaves the dark mass swirling around us and floats toward the one in my arms. They greet each other like children on a playground, and in a gesture almost human, the small Shadow reaches out an inky hand and guides the Shadow from my arms. Hand in hand, the two move away from us, and I'm unable to suppress a rising feeling of loss as Prayna's wraithlike shell is absorbed into the sea of carbon-colored lifelessness the hall has become.

My bones demagnetize while my mounting sorrow causes the mass of

Shadows to swell up toward the ceiling. In response, I flip through my mind in search of an image that will steady the intemperate currents churning around us until an image of my father sitting in front of the fire manifests in my mind's eye.

I'm hidden in a dark corner of the room, watching him as he stares into the flames and recites the only language he seems to understand, his beloved Shakespeare.

> The abhorr'd ingredient to his eye, make known
> How he hath drunk, he cracks his gorge, his sides,
> With violent hefts. I have drunk, and seen the spider.

Without warning, my father shoots a condemning glance toward me and spits out his words like rotten food. "I see you, my spider…"

My mind is ripped from the scene by the sound of voices creeping toward me from all sides. I feel my skin go cold as each of the Shadows' whispers lands on my body like a poisonous insect. "I see you, my spider…"

Heart racing, I stare at the Shadows that are dangling in the air around me like phantoms, whispering the phrase again and again like a thousand broken record players. I attempt to deadbolt my mind, feeling like they've violated the sanctity of my private thoughts, as Zoran moves through the Shadows, creating a path toward a panel door across the room. Desperate to escape, I follow him. Behind us, the Shadows' whispers combine with the dragging sounds of their gummy feet as they amble after us like a frothy black tide.

Unable to stand the voices any longer, I run past Zoran and push open the panel door. Once I've stepped over the threshold, I hold the door open while he enters, then watch the mobile graveyard of Shadows lurch forward and utter one last whisper.

"I see you…"

In the hopes of eradicating the thousands of hollow eyes that are fixated on me, I slam the door and force their voices from my mind. Turning into a narrow, torchlit passageway, I follow Zoran, who has already entered a dim room up ahead. The Shadows on the other side of the door have fallen silent, but the effects of shepherding them into the hall has drained the life from my body—it feels like I'm lugging my own weight along the rough stone floor.

Reaching the room, I step onto an elevated, cushion-covered floor and am greeted by Sola, who helps ease me down onto a soft cushion in front of Zoran. While taking in our surroundings, I feel the room has swallowed us whole, its creamy walls, mounted lanterns, and multicolored floor adding a welcome air of homebound comfort to what would otherwise be a bleak underground prison.

Sola sits beside me, her gaze locked on the violet sphere that bobs up and down in the back corner of the room like a skyless star.

"What will happen to her?"

"She'll remain in my care." Sola fingers Prayna's medallion, which hangs around her neck.

"She showed me things, memories."

Appearing to understand what I've seen, at least in part, Sola replies, "The pieces will all come together in time—for both of us."

Unable to hold himself back any longer, Zoran takes a few steps toward me. Sola seems on edge as Zoran drinks me in. I find the concentration of his stare unnerving to the point that I feel like I'm in danger, and when he speaks, it sounds like soft thunder.

"When you're able, you should go." A small drop of saliva leaks from the side of his mouth, and if it weren't for Sola, I'd feel unsafe this close to him. I'm confused as to what's caused such a sudden shift in his demeanor and I grow even more unsettled when I see his muscles tense like he's fighting back the starved predator he appears to be becoming. "Things are more complicated now."

My instincts tell me I can't hide from him, nor he from me. "It's because of my blood?"

He sends a cold glance toward Sola before speaking. "It never should have happened."

My mind races as Sola retorts, "It had to."

Zoran's silence tells me he knows Sola's argument is sound, and he continues, defeated, as if speaking to himself. "My redemption was almost—"

Sola counters while Zoran takes another step toward me. "Zoran, this isn't the time."

His fur grazes my skin, and in that moment, I'm able to see inside him. Flickering images rush into my mind, fractured pieces of his thoughts—all of them of me: my pale skin, the vein pumping in my neck, blood leaking from my finger, the taste of me—each coursing through his consciousness.

Looking at Sola, he speaks in a tone bordering on anger. "It should've been 'Forgiveness before bond.'"

"And even in reverse, it will come. But for now, there are other priorities."

At her insistence, I feel him trying to shut me out and shield his thoughts, but it's too late. I already know what he seeks to hide. Feeling his shame as though it were my own, I place my full palm on his chest and read the unbridled regret he feels for the life I now know he took. The buried darkness of his past indiscretion filters through my scorching hand and travels up my arm like a fire-skinned snake.

Unable to bear the pain any longer, I pull my hand away and watch sadness fill his eyes.

"At my lowest point and in my deepest shame, Prayna was a friend to me. Without her light, I would have been lost to darkness."

Although I'm no longer touching him, I feel the vacancy Prayna's death has left. Before I can inquire further, I'm stopped by the sound of the door opening at the end of the passageway.

A muffled female voice echoes into the room. "I've helped Zoran because my sister asked me to. But seeing them together tonight, the way he looks at her—they're dangerous." By the screeching feel of her presence, I know the voice belongs to Arvada, the razor-thin woman from the hall. A male voice attempts to break in but is cut off by the woman's continuing tirade. "Those Shadows are my responsibility. She had no business connecting with them. If our future is in the hands of that woman, we've no hope. If Zoran hadn't kept me from reading her days ago, I could have told you that—"

"You can't be certain."

"Yes, I can. I felt it. If there's one thing I know, it's someone's Shadow."

Again, he attempts to allay her rising ire. "Arvada, everyone has darkness."

"Not like hers. It's almost shameful how far she's strayed from the path of her bloodline."

Heavy footsteps drop like bricks down the passageway, the scent of pre-rain wafting into the room and informing me it's Daegan who approaches. When he enters, Sola and I are already on our feet.

Daegan notices the copper medallion around Sola's neck, and when his gaze drifts to the violet sphere suspended in the corner, there's no denying the grief in his eyes. With his tattoos swirling at his temples, he wrangles himself into a commander's composure. "Zoë, wait for me in the hall."

I do as he's asked. But halfway down the passageway, I halt in my tracks, unable to bring myself to face the Shadows alone.

Turning back toward the room, I catch Daegan's gaze as he waits for me to be out of earshot. I beg my feet to carry me toward the door, yet they fight me with every step, my toes gripping the floor in an apparent protest to stop any forward movement.

Reaching the door, I open it and put one foot into the empty hall while my other foot holds the panel door open, one adamant toe refusing to commit to entering the cavernous room. I scan the empty hall in every direction, wondering where the Shadows have gone, and it's not until I feel a cool hand on my arm that I realize they've merged into the walls. The Shadow holding my arm pokes a translucent head out from a painted forest scene on the wall, setting off a chain reaction whereby thousands of heads thrust out from the walls around the room.

Watching the Shadows half submerged, I realize they are living inside the painted scenes, inhabitants of the oil-colored worlds embedded in each panel. The little Shadow next to me has part of its body pressed inside a painted forest cabin, and I find the sight of it residing within a flat, imaginary home disturbing.

Daegan's hushed voice drifts down the passageway and trickles through the crack in the door. "Prayna gave you her medallion?"

"Yes."

"One of you should have come to me."

Sola explains, "The Shadows connected with her. There was no time. We had no choice but to bring them here."

Zoran weighs in. "It hasn't been like this since the Great Battle."

"How's he doing it?" Daegan queries.

"He can materialize now. Not fully, but enough to—"

Daegan interrupts, "How is he getting blood?"

"Through Ronan." Zoran's voice pierces the air as he asserts, "You can't let her go back to the Thirteenth."

Even through the door, I sense the contention between them as Daegan responds, "You and I just discussed this. She's of free will. I can't keep her here."

"I'm going back with her," Zoran asserts.

"That is not the role we decided you'd play—"

"Things have changed. It's far more dangerous for her now."

"I understand the gravity of the situation."

Again, Zoran pushes. "She needs me, and only me. You know that."

"The last time I placed my faith in you, it was a grave disappointment."

"The identical is true for me, where you're concerned," Zoran snaps.

The loaded silence between them skulks down the passageway toward me until Zoran breaks the silence. "I would never harm her."

Daegan's tone is fierce as he fires back, "There is no greater damage you can do to her than what you've already done."

The scent of pre-rain whips down the passageway, and in reaction, I close the door and move off to the right. The little Shadow holding my arm ducks back into its painted cabin, causing the other Shadows to merge into the surrounding walls.

Daegan opens the door, his gaze meeting mine as he leads me across the hall's checkered floors. Yet absent is the usual thump of his lionlike heartbeat. Instead, his pulse is faint, almost beating in delay, as though the impact of Prayna's death has threatened to stop his heart.

My ache for her surfaces and meets his in a silent, commiserative embrace. I'm comforted by his sturdy hand on the small of my back but am only half his, seeing as part of me still lingers at the precipice of Zoran's fiery presence. They are like the interlinking black and white tiles beneath my feet, and I, the grey mortar keeping their sharp edges from slicing into one other.

We're almost at the tunnel's entrance, and I find myself wanting to leave the hall. I can't wait to feel the winter air against my skin and need the moonlight to cleanse my cells of this forsaken musty Underworld. But when I step into the tunnel, my legs give out. I'm too tired to continue, my body in flat-out revolt against further exertion, and with my eyelids growing heavy, I feel like my skeleton is made of concrete.

Daegan props me against the tunnel wall and puts my face in his hands, but I'm only able to focus on him for a few seconds before my sight degrades into a blurred haze. Then I feel him take me in his arms and lean me forward into his chest until the side of my face is pressed against him. Unable to keep unconsciousness at bay any longer, I succumb to blackness.

44

MANHATTAN, UP

Zoë wrestled herself into a sitting position, eyes stinging from the morning light, then turned toward the bedside table and stared at the neon numbers glaring back at her:

11:11 a.m.

Time had become an unruly companion, wearing down the threads of her hand-stitched world until the fabric-come-skin of her existence was being unraveled from either side by two sparring forces: her dreams and her reality. Feeling the duvet beneath her fingertips, she rubbed a small section of the plush cloth between her thumb and forefinger as though the woven material could somehow repair her own threadbare, velveteen world.

Seeing her mother's journal lying open next to her, she was about to skim its artful prose when she noticed a few paragraphs of curled red script on an adjacent ivory page and realized it was her own handwriting. Although her mind was already tossing around ways in which to reject the writing, a telltale red ink stain on her index finger made her authorship impossible to refute.

Zoë scanned her alien words, then surrendered to the peculiar experience of reading private thoughts that seemed to have written themselves until the sound of her phone chirping forced her focus to the bedside table.

After retrieving her phone, she read the calendar reminders:

Giulianna Xu, 21 Club @ Noon
Dr. Lawson @ 2 p.m.

She hurried out of bed, washed her face, brushed her teeth, and readied herself in record time. Before rushing out the bedroom door, she grabbed her mother's journal, intent on investigating the phantom entry with Dr. Lawson.

Rushing down the stairs toward the foyer, she heard Lula bellowing from the kitchen, "Zoë—"

"I'm late."

Lula tromped into the foyer, eyed Zoë, and pointed to her round cheek. "Kiss."

"Lula, I'm not twelve." She planted a ruby-stained kiss on Lula's cheek.

Lula put both hands on Zoë's face. "You're a vision."

After untangling herself from Lula, she hurried to the front door. As she opened it, a blast of cold air almost knocked her over, the wintry wind a fierce reminder that she'd forgotten to put on a coat.

Turning back toward the foyer, she found Lula holding her black cashmere coat. "You'd be lost without me."

Putting the coat on, Zoë replied, "Bye."

After leaving the house, she sped down the stairs and rushed to the edge of the sidewalk, the bitter cold nipping at her fingers as she shot her hand into the air and hailed an oncoming cab.

She jumped in, closed the door, and leaned back against the grey leather seat, intent on relaying her destination. Yet now in the cab, her voice wouldn't leave the safety of her throat. The thought of meeting Giulianna Xu, or rather, of anything that reminded her of Evan, felt too weighty to endure.

The cabbie glared at her through the rearview mirror. "Hey, lady—"

"Sorry. Fifty-Second between Fifth and Sixth."

Looking out the window while the cab pulled forward, she stared at the dark clouds moving in overhead. Rolling down the window a crack, she could smell the coming storm. When a wisp of its icy draft bustled into the back seat and sent a chill up into her nasal passages, she felt the storm's snowy fingers lingering at the entry point to her brain.

Zoë attempted to bury the nagging hesitation that coming face-to-face with Evan's memory might unearth him from the graveyard inside her, a blood-and-bone-constructed resting place for those she held most dear. So palpable was the vision, she could see the carved tombstones marking their graves, black script etched by her own hand; her private stony words to Evan, her mother, and—real or dream-borne—her skeleton-gated cemetery's newest inhabitant, Prayna.

As the cab turned onto Fifty-Second Street, she spotted the colorful jockeys lining the wrought-iron railings of the 21 Club. Like being at the entrance to a frightening carnival ride, she felt her chest growing tight, knowing it had been twenty years since she was here with Evan. When a vivid memory of his kiss flooded her senses, she realized it was a kiss without equal and one she'd give anything to feel again.

"You getting out?" The driver stared at her with a mixture of annoyance and concern, making her wonder how long she'd been sitting in the motionless cab lost in thought. Running her card through the machine, she paid, then forced her unstable legs out of the taxi and onto the bound solidity of her stilettos.

After closing the door, she watched the taxi speed away, which somehow left her feeling uneasy. Shifting her gaze up toward the angry, storm-grey sky, she became starkly aware of being trapped between it and the smooth cement beneath her feet.

Shifting her focus from the swarming clouds overhead, she walked down the club's painted grass-green steps and entered the restaurant, where a well-dressed gentleman greeted her. "How can I help you?"

"I'm meeting someone."

"Certainly. I'll show you to the lounge."

She followed him into a wood-paneled room, where he led her to a red wingback chair in front of the fireplace.

"May I offer you anything to drink?"

Intent on ordering a glass of wine, she was surprised that what left her lips was the drink Evan would have ordered. "Manhattan, up. No cherry."

The man watched her for a moment, then responded, "Your cocktail should be along shortly. May I take your coat?"

"Yes, thank you."

She handed her coat to him, then sat and leaned against the chair's firm back. The man folded her coat over his arm as though it were woven from black diamond threads before walking away and leaving her in the solitary company of the room's flame-filled mahogany fireplace.

Letting the fire's warmth radiate through the hard soles of her shoes to the balls of her feet, she stared at the circumference of her heels and wished for a moment they were wider, stronger, and better equipped to stand upon the shallow graves inside her.

A tall, slim waiter appeared from thin air, his Ichabod Crane–like appearance capturing her attention as he handed her a flawless crafted drink. "Manhattan, up. No cherry."

The glass felt like it was carved from ice, and when she let her fingers rest on its cold, slippery exterior, she stared at the fiery orange liquid inside, knowing it would soothe her nerves.

"Thank you."

The man smiled, then left the room.

As she was about to take her first sip, she looked up at the sound of several glasses clinking, then felt her skin grow hot upon seeing Mr. Llewellyn sitting in an adjacent room watching her. Always impeccably dressed, he wore his pinstriped three-piece suit to perfection, all the while sending pulses of electric current toward her from across the room, each one landing like a splash of raw lust in her drink.

Taking a lengthy and lingering sip, she watched Mr. Llewellyn over the rim of her frosty martini glass and thought that if she didn't know what she knew about him, he'd be the most tempting man in the room.

Feigning disinterest, his focus drifted away from her and back to the two men next to him.

"Ms. Hall?"

Zoë shifted her focus toward a petite Asian woman standing beside her. The woman's flawless round face was framed by a black bob that made her look like a china doll in the flesh. The tailored navy skirt suit she wore gave her slate-colored eyes a strange bluish quality.

"Giulianna Xu."

As they shook hands, Zoë studied the woman's face, certain she'd seen her somewhere before. Ms. Xu withdrew her hand, and before sitting, sent a steady gaze toward Mr. Llewellyn in a manner that suggested they knew one another.

After calling the waiter over and settling into her chair, Ms. Xu crossed her legs and a line of crystals dotting the backs of her sky-high heels caught the firelight.

The waiter reappeared. "Madam?"

Ms. Xu ordered without even looking at him, removing a fat envelope from her briefcase. "Scotch. Neat." She thumbed through the papers inside, ensuring everything was in order.

Behind her, Mr. Llewellyn stood and shook hands with the two men. Zoë listened to bits of their goodbyes as the men smiled in celebratory spirit. "I can't believe you've finally sold something. You've mergered and acquisitioned half of Manhattan!"

All three men laughed as the maître d' brought their coats. Although schmoozing, Mr. Llewellyn seemed uncomfortable with Zoë's presence. Flashing a kind smile, he continued chatting with one of the men, and while observing him, she was surprised at how charming he could be, considering that he was a rigid ball of moodiness when he reached her house at the end of the day.

Once Mr. Llewellyn had exited the room, Zoë shifted her focus back to Ms. Xu, who placed the envelope facedown on a drop table between their chairs. She was about to inquire as to its contents when the waiter returned and handed Ms. Xu a perfect glass of scotch. "May I offer you anything else?"

"We're fine, thank you."

The waiter nodded and left the room as Ms. Xu raised her glass and drained her drink.

"You said it was important that we meet."

Ms. Xu put down her empty glass and retrieved the envelope from the table, revealing its block-lettered label: BLACK ESTATE. Zoë felt one of the graves stir inside her, a bit of its earth now displaced, and as a result, she pressed the heels of her shoes deeper into the soft wood floor.

Ms. Xu handed her the envelope. "I'm assuming you have an attorney?"

"Yes."

"Please, review these and let me know if you have any questions."

The label's large, bold-type BLACK ESTATE was invading her peripheral vision as Ms. Xu continued. "Evan thought quite highly of you and would like you to take a more active role in his affairs. This packet will explain everything."

A set of dirt-encrusted fingers pushed through the coffin-like floor and seemed to wrap around the top of Zoë's foot.

Ms. Xu handed her a business card and was about to speak when a slithery, heavily cologned man entered the room. "Ms. Xu, you should've called. I'd have given you a private room."

"The lounge is fine. It was a last-minute meeting. You're well?"

The man smiled, his veneers cartoonish, like Chiclets in their whiteness. "Very. Please thank Mr. Black for loaning us the painting from his collection."

Ms. Xu shot Zoë a quick glance before replying, "Apparently, you haven't been informed, Marcus. Mr. Black passed away."

Zoë swore she could see an invisible wrecking ball hitting the man's face as his gleaming smile dimmed to nothing. "I had no idea. We were very fond of him. My deepest condolences."

"I appreciate that. Thank you."

An awkward smile crept along the man's ChapSticked lips as he nodded to each of them, then walked away.

Ms. Xu's china-doll face tensed as she glanced up and to the right. Zoë followed her gaze to a small painting above the fireplace mantel, and before commanding her body to do so, she was standing and walking toward it.

Studying the painting's scenery, a familiar landscape from her dreams, she couldn't stop her mind from racing. While attempting to conceal the effect the painting had on her, she asked, "How long will this be on loan to the club?"

Ms. Xu answered, "Until the end of the month."

Forcing herself away from the painting, Zoë returned to her chair. "May I speak frankly?"

Dipping her chin, Ms. Xu urged, "Please."

"I have no desire to be involved in the day-to-day workings of Evan's company." Feeling cold fingers clawing at the top of her foot, threatening to disentomb the corpse they belonged to, she shoved her toes hard against the front of her shoe.

Ms. Xu clarified. "I'll be running the company. What is being asked of you is of a more personal nature."

Her comment set Zoë's thoughts spinning until, as if they'd been banished, the skeletal fingers clutching her foot loosened and retreated back into the floor.

"All the details are in the envelope."

The two women watched one another while Zoë's mind turned her thick thoughts into words. "I hope I'm not being too forward, Ms. Xu—"

"Please, call me Giulianna."

"May I borrow the painting for a few days?"

"Of course. Technically, you own it."

"Pardon?"

"You're the sole beneficiary of Evan's personal estate, which includes his art collection. I'll arrange everything and have the painting delivered to you this afternoon." She smiled. "You have similar tastes."

"How do you mean?"

Ms. Xu's gaze flicked up toward the painting. "She was one of Mr. Black's favorite artists."

Zoë felt her pulse begin to race. "Does he have other paintings of hers?"

"No. This one is supposedly part of a triptych, but Evan was never able to locate the other two."

Feeling disappointed, Zoë offered, "I appreciate your arranging for me to have the painting."

"You'll contact me once you've sorted through everything?"

"Yes."

The waiter entered the room. "Ms. Xu, may I get you another round?"

"We're fine. Put everything on the house account."

The maître d' walked over with their coats and helped them into their cashmere cocoons one at a time while the spicy scent of Ms. Xu's perfume drifted from her coat and stung the inside of Zoë's nose.

The waiter handed Ms. Xu a leather-bound bill, which she signed before gathering her briefcase from the floor.

"Ready?"

Zoë nodded, put the envelope in her purse, then followed Ms. Xu out of the club, up the stairs, and onto the sidewalk. Ms. Xu walked toward a black Mercedes and opened the door. "It was lovely to finally meet you."

For some reason, the word *finally* left Zoë feeling troubled, but she reciprocated with the necessary pleasantries. "Likewise."

Ms. Xu held Zoë's gaze for a moment. "The painting should arrive this afternoon." After stepping into the car, she closed the door and disappeared behind the window's midnight-tinted glass.

Zoë watched the Mercedes drive away, leaving her alone beneath the storm-grey sky while small, jagged flakes fell from above, each one landing on her like a mirrored cluster of tiny blades. Unable to pinpoint why she felt anxious, she let her thoughts drift to the memory of the painting as Mr. Sumel's premonition about the paintings replayed in her mind: "They'll find you." And, in fact, they had.

Feeling her phone vibrate in her pocket, she retrieved it and read the incoming text message from Lula: "POD wants to see you tonight."

She would see him, the Prince of Darkness. Welcoming a chance to re-pay him for their last exchange, she'd exact two proverbial strikes with one sword, coaxing him to reveal what, if anything, he knew about Giulianna Xu.

Taking in a deep breath, she reminded herself that Evan must have trusted Ms. Xu, seeing as he'd left his estate in her care. Yet something didn't feel right. Ms. Xu was excessively smooth, like a perfectly drawn character on an artist's page: realistic, but fabricated nonetheless.

45

WIRED

D r. Lawson adjusted his glasses before sitting down and focusing on Zoë. Stormy-eyed, she watched him, then crossed her long legs and settled into his chair.

This was the second session in which she'd chosen to seat herself in what was customarily his chair, a move to dethrone him from his kingly perch, but he would remain unruffled. The power thrusting from her shot around the room as she examined the contents of the bookshelf behind him.

Judging from her appearance, it was difficult to detect the vulnerability he sensed beneath her impeccable window-display exterior, as she never entered his office without bright-red paint emblazoning her lips. Part of him wondered if it was an everyday occurrence or a subconscious message to remind him, "Danger: Live Wire."

Yet beneath her steely, poised demeanor was a nurturing presence; there was something comforting about her. Not to mention the obvious, un-apologetic, raw sensuality that seeped from every pore of her body, which made it easy to understand why a man would engage her company—and pay to do so.

Focusing his thoughts, Dr. Lawson held her gaze while thinking that her willingness to let him read the letter from her former lover, Evan, had opened an opportunity for him to explore a few of his hunches. But the key question was whether that opportunity remained.

"May I ask about your relationship with Evan?"

The loose wire shot around the room, throwing sparks and dancing close to his face as it did so. His leather chair appeared to smolder beneath Zoë's supple frame as she tapered her gaze. "All right."

Feeling he had only one shot, one question he could ask, he let his mind circle the sparking wire of her stare while choosing his words. "When and how did your relationship with Evan end?"

The wire ceased to spark and dropped to the floor as a bulb in the lamp next to him popped and went dark. Zoë turned her head and looked out the window. "Five years ended by two lines. 'My love for you is stronger than ever, but I've promised to let you go. I am always with you.'"

"A letter?"

"With a stack of stock certificates and a phone number." She fidgeted with a bracelet on her wrist.

"To whom did the phone number belong?"

"A man named J.T. He was a financial advisor, and, sort of by accident, my first client."

"Did you and Evan ever—"

"I never saw him again."

As she pulled her gaze from the window, the wire lit a blazing red and flew from the floor, signifying that this portion of their conversation was over.

"Can you dream while you're awake?" she asked.

A surge pulsed through him. "Yes. There's a phenomenon called wake-initiated lucid dreaming, or WILD. It occurs when the dreamer goes from a normal waking state directly into a dream state with no apparent lapse in consciousness."

"How real would these dreams feel?"

"It depends on the individual."

After a moment, she inquired, "Experientially, could they alter your reality?"

"In rare cases, I suppose."

After seeming to mull over his answer, she pressed further. "So, it could seem to a person that they were actually somewhere else."

"It could. Yes."

Her mind appeared to be working—on what, he wasn't sure—but the visible heartbeat pounding at the side of her neck was telling him far more than she was.

Softening his voice, he suggested, "Keeping a journal could help ground you. It can provide clues as to what needs to be addressed."

Zoë pulled something from her purse and placed it in her lap. It looked like a journal, but that was too much to hope for. She opened it, flipping to a marked page before leaning forward and handing it to him.

The wire flew around the room, sparking and crackling as she settled back into her, or rather *his* chair. Feeling his face flush, he looked down at the curled red script and read to himself:

> *Charles Dickens said: "No one is useless in this world who lightens the burdens of another."*
>
> *I believe I lighten their burdens, Mother. I believe I carry for them the weight their own souls cannot bear. My modalities may make Mr. Dickens blush, but the ends justify the means.*
>
> *So, I sit, rosy-cheeked and bulging with the burdens of others, I stuff myself with their wantings in the hope that—*

Her writing stopped, as if she'd left a beautifully prepared meal uncooked and unserved. He reread the passage several times, then met Zoë's gaze. "Why did you stop writing?"

"I don't know." Staring at her bracelet, she continued. "You honestly believe that participating in my dreams will be a useful exercise?"

"I do. Wholeheartedly. It's a magnifying glass into your psyche."

She looked out the window again, and in that moment, he wanted to look through her eyes and see whatever it was outside that comforted her.

Thirty-five minutes remained in their session, but they had yet to ever go a full hour. He knew she was done, ready to put him away in the closet like a piece of clothing until she wanted to wear him again. "I have no problem with us ending early."

Pulling her focus from the window, she spoke. "Thank you."

He returned the journal to her, their hands brushing as she took it from him with the utmost care. The wire danced around his face, now without its danger sign, searching him, looking for a place to repair its frayed ends.

Staying seated, he watched as she stood and walked past the unlit lamp next to him. He heard his door open, and after a long pause, her pale hand came over the back of his chair. He took her hand, holding it for a moment before feeling her let go and leave his office without a word.

46

OUT OF OZ

Staring at the painting Ms. Xu had sent over from the 21 Club, Zoë couldn't wait to have time alone with it. Taking in every brushstroke of its dreamscape, she wondered if she was indeed still entrenched in a dream, as it was the only way the painting's landscape—one she had been in before—made any sense.

Dr. Lawson's words mixed with her thoughts. "WILD, wake-initiated lucid dreaming..."

Lula instructed, "Exhale."

Zoë shifted her focus away from the painting and pushed the air from her lungs while Lula yanked the laces of her pale peach corset outward. Gripping the bedpost, she held her breath as Lula went about reducing her midriff to the size of a music box ballerina's.

Half of her mind was processing the idea that her real and dream lives were separated by a cellophane-thin wall, while the other pondered how her consciousness seemed to be working against her, behaving wildly in both the literal and acronymic sense. The anxiety it aroused felt like a coiling rattlesnake in the pit of her stomach.

After one last tug, Lula's nimble fingers tied off the corset laces and tucked away the stray ends. Taking in a deep breath, Zoë felt her lungs constrict against the corset's unyielding grip. Yet she was grateful to be bound, the silk and boned armor encircling her waist confining, even suffocating, the snake twisting inside her.

Lula turned Zoë around and inspected every inch of her corseted frame before draping a silk robe over her shoulders. "You're a vision." The doorbell chimed and Lula's body tensed. "Sure you're up for him tonight?"

"Yes."

After eyeing Zoë, Lula left the room and closed the door without a word.

Now alone with the painting, Zoë felt it was speaking to her and demanding that she reunite it with the others so that they might live in triptych harmony. Stepping closer, as though pulled in by the color-stroked fingers of the vibrant scene, she again studied the canvas in detail, recalling the incomplete meadow of the center painting she had received from Mr. Sumel and how it looked like someone was walking off the canvas into the missing painting beside it. With the last painting of the triptych now in her possession, the meadow was complete, and she could see the identity of the person in question. It was her.

Even in profile, her features were a flawless duplicate of those of her living flesh, a version of her likeness in perfect, pigmented form, and standing beside her was her midnight-tainted beast, Zoran. The landscape was so real that she could almost detect the faint floral scent of the meadow drifting from the fibers of the canvas. She wanted to study the painting further, but hearing the door to her bedroom open, she stood and turned toward Mr. Llewellyn, who entered in a deliberate, focused manner.

Still clad in the pinstriped three-piece suit from earlier, he walked toward her carrying a red shopping bag. Moving away from the painting and sitting on the edge of the bed, she watched him make his way across the room, noticing that the usual moodiness residing beneath his expensive suit was nonexistent, or at the very least on temporary leave. Stopping in front of her, he placed the bag in her lap, its color matching the shade of her lips and his tie to perfection in a fiery trinity.

Zoë opened the bag and removed a shoebox, then opened it. Inside was a pair of the exact shoes she'd seen Ms. Xu wearing at their meeting earlier, only hers had been navy while Zoë's were covered in ruby satin with a fine line of red crystals along the back seam.

Feeling the intensity of Mr. Llewellyn's stare, she met his gaze. Even through the thick wool of his suit, she could see his breath quicken as he loosened his tie. "Put them on."

As instructed, she removed her nude satin shoes one at a time before stepping into the exquisitely constructed platforms. Still sitting on the edge of the bed, her feet burrowed into the restraints of what looked like flame-blown glass slippers. She watched him staring at her, his scarlet-footed muse, while his facial expression bordered on worship. It was an exalted state she'd accept, seeing as a man living such a confined life, a self-proclaimed king of his own mounted kingdom, needed an oceanic Venus to crash into his shores and level the throne upon which he'd become rooted.

Appearing compelled to eliminate any form of barrier between them, he unbuttoned his vest. She wondered how much exposure he'd allow; they'd been together for a year and she'd yet to see him naked, let alone feel his bare skin against hers. A restriction of his choice, the result of a self-imposed exile from intimacy, had left them an unconsummated pair: They were the sun and the moon, never visible in the sky at the same time.

She continued watching him undress, his hands smooth and strong as he unfastened the buttons of his starched white shirt. The closer he came to freeing himself from the boundaries of his clothes, the more intense his breathing became.

The sound of his deepening breath sent an electric current through her, one she sought to quell. Sensing the heat building inside him, she shifted her gaze upward and rested her attention on the vein in his neck, which pulsed with the flow of his rushing blood.

He opened his shirt, eased it over his shoulders, and let it fall to the floor. Bare-chested, his armor disassembled and removed, he appeared willing to sacrifice his well-established façade.

Readying to stand, she shifted her weight, feeling the ruby shoes grip her feet.

"Don't move."

After moving closer, he knelt and ran both hands down her calves until his fingers found the peeking arch of her platform-clad foot. Closing his eyes, he lowered his head and kissed the tops of her thighs before moving down toward her knees, then her calves.

The room felt hot and the featherlight brush of his lips only served to raise the temperature further. Feeling his soft mouth and tongue along her skin, she watched him exhibit an eroticism she'd thought him incapable of possessing.

After kissing each of her ankles, he lowered himself to the floor and rested his head on the tops of her feet. The king, before his Venus, was now dethroned, living only for the satisfaction he hoped she could provide.

He kissed the arch of her foot, then ran his tongue up toward the inside of her ankle. Watching him caress and mouth her ivory skin, she found it hard to imagine the violence she'd suffered at his hand on their last encounter.

Wrapping his hands around her heels, he stroked the edges of the shoes where her skin was pressed tightest against the satin. Feeling her bound feet, he let out a rough moan, and with his mouth poised open, she felt he might actually bite her.

Keeping his head at her feet, he rotated his body until he was lying stomach-down and parallel to the edge of the bed. He lifted one of her feet and placed her sharp, dangerous heel on his upper back. With her right foot still on the floor above his head and her left jabbing into the skin below his neck, he was reduced to a fleshy footrest, one that wanted nothing more than to feel the weight of her unforgiving heels.

Forcing her left heel deeper into his skin caused his cheek to press harder against the hardwood floor, and she watched the heat from his breath form a small, steamy circle on the wood's glossy surface. Unable to control the rush of heat within her, she removed her robe and propped both feet in the middle of his back, letting them rest against his skin with the teasing promise of both pressure and pain.

The firelight was reflecting on the surface of his skin, making it seem as if the soles of her shoes were resting atop hot coals that were all but daring her to walk across them. As if echoing the challenge, he arched his back up against her feet until she thrust both heels into his back.

Supporting herself with the thick bedpost, she stood, then rocked back into the heel of each shoe. The look on his face was one of undeniable ecstasy, yet it was impossible for her to comprehend how he was managing the pain.

She moved toward his tailbone on delicate tiptoe, putting one foot in front of the other as though strolling along a precarious, fleshy sidewalk. Feeling his breathing grow heavier, she let more of her weight press into his lower back before pivoting on one foot and walking back up his spine. Upon reaching his shoulder blade, she dug a ruby heel into the bone, and in response, he gripped the bottom of the bedpost with both hands.

At the top of his back, inches from his neck, she picked up her left foot and rotated on the ball of her right toe, preparing to amble toward his clenched backside. Her left heel had yet to come down, but the anticipation of its piercing arrival drove him mad, and in that moment, they were equally roused, him wanting to feel the maiming, her wanting to deliver it.

She let her left heel find a home in his rosy flesh before walking down his spine. Her steps were deliberate and cruel in their lingering, heavy-heeled gait, and at the small of his back, she lifted her foot and let her heel linger just above his skin before pivoting on her toe and readying for another pass up his now-bloodied back.

Taking a deep, puncturing step, she heard his breathing become harder, hastier, as though on the verge of sexual detonation. Putting both feet down, she rocked back into her heels with all her weight until his mouth opened and he let out a guttural moan.

Rocking back a second time, she was hell-bent on repeating her ruby-footed daggery, and as blood seeped around the edges of her heel marks, the sight of her bloody imprints caused her skin to flush with heat. She walked up his back again, this time releasing her hands from the bedpost and letting her unsupported weight bear down on his skin, her pinup figure nimble as she navigated his spine-turned-tightrope, her corset the costume of a bloody ballerina balancing on the thin line of his vertebrae in what had become their private, macabre circus.

Trying to suppress the fire rising inside her, Zoë felt it grotesque to be growing more aroused during an act of such calculated viciousness, but as his moans deepened, she couldn't stop herself from becoming charged. Making her way toward his upper back, she watched his body stiffen with the tension of impending release, all the while her body mirroring his desire, a transference rising through the ruby props he'd bought for her wanton and gruesome performance.

Despite all their sessions, she'd yet to see him climax, and with him so close, she was determined to inflict all the pain necessary to push him over the edge, as the more discomfort she caused, the more bloodletting at her hand, the deeper his plunge toward release.

The walk down his back was treacherous, the tightrope of his spine marred with sweat and blood and the air so hot she could barely breathe. With each step, his moans became uncontrollable, his body trembling beneath her feet.

Hearing his quickening breath and knowing that pleasure was overtaking him, she stepped down from his back, wanting to be near the sweetness of his release. When she turned him over, he grabbed her shoulders as his stomach muscles began contracting.

Opening his belt and ripping down the clothing that stood between her and the release that had taken nearly a year, she watched the last of successive convulsions gripping him until she, too, longed to unleash. With her hands on his underclothes, she was set to remove them when he clutched her wrists. "Please. Don't—"

Watching his back arch and hearing the sound of his climax, she ignored his plea and pulled down his underwear. His cries of pleasure traded places with those of anguish as the lifeless, truncated flesh between his legs released. As he tried to cover himself, she moved his hands away. "You don't have to hide from me."

Lying down beside him, she took his mutilated flesh in her hand and bathed her fingers in its white blood while letting her lips brush the side of his face. It was just the two of them, his burden lightened, a toy soldier beyond repair but cherished nonetheless. She stroked him, each of her fingers seeking to remove, if only in part, the emotional and psychological barriers he'd built to encase the shame his impediment had caused.

The pungent scent of iron filled the air; the hardwood floor beneath them was marked with the stains of his blood, the stairway to his release a vicious and cutting ascension.

"I was told I could never—"

Cradling his flesh in her hand, she kissed his cheek. He made more sense to her now: a crusader after the storm of his own gratification, lightning that would only strike from her skies. Even with his considerable power and prestige, he was incomplete, the hope of his wholeness solely resting in her hands.

Both of their bodies were growing heavy, sinking into the floor as if the wood were soft earth, until the scent of pine and cedar floated through her senses and lulled them both toward needed sleep.

47

IN VEIN

awake to the sound of the wind outside howling as if
seeking to coax me from my coma-like sleep. Forcing my
eyes open, I attempt to focus on my blurred surroundings while waiting
for my vision to regain full clarity.

Beneath me is a layer of soft fur lining a mattress that feels like a cluster
of clouds have been knitted together to form a heaven-ready bed. After a
moment, my sight sharpens and I take in the paper-thin fabric panels that
are draped around me like a tented canopy.

Raising my head, I look through the gaps in the panels toward a fire
raging in an inset copper-plated fireplace beyond the foot of the bed, which
adds to the wind's faint cry with a series of percussive pops. A tufted leather
chair sits to the right of the fireplace, and although it is empty, I feel the
weighted thoughts of its owner as though they've been left behind by a
person too burdened to continue carrying them. The scents of cedar and
pine permeate the air, and as I study this large, circular, one-room cabin,
I find it familiar.

Hearing a bottle being uncorked, I look to the far left and see Sola and

Nikolai standing in front of a thin floor-to-ceiling cabinet while Nikolai pours milky white liquid out of a long-necked bottle. "I don't feel right about this."

Sola takes the bottle and sets it down on the cabinet's small counter, then turns to face him as she pulls up his sleeve and examines his skin. "We don't have a choice."

Even from across the room, I can see the jet-black veins in his hand and forearm; it looks as though an alien-like substance has invaded his bloodstream. He speaks in an almost defeated tone. "Lukaes has never been this strong, this bold…"

His voice trails off as if he's unable to finish his sentence, and Sola caresses the side of his face and reassures him. "He underestimates you."

"I can't ask her to do this."

"With a bloodline in common, the risks are minimal," Sola counters.

Nikolai pulls his hand away before turning back toward the cabinet. Watching him mix several liquids into a small glass bowl, Sola continues. "Once you're joined, she can see." He stops mixing as she hesitates to complete her thought. "Just be mindful."

Nikolai turns to look at her, and they are both shrouded in disquiet as the wind outside ceases to howl and falls prey to the silence gripping the room. They break their stare and walk toward the bed.

Feeling guilty at having eavesdropped on their conversation, I close my eyes and pretend to sleep. Yet after having seen the effect my blood had on Nikolai in the Blacksmith's shop, I have little doubt they're seeking the same remedy, one which I'll provide, seeing as for reasons I don't understand, I want to help him.

My regard isn't a romantic interest, but rather a kind of kindred-spirit connection. I know that Nikolai suffers and, to that end, as seems to be my custom, I cannot refuse the reprieve my blood offers—to me, the risks seem nil. What harm can come from a good deed performed within the confines of a dream?

My thoughts are interrupted by the potency of Sola's honey-rose perfume as she sits beside me. I open my eyes and see Nikolai easing down on the bed next to her, both of them focused on me in a manner I find disconcerting.

"What I'm about to ask is—"

I interrupt him. "I know."

Nikolai takes my hand in his, and when I look down, I try to hide my revulsion at his veins, which are thick and pulsating, like black tentacles may rip through his skin. "Are you sure?"

My hand aching from being in contact with his, I confirm. "Yes."

After getting up, Nikolai crosses to the cabinet while, without a word, Sola leans down and kisses me. However platonic her intention, I feel the heat of her lips throughout my body like a controlled fire. Pulling away, she lets her gaze meet mine, and I see how much my willingness to help means to her.

She takes my forearm and lays it in her lap, stroking my skin as Nikolai returns with the small glass bowl. Sitting beside me on the bed, he takes a paste-like mixture and draws two parallel lines on my wrist. Once in contact with my skin, the paste turns a deep, almost brownish black as my fingers curl inward until I'm making a tight fist.

He exchanges a quick glance with Sola before taking a knife from his belt and puncturing a small hole inside the lines he's just drawn on my wrist.

Sola places her hand on my forehead and whispers, "Close your eyes."

I do as instructed, then take a deep breath while falling into a trancelike state. My body, or rather, my consciousness, drifts into a cloudy grey room where eight colored glass panes are floating midair, stacked on top of one another like suspended, frameless windows.

Although only tangentially, I become aware of my physical form upon feeling an intense pressure on my forearm. The sound of rushing blood floods my ears like my veins have converged into one living river leading into and out of the pinprick opening in my wrist.

My awareness glides back into the cloudy room, but rather than being alone, I am with Nikolai. Both of us are fixated on a thin beam of light shooting down through the stacked panes like a single sun-infused ray has been aimed from above for the sole purpose of turning the room into a kaleidoscope of dancing, prismatic light.

The layers of glass grow deeper in color, each shade seeming to correspond to an element, with the sixth pane solid black and covered in a smoky film that ebbs and flows along its surface.

Nikolai takes my hand and leads me across the room until we're in front of the panes. Raising our hands, he places my palm, then his, on the black glass as thousands of images whiz through my thoughts, until everything slows and focuses on an image of Nikolai's face. Growing larger as if merging into the very tissues of my physical brain, the picture pixelates and gives way to a scene of a young boy I sense is Nikolai.

As though we're one, I feel the steady, rhythmic pumping of the blood in his veins—blood that will soon be cleansed and purified by our current union. The synergy of this experience is ours, and I recognize it's an interaction to which we must both submit wholly and without prejudice. I know this to be true as if it were projected onto the surface of my spirit. Without an unadulterated willingness to share our blood, our souls, Nikolai is in danger of being engulfed by the darkness I feel stalking the edges of his being.

Nikolai is ill at rest, and both of our pulses race as a fractured memory darts through our mind's eye: pieces of a squalid, iron-barred hell, of being filthy and caged in a dark room without windows or, at times, even a speck of light. He can't be more than seven or eight years old in the memory, and it's heartbreaking watching how he's carved a window into the iron floor of his misshapen cage. Outside the etched window, he's engraved a detailed forest of tall trees surrounding a lake, as if drawing the wooded sanctuary line by line would make it real.

Judging by the pain emanating from him, it feels as though the lightlessness he experienced as a child has perforated his soul, the bleakness of his early existence still visceral, like a hole inside him that can never be closed. Far deeper than a wound or puncture, it seems to have reshaped him to the point of almost circumventing his faith in humanity.

Resurrected from his memory, a smoky darkness closes in around our mind's eye, carrying with it a trace of Lukaes's sickly sweet scent, and while he stalks Nikolai like a voracious, vein-caged viper, I hear a calming male voice drift into our thoughts. "You are of him, Nikolai, but you are not like him."

An image of the man with the holstered swords I met in the forest appears and overtakes the smoky blackness like a beacon of light on a dark sea, his angular, almost Native American–looking face otherworldly in its backlit transparency. With him as a focal point, I feel tranquility sweep over Nikolai until I'm certain that other than Sola, this is the only person in the world he trusts.

Yet Nikolai's calm is short-lived, as the man's image is smothered by the plume of shadowy smoke growing larger, the cloud now acting as a backdrop for the scene of Nikolai, hopeless and bound to his cage. Then, as if I'm being infused with a liquid memory poured into my consciousness, I understand that Lukaes is the predator forcing this vision upon us; he is not only Nikolai's childhood captor, but also his maker.

Before I have the chance to process the realization, a picture overtakes our mind's eye: me, stormy-eyed and standing next to my mother, both of us chanting while a gentle wind tosses our long, dark hair around our faces, faster and faster until the strands become fingerlike clouds that swirl until the scene goes black.

The darkness clears and I see myself, older now—alluringly strange and striking—sitting on the lap of my plump, rosy-cheeked grandfather. My stomach tightens as my gaze moves down toward his hand on my knee while he reads aloud:

> "But I don't want to go among mad people," Alice remarked.
> "Oh, you can't help that," said the Cat: "we're all mad here. I'm mad. You're mad."
> "How do you know I'm mad?" said Alice.
> "You must be," said the Cat, "or you wouldn't have come here."

He lets his forearm slip up my thigh and brush past my groin as he lifts his hand to turn the page. I hop down from his lap, and his reaction to my dismount is a prompt slap to my bottom. In response, my pale skin blushes and my eyes mist over, attempting to hold back a flood of tears.

Embarrassed at what Nikolai is seeing and no longer wishing to be embedded in this memory, I'm tempted to sever our connection until I feel his hand come down over mine. In response to Nikolai's touch, our mind's eye clears and presents only clean, white space before I feel myself pulled from the cloudy room and back into my body.

My eyes fly open, and I inhale as Sola helps me into a sitting position. "Just breathe."

Taking another full breath, I see Nikolai lying beside me as if in anesthetized slumber. Both of his sleeves are rolled up, and I notice that the veins in his arms are without any trace of Lukaes's black blood. He is peaceful, and for the moment, free.

Absolute enervation saturates my cells. I'm too drained to think, talk, or continue holding my body upright, and feel myself collapse into Sola's arms as my mind goes blank.

48

[W]UNDERLAND

E ven asleep, I'm aware of memories dislodging from my mind, images that spring upward one by one like they're vying for my individual attention. I'm recalling scenes I've kept locked away in custom-fitted coffins since I was a young girl: a Celtic ritual my father taught me, being read to by my grandfather and how his hands always found my bare skin…

My preference was to call him by his first name, Killian, never Grandpa. It seemed impossible for me to accept we were related, and separating myself from calling him by a familial name suited my need for dissociation.

I can still see the Frankenstein-like vertical scars on his chest from the bypass surgery that left him with an arrhythmic and ill-functioning heart. It seemed fitting that his heart's valves were replaced with those of a pig—or so he told me—and that those mixed parts could merge and find a semblance of what made them the same.

Forced by my father, I would sit on Killian's lap, hating every moment that his big shirtless belly rested against my back like an overstuffed leather sack. His thick Irish accent and jangling cross necklace never convinced me to believe the constant religious rhetoric he spouted: "The good Lord loves an obedient child."

Perhaps that was true. But to me, the "good Lord" could keep his misbegotten affections and all the holy babble that came with it. I'd been better served by my mother's beliefs—a day in the forest with her, our feet upon the skin of Mother Earth, and our spirits warmed by the rays of Father Sky were all I needed to feel loved.

With my mind still spinning, I feel someone touch my face and my consciousness retracts from the memories of my childhood and filters into the present. I'm aware of how depleted I feel on a physical level, but mentally, I seem to be at the mercy of a curious mind, one that is pushing me toward a waking state until I'm able to open my eyes.

"I was starting to worry."

Turning my head to the left, I meet Nikolai's thoughtful gaze. He's kneeling beside the bed, the smell of cedar drifting from his clothes and a few of his loose, pepper-colored hairs hanging next to his right eye as though wishing to get a better look at me.

He eases himself onto the bed and helps me into a sitting position before offering up a small glass of bright green liquid. "Drink this."

I'm about to refuse, but when he raises the glass to my lips, I feel compelled to drink.

"It tastes terrible, but it'll bring your strength back." Smiling, he waits.

I take a sip and conclude that terrible is not the word. Vile is more accurate, and once I've controlled the revolt in my stomach, I bring my hand away from my mouth as the quilt covering my torso slips downward, revealing the top half of my bloodstained corset.

Taking my glass and setting it on the floor, Nikolai seems agitated by the sight of me. The longer silence exists between us, the more I feel my cheeks flush with heat; outside my staged environment, my costume borders on ridiculous.

He inquires, "Your blood?"

I get a sense that he's protective of women in general, but in both my and Sola's cases, it feels primal. While awaiting my response, his right eye twitches a few times like he's holding back a rush of questions ready to spew forth were I to affirm it is, indeed, my blood.

I answer him in earnest. "No."

"Whose, then?" He continues studying me.

Flashes of Mr. Llewellyn's brutal ascent flicker through my thoughts like lightning in a dark sky until an image of him lying in my arms locks in my mind's eye. It's then that I understand he's been reborn. This ushering in of a parallel, yet freer version of life—a kind of midwifery—is what I love most about being alive, and no matter the stage, scene, or accouterment required, I have constructed the patience required to see the process through to the end, bloody or otherwise.

"Someone I couldn't let go into battle alone," I answer.

Nikolai is about to speak but is interrupted by the sound of something crashing onto the cabin's thatched roof outside. Bits of dust, splintered wood, and thatch fall to the floor, indicating that the structural integrity of the vaulted ceiling above us has been compromised.

He stands and rushes toward the front door while whatever hit the roof slides down, picks up speed, then collides with the ground. A few more clumps of thatch and debris tumble to the floor as I throw my legs over the side of the bed to follow him.

Beside my bare feet, which seem to falter as I ask them to sustain my weight, are the satin stilettos given to me by Mr. Llewellyn. Still encrusted with dried blood along the edges of the red lacquered soles, they appear almost cruel, like mini war machines gathering dust after having won a long-coming and fiercely fought battle.

A rush of cold air whips across the room, carrying a trail of icy snow as I shift my focus toward Nikolai, who has already opened the door and is about to step out into the wintry night. Taking a quilt from the bed, I wrap it around my shoulders and force myself onto my shaky legs, then walk across the room.

I've almost reached Nikolai when a carved plaque above the door catches my eye: "Into the woods I must go, for its secrets I'm to know." Taking the last few steps until I'm standing inside the door's sturdy frame, I notice

Nikolai surveying the damaged roof from the center of a small forest-flanked clearing, which is covered in a deep, sleepy layer of fallen snow.

I recognize the thickets lining the grounds. This is the very same cabin the white rabbit led me to prior to its gruesome demise in a previous dream. I realize now that it was Zoran who was hiding in the thicket's rough brush, and the fact that he caused the rabbit's death is a truth I find bothersome.

Nikolai studies the ground around him, which glistens and catches the bluish moonlight as though it's blanketed in crystalline sand. Observing him in his concentrated state, his tall, tree-trunk-like frame rooted to the ground, I feel like the mammoth trees surrounding him are his wood-clothed kin, his tribe.

Nikolai walks back toward the cabin and I inhale the night's glacial air, feeling it sting my lips and mouth. I exhale but find it peculiar that rather than dissipating, my breath remains suspended in front of me, a stationary patch of fog. It's as if the substance that left my lungs is foreign to the forest's frozen atmosphere, and the little cloud is all but forced into a floating quarantine.

"A branch broke off from one of the trees. The roof is stronger than it looks. I think we're fine." Taking a last step toward me, Nikolai unknowingly knocks into the suspended cloud, which tumbles sideways like a raft on a stormy sea, never breaking apart or losing opacity.

Still examining the breath-borne cloud, I see it starting to melt like plastic on a hot stove while it drifts back toward me in a goopy mass, and for reasons I can't explain, a sense of dread rises inside me.

Like Alice, I feel as if this strange and dream-bound land is taking on a disturbing quality. What was up is now down, what was peaceful is now upheaved, and the very laws of its nature seem to be eroding into a perverse version of a once-pristine and organically functioning set of rules. In quiet truth, something is very wrong, and I feel it all the way through me like I'm connected to a malfunctioning electrical current.

Nikolai is set to usher me inside when an earth-shaking rumble pulls our focus skyward. Above us, the sky twists and folds in on itself like great crashing waves of bruise-colored water, and inside the cluster of churning clouds, lightning flashes as though something baleful and furious is imprisoned within them.

For a split second, dread gives way to sadness and the blood flowing in my veins decelerates; I feel my muscles contract like I'm somehow embroiled in the sky's roiling distress. Sensing my altered state, Nikolai takes my hand, and although it's a gesture meant to offer comfort, his touch unnerves me further.

Beside me, I hear a crackling sound, and when I look down at the hedges along the front of the cabin, I notice clumps of snow falling from the damaged hedges as their tiny leaves melt like wax exposed to a toxic flame. Seeing movement in my peripheral vision, I shift my focus and watch the forest canopy wilting and audibly sinking several feet toward the ground.

Seeing the forest's serene beauty disintegrate into a feeble, flaccid version of itself has a visceral effect on my system. As though we're one, its rapid demise is mirrored inside me, and with a wave of nausea sweeping up from my stomach, I'm about to go back into the cabin but am stopped by voices chanting in the distance. "The final offering…"

I'm resolved to ask Nikolai what he means when the sound of what I can only describe as millions of small bones cracking ricochets through the air. I watch in disbelief as the forest canopy deflates, the treetops collapsing en masse like giant, mangled umbrellas.

The ill-fated forest continues to wreak havoc on me: my blood runs cold; the sinew within me weakens, growing brittle and inelastic like a frozen rubber band, and my ribs ache as if I too am succumbing to its swift and vicious decline.

Silenced by the forest's instability, the chanting ceases, and when Nikolai puts a kind hand on my shoulder, I look at him and see the penetrating pain in his eyes. I wish I could tell him I feel nothing, that I'm immune to what's going on inside me, but it would be a lie, and he knows it. The truth is that I feel sick, and as the sour scent of decaying wood slips into my nostrils, I'm pressed into a panicked form of angst I can't rationalize away.

"This present darkness has but one end." With tenderness, he brushes a stray hair from my cheek. "You."

Nikolai holds my gaze until I feel we are of the same mind. I not only hear his words repeating in my mind, but also see pictures of all the thoughts associated with what he's just said, the most vivid amongst them being a flash of me cleansing Lukaes's black blood from his veins. I am, at least for Nikolai, darkness's countermeasure.

Forcing our connected thoughts from my mind and unable to withstand the weight of Nikolai's gaze any longer, I look out into the clearing, hoping to see the forest renewed and robust against the life-sucking force that has brought it to a deadening heel. But it is not to be, and if anything, the once-grand trees are in an even graver condition, dripping a tar-like substance into the pure white snow as if they're rotting from the inside out.

Nikolai puts his hand on my back and is about to lead me into the cabin when he stops and stares out into the clearing. I follow his pinpointed focus and see something tunneling through the snow toward us. Whatever is making its way in our direction is exerting great effort to do so—this evidenced by short bursts of laborious movement followed by periods of rest.

Once what I could swear is a small white rabbit is close enough, Nikolai crouches down and its small, furry head pops up from the deep snow. Nikolai picks it up and cradles it in his arms before going back inside. I trail in behind him and close the door, grateful for the radiating warmth of the fireplace chasing away the pervasive chill lodged in my bones.

Sitting on the bed, I wrap the quilt around my shoulders while Nikolai dries the animal off with a woolen cloth. My mind relaxes and becomes numb as my body settles into a more normal state, the nausea and internal reactionary effects of the forest's decline subsiding as though the cabin's walls provide a sanctuary from the apocalypse-like events outside.

Nikolai sets the animal down, and as soon as its feet hit the ground, it waddles toward me. Watching it approach, my vision blurs and thoughts bounce around my skull like rogue Ping-Pong balls, none making any real sense, just flickers of words and pieces of fractured imagery coming together enough for me to regain some sense of coherence. When I feel tiny padded paws against the top of my foot, I look down and stare into Ziggy's beady black eyes.

Ziggy crawls up the quilt, and rather than watch him haul his rotund body upward, I reach for him and place him in my lap. Nikolai sits in his chair by the fire, watching me.

"'All the world's a stage, and all the men and women merely players.'"

As I pet Ziggy, he flattens out like a pancake, and my psyche sharpens and comes alive with a prosecutorial debate. My mind is not my friend, and whatever it's seeking to reveal through my dreams is either something I don't care to know or something I *do* want to know but don't care to face.

Of course my own cleverness and dexterous wits will be used against me, and to my mind's advantage, including the quoting of this particular line of Shakespeare that alludes to the seven stages of a man's life, each one fraught with some form of codependency, until the final culmination, or rather realization, that nothing was as it seemed. Everyone was just playing a part, up to their eventual end—and once this knowledge is grasped, it's too late to turn back time and live an unscripted life.

Ever my father's daughter, I recount the seven stages as he taught them to me: infant, schoolboy, lover, soldier, justice, Pantalone, and old age, and wonder on which of them my mind wishes for me to focus. What is *it* that I'm meant to see? Or can I not see it until I've decided whether I wish to be privy to the information attempting to be revealed?

Furthering my pursuit of the white rabbit into the proverbial hole is the presence of Ziggy. This is the first time my waking life has invaded a dream, and I deem his arrival significant, but to what end, I'm not certain.

"Penny for your thoughts, nickel for your dreams?"

Looking up at Nikolai, who smiles, I stare into his eyes and find a sense of home. To me, he is solid and familiar in a way I haven't often experienced in my waking world. Nikolai feels real to me, Ziggy lying in my lap feels real…

But based on what I've learned from Dr. Lawson, lucid dreams can feel real, tricking the mind in a trip-the-light-fantastic slip between dream and reality. Who's to know what I should consider peculiar, or what my reality consists of, under those circumstances? With this thought, I build myself back up into a more balanced state.

In keeping with my attempt to remain clearheaded, I recall the instruction I've been given, which is to explore these dreams and scenarios to the best of my ability. Considering that the line from Shakespeare's play concludes with the seventh stage ending in "mere oblivion," I resolve to find my way to the truth before such a grim outcome is cemented as my fate.

With this impetus, I crawl the rest of the way into the rabbit hole and acquiesce to the resulting fall.

"When you say 'All the world's a stage,' what do you mean?"

Nikolai leans back into his chair as his eyes brighten. "Everything is connected. You see two worlds, but there is only one. We're all players, but you'll decide our fate." With a note of concern in his voice, he continues, "My hope is that you realize the truth in time."

Of all the conversations I've had on this subject, with myself masquerading as dream-role characters, this one is the hardest to dismiss. There is something about the look in Nikolai's eyes; he is without an agenda on this front, and when he gazes at me, I know I represent to him the one thing even I can't live without: hope.

I see the inscription in my mother's Cherokee book materializing in my mind's eye: "Do as did Pandora, save for don't leave hope inside. In bocca al lupo."

The two phrases fit seamlessly within this current world—my stage— for I can fix Pandora's mistake and offer hope, but to do it, I'll have to leap "into the mouth of the wolf."

Yet when I think of submitting to what is required to bring hope, I can't do it. Everything in me rejects allowing myself to act, even in a dream, as some kind of savior. Why has my mind not chosen martyr? Why must it be redeemer?

The truth is, I'd much rather submit to the experience of dying, as it's a far more interesting mode of exploration. Many cultures believe that death while still living is one of the most powerful tools for metamorphosis, whether it be of the body or of the spirit. To me, discovery by death possesses a deeper form of honesty and requires greater self-sacrifice.

In comparison, how difficult is it to accept a preordained savior status, after which this world and all the suffering within it magically washes away? Where's the sacrifice in that? It hardly seems a path, dream-world or otherwise, on which one can become enlightened, at least not in any real or lasting manner.

Nikolai interrupts my spinning thoughts. "Have you been in Phinneass's basement?"

Hearing Nikolai ask such a question, let alone use Mr. Sumel's name, causes the moisture in my mouth to evaporate as Ziggy's body becomes stiff in my lap. My mind, ever the agile opponent, has unleashed a house-sized cannonball into my psyche's camp, rendering it incapacitated to the point that I'm unable to respond. Then, as though I've given myself a well-timed reprieve, I hear a deliberate knock on the door.

"They've come for us."

Nikolai is already on his feet and moving across the room, but with my blood pushing up and forward, I know who stands outside, jet black against the night's fresh snow, my mind appearing to have called forth the mouth of the wolf into which I must jump. I place Ziggy on the bed and move to the center of the room as Nikolai opens the front door to reveal Daegan and Zoran standing outside.

Beneath the falling snow, Daegan's porcelain skin seems to glow while Zoran's fur soaks up the surrounding night. With Daegan so close to Zoran, their dislike of one another is palpable, the two of them like opposing chess pieces forced to stand, mismatched, in the other's square.

Daegan shifts his focus from Nikolai to me, the look in his eyes one of severe disapproval, which I don't understand until I realize I'm standing in the center of the room in just my bloody corset and underwear. After a moment, he steps inside and walks past Nikolai without a word, his presence so sizable it feels he wears the room like a piece of clothing.

Still outside, Zoran takes a step closer, and in response, my bones vibrate and magnetize. Nikolai's demeanor grows stone cold, making it clear he's less than fond of Daegan; but his pure, unadulterated hatred for Zoran is so noxious that it severs our connection and demagnetizes my bones, and the thick tension in the room rises upward like a suffocating fog.

Now in front of me, Daegan examines the stains on my corset as he removes his cloak, wraps it around my shoulders, and fastens it beneath my chin like I'm nine years old. He takes my hand and prepares to lead me out of the cabin just as Ziggy topples from the bed to the floor. In response, the tattoos at Daegan's temples fan out, shooting past his hairline like unrestrained snakes while he stares at Ziggy sitting motionless next to my blood-crusted stilettos.

Still focused on Ziggy, Daegan leans down to pick up my shoes, and I swear his palm grows rough against my hand, like sharp scales have erupted from his skin. After he hands me my shoes, I bend down and struggle to force my swollen feet back into my satin platforms, which are violently out of place in Nikolai's rustic and stifling cabin.

Once I've finished jamming my feet into my proverbial ruby slippers, I feel absurd as I straighten up and find all three of them staring at me. Silence sits inside the room like a rootless tree, unstable and dangerous as it rocks back and forth in the cold storms discharging from each of them. There is so much subtext going on, I can't figure out if they all detest one another or if their eerie lack of conversation has something to do with me.

Daegan turns toward Nikolai. "Has it worsened?"

I'm not certain what's going on between the two of them, but Nikolai appears unwilling to answer; instead, he crosses to the small cabinet and retrieves a drawstring pouch before placing several tiny blue vials inside. After gathering two small knives from a cabinet drawer, he attaches them to his belt and walks out.

Daegan leads me out of the cabin and past Zoran, still laser-focused on Nikolai. "Show me. Please."

Nikolai glances at me for a moment before grudgingly rolling up the sleeves of his woven shirt. Daegan hasn't missed the exchange between Nikolai and me, and if anything, it's unsettled him further. But when he sees Nikolai's hands and arms, clean and free of the black blood that plagued them, he appears to implode.

Daegan grabs my arms and studies my wrists, one of which still harbors two paste-dyed lines. I never thought I'd see him lose control, but when he refocuses on Nikolai, I'm almost afraid of what will happen next.

Taking a step toward Nikolai, Daegan demands, "How could you have done this?"

Again, Nikolai glances toward me before leading Daegan off to the right of the cabin. Yet despite their attempts to have a discreet conversation, I hear every word.

Nikolai asserts, "She agreed."

"What does that matter when she knows nothing of the consequences or risks?"

Refusing to back down, Nikolai contests, "She's stronger than you think."

"That isn't the point. We need her—all of her—and whether you realize it or not, you've set us back. I can't take her to the gates now. She's far too weak."

"The gates have been forged?" Nikolai appears taken aback.

Ignoring the question, Daegan continues berating him. "We agreed you'd wait. You gave me your word."

This seems to have struck Nikolai, and it's quite some time before he responds. "It's a promise bent, not broken."

Daegan eyes him. "Either way, it's not what we decided."

Nikolai lowers his voice. "I saw the Book when I mirrored her. It was an older memory, but…"

The look on Daegan's face leaves Nikolai unable to finish his sentence, and the two watch one another for a long while before Daegan speaks. "We should discuss it later. I have to get her back to Laksha. Zoran will go with you to fetch Sola. We'll need Prayna's medallion to mix the blood."

Daegan is about to walk away when Nikolai takes his arm. "The Scribe gave you the birth blood of the Asdans?"

"Yes."

With a note of fear in his voice, Nikolai inquires, "Is it wise to invoke the Elders? To release such a force could—"

"We don't have a choice."

While they continue talking, Zoran moves closer to me, and in response, my blood pushes against my skin and his piercing stare makes me feel I've somehow distressed him by helping Nikolai.

Watching one another like we're the only two people left in this apoplectically decaying land, my breathing quickens, as does his. Within the isolation of our connection, he's the only thing I see until Daegan brushes past us like a white-blurred storm. Daegan walks away from us, his stride intense and his frame stiff against the cold as he flattens a clear path through the snow for me. Although he doesn't look back or speak, I understand that I'm expected to follow.

Reluctant, I turn from Zoran and trace the footsteps Daegan has made for me, feeling each stiletto-heeled step that takes me from him is one of pricking, satin torture. But rather than look back, I glance down at my feet and examine the places where my pale skin ends and my scarlet shoes begin.

Treading through the snow, I feel my right foot is divorced from my left, devoid of its commitment to follow the pattern of forward motion. Sweeping my gaze upward, I take in the scenery around me, noticing that despite the shriveling forest, the landscape feels familiar.

Nikolai's voice drifts into my thoughts. "Everything is connected."

An image of Ziggy in Nikolai's house flashes in my mind's eye until I begin walking faster and tilt my head skyward, hoping the falling snow will wash the image from my mind.

I find release in my now-brisk walk, freedom from my circus of circular memories. Overhead the sky pulses in deep greens and purples, a cornucopia of swirling light and folding color that gives rise to a gust of wind whipping through the trees and bringing with it a chill that bites my skin and stings my eyes. Seeking refuge from the icy tempest, I look down and wrap my arms around my torso, wishing Daegan's cloak was made of solid fur to better shield against the bitter cold.

My mind feels jellylike, and in response to my viscous thoughts, the snow thickens, wetting my legs and changing the bloodied satin of my shoes to watery fuchsia. Dye leaks freely from my daggered platforms, and when I look over my shoulder, I see the stained footprints of night's deeds in the pure snow behind me.

Refocusing my gaze forward to navigate the winter-licked ground, I almost slip and fall before halting in my tracks in an attempt to stabilize my weakening legs. Daegan turns around, comes toward me, and scoops me up in his arms, and his heartbeat thunders in my ears.

I'm taken by the ease with which he carries me, as I'm neither small in stature nor lacking a curvaceous frame, but the way he cradles my body makes me feel more delicately built than I am. My arms are around his neck, my lips inches away from his skin, his defining pre-rain scent permeating my cells. I'm holding him tighter than I need to, feeling like he's doing the same, as together we move beneath the undulating skies of a Van Gogh night.

49

INSCRIBED

Surveying Daegan's rotting garden, I nestle deeper into the threaded warmth of his cloak as a frigid gust of wind whips a few strands of raven hair around my face. Although the night air delivers an ice-fanged bite, it feels sticky against my skin, like a layer of melted sugar has coated each of its packed molecules. Inhaling, I let a frosty breath pass over my lips and filter down into my waiting lungs, its sweetness lingering in my mouth before turning sour and leaving a swampy, bitter aftertaste.

The once-vibrant garden has continued to succumb to the forest's defoliant-like demise, and in seeking refuge from its putrid deterioration, I shift my focus out over the wall. Below, two violet flames still blaze in cauldrons mounted at the cardinal points of the circular city where thousands of people line the perimeter, their collective voices forming a lingering lament that reaches upward like the searching arms of a forlorn child.

I understand that this is the imploring chorus of those on the precipice of death, and in knowing this, I wonder if, in their eyes, I've gone from negligent Guardian to barbarous witch in what is becoming an unraveling domain. But I find myself countering the concept that I am cold-hearted, insomuch as I don't know myself to be unkind, but rather practical. It is my truth I seek in this complex dream scenario built upon my own memories, psyche, and unconscious mind, the trio of which I've yet to wrestle into one fine-tuned exploration.

Nonetheless, I'm perplexed that I've bestowed upon myself the role of Guardian—savior—when it's so richly undeserved. What do I know of saving? Not my mother, not my father, nor Hannah or Evan. Were someone to judge from the outside looking in, they might view me as an anti-savior, a bringer of great and destructive death. Perhaps the riddle to be worked out is, how does death's handmaiden atone and become life's liberator?

My thoughts are interrupted by the tinny, scratching sound of spidery legs scurrying toward me through the snow, a single uniform line of shiny round foot soldiers that trails Daegan as he emerges from the path leading to the cottage. Head tilted back and focused skyward, Daegan walks toward me as he examines the twisting, blue-black clouds above, which to me look as though they may implode at any moment. With thunder rumbling to the point of nearly rupturing my eardrums, I feel my guts coil inward like a compressed spring.

Daegan is beside me now, looking out over the city, and with each wave of cries echoing upward, his tattoos swirl in wilder, more misshapen circles. Turning toward him, I'm aware that from the fertile soil of my own unconscious mind, the man before me has been born into a flesh-and-bone being. A person to whom I'm accountable, a dream counterpart whose words and actions can reveal the inner workings of my psyche. In so knowing, I understand that he is my proverbial coat of many colors. I've stitched him together from the tattered remnants of hopes, memories, experiences, and interactions. He represents bits and pieces of the men I've loved, lost, hated, wanted, mended, and saved—each fragment rinsed of its life-blotted mark, then sutured together with blood-woven thread to form a quilt of pure, unsoiled white.

What remains of each of those fragments, now cleansed and drained of their sin-dyed pigments, drips to the floor and comingles to form a pool of inky blackness. And from that watery grave made of all my wrung-out colors arises the midnight-tainted form of my wet and hungry beast, his aqua eyes the only indication that he was created from anything other than darkness itself.

Daegan shifts his focus to me, and when I study the bright green of his irises, I feel like they personify the vibrancy of the forest my mother loved. On the canvas of my mind, Zoran's face appears, his aqua-eyed stare embodying the one thing that could calm my father's restless soul: the sea. It's clear I've made and chosen them for the sole purpose of guiding me on this journey; they are the manifestations of my days and my nights, both resurrected from the stained scraps of my life, and together we stand at the edge of a world nearing fiery collapse.

Feeling like I've sorted out how we move through this exploration as a unified trio, my churning thoughts are slowed when I see movement in my peripheral vision. I shift my gaze left and notice a woman walking toward us from the far end of the garden, and while watching her, I'm perplexed as to how she skims across the vast grounds like she's floating above the deep snow.

Around her, the landscape ripples as if it's a watercolor painting rather than solid land. To me, she is ethereal, and I find myself entranced enough by her presence to search for traces of emotion, for a soul. But all I detect is the vastness of empty space. It feels like star-dusted consciousness merged with matter, matter borrowed flesh, and together they moved toward us under the guise of a statuesque feminine form.

Her medieval gown is blood red with a structured bodice that bears an embroidered crest, and draped over her head and face is a thick, billowing veil of the same deep crimson hue. With her gloved hands clasped in front of her, she advances in a manner that suggests she's propelled by a need for truth, whether delivered or revealed.

She slows her approach, and although I can't see her face beneath her opaque veil, I'm certain she's focused on me. I feel her essence surrounding me like particles of celestial light seeking to illuminate a restless darkness. Of their own volition, my cells are succumbing to her particles' resonant light, like they wish to be freed from the monotonous existence of making up my human form and instead would see me broken apart and unleashed so as to join her.

Now standing in front of us, she utters not a word—the only sounds coming from her are echoic breaths, quiet yet powerful, like she's inhaling our collective consciousness, then exhaling the dusty debris encrusting our human souls. I study the embroidered crest on the bodice of her dress, four interlocking circles that form a vertical line: black, white, violet, cobalt. The bottommost circle has tentacle-like cobalt veins that extend downward from its embroidered edges and cover the lower half of her bloodred dress, causing my sight to flicker, as though my brain is straining to take in both colors at once. Leaving the field of my physical sight, I slip into my mind's eye, where radiating particles of neon-blue light are dancing around me in a uniform glow. And were I not planted on the ground—bone, blood, and flesh—I'd swear I was floating, then splitting into a million pieces until I'm part of the array of light encircling my consciousness.

Beside me, Daegan inhales and raises his sleeve to reveal the inside of his forearm, where words are being etched into his skin in cobalt ink, as if by an invisible pen: "The gates have been forged?"

Daegan appears calm as he looks at the woman, but as evidenced by the tattoos churning at his temples, he is far from it. "Yes."

With the previous phrase having disappeared, or rather, healed, another set of blazing words materializes on the canvas of his skin: "Too far gone now. Asdan blood not enough. Need the blood of the Thirteenth."

The woman raises a gloved hand toward me until it's hovering over my heart, and as she does, the hems of her glove and sleeve part. What I'm seeing must be an illusion brought on by the dark, churning night, for rather than the flesh of what should be her wrist, I see nothingness—empty space—save for a smattering of coursing, neon-blue veins.

Letters carve themselves into furious existence while Daegan and I look on. "Thirteenth unstable. Fire, unchecked. The Rose, wild."

Daegan winces as another phrase forms, this time deep enough to draw blood: "Night will end. But the blood path will not."

The woman moves my cloak aside and puts her hand on the skin above my heart; I feel like my body is losing form and becoming light-filled mist. She takes a step toward me and I inspect her veil for traces of a face beneath, but I find nothing—no indication of flesh, nor any definable features.

An excruciating ache rips into my forearm; I look down and read the forming phrase. "One cannot see what one cannot give."

My sight is taken over by an image in my mind's eye: She is sweeping through my thoughts like a lithe probe comprised of light-infused particles. Around me, the landscape disappears, as if my vision has inverted, and I'm now in the archives of my own thoughts. Inside my mind, upon the shelves of my consciousness, the particles weave in and out of the leather-bound volumes that make up my life as they search, studying the script-titled spines of each closed book.

They locate the volume they want and contract around the leathery journal as though absorbing the pages through transference. They're compacted so tightly I'm almost unable to read the title on the book's spine through their mist-like cloud: *The Woods*.

I remember writing this diary as a child during the last summer I spent with my mother at our cabin in the forest. It was at her insistence that I chronicled our time together, but mostly it was a sort of reference book for all the Cherokee rituals and Clan history she worked to instill in me on those long balmy days. I wrote the journal for her because she asked me to, but my heart was scarcely in it, as all the hours spent writing were ones not at her side.

In vivid detail, I recall one line from the journal, the day I wrote it as clear to me in this moment as if the pen were still in my hand. Watching my own handwritten words float across my field of vision, I can't breathe: "Mother thinks I'm better than I am. She thinks I'm like her, and for her sake, I pretend."

I'm pulled from my mind's eye and thrust back into the cold-handed grip of the winter night as the woman takes her hand from my heart. She shifts her gaze toward Daegan, and although his sleeve is covering his forearm, I can tell by the look on his face that something is being etched into his skin.

Rather than lift his sleeve and reveal the phrase, he remains focused on her.

After a moment, she makes her way back across the garden, and the landscape around her ripples like water being disturbed on a snow-covered lake. As when she arrived, I sense no emotion, no identifiable human traits, and the farther away she moves, the harder it is to continue thinking of her, as though she's erasing the memory of our encounter.

Once she's stepped onto a stone path and rounded the corner, Daegan's voice is almost drowned out by the wave of pleas still rising up from the city.

"Our Scribe, our fate." His voice trails off as he pulls up his sleeve, angles his forearm away from me, and reads what she's written. With his tattoos twisting into bunched knots and his face solemn, there's no mistaking the effect her message has had on him, and I'm certain it has something to do with me.

50

BIRD & HOUND

Sleet pounded against the window as an icy storm raged outside. Unfazed, Phinneas inquired, "How long did you work for Mr. Black?"

Lula shifted in her chair. "Quite a stretch." The thickness of her accent stayed in the room even though she had finished speaking.

"How did you two meet?" he asked.

A thin streak of pain flashed in Lula's eyes. "I'd been left penniless by my husband. Without any office skills, I had to take a job in the only field I ever cared about: mythology. I love anything ancient and hard to explain."

Laughing, Phinneas retorted, "Then you'll love me!"

Lula recounted while smiling, "Anyway, I was working in a Celtic bookstore. He walked in and that was that."

Ziggy rooted around the table in circles like a dog chasing its tail while Phinneas continued getting to know Lula. "So, what did he hire you to do?"

She brushed an unruly hair from her face. "Keep things sorted for him." She twisted a large amber ring on her finger. "An all-weather girl, you could say."

"Why do you suppose Evan put us together?"

"I suspect because she needs us, and we need each other."

Giving a terrible yet heartfelt Bogart impression, he quipped, "Perhaps this is the beginning of a beautiful friendship."

Lula smiled as she reached down, retrieved her purse from the floor, then pulled out a few pieces of paper. "Stab in the dark, but do these mean anything to you?"

Phinneas took the pages from her and examined each one before happening on the typed headings at the top of two columns that formed a makeshift family tree: "Wolf Clan" and "Blackwood." Moving to the next page, he read the heading recipes, and the words "slowing ascension" and "speeding ascension," and his pulse started to race.

After putting the paper down on the kitchen table, he inquired, "Mind if I ask where you got these?"

"Evan left me an envelope filled with papers. These were the only ones I could make heads or tails of."

Phinneas knew Nilah and Evan had had a friendship, but he hadn't realized they were close enough for her to have given Evan information so dear to her. Setting the pages back down, he reached for his pipe, then lit it, the smell of tobacco filling the room. "Zoë's mother, Nilah, was a descendant of the Wolf Clan. These recipes are from a book passed down by her Clan Elders."

Looking at the recipe page, he studied the ingredients. "The book contains everything from ways of contacting spirits to the history of the Wolf Clan to the usage of herbs, plants, and whatnot." Ziggy waddled across the table. "Supposedly, these recipes were used on young Clan members during a vision quest, a rite of passage or coming of age."

A lock of Lula's red hair fell from its pin and hung around her shoulder like a curled flame as she waited for him to continue. But rather than say more, he elected not to divulge that before her death, Nilah had provided him with herbs to give to Zoë, a potent concoction he'd been dispensing into her cocoa.

Lula pushed one of the pieces of paper toward him. "Halfway down the page in the Blackwood column, looks like the names change to Black. Below that, if you keep going, you'll see a box with Evan's name." She tapped her finger on a faint line of cursive at the side of the page. "And then there's this."

Bringing the paper closer, he strained to decipher the small cursive handwriting:

M. Blackwood: DOB: 1831, DOD: unknown
(no vital records?)

Lula traced her finger along the page. "There's a line from this Blackwood note to a woman in the Wolf Clan column. Zoë's a direct descendant." With an undertone of anxiety in her voice and as though a new thought was forcing its way to the surface, she commented, "I wanted to research it more, but he asked that I not interfere. Those were his last words to me, actually."

"What do you mean?"

"He said, 'In all chaos, some order exists.' But things go on in that house—I find wee vines, leaves, bits of trees everywhere. It takes nearly all my time to keep the house free of them. I swear if I were gone for more than a day, a bloody forest would grow in her bedroom. I'm supposed to ignore that?"

Wanting all the information Lula could give him, he kept quiet and waited for her to resume.

"As if that wasn't enough, I've seen a strange man watching the house from across the street on more than one occasion. I keep waiting for 'chaos' to become 'order,' but it sure seems bloody unlikely."

An image of the man with the wingtip shoes crept into Phinneas's mind. "Trench coat, hat, and wingtips?"

Lula's face drained of color. "He's turned up here as well?"

Seeing the anxiety in Lula's eyes, he debated how much he should reveal about his interactions with the man, for fear of adding more to her weighted state of mind.

Seeming to sense his churning thoughts, Lula inquired in a manner suggesting he were Sherlock and she, Watson. "What is it?"

He'd only ever revealed his past to Nilah, but in knowing that it was she, even if by proxy, who had brought him and Lula together, he spoke. "I was a young man. It was a one-night stand." He could still see the woman's face in his mind's eye, so beautiful; and to this day, the only time in his life he'd been with a woman. He continued. "There was a child. The man knows who my son is, and I don't."

Lula's expression turned solemn. "He's threatened you?"

"Not exactly."

Genuine in her concern, she pressed. "What are you going to do?"

He took a puff of his pipe. "She's the priority." With his heart heavy, he pulled a small journal from the pocket of his robe and ran a finger over the inscription, THE WOODS, which was carved into its thick leather binding. Opening it, he flipped to a page in the very back before setting the open book on the table. "Quid pro quo? With your mythology knowledge and whatnot."

Lula took the book from him and examined a hand-drawn picture of five rings that formed a bull's-eye-type wheel. The wheel was cut into four quadrants by vertical and horizontal lines comprised of sticklike symbols, with a burnt-out circle at the center of the wheel.

Evan's reasoning for putting Lula and Phinneas together was becoming more evident with each passing moment. "It's called Fionn's Window. Some call it the Wild Rose because of the pattern of rings and symbols. It's similar to a medicine wheel," Lula explained.

"What's its purpose?"

Still inspecting the drawing, she replied, "Technically, it's for pathworking, or the Walk. It's the Celtic Druids' form of the vision quest you mentioned earlier. It's used in a ritual that opens the path to both an inner journey and another realm or dimension." Bringing the book closer, she felt the paper around the burnt-out circle. "It's hard to tell with the scorch marks, but I think there's dried blood around the opening."

Phinneas sat back in his chair. "Is that significant?"

Without answering him, she queried, "Who drew this?"

A hostile gust of wind battered the house as the two candle lanterns sitting on the kitchen table flickered. Reaching out to soothe a storm-shaken Ziggy, he responded, "Zoë."

"Recently?"

"No. It's from the last summer she spent with her mother. It was in a box Nilah left me after she died."

Setting the book back down on the table, she opined, "Well, if memory serves, this is a powerful ritual, and assuming she's begun the Walk, a door has been opened—she'll have to complete the journey or face irreparable harm. At least, in theory."

Ziggy waddled closer as Mr. Sumel asked, "Harm?"

Lula fidgeted with her ring. "Madness. The death of the soul. But again, that's just theory."

They sat in silence until Lula turned the book toward him and continued, thinking aloud. "According to tradition, the reason for getting on the path is to become 'wise like a tree.'" She pointed. "See the markers here? They're based on different types of trees, and each ring symbolizes a phase of the Walk, with the final, innermost ring surrounding the tree of knowledge."

Lifting the page away from the book, she explained. "The center ring on this wheel was burned away to create a 'window' into the spirit world, through which the journeyer can travel." Puffing on his pipe, Phinneas let her words toss and tumble in his head. "But theory or not, I'm worried." Passing the journal back to him, Lula met his gaze while he waited for her to finish her thought. "It's unusual that the window was burned, then sealed from a vein."

He dug deeper. "I'm not sure I understand."

The room seemed to darken around her. "It means that her Walk will be fraught with the wildest of fires and her path paved in blood."

51

FIREWALL

Beneath the moody moonlight, the meadow is untouched by the forest's pervasive decline, and stand-
ing at its center, I feel in another world, one blessed with the heavenly,
blanketed whiteness of pure, undisturbed snow. Daegan is surveying the
ice-covered trees along the meadow's edge, each of them determined in their
wooden-armed reach toward a still-furious sky, which twists and writhes
like a dark celestial sea of bodies overhead.

Shifting my focus toward the willow tree, I notice that it's grown lusher,
refusing to succumb to the death closing in on all sides. From beneath its
tentlike canopy, a line of black spiders makes its way toward me, struggling
through the deep snow and at times sinking below the surface, making
their progression more one of tunneling than walking.

One by one, they walk across the threshold of the meadow's circular
border, around which are twelve iron gates, formidable in size and structure.
Just as with the old gates in the cathedral, each re-creation harbors a large
Roman numeral within its thick bars.

After studying the open twelfth gate, I scan the others, which are beautiful to me, almost sentient, their artistry radiating the symbiotic sense of the adept hands that crafted them. For a moment, I suspect the Blacksmith may have imparted DNA-like slivers of his spirit into each of them, seeing as they feel alive, like a separate soul-filled person inhabits their metal frames; how peculiar to have the innate feeling that I'm connected to them, like my flesh encases our conjoined, iron-boned skeletons.

With the sudden pungent odor of rotting vegetation drifting over my shoulder and pushing up my nostrils, I turn toward the marble rose behind me, peer into its open center, and find it filled with a small amount of foul-smelling liquid. Recalling the living elements of its once syrupy sweet liquor and radiant, conscious aura, I'm aware of the life draining from this realm like blood from an untended wound, and the longer I'm exposed to the rose's cold and lifeless presence, the more disturbed I become.

One of the larger spiders enters my peripheral vision and moves near the rose's base to garner my full attention. The spider's back has greyish-white scorch marks like it's been recently burned, and for a moment, I wonder if it's the same flame-bodied spider that saved me from the robed man, Ronan, and served as my fiery beacon in the dark forest. In what feels like a silent confirmation, the spider watches me for a few seconds, then turns away and joins its comrades, who have formed a tight circle around me like a black-shelled army.

Beyond the ring of spiders, I see Nikolai, Sola, and Zoran emerge from the forest near the willow tree, their collective demeanor sullen and pulled down by the weight of their thoughts. Daegan joins them in front of the open gate while the spiders fan out into a wider circle, flanking the perimeter like miniature watchmen.

With my bones becoming magnetized, I feel my skin flush with heat, the intensity of the vibration increasing as Zoran speaks. "It's begun."

Daegan inquires, "How many?"

"Several hundred," Sola responds. "Mostly the young."

The smooth, iced state of the forest creates a cave-like echo, and even though their tones are hushed, I can hear their conversation.

Nikolai weighs in. "They're suffocating. Then their hearts just stop."

Even from where I'm standing, I feel the burdened heaviness of Daegan's demeanor as he speaks. "For now, we must focus on the invocation of the Elders. At this point it's our only hope for realigning the gates and safeguarding the portal and realms from collapse."

Sola exchanges an anxious glance with Zoran, then interjects. "Before we begin, there's something you should know." Sola takes a step toward him. "Their blood has been mixed."

Tempering his tone, Daegan responds, "I'm aware."

"It had to be done. We couldn't let an Asdan perish."

Daegan leans toward Sola and speaks with equal parts concern and reproach. "But there's to be an order to things, and my concern is that forgiveness will come too late or not at all."

Nikolai takes a step forward. "Daegan, it's between them now. It's always been between them."

Daegan keeps his focus locked on Zoran. "Reluctantly, I've agreed to do this your way. But when she finds out who you are and what you've done, she may never forgive you. Are you prepared for the consequences?"

Zoran replies, "I am. And I'll do what we agreed—when I do, you'll bring Elli back."

"Assuming she's done her part, then yes."

My mind ignites with questions around who Elli is, and why Zoran's longing for her is draped in such intensity.

"Come," Daegan instructs. "We don't have much time."

Daegan turns, then walks through the open gate and toward me while the others trail behind him, all of them wearing long black cloaks and appearing to float above the snowy ground like phantoms. With Sola's gaze set on me, I sense a grounded peace emanating from her and feel my bones cease to vibrate as if my frame is comprised of wood-formed roots.

Part of me suspects she is purposefully anchoring me. And when I inhale, it feels like my body is under the fluid tranquility of her command, a sensation I haven't experienced in many years; my mother was the only other person who could temper the heat in my veins.

The four of them join me and surround the rose in a perfect circle as

Daegan reaches beneath his cloak, takes a small knife from his belt, then raises my hand and deepens the unhealed cut on my right index finger.

Taking my finger, he draws a circle on his palm, where a tiny white flame sprouts from his skin and hovers in the center of the blood-inked circle. Daegan walks to the rose, and with great care, as if handling a volatile chemical, transfers the flame into its center, causing an instant reaction that results in a long, wispy flame shooting up from the rose like a white rope reaching toward the black-churning heavens above.

The flame twists and undulates like it's alive and serpentine in both body and expression while Daegan tightens our circle around the rose. The flame's white heat warms my face and electrifies my insides to the point that my skin feels too tight, like the current is unsatisfied with what's within me and wishes to break free and find a more expansive point of conduction.

Daegan looks to Sola, whose scar seems to have almost disappeared beneath the brightness of the flame, then nods. With authority, Sola speaks. "At the Scribe's behest and with the birth blood of the Asdans, I invoke the spirits of the Elders."

Sola opens her cloak, removes Prayna's copper medallion, and holds it inches from the flame as Daegan pulls a small glass bottle from his pocket. He releases the cork, and I watch as four thick strands of smoke drift from the bottle, each floating toward what appear to be chosen counterparts: Nikolai, Daegan, Zoran, and me.

Daegan's focus is on the small strand-turned-cloud in front of him as he exhales a gentle breath, causing the little cloud to glide toward the medallion. Zoran echoes Daegan's actions, his cloud following the same path until it, too, hovers over the copper disk. Daegan then looks to Nikolai, who exhales onto his cloud, except his actions fail to cause any movement.

Tattoos swirling at his temples, Daegan offers, "You'll have to let Lukaes in, Nikolai. Just enough to activate the bloodline."

Nikolai closes his eyes, his skin turning stone pale and his body tensing as the veins in his hands become leviathan black. Seeing him clench his fists in pain, I can barely control my compulsion to force Lukaes's darkness from his body. Then Nikolai exhales, and his muscles relax as his cloud travels toward the medallion.

Deducing that it's my turn, I exhale, feeling ridiculous when my smoky cloud refuses to budge. Daegan walks over and stands behind me, then pulls me toward his chest while putting his palm over my heart. Along with the great rhythmic beat of his bass-drum pulse, I feel electricity coursing through my body with such intensity that it's causing my muscles to contract.

In my mind's eye, I'm moving through a tunnel comprised of nothing but numbers—a peculiar form of binary code—and every few seconds, I see a flash of what looks like a counter, identical to the ones that played before old black-and-white movies.

Moving faster through the tunnel, as though traveling through time, the code grows more complex and the counter continues flashing. When it reaches the number thirteen, I see a split-screen image of my parents, their eyes clouded over like they've been frozen in time; when they open their mouths, thick roots burst forth and merge to form a single taproot that shoots toward me. Then my mind goes black.

I hear Daegan's voice in my ear: "Exhale." When he releases his hand from my heart, the electricity inside me diminishes. I do as instructed, and in response, my cloud ambles toward the copper disk like it lacks the energy to complete the journey.

Once all four clouds are hovering above the medallion, they unite and begin raining down what looks like blood, every drop collecting in a dip at the medallion's center until the clouds fold in on themselves and dissolve into the pool below.

Sola moves toward the white flame, then pours the mixture into the rose's center. I hear the rumble of thunder overhead as twelve steady streams of lightning erupt from the skies and join the white flame like it's a conducting rod. From storm to serene calm, the lightning ceases and the flame reduces to a tiny fire-filled spark dancing above the center of the rose.

"Considering our blood has been mixed and that a debt is owed, it should be me who stays with her," Zoran proposes.

Daegan and Zoran are now facing each other, watching one another from the turreted tops of their separate stony structures.

Daegan breaks the silence. "I'm forced to agree."

I have the profound feeling that this realization distresses him somehow, like my supposed dependency on him is what makes up part of his existence. This idea—one in which I carry such an absolute importance in his life—makes me feel rather narcissistic, and as the creator of the dream in play, I wish to release him in some way. For rather than continue allowing him to believe I'm a savior of sorts, I find myself wanting to illuminate the reality he fails to see, which is that neither he nor his plight exists.

While in the trenches of my thoughts, I discover a set of questions I find intriguing—like buried bones they lie just below the dirt-encrusted surface of my mind. Is it possible the characters in my dream believe they're real and that my mind has perpetuated this deception?

Knowing little about the inner workings of the unconscious mind, I haven't a clue how such a thing would be possible; yet just as the mind splits to form multiple personalities, could a mind halve itself and live in two separate realities? Has my mind created these characters and given them a slice of their own consciousness? Perhaps each possesses a small part of my intellect and, in turn, knows how to negotiate the complexities of their survival, which makes these proverbial monsters of my creation, in essence, my mind's own manifestations gone rogue.

This means my fictitious animations have, in dream-true fashion, made themselves believe they have a world to save, and furthering the plunge down the rabbit hole is the fact that only I can end their suffering and impending destruction.

It makes sense to me, if only in part. I'm replaying the happenings of my childhood in opposing form—where once the child was helpless to save or be saved, she is now both redeemed and redeemer. I've cordoned off a portion of my mind to lay the beasts inside me to rest, and for them, I've crafted a forested showground in which to play out their final scenes.

I take a deep breath and feel my body relax, knowing this madness will end soon, my mind having given this partitioned mental space a lifespan and the resulting countdown reaching its imminent close. Soon I'll be rid of sleepless nights, merciless bloodletting, and ruthless specters, and as in my childhood, the forest will set me free. It's no accident I've chosen the woods as a backdrop for this peculiar yet cathartic experience.

Therefore, I will give these characters, my beloved unhinged beasts, whatever they need to be put to rest. I'll submit to the experience of them being real—not as a watcher but as a doer. I'll relate to them as if their hearts and minds are not separate. I'll listen and take them in.

All this is manageable, but the one thing I refuse to do is accept the role of savior. There must be another ending to this story, one that allows me solidarity with myself rather than the exalted position of redeemer. I cannot stand above my beasts and command them from an unreachable throne; the untamed creatures inside me will only rest if I acknowledge their existence and lie down beside them.

In apparently orchestrated timing, Zoran moves toward me, one of the beasts lured to its maker in hopes of oneness. With a newfound awareness of my mind's true intent, I'm willing to submit to him and take in the experience of being fused with my creation.

Glancing around the meadow, I notice that, save for the spiders now forming a perimeter outside the gates, the others are nowhere to be found and the twelfth gate is now closed. I've no idea how much time has gone by; the labyrinth of my thoughts seems to have sucked up hours, leaving Zoran and me alone in the iron-encased meadow.

Turning toward him, I stare into his aqua eyes and resolve to withstand the fiery torture of his fur against my skin, my mind having decided the pain is well worth a fleeting moment of connection with my beast. Why he affects me in this way, I cannot reconcile, nor do I care to. I'm only concerned with touching him, and when my fingers graze his chest, his fur feels like strands of fiery silk. Forcing my burning hands to glide along the contours of his body, I'm lost in wanting to feel him against my bare skin, warmed by the heat radiating from him.

My hands sear with pain, but I push my fingers deeper into his fur, and when he leans forward and takes in the scent of my skin, I feel him grow wild inside. Bones remagnetizing and buzzing like they might split and burst through my skin, I imagine myself breaking into scattered splinters only to be repurposed and reconstructed in accordance with his desire that I be reassembled with skin that doesn't keep us apart. What a strange and incomprehensible circumstance I've created in these dreams, a primal draw to something I can't touch without excruciating consequence. Metaphorical, I'm sure, but frustrating nonetheless.

Zoran takes a step toward me, and despite the frostbitten night, I feel myself starting to sweat as he opens his mouth enough for me to see his razor-sharp canines. I know what he wants, or rather, needs, and if it aids in striking down the first of my beasts that they may all fall like dominos, I'll give him what he craves.

Turning away from him, I kneel on the round base of the rose—the very place where he'd asked me to read the carved inscription that spoke of an Eternal Night—which is now blanketed in a thick layer of powdery snow. Moving my hair to one side, I tilt my head and expose my neck. I'm giving him license to bleed me dry, tear me apart…devour me.

As Zoran's breath drifts down on my neck, I can hear him panting and feel the quickening of his pulse, like our hearts are pumping the same blood. Tilting my head closer to my shoulder, I close my eyes and wait for the piercing pain of his teeth, knowing it will all be worth the suffering when my beasts are laid to rest.

Feeling him move closer, I sense he's close to penetrating my skin, the heat and force of his breath telling me the side of my neck rests between his waiting jaws. Blood rushes up from my legs, torso, and chest, racing into the side of my neck as if eager to quench his thirst, and as a few of his teeth graze my skin, my jugular vein pulses, then pounds until I find myself wanting to release into him.

I'm in a state of submission I've never allowed myself to explore, as this kind of vulnerability, sexually or otherwise, would be far too dangerous in my waking world. But with him, in this dream, I can pledge myself to pure, undiluted capitulation. The truth is, I want it to happen—I'm apt as surrender's concubine.

With Zoran's tongue resting against the vein in my neck, soft and velvet-like, not rough, as I'd expected, my body surges with heat; but as I prepare myself to be bitten, he pulls away. The restraint he's shown has taken a toll, and I notice him trembling from the strain while disappointment lodges within my demagnetizing bones.

With a stern, controlled tone, he instructs me, "Your blood completes the invocation. One drop, nothing more."

Still facing the rose, I hear him walk away, and although my body is beginning to cool, the heat from his mouth lingers on my neck as if his hunger is still clinging to my skin. It's like he's left a part of himself behind, a fiery piece of his desire that requires my presence to survive—a flame of wanting that makes him feel alive.

After standing, I turn from the rose and watch him stop in front of the ninth gate, its Roman numeral bulging from its iron bars. Although I'm sure it's the angle, or perhaps the moon's bluish light, I'd swear the entire gate is bowing inward.

Zoran looks toward me without saying a word, and I raise my finger, squeeze below the cut, and let a single drop tumble past the white flame hovering above the rose's center, hoping my blood will be the anesthetizing serum that coaxes my beasts to their knees.

The air around me is charged, as if its molecules are heaving with weighted expectancy, when the ear-splitting sound of dense stone grinding mixes with the stridency of creaking iron. For a moment, I swear the scent of musty grease drifts through the meadow.

From beneath each gate, stone slabs extend outward, shaving snow and ice from the ground like great knives. Watching Zoran jump onto one of the encroaching wedges, I realize the vegetation-covered edge of the meadow is raised, like the meadow itself is sunken below the level of the forest floor.

With the slabs mere feet from the rose's base, I notice that their tips are made of a more transparent, quartz-looking stone, and when they lock into the base, they create a smooth floor. The stone beneath my feet radiates with heat and in my mind's eye streams of bluish-hued air flow toward me from each of the gates as though I'm the center point, like a cog in a wheel.

Tumbling back in time, I close my eyes and am transported to a memory of my mother relaying the story of the Mystics, saying that Great Spirit created the twelve sky-bound deities and placed a portion of the universe in each of their palms. I remember her sketching a large circle while she spoke of them, her steady hand drawing what looked like a cross between a medicine and zodiac wheel. As if my mother's words are giving birth to form, in my mind's eye, I watch extraordinary, tall, translucent bodies materialize in front of each gate.

It's clear my imagination is overactive in this vivid depiction of what I'd describe as my mother's beloved Mystics—or perhaps the Elders Sola sought to invoke—emerging within my mind's eye. Although their bodies are like jellyfish in a deep sea, I'm able to see their hearts pumping what looks like liquid silver through their thin veins.

Warm air is still streaming toward me, and when I look up at their faces, I realize the gentle breeze gracing my skin is emanating from them. It's their collective breath, a life-affirming current sent like an aiding wind to a stationary sail. They wish for me to come alive, for my fire-filled sparks to create a unified flame. Almost outside myself, I send a message to them: I am only the spark's strike point, not its evolution. With unapologetic truth, I insist that I'm merely a flint, built to ignite but not to burn.

In a display of apparent protest, they grow taller and extend toward the night sky like an elongated vapor. With my mind's eye under their control, I'm a captive audience and feel they're jubilant in their creative freedom as they lean inward, join hands above me, and form the illusion of a dome.

Their bodies seem to be liquefying as their arms meld into what is now a semitransparent gelatin covering the meadow, a viscous dome pulsing as if connected to an invisible heart. Silvery fluid shoots throughout the dome's surface, traveling inside tiny veins like smelted neon light, making it appear the meadow and surrounding gates are encased in a living, breathing sphere.

Echoing a night sky, the dome forms its own constellation in miniature, a condensed, star-filled night sky so luminous it appears to be lit by millions of diamond-size pieces, and I'm moved by the beauty of a mirrored universe so pure and close. Possibly, it is as my mother said: each of the proverbial

Mystics holds a portion of the universe in their hands, and upon joining together, they have shown me how sparks become flame.

Yet as glorious as they are, a sight to behold, I must remind myself that they and this dream-constructed world are near an inevitable and deliberate end. So I'll await the implosion of my personal multilayered realm, complete with its own representative heaven and hell, one inhabited by the Mystics, the other by my intractable beasts. When all is said and done, I'll be content making a home cradled between the two blown-out craters that once housed the best and the worst of me, as in essence, I suppose that is the art of true surrender.

Zoran's booming voice rips through the meadow. "ZOË!"

Yanked from my thoughts, I open my eyes and follow his fixed gaze to a small pool of blood seeping into a seam between the rose's stone base and marble stem. Before I can pull my hand away, like ignited fuel, the tiny white flame hovering above the rose erupts into a raging column of bright red fire that shoots skyward.

Liquid pours from my finger, drawn out as if the rose is somehow seeking my blood to further its ravenous burning. With a corner of my cloak, I wrap my finger to stop the flow, but when a forceful blast reverberates throughout the meadow, I realize my actions have come too late.

Scanning the gates, which are now engulfed in a wall of rancorous flames, I notice that every bar is wrapped in a casing of angry red fire. As if we're conjoined, the marrow in my bones feels like molten lava, my skeleton seized by the same inferno gnawing at the gates' weakening frames.

Zoran rushes to my side, and when I turn toward him, the look of panic in his eyes causes my pulse to race. In response, the wall of fire closes in, leaving us trapped and defenseless against the tightening ring of flames. The spiders dart through the flames and form a circle around us as the wall of fire inches forward. At their black-shelled perimeter, the fire stops its approach and sets their bodies ablaze.

As if enraged by the inability to continue forward, the flames shoot higher. I stare at the tips of their fiery fingers, realizing that the same viscous, diamond-starred constellation I saw in my mind's eye is real and pulsating above us. The dome's unified heartbeat is alive and pushing silvery liquid through what I'm afraid will soon be a network of cauterized veins.

My fear becomes reality as barreling winds sweep through the meadow, stoking the flames higher. The winds send a thin wave of fire across the dome's gelatinous surface, extinguishing each of the stars' brilliance and making the dome look like a sprawling city losing power.

The wind intensifies and merges with a low, yearning moan as the Mystics succumb to the crucible I've created. With my feet blistering from the scorching stone floor, I pull my focus from the dome and ready myself to face the blazing ring around us.

Faced with my imminent quietus, adrenaline floods my system, which, like gasoline, sends the flames ever higher as the spiders, still positioned within the ring of flames, shudder. Their bodies are unable to withstand the unforgiving wildfire fueled by the combustible mixture of my adrenaline and blood, and like thousands of fireworks, they begin exploding around me, leaving nothing behind but crumbled piles of white ash.

Without the spiders' living presence, the fire moves past their powdery remains and resumes its unyielding advance while the wind continues whipping through the meadow. The low moaning intensifies into thunderous screams as my mother's Mystics protest their imminent, fiery deaths.

With my feet raw and the infringing firewall inches from setting my cloak ablaze, Zoran and I are trapped. There's nowhere left for us to go, no escape and no retreat from what has become a nightmarish end to my fabricated dreamscape. Hardening my body, I clench my fists and wait for the sea of flames to suck me into their savage undertow, but instead I am knocked to the ground as Zoran lands on top of me.

Like predator to supple flesh, the fire rips into his body, and I hear him let out a gut-wrenching cry as his muscles stiffen in response to what must be inexorable agony. When he lets out another guttural wail, I realize I cannot endure another moment of him being burned alive.

Trying to nudge myself out from under him, I inch my body to the left, only to feel him bear down with his considerable weight as the scent of his scorched fur, skin, and blood swirl around me like a noxious cloud.

Letting out another howl, he convulses while struggling to shield me from the flames. Bleeding freely now, his skin having given way to the fire's gnashing teeth, his blood cascades onto my thighs, hands, and arms. Yet still he holds himself above me and withstands the torture of what I know to be an excruciating demise.

Feeling his heartbeat slow, I lie beneath my beloved beast, knowing it's not slumber overtaking him, but death, and faced with his extinction, I refuse to allow it. He is my creation, my responsibility, and it's gutless of me to stand by as he's torn from his existence, fictional or otherwise, in such a gruesome manner.

With his heartbeat thumping a few last times like a distant drum and his frame becoming dead weight, I use all my strength to maneuver myself out from underneath him before drawing in a needed breath. The stench in the air is like poison; my stomach lurches and my eyes water, but I can see well enough to know the fire has burned out.

I work to release my lower body from beneath Zoran's frame, and it's not until I pull my legs out from under him that I'm able to take in the severity of his injuries. He's been mutilated by the flames and looks like carrion left to rot in the sun, his flesh hanging from his bones, thick blood running from his open wounds and trailing along the scorched stone floor like lava.

Watching his blood trickle toward the blackened rose, I reach for one of its protruding stone thorns and gouge my finger until it spurts like a fount. Turning back to Zoran's mangled body, I open his mouth and let blood drop onto what's left of his tongue. Feeling helpless and alone sitting on the meadow's burnt-out floor, I'm confused as to why my architected realm is still intact, as I'd expected it to collapse and catapult me back into the reality of my waking world.

Exhausted, I lie down beside Zoran, continuing to let my blood flow into his mouth. I scan his body for any movement, a breath or twitch, but there are no signs of life. I stare into his deadened aqua eyes and notice that one of them looks like charred black glass.

Shifting my focus upward, I watch the dome's gelatin membrane emulate the moon's bruised light while a few lone stars shine in rebellion, their lively diamond sheen highlighting a small network of silvery veins still pulsing with a modicum of life.

The air reeks of death, iron, and blood, the uncompromising evidence of the battle within me, my mind and psyche waging war against one another, one unwilling or unprepared to let this night-realm be destroyed, the other unremitting in its desire to have my day-waking world reign supreme. In my mind's eye, I imagine my blood as a sea surrounding two adversarial islands, and although I control the tides, the islands are impervious to my commands, as they are self-governing and loyal to their opposing causes.

Yet there is a bridge between them, built not of steel but of oak; constructed from the forest's trees and pockmarked by the knife-heeled platforms I wear when walking from one island to the other. It's a bridge I must continue to cross, for it's on this moonlit island that I have elected to resurrect my beast. Perhaps it's better he is awake and walking beside me as both shadow and companion: he has learned to wear the night as a second skin, and to know myself more deeply, I'll demand he teach me to do the same.

Am I not better for choosing both night and day? Shouldn't I be on equal footing with both? This question lingers in my thoughts as my mind dips to moonless darkness.

52

MOONSTRUCK

Zoë lay on the floor, attempting to force her thoughts into some semblance of awareness, the only thing visible in her mind's eye the emblazoned image of Zoran's fire-eaten face surrounded by a ring of flames. How disturbing to have seen his majestic form reduced to a mutilated shell, the lush meadow now a graveyard in which he lay untended and unburied. With this thought occupying her consciousness, the flames in her mind's eye shot higher, as if representing the angst her most recent dream had inflicted.

Forcing her eyes open as one would a sealed attic window, Zoë watched the fire-rimmed vision of Zoran disappear from her thoughts. Mind clear, she took in the hazy view of her cold bedroom, where she lay on her back with her limbs awkwardly placed like she'd been standing and had crumpled to the floor. With her lungs aching and her skeleton misaligned—seemingly assembled from iron that had been heated and pounded into malformed shapes—she untangled her limbs, then eased into a sitting position, feeling like her spine was struggling to hold her upright.

Inhaling, she ran a few fingers through her hair and found it wet, indicating that she'd bathed and changed into a fresh white nightgown. Yet rather than being clean, her gown was soot-covered and dotted with bloodstains from the leaking cut on her finger.

Hearing a loud thump on the hardwood floor, she shifted her focus to the corner of the room as Lucille leapt down from the vanity and walked toward her with a probing gaze, as if she suspected Zoë was somehow an impostor in what she considered her domain. Stopping a foot or so away to further investigate before approaching, she arranged herself into a tidy sitting position, then swept her tail along the floor, wrapping it around the base of her body and causing a fine cloud of dust to plume into the air.

After focusing on the tiny particles that were drifting down through beams of watery blue moonlight toward a thin layer of what looked like ash, Zoë turned back toward the lifeless fireplace in front of her, finding its flameless quiet disconcerting. Based on the amount of dusty soot around her, there had to have been a recent fire, albeit one that had been smothered enough to cause residue to scatter into the room like an ashen blizzard.

Standing, she surveyed the layer of charcoal-colored powder, noticing a set of her footprints leading from the bed to the outlined space on the floor in front of the fireplace where she'd been lying. Rooted in the surfacing scene playing in her mind's eye, she saw herself entranced, pulled from the comfort of her bed, and drawn toward the blazing fire by whatever arcane force had snuffed out its raging flames.

Feasibly, as in her nightmare, it was she who had created a true trial by fire, unconsciously forging a path of flaming embers in her own bedroom. Although this was frightening, she wondered if it was irrefutable proof of the two islands inside her: one controlling the episodic story of her dreams, the other directing her physical body as if she were a marionette in a puppeteer's box.

Then, as though her dreamscape was becoming reality, the moonlight in the room turned an ominous fiery red, making it seem like the meadow's inferno had followed her home so as to encase her house in a ring of fire. Like mistress to master, she walked to the window and stood transfixed, gazing at the bloodred moon's eerie light bathing her nightgown in watercolor flames.

Recalling a similar moon on the night of her mother's death, almost twenty-two years ago to the day, Zoë imagined the bloodied sky covered with the mist of her mother's spirit, the fanning array of her soul merging with the moon she so dearly loved. With her mother at home in the arms of the ancestors, it seemed they were again demanding the winter solstice bring a rare lunar eclipse, making it appear like the apoplectic moon was drenching itself in a sea of blood in honor of her death.

But on this night, she found the moon's presence unsettling, knowing her mother believed their bloodline was sacred, carrying both the knowledge of their Clan and the spirited whisperings of their ancestors' secrets. It was a belief Zoë neither shared nor had any interest in pursuing, and she almost couldn't bear to hear her mother's voice echoing in her thoughts: "The fire in your blood can cast death or life. Courage is in knowing which to use—and when."

Having come from a long line of courageous women who were far more devoted and brave than she could ever be, Zoë knew that high above, looking down from their sky-swing perch, her ancestors' fire-ringed moon was sending a message. A reckoning was coming, an exhumation of all she had buried in darkness. She would be held accountable, and like the ancestors of her Clan, she, too, would be forced to face the death-hungry beasts inside her.

Standing at the window, clothed in white, feeling the biting air creeping through the paned glass, she felt like a sacrificial bride before her winter-groom's bloody altar. With the anniversary of her mother's death fast approaching, she understood the moon's demands, even though she wasn't ready or willing to comply.

After moving away from the window, she walked across the room to sit on the edge of her bed; on the bedside table, neon monsters shouted from their silent, electric mouths: 3:11 a.m.

Next to the clock was a lukewarm cup of Lula's cinnamon tea and the unread book she'd given her nearly two weeks prior, *A Tale of Two Cities*—a title befitting her circumstances. A book that could figuratively portray her relationship between the forlorn "cities" of night and day, neither of which was getting the best of her, nor she the best of them.

Next to the book, her phone blinked, and seeking a distraction from her thoughts, she picked it up and read the previous night's texts.

"Brave the beastly cold for cocoa? -ps"

The thought of a cup of cocoa felt soothing, but first she needed a night of dreamless sleep. "Be there at 10."

She scrolled down to the next text. "Can I stop by tomorrow tonight to talk? 9? Not for appt. —Bill"

While responding, she found herself wondering what he wanted to discuss. "9 is fine."

After putting down her phone, she removed her nightgown, dusted off her feet, then lifted the covers and slipped beneath them as Lucille bounded onto the bed. Although she wouldn't normally allow Lucille such latitude, for some reason her presence was comforting, like an anchor in a turbulent sea.

Inching deeper into the covers, she focused on her mother's journal, which lay open beside her, the writing shaky and light against the page. Pulling it closer, she read the words lit only by the bloodied moonlight streaming into the room.

> *The Watcher comes with sweet, spice-laden cocoa hoping it will soothe the ravenous beast, or perhaps distract it from its steady consumption.*
>
> *Yet although the beast inside me fights viciously, I do not suffer. I feel Great Spirit's arms hold me closely, as the Gardener does you, dear daughter, tilling a soil newly suited for spring's embrace.*
>
> *The Gardener has been to see me, a seed of understanding he plants, his words tending to the wounds he supposes your absence from me has left; he is a genuine soul even though the fruit of his own tree rots.*
>
> *I pray you tame the snakes that writhe within, as I know the sight of my decay damages your spirit, and I understand your pain overshadows mine by a world's length. I forgive you, I breathe you, and through you, my life takes on new meaning.*

HalfLight breaks from doctor's orders, again doubling my medicine, masking the pain not for my sake, but for his. Behind his eyes, a storm of icy wind circles. He doesn't know it yet, but it is your flesh for which he hungers, so I have offered my own.

The time is soon. He grows restless. I have seen my hasty crumble in HalfLight's frozen eyes.

But I welcome the beast's bite, its venom quick, thorough, and calculating. I am ready. It is not death the beast brings, but redemption. For in time, from the prisons of fire and earth, I shall be freed…

None of them know.
Like the silver fox, I am sly.
All are tricked.

—Mother

Native American legends had graced Zoë's ears from the time she could remember—stories of life, love, and caution—but her mother's favorite was that of the silver fox. "I am like the silver fox," she would say, "small, clever, and silent." She would tell the story, then laugh at the sight of Zoë's stature. "How ever did the silver fox give birth to a bear!"

Zoë's thoughts drifted to the sound of her mother's boisterous and contagious laugh as a flood of memories hit her mind. While a smile etched along her lips, she let the memories wrap around her consciousness until in her mind's eye she could almost see the silver fox curled up beside her.

53

TAPROOT

Tap...tap...tap...

Lula opened her eyes and focused on the ceiling, which was bathed in peculiar fire-hued light.

Tap...tap...tap...

With her heart racing, she shifted her gaze left and watched as a large raven sitting on the ledge outside pecked away at the bay window.

Throwing back the covers and walking across the room, she studied the raven's piercing cobalt eyes. It appeared to be staring right through her, its intellect far outweighing the known cleverness of its species; this bird was determined and systematic in its desire to not only garner her attention but to also keep it.

Inching sideways along the ledge with its body facing her, knocking clumps of snow to the ground as it moved, the raven dragged its sharp beak along the window while continuing to examine her. Back and forth on the sill it went, attempting to cut through the glass to whisper whatever secrets were swimming in its lake-like eyes.

With the room's light deepening to a shade of blood red, Lula gazed up toward the fire-ringed moon and felt her heart sink, her mind drifting to the image of the Fionn's Window she'd seen in the journal Phinneas showed her. Such a rare and ominous moon only served to anchor her suspicion that Zoë was walking a fire-lined path paved with blood, and in so knowing, she couldn't bear the thought of how isolating it must be for her to undertake such a journey alone.

Tap…tap…TAP…

Shifting her focus back to the raven, Lula noticed that it was pecking in the bottom right-hand corner of the window frame, grabbing hold of a vine that clung to the front of the house like it was a worm in the grass. The raven yanked and pulled at the vine, and as Lula leaned forward and put her palms on the sill to watch, she felt something move against her right hand.

Bending down, she stared at a small vine that appeared to have burrowed through the walls of the house and into her room like a stone-hungry snake. The little vine jerked, then slid backward as the raven tugged at it one last time before launching from the windowsill and vanishing into the firelit night.

Needing more light to examine the vine, Lula walked to the bedside table and turned on a small antique lamp that cast a bluish glow into the room through its sea-colored stained-glass shade, as if seeking to douse the moon's fiery light. She stepped back to the window, peered outside, and felt her body go stiff when she saw a man standing on the sidewalk beneath her window clothed in a telltale trench coat, hat, and wingtip shoes.

Although her view was from the second floor and his face was hidden by a fedora, Lula could see he was focused on the front door. She was certain the entry was bolted tight and the alarm armed, and with that top of mind, she wondered what on earth he was hoping to achieve by gawking at the entrance to what was an impenetrable brownstone-turned-fortress.

Half of her brain was telling her to call the police, but the other half was caught in the invisible web he seemed to be weaving around the house. She felt like he'd rendered her immobile, like spider to fly, in a cocoon of silken thread. As if sensing her penetrating stare, he glanced up for a split second, then walked down the street in a slow, deliberate manner she found disturbing.

Watching him approach the street corner, a shadowy image of the man's face surfaced in Lula's mind; his smooth skin, strong jaw, and piercing gaze all adding to the peculiar and anesthetizing allure of his presence. And when the tiny vine resting on the windowsill twitched against her skin, she swore it was somehow at his command.

Once he'd rounded the corner onto Greenwich Street and disappeared, Lula knelt beside the sill and studied the vine. It appeared to be connected to a cable-like cluster that clung to the wall, running from the window frame to the floor, then along the baseboard and out into the hallway like an inconspicuous telephone wire.

After grabbing her phone to use as a flashlight, Lula followed the tiny vine cluster down the hallway to the staircase, where it trailed along the base of the railing before curving around the last spindle of the banister. Stepping from the final stair to the oaken floor, she turned into the foyer and tracked the vines until they disappeared beneath the door to the basement.

She opened the door, then reached inside to flip on the light, the strong scent of damp mustiness infiltrating her senses as she trained her gaze back on the small cluster of vines that traced the stairs leading down into the basement.

Zoë had intended to convert the basement into a cozy room with an adjacent wine cellar, but it was a project that never got off the ground. Each time she sought to engage an architect, something derailed the project; either her diverted attention or an inability to find a project partner who shared her vision. As a result, the basement had remained untouched since the house's original construction, and as Lula completed her descent and made her way into the large, brick-walled room, it was like going back in time.

She tracked the cluster of vines along the planked wooden floor until they converged with something in a dark corner of the room. Using her phone as a light, Lula approached what appeared to be a coffee-table-sized medicine wheel. As she examined it, she could that see the vines merging into the wheel's outermost ring had traded their bright green exterior for deep maroon as though they were pulsing with rich, oxygenated blood.

Kneeling down, she studied the wheel, which seemed to have been laid out in a ritualistic manner with an outer ring of thick, leafy vines; a second, inner ring of shiny bones that appeared to have been lacquered in blood and fire-set; a third ring of black feathers encasing a fourth ring of crushed petals; and a fifth and final inner ring made of what looked like ash. At the wheel's center, a small seedling had pushed up through the wood, its phosphorescent leaves a brilliant bright green.

Next to the wheel was a makeshift knapsack that had been created by tying together four corners of a filthy piece of cloth. Upon further inspection, Lula realized it was the same sack carried by the creature she'd seen enter the house a week or so prior. Next to the sack were her mortar and pestle from the kitchen, along with a small glass of water and two twine-tied sprigs of dried rosemary from the spice pantry, stocked and tended by her own hand.

Reaching forward, Lula took one of the crushed petals from the fourth ring and rubbed it between her fingers until it released the scent of lilac. She dipped her finger in the fifth ring and brought it to her nose; the powder was ground black pepper.

Examining each of the rings, she constructed the story of the wheel, calling upon the myriad collections of mythology she had studied, until each ring spoke to her:

> Vines give rooted strength,
> Bones call upon the wisdom of the ancestors,
> Feathers give a warrior agility in battle,
> Lilacs soothe the spirit of a restless traveler,
> Black pepper expels that which is hidden in darkness,
> The seedling speaks to a gate being opened.

Lula's pulse raced as she wondered who could have formed this intricate fusion of Celtic, Native American, and Aboriginal spiritual wheels, seeing as the work before her was complex in both execution and purpose. This was crafted by someone who knew Zoë and her current plight intimately—or perhaps, as with many of the peculiar things going on in the house, Zoë had somehow contributed to or performed this task while in one of her trancelike slumbers.

Whoever created the wheel, it was meant to be a companion to the Fionn's Window from the journal, and it signified the final push to attain the key of knowledge, which would in theory unlock the gate to the realm of one's soul. But such a passage was never undertaken alone, as it was both dangerous and frightening; she had never heard of a traveler attempting such a feat without the aid of an experienced tribal Elder or master spiritualist.

Based upon the advanced elements of the drawing she'd seen in the journal, someone had to have started Zoë on the Walk, but who? And why would they have left her in the throes of such a perilous crossing on her own—one in which she could fall into the arms of permanent madness?

As Lula's mind flooded with questions, she opened the text window on her phone and typed, "Phinneas: Can we meet? I think our party of two just gained a third. Tell you more in person. —Lula"

It was her hope that reading the journal Phinneas had shown her in its entirety would shed some light on Zoë's current situation. The more information she could gather, the better—and that included trying to find out more about the man outside her window. Specifically, why he seemed so interested in Zoë, and what, if anything, he might have to do with what was going on in the house.

54

LET SLEEPING DOGS LIE

Sleet was beating the outside of Mr. Sumel's house like thousands of tiny fists demanding entry. It felt as though each piece hit the base of Zoë's consciousness with the sole intent of clobbering it into a pulped mixture of memories, dreams, and questions; whereby milled and strained of identifiable matter, her intellect and ability to reason would resemble little more than pulverized mush, void of clarity or anything tangible for her to grasp.

Mr. Sumel's inquiry halted her spinning thoughts. "What do you think of the new recipe?"

She took a sip and the spicy cocoa burned her tongue. After letting the flavor of what she swore was chili oil linger, she commented, "It's interesting."

Mr. Sumel let out a hearty laugh and took a drink of cocoa. Surveying the cozy upstairs sitting room, she shifted her weight and attempted to inch away from one of the springs that was pushing through the time-thinned padding of the couch cushion like a steel snake.

Once comfortable, she watched the crackling fire in the inset copper fireplace in front of her. While she fixated on the flames, the movie of the previous night's dream played on high speed until her liquefied mind reflected images of the burning meadow and fire-chewed face of her midnight beast.

The stormy fists beating against the window behind her intensified, their incessant pounding jerking her mind back into the room. When she looked at Mr. Sumel, who was sitting beside her, he appeared a million miles away, his gaze locked on the fire as though he too was immersed in a collage of unnerving recollections.

Waiting for the heaviness of his thoughts to lighten, Zoë examined the mounted iron lanterns on either side of the fireplace, listening to them sizzle and guzzle fresh oil. Sending her gaze downward, she noticed that an electrical outlet on the wall next to the fireplace was charred and burnt at the sides. With a stack of old magazines and newspapers sitting below the scorched outlet—not to mention every room being lantern-lit—she was amazed the house hadn't yet burned to the ground.

In continuing to examine the blackened outlet, an inquiry was triggered. "Why did you give me the Black Industries article?"

Feeling a charge ignite in the room, she focused on Mr. Sumel as he answered, "You know, Alice, the rabbit hole won't always lead you to Wonderland."

Synchronizing their sips of cocoa, they sat in silence long enough for the air to lose its charge and settle to the ground like a sleeping hound.

"In this light, you look so much like her."

Feeling her guts tighten, she queried, "You were with her near the end?"

He answered while shifting his gaze back to the fire. "I was, yes."

Zoë set her mug down on a side table and fidgeted with her bracelet, watching its red stone glow in the firelight, feeling like her mother's love was visible in every strand of its woven copper wire.

"I hope you know…not even death can break the bond between the two of you."

A black shroud came down over her thoughts, echoing the guilt she felt for not having been there the day her mother died. Against her will, it was forcing her to see the room through a dark and shadowy veil. "She called you the Watcher."

The angry clouds outside grumbled in response to the clear and present ache in his eyes. "I tried to be. When I could get past her nurse, that is."

Recalling a recent journal entry, she wondered if he was referring to the man her mother called HalfLight. Before she could inquire, Mr. Sumel eased himself up from the couch and rustled down the hall to his office, still talking as if he were right next to her. "Such a depressing fellow."

She listened to him rattle around in his office and was about to prod him when the charred outlet flickered with neon-blue light. Tiny licks of electrical tentacles slid from the outlet, buzzing faintly as Mr. Sumel's voice and shuffling steps approached. "His eyes could razor right through you."

Entering the room, pipe in hand, Mr. Sumel trundled back to the couch still prattling on about the nurse while pipe smoke trailed in behind him like a phantom companion. "He barely tolerated my presence." As he lowered himself to the couch, the tentacle of electricity disappeared back into the socket. "But she was stubborn, your mother…"

Studying him, she waited for the smoke exhaling from his mouth to draw out the remaining thoughts still rooting around in his brain.

"My bladder's like a damn sieve. Was only gone a minute or two." Staring at the fire, he gummed his pipe like it was a pacifier, tension knotting up his face. "She died while I was out of the room, with that nurse at her side. Always hated that."

Like hundreds of hornets were stinging her at once, Zoë felt her skin flush and swell in response to what she'd just heard; she'd always believed her mother had died in her father's arms, not in the presence of a virtual stranger.

Juxtaposed to the stinging venom coursing through her system was the gentle caress of warm fur against her hand; when she looked down into Ziggy's beady black eyes, she felt even more unsettled. Flickering pictures of Ziggy in Nikolai's cabin flooded her thoughts, and as she ran her hand down Ziggy's back, she couldn't help feeling like reality's assassin lay in her lap.

Mr. Sumel inquired, "Penny for your thoughts. Nickel for your dreams."

Nikolai had used the same phrase while they sat together in his cabin in front of a copper fireplace she now realized looked almost identical to the one blazing in front of her. Eclipsing all other thoughts, she feared she was going mad, and the resulting dread gripped her like a fever, holding her breath hostage and making her long for the only person whose counsel she had ever trusted.

As if to herself, she reminisced, "I miss her wisdom."

In a soothing tone, he remarked while puffing on his pipe, "'Let him that would move the world first move himself.'"

Running a hand down Ziggy's back, she played along. "Socrates."

He flashed a beaming smile. "Your father's daughter, I see."

That was true in name only, seeing as she and her father had just two things in common: a love of books and her mother.

Ziggy, her personal fur-armored assassin, crawled from her lap onto the threadbare couch and waddled toward Mr. Sumel while her thoughts spun themselves into words. "Strange things happen—" Forcing herself to continue, she met Mr. Sumel's gaze. "In my house, in my dreams."

Mr. Sumel was about to speak when Zoë's phone rang. She retrieved it from her purse and studied the screen, which was without an incoming number.

He joked, "Go ahead and take it. Might be a handsome fella!"

She pressed answer but couldn't seem to say hello. After a brief pause, a man spoke. "Ms. Hall?" Dripping with the melted fat of beefy sensuality, the man continued, despite her silence. "I understand from Mr. Sinclair you've agreed to a meeting."

Silence stretched between them like a weighted rubber band until Zoë willed herself to inquire, "Whom will I be meeting?"

Curt and matter-of-fact, the man replied, "Malcolm Blackwood."

She felt anesthetized, like an insect caught in an expertly woven web. Time stood still as if this man were the master of both minute and hour.

In a casual manner, Malcolm Blackwood commented, "Art can be such a lovely form of introspection. I do hope the painting from Mr. Sinclair's shop has brought you joy." Without waiting for her to respond, he confirmed, "We have much to discuss. I look forward to seeing you."

With that, he ended the call, and as her heart pounded in her chest, she turned toward Mr. Sumel, whose face was chalky white as he spoke. "It's impossible for you to meet with Malcom Blackwood."

"Why?"

In an uncharacteristically serious tone, he responded, "Because Malcolm Blackwood is dead."

55

NEVERMORE

Bill stood on the sidewalk staring up at a large raven perched at the top of the stone steps leading to Zoë's house. The bird was looking right through him and into the memories its presence had dislodged.

"The ravens, I have to go with them." Those had been his father's last words before he leapt from the fire escape of their five-story walk-up.

A decorated officer, Bill's father was one of the city's guardians, a wingless angel with a gun on his hip and a shiny shield in his pocket. It had always been just the two of them: him and his hero. But something had gone horribly wrong. Grown men didn't change from functioning adults to gibberish-babbling madmen without a reason. Yet no one had answers about his father's death. No one would talk.

Bill had amassed a small entrepreneurial fortune, which permitted him the luxury of employing those who would help feed his voracious appetite for investigating what forced his father off the fire escape and to his death that night. From what he'd gathered, it had to do with something his father had seen, something that had—almost overnight—ripped his sanity out from underneath him.

His father's voice filled his thoughts. "The ravens, son, can't you hear them?" Bill couldn't, in fact, hear them, nor could he recall seeing one in the city until now.

The raven lowered its head, then lifted into the air with great effort as though it were held down by the magnitude of its own memories and thoughts. Watching it fly past him and toward the intersection, Bill found himself fixating on a bent street sign on the corner that read Jane Street.

Shifting his focus back toward Zoë's house, he stared at the front door and imagined three words carved into the door's dark wood:

Sanctuary. Battlefield. Valhalla.

Bill moved up the stairs toward Zoë's room, her perfume lingering in the air, sweet and pungent. The purpose of his visit was weighing on his mind, the lives of him, Zoë, and his dead wife united by an almost cruel circumstance. A part of him wished he hadn't discovered the connection, information that had been haunting him since he saw the Black Industries article on Zoë's vanity.

Reaching the top of the stairs, he ventured into the dim hallway toward her bedroom, feeling his pulse quicken. There was no questioning the effect she had on him. He took a deep breath and steadied the thumping, rhythmic drum inside, reminding himself that allowing the development of any further feelings for her was unwise.

The door to her room was ajar, leaving a sliver of her visible. He stood watching the room's muted light surround her. After a moment, it seemed she was the room's sole source of light. Warmth from the fireplace next to her flowed from the room and wrapped his chilled skin in a thick ribbon of heat. Taking a step closer, he noticed that she was staring at an old Polaroid and that the longer she examined the photo, the more rigid her body became.

After a few tension-riddled minutes, Zoë shoved the photo back into an open book on her vanity then slammed the book shut. A sconce beside him popped and went dark, and she shot a glance toward the bedroom door. Bill took a step backward, but it was too late. She'd already seen him and was crossing the room like a silken storm.

He stood planted in the hallway, embarrassed and without an excuse for failing to announce himself. After opening the door, she met his gaze. It was frightening how she composed herself, shifting her demeanor like a chameleon blending into changing terrain. Placing a calm hand on his shoulder, she beckoned him into the room.

He hadn't commanded his legs to walk forward, yet they were already in motion and carrying him into the warmth of her bedroom. She walked toward the bed, crimson silk trailing behind her while he followed, moth to flame.

Once at the bed, she looked at him. He could see a residual spark of anger in her eyes, contained voltage resting below her smooth, controlled exterior—he found himself curious as to why the photo had upset her. But there was something alluring about her forced state of calm, like being caught in the eye of a storm, and when she sat on the edge of the bed, he felt her commanding him to do the same.

Easing himself down beside her, a shot of adrenaline coursed into his system. With his heart racing and his mouth growing dryer by the minute, ineloquent and intrusive as it was, Bill pushed a waiting question from his lips. "Did you know Evan Black?"

Looking like a child who'd been tricked, she searched him for some time before responding, "Did you?"

Despite the pain that had flashed through her eyes, he answered, "Through business only. My wife knew him—personally."

Seeing her obvious longing for Mr. Black, Bill felt an unexpected hint of jealousy rise to the surface. It was a juvenile response and one he sought to suppress.

"Your wife's affair—it was with Evan?"

He met her gaze. "Yes."

The battle within her was apparent. "It seems sadistic of J.T. to have introduced us."

Bill swore the air around her was growing hotter; the room was charged to the point that it made him uncomfortable. "Actually, J.T. introduced them as well."

It was clear that her mind was sifting through a bevy of weighted thoughts. After a moment, she commented, "Evan had to have had a reason—"

Bill interrupted with more bluntness than intended. "For having an affair with my wife?"

With her hands folded in her lap, she looked like a statue whose insides were filled with frayed wires. "Is this why you came? To ask me about him?"

It was his intention to answer her, but his mind had gone blank. The color of her cheeks flushed a deep red and her lips were swollen as if they were holding back the raw voltage inside her. All he could think about was kissing her, and without hesitating, he did.

The way she tasted, the softness of her lips, made him want to devour her. Never in his life had he been sated by a kiss; an act that was usually precursory was with her almost consumptive. She pushed against his chest while he pulled her closer, his mouth hovering above hers, their breathing in careful and meticulous trade. He was struggling to find a balance between caring for her and wanting to satisfy his overpowering drive, and such tense negotiations to reach a compromise caused his deliberate patience to wane.

Laying her down, he guided his hand beneath her underwear and slipped a finger inside her. She was perfect, wet. His rational thoughts were backseated by the cruel but coveted drug of male desire, the feel of her beneath him such a swift and potent high that he had to stop himself from ripping off her robe.

She removed his belt, unzipped his pants, then wrapped her fingers around him. There was wildness between them, the power of her appetite male in its intensity, her kiss deep, her hands adept, and for a moment, he teetered on the edge of coming.

Desperate to feel her skin, he removed any remaining clothing and pressed himself against her until their bodies were so intertwined it felt like they were of the same flesh. She opened her legs wider; he was seconds from being inside her and so hard it was almost painful, but just as he went to enter her, he felt her body stiffen.

In an instant, she tore herself from him. She was up and away from the bed like naked lightning. Both were breathing heavily, his gentility at odds with the animalistic state of his desire, while she, no less at odds, walked back toward him in silken bareness.

"I can't."

Confused and jilted from the release he didn't realize he needed, he uttered something thoughtless and asinine. "I'll pay you."

He would have traded all his possessions to take back the words that had just slapped her in the face.

He stood and went toward her, frantic to repair the damage he'd done. Hoping for a chance to explain his actions, he searched for a way to get back to the point where she would let him in. But it was apparent she wanted him to leave.

She put on her robe and stood in the center of the room while he gathered his strewn clothing and dressed. It sickened him to know he had hurt her, a fact she would never admit but one he knew to be true.

Dressed and feeling foreign in his own clothes, he went to her and put a gentle hand on her cheek. Her skin was like ice, an arctic wall meant to shut him out, a wordless "Fuck you." So although it killed him, he kissed her cheek and walked from the warmth of her room.

Once in the hallway, he let the door close behind him, locking her in and himself out. The scent of her perfume was inside his skin; he could smell her everywhere, and with each inhale the scent grew stronger. The house was silent, dark, and cold, and it seemed even the walls were moving inward to force him down the stairs and out into the winter night.

In a slight daze and halfway down the stairs, he felt a gentle hand on his shoulder. She turned him around, the moon lighting her like a radiant ghost. "Thursday. Nine."

He watched her walk back up the staircase, the bloodred silk of her robe cascading behind her, and once in the hallway, she looked over her shoulder. "And leave your wallet at home."

56

IN BOCCA AL LUPO

With her lips still inflamed, Zoë closed her eyes and could almost feel Bill's mouth on hers, his hands in her hair, his strong arms around her.

Most men had an element of greed in their kiss, a demanding kind of entitlement, but the hunger behind Bill's desire was deliberate and searching, as though he were seeking to know her, to see her in the rawest sense. In many ways, she had wanted to give in to him, as it had been ages since she'd allowed herself to feel the full force of her own unbridled sexuality—not since Evan. But after having been told of Evan's affair, her mind was unable to cope with the intimacy her connection with Bill had demanded.

As if her sensorial perceptions were layers of transparent film, the memory of Bill's hands on her skin was overlaid with the feeling of Evan tracing the curves of her body, both sets of experiences playing simultaneously like they were two men expressed as one. Evan's face then overtook her mind's eye until she felt like her blood was pumping in reverse, as if time itself was edging backward to bring them closer together.

With Evan's presence mixing into her heated blood, her mind caved beneath the weight of knowing that he'd moved on with someone else and found a way to live without her—a childish notion, but one that surfaced nonetheless. It was naïve of her to suppose he'd never find love again, assuming theirs was a union even based on love, but on that topic she'd have preferred blissful ignorance—especially as it related to J.T. bringing Evan and Bill's wife together.

A mass of coiled cords forming in the pit of her stomach sent a wave of bound tension snaking up through her abdomen until they settled in the space around her heart, and as she picked up her phone to text J.T., her fingers were hot enough to leave fire-forged prints on the screen.

"Need to meet. Urgent."

To her, the mass of strings winding inside her mirrored the mayhem of Fate, a cruel and petulant mistress toying with the strands that held the lives of her subjects together. Fate was a master weaver, caring more for her own entertainment than for the tempestuous twists and distorted, misthreaded messes she made of people's existences.

Feeling the coil expanding, there was no denying Fate's officious hand was wreaking havoc on the tapestry of Zoë's own life by entwining Bill's wife with Evan in such wicked fashion. In a final loom-driven act of mercilessness, Fate had cross-stitched Bill's life thread with hers.

Having seen the newspaper article on the Black family with Evan's grandfather pictured in front of his home—66 Jane Street—she knew that even through her house their lives were interwoven. When she closed her eyes, she could feel Evan around her, his essence drifting through the windows, his vessel-less soul floating along the oaken floors, his whisper within the walls.

Like a thread being dip-dyed, the echo of Evan's spirit merged into the sound of Nikolai's voice as it glided through her thoughts. "You see two worlds, but there is only one." Perhaps Fate's loom was active even in her dreams, reminding her that the separate and solitary life she'd chosen could, in fact, be a constructed illusion.

Letting her gaze sweep down toward her vanity top and settle on the old Polaroid that slipped from her mother's journal before Bill's arrival,

Zoë felt all other thoughts fade into the recesses of her mind. The photo displayed her mother's severe physical deterioration, yet somehow, tubes, wires, unnatural thinness, and interminable pain had done little to suspend the ethereal nature of her beauty.

Behind her mother, standing in the background and clad in nurse's scrubs, was the man her mother called HalfLight. Knowing that her mother had taken her last breath not in the presence of family, but rather in the company of this frozen-eyed shell of a human being caused Zoë's blood to boil. How her father could have lied, reciting a theatrical tale of her mother dying in his arms, was unimaginable and unpardonable, and if he weren't already dead, she would make him suffer for uttering such a self-serving falsehood.

Cooling her lava-like blood, she studied the three vestiges of her mother sitting on the vanity top, scanning every detail and trying to make sense of how, or if, they all fit together: the photo, the journal, and the paintings were speaking to her, so as to be reunited with the tapestry from which each had been unwoven.

With the voice of the paintings the most exigent, Zoë put the three of them together until the copper strips at their sides touched. Just as the first two had previously, all three now came alive as if electricity was pulsing through them and causing each one to change.

Feeling her hands becoming charged, she watched the left-hand painting—a monochrome version of 66 Jane Street—turn a murky grey while the crescent moon above ran red with blood. The small tree on the sidewalk in front of the house—the raven on one of its spindly branches appearing to grow larger and more pronounced—extended a thin, spidery root across the bottom of the canvas toward the center painting's partial meadow before passing beneath the inscribed stone and marble rose where she first met Zoran.

Leaving a trail that burned like acid behind it, the root slithered from the center painting into the far right painting, then turned a gruesome, bloodied red before reaching the outermost edge of the painting's frame.

Feeling the charge in her hands intensify, she gripped the paintings harder while twelve iron gates materialized around the meadow. With the gates now visible, she noticed that the root had stopped in front of the open ninth gate; her painted doppelganger was standing beside the gate in a crimson-hooded cloak that concealed part of her face as well as whatever she was carrying in her arms.

Resurrected from his fiery death, her midnight-tainted beast, Zoran, was at her side, looking toward the gate with an expression of apprehension and fear. Yet despite his trepidatious demeanor, there was a determination to his stance that made it clear he intended to lead her through and into the realm that lay beyond it.

A feeling of dread washed over her as the meadow transformed into the familiar remains of charred stone, and she swore she could almost catch the scent of hot iron in the air as all the gates but the ninth began to disappear. Then, like a deadening plague ripped across the right and center paintings, their landscapes grew dark and lifeless until they blended into the shadowy monochromatic painting on the left.

Removing her hands from the sides of the paintings, Zoë took a shallow breath and, with her mind reeling, attempted to steady her racing pulse. As evidenced by the triptych's contents, the twelve gates in her fictitious dreamscape had been moved just before the meadow burned; details unfeasibly present in a living triptych painted by her mother thirty years prior.

Brighter and more vivid than before, the letters hidden in the paintings surfaced from the dingy scenery and begged for her to unite them. After bringing a lamp closer, she pulled out a notepad and finished the inscription:

> A ring 'round the rose are the gates that lead,
> A crimson stone its nestled seed.
> By the night of twelve, it must be free,
> Or all that was will cease to be.

Overwhelmed, Zoë wanted to run from her house, tear down the street, and thrust herself into the arms of the waiting winter night. Standing, she knocked her mother's journal from the vanity, its ivory pages mashing into the wooden floor. When she bent down to fetch the journal, she noticed it was open to the page she'd dog-eared days before.

Reading the entry containing her mother's Cherokee script, she felt darkness closing in on all sides of her mind while the coil of thread inside her whipped up into a brewing storm.

> *I see shadow in his eyes (I have named him HalfLight) and ask Great Spirit to bestow pardon upon him, though he's the ᎬᎧᏴ ᎦᏉ ᎠᏟᎢᎾᏙᎫ ᎠᏟᎭᎾ.*

Almost outside herself, Zoë flipped through the rest of the journal as passages, phrases, and letters appeared to be lifting up and away from the ivory paper.

> *HalfLight breaks from doctor's orders, again he doubles my medicine…I have seen my hasty crumble in HalfLight's frozen eyes.*

But one phrase punched her in the gut with blunt, inky fists:

> *…and so shall it be, even after the pierce of midnight's clawed foot.*

Never had she moved so fast in all her life. With the journal still in hand, she flew down the stairs into the firelit sitting room and straight to her mother's end table. Lilac petals floated to the floor as she moved the vase between her and the books her mother was never without.

The slim red book that led Zoë to Mr. Sumel was on top of the small stack, just where she'd left it after first meeting him, its cover tattered and worn in her hungry hands. She flipped through a section of Cherokee poems and stories, searching for anything that could help her decipher the script in her mother's journal.

Locating the glossary and alphabet in the back of the book, she translated her mother's Cherokee script and read the full passage aloud.

I see shadow in his eyes—I have named him HalfLight—and ask Great Spirit to bestow pardon upon him, though he's the black wolf, death bringer.

With her knees giving out, she slumped onto the sofa and stared into the blazing fire. Her mind flickered with a montage of voices and pictures, the most prominent being Daegan shifting forms in one of her dreams. A portion of a previous conversation with him, where he'd referred to himself as a Satient, floated through her thoughts as she grappled with the true meaning of the term: he was two in the body of one.

A flash of the Polaroid that fell from her mother's journal sat lodged in her thoughts, the nurse lurking in the dim background like a night-stalking predator. Yet even with his unmistakable stare boring a hole through the fabric of her waking world, she wanted to refute who he was.

Deconstructing the wall of her denial, in the backdrop of her mind's eye, Daegan's voice crashed into her consciousness, his terse words to Zoran like daggers in her brain. "When she finds out who you are and what you've done, she may never forgive you." Another phrase from her mother's journal lit up like a cluster of stars on a dark night. "I fear the parting I know lurks on padded feet…"

Usurping her mother's starlit words was a clipped, burning memory of digging deep into Zoran's soul and unearthing the buried secret that resulted in his unrelenting shame and purgatorial existence: he had taken a life. It made her feel insane to admit it, but from within her storm-ridden guts, she was certain Zoran was somehow responsible for her mother's death.

For a moment, she was a child again, sitting alone as she had the night her mother died, when she had cried out and cursed Great Spirit for stealing the one thing she couldn't live without. But as Fate dethreaded the tapestry of the world around her, she realized it wasn't Great Spirit who had snuffed out her mother's life—it was death incarnate. A shift-to-blackness reaper who had pilfered her mother's last breath, then dared to masquerade as her dream-borne companion.

An inscrutable and callous hatred gripped the edges of her soul, and as the storm inside her plumed into an ice-force gale, her blood grew so cold she ceased to breathe, and with atomic force, her hand-stitched world exploded.

Defenseless against the sudden blast coming from the arctic tempest inside her, the fire's raging flames extinguished. Enclosed in hushed darkness—like Alice plummeting into a black abyss—she let herself fall, body squeezed, mind shutting down until only one thought formed inside a midnight-tinged corner of her mind.

When I find you, I will kill you.

57

RECKONING

I am rage in the flesh, the speed at which I'm running almost inhuman as I cut a straight line through the forest like a knife. My instincts have taken over, and the only sensation rising through my ice-laden body is the scorching ball of fire that has traded places with my heart.

With the two islands inside me doused in flames and melting into a bloody sea—the solid bridge between them blown apart—I balance myself on a floating wooden remnant just large enough to hold the weight of both my body and my hatred: it has its own identity now, my loathing, like a dark companion chained to my side, and together we will ensure brutal and swift retribution.

Even though my vision is focused forward, I can't ignore the fact that the forest around me is dying an excruciating death. I hear the screams of the trees in my ears while images of splintering black wood flicker upon the screen of my thoughts, and beneath my feet I feel the life-giving root systems of the trees fighting their encroaching end.

Though it is mind-bending to admit and even more challenging to comprehend, the fabric of time and space holding Loryian together like a living and breathing three-dimensional grid is visible in my mind's eye, as if I've been given an unobstructed universal view. This high-minded awareness brings with it a sensorial confusion that is disorienting and frightening, my brain grappling with its newfound perceptive abilities like a child relearning to walk.

Desperate to reorient my thoughts, I imagine the fire inside me burning out all other imagery, and as I run faster, pushing my legs until the muscles inside them ache, the only picture remaining is that of Zoran's flame-eaten carcass in the meadow. If I'd known then what I know now, I would have reveled in the horror of his death as he writhed on top of me, the scent of his singed fur and melting flesh creating a state of compound and complete bliss. But instead, in my ignorance, I bled to save him—I chose to resurrect my traitorous beast.

The blood rushing through my veins carries with it my mother's lightness, her effervescent grace, and although tricked and unwitting, I'll never forgive myself for funneling a part of her spirit into the very vessel that took her life. Seeping into my marrow, my loathing for Zoran is immeasurable; and knowing he has her blood, even a trace of her vibrant soul, feels like a glass shard lodged inside my guts.

Triggered by my ire, a flood of adrenaline hits my system and forces my stride to lengthen. Like a flesh-covered bullet, I shoot through a tree line and out onto snow-covered grass. Sprinting toward the wheel-shaped city lying before me, I realize I've no choice but to run down a small hillside and around a portion of the city's walled perimeter before I can realign with my current trajectory.

While racing down the incline, I watch lantern light flickering along the wall. As it mixes with the moon's bloodied purple haze, it casts a kaleidoscope of beaten and bloodied light onto the thousands of copper-dipped skulls embedded in the rectangular stone blocks. From inside their rocky crypt, the skulls speak to me, recounting the horrors of their shadowy, gruesome deaths until I hear their discordant voices calling out and begging for me to relieve their pain and fear.

Thunder booms from above, and when I look toward the sky, I see it twisting with patches of misshapen, black-cotton clouds until flurries of foul-smelling snow begin falling, like the realm itself is starting to rot and release bits of its icy, rancid entrails.

Refocusing forward, I slow my pace while trying to comprehend what I'm observing: hundreds of cloth-wrapped bodies are lined up in front of me, their heads butted up against the wall's rough stone. White on white they lie, their burial shrouds against the snow and blending into the ground like they're sinking into a milky graveyard.

The corpses closest to me are adults, but the rest of the bodies are children. When my gaze locks on the mummified remains of an infant, its form small and fragile like a doll lovingly wrapped by its maker, I want to stop running. But instead, I pass by, unable to halt my legs from their relentless quest for advancing motion.

The smell of death seeps into my bones, the combined demise of the forest to my left and the corpses to my right, a joint decomposition of wood and flesh that's making me feel claustrophobic inside my own skin. With my chest tight and my lungs too tense to expand, I must coax myself to breathe and am about to swallow down a gulp of malodorous night air when I'm overcome by a vision of Zoran. He is near, so very close.

Sucking in a deep breath, I taste ash in my mouth. Sour and sooty, the tainted air spills down my windpipe and oxygenates the fire burning in my blood. Refueled, I run past the last of the corpses toward the other side of the forest, following the invisible trail Zoran is forging for me.

With my blood pushing up and forward, I know how to locate him. I need only expand my senses into the three-dimensional grid and use it like a mind-to-map guide, since despite my purposive hatred, we are joined by a blood-woven cord that I'll use to strangle the life from him.

Leaving the city behind, I run up a small hill near where I first met Sola, then break through a dense tree line until I'm back inside the disintegrating forest. Up ahead, I see Ayalah step into my path. With no choice but to slow down, I wrestle my speed-hungry legs into a form of unwilling submission while she moves toward me bathed in rays of battered moonlight that stream through the trees like liquid sorrow.

I need only look at her to see her link to the dying forest, as like the withering trees, her sienna-colored hair has become dull and stringy and her skin has faded to a gaunt and pallid green. Coming close enough that I must halt in my tracks, I meet her burrowing stare while the scent of rotting flowers drifts from her skin, carrying with it a jet stream of her piercing words. "Death is all you know, so death is what you bring."

I've heard what she's said but am lost within my own mind. What was once a fictitious cast of dream characters is a flesh-and-blood inhabited world. I've had no time to process the collapse of my reality or its implications to those I've met on my dreamscape journeys. With no idea how to respond to her and little interest in sorting through the debris of my shattered life, I refocus on my solitary desire and decide that unless Ayalah can further my pursuit, I have no use for her.

I'm about to start running when the sound of cracking branches ricocheting throughout the forest freezes my feet in place. Behind Ayalah, a grand canopy of trees sinks toward the ground as if their roots are being yanked into the pit of a hellish Underworld.

After a long and tension-filled quiet, Ayalah offers, "To get to him, you'll need me."

While searching her, I'm quite certain she has an agenda—it's evident she's made herself useful to me and knows I've no choice but to accept. I've no doubt this is a mutually beneficial arrangement: she's helping me, but I'm quite confident that I'll also be giving her something she wants or needs.

Without a word, she turns around and makes her way deeper into the forest while I follow behind her, feeling frustrated that I can't leave her behind. Veering off the path, she leads us into thick underbrush and dense patches of ivy. Yet despite the unfavorable terrain, Ayalah is surefooted and determined, appearing to know the landscape like she herself has formed every dip and mound.

With each step we take, the trees around us sink farther toward the forest floor, their trunks buckling beneath their own weight, and from every direction the sounds of snapping branches and cracking wood assault my ears.

Ayalah looks over her shoulder at several listing colossal trees. "We're running out of time."

The two of us are now unified in motion, flying through the desecrated forest. Behind us, I hear trees crashing to the ground, one close enough to send a gust of wind rushing toward my back when it smacks against the forest floor.

Side by side, we push ourselves to move faster as trees topple to the ground like great wooded dominos. When we pick up the pace, Ayalah's breath becomes labored—not due to our speed, but because the forest's annihilation is killing her.

Catching the scent of charred stone and iron in the air, I look left and see the burnt-out meadow, the willow tree at its edge appearing to have grown even more phosphorescent and now oozing what looks like liquid light from its swaying branches.

Ayalah breaks from my side and swerves toward the entrance to the Hall of Shadows while I run full speed behind her, my heart pounding a hole in my chest knowing Zoran is almost within my reach. I navigate the forest floor with far less grace than Ayalah, who races across a wilted carpet of ivy before stopping in front of the Hall of Shadows' newly sealed entrance.

After studying the stone slab blocking the opening, she pulls ivy from the frame around the entryway.

"There's a symbol."

Joining in, I thrash through the ivy like a machete, tearing vines and leaves from the stone, my fists filled with bludgeoned greenery. Brushing away a few stray ivy leaves, I see a reversed triangle with a line at the top carved into one of the stones.

"Here."

Ayalah takes a step closer and warns, "It's the only way in, but there's risk. If this cardinal element is subsumed, you must do the same with the other three."

I hear what she's saying, but the truth is, I don't care. Zoran is so close I can taste it. It's driving me mad that I can feel him lurking beneath my feet, sulking somewhere inside his stone room with life still in his body.

Taking my finger, Ayalah pricks it against a sharp piece of stone next to the symbol. Using the leaking blood, she traces the symbol's deep grooves until the triangle opens to reveal a small stone compartment filled with a pile of soil.

She reaches inside, extracts a handful of earth, and squeezes enough of my blood into the soil to make a paste, which she uses to draw the symbol on the stone slab blocking the tomb's entrance, then on my chest.

I feel the crushing weight of the forest's state of demise: my limbs aching, my throat burning, my stomach twisting into a form of knotted wood. Yet the discomfort I'm experiencing is eradicated by the euphoria I feel when I hear the slab unseal and begin moving.

I don't even wait for it to open fully. I squeeze through and fly down the stairs, rushing into the dim tunnel that leads to the Hall of Shadows. Flickering torchlight illuminates a wide, bloody trail that runs along the center of the tunnel, and as though in a trance, I place one foot, then the other onto the living path of wet blood covering the floor, feeling certain that it's his.

Following the trail, I round the corner and begin the sharp descent toward the Hall while my mind whirls with images: visions of my mother, the sun blazing behind her like a radiant halo—she is young, lively, smiling. Not a trace of sickness is evident in her face, her cheeks full and flushed with color, her lips supple and giving birth to the words of wisdom I'd give anything not to have taken for granted. With all that's inside me, I can no longer deny that I'd do anything, even debase myself completely, to get her back.

I'm starting to sweat, the heat inside me an unchecked firestorm. The hotter my blood burns, the more I feel my chest crushed beneath the soil-drawn marking on my skin. At the end of the tunnel, I enter the Hall and a sip of air drifts over my lips and filters into my lungs, bringing with it the overpowering scent of stale, unwashed human flesh.

I follow the thick trail of blood across the symbol for earth embedded in the Hall's black-and-white checkered floor until it stops dead at the closed door inset in the mural-covered wall. I'm about to open it when I notice the mural beside the door coming alive as several Shadows in the painted forest scene emerge from a small painted cabin to get a closer look at me.

Undeterred, I refocus on the door before pushing it open and putting one bloodstained foot in front of the other, walking toward the candlelit room ahead while my heart thumps within my heavy chest. Blood lurching up and forward, pulse like a hummingbird's, I'm almost at the room when the tall, razor-thin woman, Arvada, steps into the doorway.

Although her snow-white gown is covered in blood and her pale face is drawn and tight, Arvada's dark eyes harbor a brightness inside them, a fervent spark of light that belies the shrill dissonance of her presence.

"You need him."

Seething at her inference that I could "need" him for anything, I feel my blood boil.

Faced with my surfacing wrath, Arvada's pale skin flushes as she stands in the doorway while I, furious and unable to hold back any longer, realize I will harm her to get into the room. My fingers curl toward my palms until my hands become cemented fists and the stone walls on either side of the doorframe form hairline cracks.

"Zoë, no greater damage can be done to him than what's been inflicted already. His suffering is—"

Interrupted by his tormented cry, Arvada stands still while I delight in his agonizing scream, finding it beautiful. For me, there is ecstasy in his pain. About to do whatever's necessary to remove this woman from my path, I feel a cool spot of air swirling around my shoulder. I turn my head and see a small, familiar Shadow hovering beside me, its tiny voice seeping into my mind like water from a mountain stream. "Little Dragon…"

"He either gives back the life he took, or he pays with his own," I command.

The exchange I've proposed isn't humanly possible, and even though it's left my lips, I'm still not sure why I've demanded it.

In what I know is a tactic meant to stall my stalk-to-kill hunt, Arvada weighs in. "What you're suggesting has never been attempted."

Feeling out of my body—and my mind, for that matter—I probe further.

"Are you saying it's possible?"

Watching her step aside and shift her focus into the cushioned room, I follow her line of sight and see a man with his back to me lying curled up on the floor in a bed of rotting skin and blood. "Not without his help."

Walking past Arvada into the room, I'm bowled over by the stench, and as I make my way along the wall until I'm able to see his face, I'm ill prepared for the sight. He lies at my feet, a gruesome creature crossed between human and canine, his musculature exposed and his deteriorating skin rife with gaping sores that bleed freely to the floor.

Pain fills his eyes, or at least what's left of them, and when I bend down, his looming death soils my senses so completely that I will myself not to vomit. The degree to which his suffering pleases me is sickening, and I can't find my way to even one thread of human compassion.

"She had a name for you."

A large strip of decomposing flesh peels away from his neck as he cries out in agony, but I'm undeterred. I need to hear him utter the words, if only to stop me from feeling like I've gone insane.

"Say it."

The shiny sinew of Zoran's exposed muscles contracts with regret and self-hatred as he forces the thinnest strand of sound from his decaying vocal cords.

"Half...Light."

58

REQUIEM'S GATE

H olding the Shadow in my arms, I follow Zoran up the steep incline leading out of the Hall of Shadows, my finger throbbing as the memory of him drinking from me plays in my mind—my blood his fountain of life.

I've almost bled out to resurrect him, a task no normal person could have performed while continuing to breathe, to live. Now I wonder if my humanness, along with my sanity, is in question. What am I, and in discovering what, or who I am, will I ever find a place to settle the fractured pieces of my life—myself?

Eclipsing the chatter in my head, my loathing ekes its way into my mind like a barbarous predator. As I walk through the tunnel with Zoran in front of me, strong, determined, and alive, I deem him the epitome of living injustice, and when he ceases to be useful in my current quest, I'll rip the life from him with my bare hands—this is the irrevocable fate of my beast, my Judas.

Since I can't yet drain him of life, I decide to bleed him for information. "Tell me why."

"It was a trade."

Unable to accept this as a reason, I press further. "For what?"

Zoran stops walking and stands in the darkest part of the tunnel like a thief hiding in the shadows. "Lukaes took someone from me."

Incensed at the notion that anyone was worth my mother's life, I demand, "Who?"

"Elli."

The name lingers around me like rancid perfume as my mind prepares to facilitate the barrage of inquiries lining up to be loosed. "In taking her, he must have wanted something from you."

The muscles in his chest tense. "When the time came, I was to deliver Nilah to him in exchange."

Hearing him say my mother's name causes my blood to boil, and while I'm barely able to grasp, let alone accept, what he's suggesting, I probe further. "You're saying he wanted my mother—specifically?"

A flash of distress registers in his eyes. "He wanted her above all else, which is why I never considered that he'd Excise her."

"You were there?"

In a disconnected and almost detached manner, he verifies, "Yes."

I want to scream, but my voice is lodged in my throat like dynamite detonating underground, the surface undisturbed save a small shockwave that displaces a few pieces of encrusted earth still inked onto my chest. Memories of Prayna's death tear through my consciousness like serrated shrapnel, and the thought of my mother perishing in the same vicious manner becomes so unbearable that I feel my stomach lurch, as if it's desperate to disgorge the shattered debris inside me.

Offering comfort, the Shadow intensifies its grip around my neck, then presses its cool, arid forehead against the side of my face until I feel we are one person, halved: I, a shell of flesh and bone; the Shadow, a soul remnant of spirit made matter.

My thoughts birth themselves into words before I can stop them. "What reason could he possibly have for killing her?"

Taking a step toward me, Zoran responds in earnest. "Retribution. Flesh for flesh. He had hoped she could make him whole, and when she refused, he took her life."

The words he's spoken have entered my consciousness, but their meaning, their inscrutable essence, is stuck somewhere inside my psyche. Even with the mounting evidence of my mother's connection to this place—her turncoat before me, midnight-tinted, just as her journal described—I fear I'm at the precipice of utter madness.

My mind pushes back against the tide of my thoughts and sends a resounding message that echoes inside my skull like the rhythmic beat of a hawk's wings. "Darkness shall light the way." These were Prayna's last words to me, and they shall now serve as a steady beacon in the night, a reminder that I must travel deep into the valley of my blackness to find the truth of what is real, no matter how burdensome or treacherous the path.

Almost outside myself, I inquire, "How could she have made him whole?"

"The same way she helped change him into what he is now."

I ache to understand everything, to know the story in its entirety without a detail spared. But when the air around us becomes charged and a gust of wind whips through the tunnel, causing the torches lining the walls to flicker, I elect to prune my flowering pursuit for specificities and ask only the questions I can't bear to leave unanswered. "Why did he choose you?"

The Shadow squirms while Zoran explains. "She was powerful. He needed an Asdan. Of the four, I had the greatest point of weakness he could leverage."

Zoran turns from me and makes his way up the rest of the tunnel's incline. Without my urging, he continues offering additional information, like he's desperate to free himself from the weight of the guilt he's been carrying. "From the beginning, she knew who I was and why I was there."

"How did you get her here?"

Appearing uncomfortable with the question I've asked, he hesitates before responding. "Satients can move between realms without the Guardian's portal."

My blood pushes through my veins. "You forced her here?"

An element of defiance coats his voice as he counters, "Knowing who you were, she did everything in her power to protect you. She came back willingly."

Like rain to scorched earth, I'm infused with the knowledge that my mother is woven into this dreamscape realm. Although I don't understand her role yet, in my mind's eye—as though offsetting my supposed madness—I see her delicate footprints in the settled dust of my exploded world. She has left a trail for me, a guided path through the devastation and perhaps even a way back into her arms.

I press the Shadow against my chest. "When you say 'back', you mean she'd been here before?"

He's about to respond when the tunnel begins quaking; the torches along the corridor throw greyish-blue light onto tiny cracks forming within the walls.

Zoran calls out, "We have to go."

With the sound of grinding stone grating my ears and the walls buckling, we rush from the tunnel into the main room while petrified earth tumbles in large chunks from the ceiling and crashes down around us like blackened ice. As the giant roots making up the walls disintegrate, we cross the room and race up the stairs, taking steps two by two.

My senses combine to form a warning bell that rings throughout my body with bone-rattling resonance. Real or imagined, the realm in which I now find myself is on its heels and prepped to topple to the ground in an apocalyptically triggered fall. Pieces of my childhood flit through my thoughts, my life flashing before my eyes, while like a hand coming up from the grave of my consciousness, a scripted prayer of my mother's appears in my mind's eye:

> Mother Earth, shelter me and I shall sleep.
> Provide food for me and I shall eat.
> Rain down upon me and I shall drink.
> For we are soil to flesh, bark to bone, river to vein,
> So it has always been and so it shall remain.

At the top of the stairs, we run toward the tomb's entrance, and despite the shockwaves rocking the stone beneath us, I stop, close my eyes, and for the first time since my mother's death, I pray. I ask Mother Earth neither for my survival, nor for the saving of my worlds—both known and unknown—rather, I pray for something I've taken for granted: time.

I beg her to blow an icy breath onto the hands of her celestial clock and transform this decomposing dreamscape into a frozen, time-locked realm. Though prayer has remained unpracticed in my adulthood, within this unorthodox yet essential communion, Mother Earth is with me, her presence so visceral I feel her expansive spirit pulsing through my veins.

Lightheaded, I take a breath while my blood cools beneath the earth symbol on my chest, which rests like a block of ice against my skin and causes the Shadow to relax into my arms like it's been given an anesthetizing drug. The trembling stone ceases its merciless shaking, and when I open my eyes and step into the archway of the tomb's entrance, I watch the wispy traces of my prayer manifest before me as cottony flakes of pure white snow fall from the night's bruised sky.

Around us, the tree trunks have turned a smooth icy-looking amber as though they've been petrified and are now more crystalline than wood, an indication that Mother Earth has breathed in my direction and, in so doing, turned this decaying woodland into a glass-like menagerie.

Even the melting tree canopies have succumbed to her command, their waxen, burnt leaves resembling a cluster of evergreen-hued handblown glass. As Zoran stands in front of me taking in the forest's altered state, my focus is pulled to two figures walking toward us from the left, their approach like bold spirits clad in heavy cloaks, one midnight black and the other cardinal red.

Stepping from the tomb's entryway into the snowy night, I watch them lower their hoods and am relieved to see Sola and Nikolai. Once they're in front of us, they notice the Shadow in my arms and send synchronized, disapproving looks toward Zoran, who is rooted beside me.

It's clear I'm bearing witness to a wordless argument. While watching their silent exchange, I become aware that the three of them possess the collective knowledge I need to fit the pieces of my and my mother's lives together.

Shifting my attention to Sola, whose alluring and arcane beauty is enhanced by the deep scar across her cheek, I notice her stare is filled with a spark of knowing I find unnerving. She seems to me a mythological entity manifested, an oracle in the flesh, and in dreading that she's come to foretell the annihilation of a hope I hold dear, I silently request that she shield me from that which I cannot bear to be shown.

Stepping toward me as if she has heard my soundless plea, Sola removes her cloak, puts it around my shoulders, and fastens the first of many heavy clasps while I stand stone-still and allow her to cocoon me within the fiery threads of her rose-scented shroud. Our faces are inches apart, her breath falling onto my mouth, and with a potent, male-laced desire gripping me, I find myself wanting our lips to touch. Sensing that I'm not alone in my longing, I lean forward just enough to detect the floral perfume drifting from her skin as we inhale one another's breath, trading the elemental life-blood sitting beneath the canvases of our heated flesh, her oxygen to my fire.

Feeling the combined weight of Zoran's and Nikolai's stares, I ruminate on what a peculiar temporary universe we've formed: Nikolai, the night sky in which we are suspended; me, Mother Earth's delegate; Zoran, a mournful moon; and Sola, the sun who keeps us all unfrozen inside this ice-crystal forest.

After fastening the last few clasps, Sola pulls the sides of the cloak up and over the Shadow's body until its head rests against my chest as if lulled by the cover of darkness.

Sola removes Prayna's medallion and puts it around my neck.

"Now we'll both be with you."

With the disk resting on top of the cloak, I notice one side is still covered in Asdan blood from the invocation of the Elders.

Nikolai urges, "You don't have much time."

I reposition my arms around the Shadow while focusing on Nikolai, whose eyes register a state of unveiled anxiety. In this moment, I'm certain he's afraid for my safety, but truth be told, I'm not sure if his concern is born from a fear of losing me or losing access to my blood—an infusion of which I sense he desperately needs.

Manifesting as if called forth by my thoughts, a single black line snakes up from his neck and comes to rest at the center of his cheek like a waiting serpent. But before I can react, Sola and Nikolai turn away from us. Watching them make their way back into the forest, I see a fine mist leaking from my wrist, my veins aching and engorging with blood like they're priming to purify him.

I hear Zoran walking away from me, and I follow him toward the meadow while of its own volition, my mind drifts to Elli—the woman for whom he traded my mother's life—and with his half of the deal met and my mother dead, I wonder where Elli is now. In pondering her fate, I'm angered by my paradoxical curiosity and remind myself that I should care nothing for the life or love of my false-hearted beast, seeing as his suffering is my bliss; and in this, I wish they were never given the pardoned grace of being reunited.

Wrapped in our respective thoughts, Zoran and I move through the forest together yet in separate worlds. When we come upon the threshold of the burnt-out meadow, I notice the gates that lined its perimeter are absent. Stepping onto the charred stone and gazing upward, I sense the presence of my mother's Mystics, and while studying the gelatinous dome overhead, I see a smattering of silvery veins pulsing with signs of life.

At their silent urging, I move toward the rose in the center of the stone floor and notice an ash-white ring a few feet in front of me; a memory of the spiders holding back the meadow's incessant flames erupts into my thoughts. I reviled them, yet they bore the brunt of my all-consuming fire until it reduced them to dust; for that, I send up an offering of appreciation through Great Spirit's cloud-bonded channel.

After walking across the chalky line of the spiders' disintegrated carcasses, I stop in front of the soot-covered rose and focus on the bloodstained outline where Zoran's fire-eaten corpse once lay. Fixating on the rose and feeling my thoughts within the control of my mother's Mystics, I watch details of her triptych's hidden inscription appearing in my mind's eye:

A ring 'round the rose are the gates that lead,
A bloodied stone its nestled seed.
By the night of twelve, it must be free,
Or all that was will cease to be.

Letters swirl inside my skull like phantoms while I examine bits and pieces of the phrases as if they're a complex math equation seeking swift resolution: "A ring 'round the rose are the gates that lead, a bloodied stone its nestled seed…"

The Mystics send a series of images that flicker through my thoughts like wildfire. Once I'm able to string the flashing pictures together to form a cohesive set of collage-like directives, I look down at my bracelet and recall my mother telling me the stone was made from the blood of our ancestors, and that through it, they could watch me from the edges of Great Spirit's sky-slung world. Hearing her melodic voice inside my head, I experience her words as equal parts prayer, edict, and warning: "The blood of our warriors is inside this stone. It is the seed of who we have been, who we are, and who we will be."

Feeling out of my body, I unwind the copper of my bracelet, remove its ruby stone, and drop it into the rose's center. As if succumbing to a chemical reaction, the rose emits a thick, viscous haze, causing Zoran and me to back away while the sound of grinding metal reverberates throughout the meadow.

Like an iron hand reaching up from a charred necropolis, one gate emerges, rising to its towering height with a slow grinding ascent, and once it's poised at the meadow's edge, the gate looks out of place to me, like an abandoned soldier left to guard its post alone. Drawn toward it like we're comrades gathering at the borders of a battlefield, I walk forward; the scent of iron overpowers my senses, a spoor so pungent it could be mistaken for fresh blood.

Stopping inches from the gate, I examine its wounded inlaid and flourished ironwork, which resembles little more than melted twists of rotting metal. After running my finger along the inset Roman numeral IX at its center, I trace a single horizontal bar that leads to a hook-and-eye latch as bits of caked iron flake away and turn my fingertips rust red. It appears the gate, sentient and iron-fleshed, is bleeding from its open sores to expel that which has left it fire-beaten and lifeless, while the latch leaks a putrid tar-like substance that reeks of burning sugar.

Driven by a force outside myself, I lift the latch and pull the gate open enough to see it unseal from what appears to be a transparent frame. A wave of humid heat blasts toward me, and as the Shadow presses its cool body against my skin, I rub its back with one hand and open the gate with the other, and walk through with my heart pounding and my duplicitous beast in tow.

Once we've passed through, Zoran darts out and surveys the bleak landscape while I examine the space around me, confused as to why there isn't a visible trace of the gate we've just used to cross into this barren land, one covered in oily black sand and contorted trees as far as the eye can see.

Up ahead, a tall man is walking toward us. He weaves his way through the forest and it looks like he's displacing the air around him, like the landscape across which he moves is nothing more than an elaborate cellophane-woven fabric he can manipulate at will. Although his demeanor could be deemed threatening, when Zoran comes to my side and locks eyes with him, it's clear they know one another.

The man breaks Zoran's gaze as he reaches us, but rather than speaking, he scans the area to our right with military precision, his oceanic-blue eyes assessing every inch of our surroundings in what I assume is an effort to ensure we're alone. When he turns his head and inspects the forest to our left, I notice an L-shaped Luminary tattoo carved into the side of his neck along with the script "Bleed darkness, swallow light." A memory of the Butcher's rough, ring-covered fingers rips through my mind.

Wondering why Zoran would consider trusting anyone associated with the Butcher, I examine the man and notice that his hair has been shoddily shaved to within an inch of his skull and the bony parts of his head are covered in wounds, like whoever sheared him did so with cruelty in mind.

Considering that his clothes are tattered, soiled, and releasing an odor of dank moldiness, it's clear that wherever this man lives—or is kept—bears little resemblance to any kind of home. He's untended and underfed, and when he shifts his gaze to me, then to the medallion around my neck, the muscles in his jaw clench.

The reluctance in Zoran's voice is evident as he speaks. "Cassian, Lukaes—"

The man, Cassian, interjects while grief floods his face. "When?"

"A few days ago."

With Cassian's stare fixed on me, I feel his hatred all the way through my body like I've been injected with lethal poison. It is I, and I alone, whom he has deemed responsible for Prayna's death. In knowing that both she and my mother willingly walked into the arms of their executioner on my behalf, I realize his antipathy is warranted.

Even though his voice is calm, Cassian's glower seethes and he reprimands me like an elder would a petulant child. "If you'd taken your rightful place, she'd still be alive—they all would."

The Shadow wriggles in my arms as Zoran interrupts. "We need a way into the city."

With dirty, yellow-nailed fingers, Cassian pulls one side of my cloak aside; the Shadow moves left and cradles itself in the crook of my arm. Cassian's mouth grows tight as he speaks to Zoran. "Do you know what he'll do if you're caught?"

I can only assume Cassian is referring to Lukaes, and despite his obvious panic, I remain undeterred.

Softening, Cassian continues, "I can't protect you. I'm bound to him." Pulling down the collar of his shirt, he reveals a small glass sphere containing a violet-colored light that hangs suspended from a copper chain around his neck like a fractured star. Examining the bluish tentacles reaching out toward the sides of the glass, I feel my heart grow heavy, as I'm certain the sphere contains a splintered remnant of his soul.

Zoran forces himself through the palpable distress Cassian's plight has inflicted, then urges, "I'll ask nothing more from you than a way in."

Cassian eyes us for a moment. "With the twelfth night nearly upon us, the city will rise to meet the blood moon, and when it does, you'll see a path. Take eighteen steps west, fourteen steps north, then another twelve steps west. I can buy you some time, but not much."

They stand watching one another long enough for me to sense the layered history between them, then Zoran moves off to our right. I'm about to follow when Cassian grabs my hand, his touch causing a miniature shockwave to shoot up my arm and into my shoulder. Once Zoran is out of earshot, he asserts, "He's the only hope you have." Leaning toward me, he continues, "And if you succeed, he should receive your forgiveness, then your blood."

Yanking my arm away from him, I hold my tongue with every inch of my will. How dare he demand that I spare Zoran from the retribution he so deserves? He's received my blood because it serves my purpose, but he will never know the freedom of my forgiveness. Not ever.

Cassian turns away from me and walks in the opposite direction before stopping to look over his shoulder. "There's good in him. Perhaps even a brighter light than you possess."

After holding my gaze for a moment, he slips back into the barren, wicked-looking forest as I walk toward Zoran, fuming. Upon reaching him, it's all I can do not to strike him down.

Zoran moves closer as though drawn into orbit by the sheer gravity of my hate, and when he searches me, I sense he believes my vengeance will wane. He trusts that the light inside me will prevail until the darkness is all but an inkblot on a universal canvas of white. But he is mistaken.

Cassian's assessment may be accurate after all, seeing as where Zoran is concerned there is an abyss of solitary blackness, and the only light I'll allow is the momentary spark of lethal flame I'll use to destroy him.

59

STRANGER STILL

Now out of the twisted, tar-dripping forest, Zoran and I walk forward toward what looks like an apocalyptic wasteland, where nothing exists as far as the eye can see—save black, sandy soil that stings the soles of my feet as though each granule is coated in venom. Every molecule, particle, and solidified portion of matter seems to have manifested from the bowels of a bitter and malevolent anti-God, an entity who has thwarted the growth of any living thing.

With no evidence of the path Cassian mentioned, I'm about to inquire as to our course of action when the area in front of us comes alive with self-churning soil. Catching a glimpse of coiled green bodies squirming below the surface, I realize the ground is infested with what appear to be buried snakes.

Zoran and I take a unified step backward as, one by one, serpentine bodies push up through the sandy soil and unfurl themselves until they're stick-straight and aiming toward the bloodied moon like murderous arrows. Upon further inspection, the skin covering their bodies is smooth, almost plantlike, and the heads, or rather tops, of the stalk-like serpents are beginning to bloat, swelling into fat round bulbs.

Bursting from the pressure of rapid expansion, a bulb in front of me blasts open, releasing a hail of fiery, colored powder inches from my face. As my eyes begin to burn, I cover my nostrils and mouth with my cloak to stop myself from inhaling the toxic cloud permeating the air around me.

In a chain reaction, the other bulbs explode like gunpowder-loaded grenades, sending billows of orangey-red dust erupting from each bulb and forming a thick haze that hovers over the field like a nuclear storm.

The sound of the rupturing bulbs ricochets in my ears like gunfire before trading places with sound-sucking silence as the landscape's fire-dusted overlay dissipates and reveals a field of thousands upon thousands of waist-high poppies. The flowers' heads and bloodred petals are giant and violent-looking, and the contrast between their vibrant hue and the bordering wasteland makes the field appear to glow.

Truth be told, I'm certain my mind is altered, as the environment feels sentient, like that which was once inert is now alive and watching me, waiting—the very air pressing against my skin like it's demanding we become one. Standing in this velvet-petaled sea, I'm wedged somewhere within the scrum of my heightened senses and the noxious fog that has befuddled them: the night tasting like poison, the moonlight stinging my eyes, my cloak feeling like weighted steel against my flesh, and Zoran's voice sounding as if every word is a hammer pounding inside my eardrums.

"They'll attempt to distract you. Just stay beside me and focus on the path."

Side by side, we walk toward a narrow path—one I'd swear has appeared from thin air—that cuts through the poppy field like a strip of black leather.

Zoran stops before stepping onto the path. "Eighteen steps forward, then take a sharp right. Count carefully—and out loud."

In hearing him speak to me as though I'm a child, I feel myself becoming irritated. How hard can it be to count my own damn steps, and why must I do so aloud?

I begin counting while the soles of my feet make contact with what feels like warm, smooth skin. "One, two, three…"

I inhale a sip of stale, tainted air and feel it drift over my lips and seep into my lungs. "Four, five, six…"

The poppies' velvety petals caress my hand, and in response, my mind tumbles into the catacombs of my thoughts. Images disentomb themselves, unearthed by something far stronger than me, and with every step, the poppies become more aggressive, like jealous lovers pushing and battling one another to get closer to me as I struggle to stay on the path and continue counting. "Seven, eight…"

A vision overtakes my mind's eye, a childhood memory of the Deadlings hiding in the forest and taunting me while I walked amongst the trees.

"Stupid, ugly little savage." Gracie, the meanest of the three, grabs my shoulders from behind and whispers, "She's gonna die. Then you'll be all alone…"

When Gracie turns me around to face her, I stare into her deep shadowy eyes and see only hatred and disgust. To her, I'm a mere insect she takes pleasure in flattening beneath the soles of her black patent-leather Mary Janes.

"Stop!"

Snapped back into the present, I realize I've almost veered off the path, and to make matters worse, I can't recall how many extra steps I've taken.

Zoran implores me with an element of fear in his voice. "You must stay clearheaded. The next step is seventeen."

Putting my right foot down, I resume counting. "Seventeen, eighteen—"

Zoran orders, "Turn right."

I do as he's instructed, then feel the path beneath my feet shifting and rotating in the direction I've just turned, growing warmer and taking on a tacky consistency while I count. "One, two, three…"

Gracie's words leach back into my consciousness: "…then you'll be all alone." Thirty years since she uttered those words, and they couldn't be more accurate, seeing as Mother is gone and I am alone. My chest tightens and the Shadow squirms against me while I fight to remember the numbers matching the steps I'm about to take. "Seven, eight, nine…"

Loneliness is not something with which I'm well acquainted, due to the fact that I never allow it in. But where my mother is concerned, in a dark corner of my consciousness, I know it lies in wait. When I think of her allowing herself to be traded by the night-stalking reaper walking beside me, I feel my aloneness stirring, and to detract from its potential surfacing, I pummel Zoran for information.

"The trade—did you get what you wanted?"

Head low, gaze forward, he answers, "I got Elli back, yes."

In hearing that they were reunited, I feel a wave of hot blood race through my veins as I wrangle my mind into focus. "Twelve, thirteen, fourteen—"

Zoran interrupts me. "Turn left. Then, twelve steps."

The path beneath my feet melts into what feels like gooey tar, yet somehow I'm able to stay just above it rather than sink into what is becoming a molten river.

I resume counting, feeling like I'm in a nightmarish trial by numbers. "One, two, three…"

With the heat continuing to rise in my blood, I inquire, "Where is Elli now?"

"As part of my penance, she was taken from me."

My blood cools and I keep counting. "Six, seven…"

I revel in Zoran's pain, which I feel emanating from him with every breath he takes. He aches for her, yearns to have her back, and knowing that they were forced apart is the sweetest-tasting bliss I could have hoped to experience.

Realizing I've lost count, I panic, and as my foot slips forward a few inches, the melted path sucks at the meat of my toes.

Zoran calls out, "Ten!"

I pause, then take a step while counting aloud. "Ten, eleven…"

The path is fully melted and spreading across the field, killing everything it touches like a liquid plague. The vibrant poppies sink into the resulting blackness, leaving only a trace of watercolor red as they drown in an oil-slick abyss.

I've one step left, but I stop dead in my tracks as sinewy black bodies rise from the sea below me, their sunken cheeks, rubbery skin, and mummied appearance making me feel like my mind is further concocting an elaborate illusion. When one of them focuses on me, its shallow, eyeless sockets lit by the bloodied moonlight, I feel my knees growing weak.

"Keep moving."

At Zoran's urging, I walk forward and count the last step. "Twelve."

My mind is becoming disoriented as I feel gummy hands guiding my feet. I look down and watch while, in a deliberate and synchronized effort, hand over hand, the creatures interweave a trestle for us to walk on.

Shifting my gaze upward, I'm certain my reality is veiled by hallucination, as it appears the night itself has given birth to a hidden stone city. Rust-colored moonlight illuminates the turreted walls along the city's perimeter, and without any visible gates or entrances along the city wall, I fear we'll be unable to penetrate the stone-blocked border.

I'm about to ask Zoran how he plans on getting us in when three giant cauldrons mounted at the corners blaze to life and begin shooting flames toward the night sky. The flaming cauldrons are identical to those in Loryian, and for a moment, I wonder if this menacing land seeks its own version of survival, seeing that it, too, seems to have lit sacred fires in the hopes that it will be spared from all but certain eradication.

The creature-constructed trestle brings us in to meet the wall, and once in front of it, I lean forward and brace one foot against a rough stone ledge while Zoran guides me. "In front of you, there should be an iron latch. Pull the handle, then twist it counterclockwise."

Feeling along the wall, I find the latch and do as he's instructed, which results in a loud clicking sound followed by a portion of the wall shifting inward and sliding to the right just enough to allow us access.

I step from the ledge, walk through the opening, then turn to see Zoran leap from the trestle and walk through the door, his gaze focused on me and the look in his eyes doing little to lessen my increasing sense of unease.

After breaking eye contact, he passes by me and makes his way down a desolate cobblestone street; I follow, keeping myself concealed in the shadows of one of the high-flanking walls. Ahead of us, the street opens onto what looks like an ancient Roman city, but instead of entering its labyrinthine structure, Zoran rounds a sharp corner and leads us onto a narrow side street lined with abandoned dwellings and market shops.

Large unlit lamps line the street every few feet, and by the looks of them, they haven't been used in years. Empty carts and tools littering the cobbled lane give the impression that the people inhabiting this part of the city abandoned their belongings mid-work, as though they vanished.

Taking an abrupt left, Zoran slows his pace and darts into an alley between two small stone dwellings. Trailing behind him, I stay pressed against the side of one of the buildings as the Shadow attempts to burrow into the space between my upper arm and rib cage.

In the distance, I hear barking dogs akin to the Butcher's vicious hell-hounds, and when Zoran stops walking and sends a fearful glance toward me, I feel my pulse race.

"We must hurry." Both of us take off down the alleyway until we cut right, onto another side street.

Zoran stops in front of a two-story stone house, the front door to which is hanging by one hinge, the shutters dangling from the exterior like lifeless limbs. The ground-floor windows have been haphazardly boarded, and the inside of the house is pitch black, filled with a kind of lightlessness that spills from the second-story windows and creeps toward us like a flesh-hungry hunter.

There's a presence here that leaves me feeling distressed. I'm reluctant even to be near the house, let alone go inside. I'm about to protest when Zoran leaves my side and slips through the decrepit front door and into the thick darkness beyond its battered threshold.

Coercing my feet into forward motion, I walk toward the house and force myself through the door into resolute blackness, my heart pounding in my ears while with every step across the creaking floor, I fight my instinct to turn around and run. The Shadow sends an electric shock into my palm as it grows cold against my skin. In order to bring our collective fears to heel, I attempt to calm both my mind and the rushing adrenaline-laced blood in my veins.

With Zoran nowhere in sight, I move toward a shaft of light streaming through a door at the back of the house, but someone grabs me from behind and throws a brute-strong hand over my mouth.

"Don't move."

From the man's heart beating against my back and the labored nature of his breathing, it's clear he's either running from or to something.

"It's Cassian. I'm going to let you go, but I need you to stay where you are."

Cassian releases his hand from my mouth, but in my blind desperation to flee this light-forsaken house, I bolt toward the back door and am moments from flying through it when I feel him snatch my cloak and ratchet me backward.

Locked in his arms, I look down and notice that my feet are inches from the edge of a plunging set of stairs that look to have been built beneath a trap door. In realizing Cassian has saved me from tumbling down them, I take several steps backward while clutching the Shadow against my chest.

Outside, the hellhounds' voracious barking grows louder, and as Zoran emerges from the shadows of the staircase and fixes a concerned gaze on Cassian, I turn and notice the fresh blow to the right side of Cassian's face. With his right eye bloodied, his lip split, and his cheekbone broken, it's apparent he has endured a vicious beating.

Zoran ascends the last few stairs, then walks toward us. "We're too late—it's been sealed."

"Then he knows." Zoran stays silent as Cassian continues. "You need to split up. The Shadow has to be taken back. If he were to get a hold of it—"

"No," I contest.

Cassian takes my arms and meets my gaze with a calmness I find unnerving. "I know what you intend to do, but it's no longer possible here. You have to let them go—for now."

Despite his genuineness, I remind myself that he's a Luminary, and on that basis alone, I deem him unfit to participate in any kind of solution. But before I can relay my thoughts, Zoran speaks. "Earth to blood, blood to heart, hand in hand, and never to part."

Memories pull me back in time with the strength of an oceanic undertow: I'm nine and my mother and I are deep in the woods, standing in front of her favorite lilac tree as she picks two sets of flowering branches and crushes the soft lilac petals into her palm. With her pocketknife, she draws blood from each of our palms, her deep earthen eyes drinking me in as she presses our hands together and recites, "Earth to blood, blood to heart, hand in hand, and never to part."

Ripped back into the present by the sound of hellhounds growing ever closer, one question keeps cycling over in my mind: How could Zoran recount a phrase my mother said to me only once, when we were alone?

"You still have the small X-shaped scar on your palm."

I'd forgotten, as it's almost invisible now, but Zoran speaks the truth.

"I made her a promise, and when it came time to fulfill it, she knew you'd need convincing," he continues.

Embedded in thought and wondering why my mother would share such a private moment with her known assassin, I fail to notice the Shadow has escaped my arms and is hovering near Zoran's side.

Seeing them together makes me feel sick, but somewhere deep inside my gut I know I must let them go.

Cassian turns toward me. "I need your cloak."

Defeated, and with a heavy heart, I unhook the cloak's clasps and hand it to him as Zoran speaks.

"There's a candle and a match on the first stair. Enter the chamber as you did the Hall of Shadows. The medallion will reveal a way back."

The weight of my loathing for Zoran is crushing. Yet I'm bound to him by a supposed promise he made to my mother, a woman whose life he stole, and as I watch the Shadow floating at his side, black on black, they are somehow one, fitting together like two night-struck companions, each incomplete without the other.

Zoran takes a step toward me. "We'll be waiting."

My cloak-clad doppelganger, Cassian, Zoran, and I turn away from one another. As I make my way toward the staircase, I'm unable to quell the rising fear that I may have just lost the only chance I'll ever have at reclaiming the missing piece of my soul.

60

THE FERRYMAN

Cupping my hand around the nubby candle's flickering flame, I make my way down the steep staircase, which feels forever descending. Like a spliced section of film, my mind loops the image of the Shadow hovering next to Zoran's side—it still sickens me to know they're together, moving through the night as a united yet soulless pair.

In some ways, I too am soulless, seeing as it was my mother's death that long ago led me to cleave my soul-filled spirit from my body. I realize now I couldn't keep the luminous pieces of my mother inside my spirit; I split in two because the darkness was easier than learning to live without her light, her love.

Like a ghost hungry to inhabit flesh, I feel my exiled spirit circling the edges of my consciousness, desperate to rejoin my body, heart, and mind. In knowing that my mother has bound me to the wretch who led her to slaughter, she has demanded I close the gaping divide I've created in her absence. Two unbalanced halves must fuse and become whole.

The darkness in my cells contracts and churns at the notion of being reunited with the light carried in my spirit. I fear that the brightest of days merging with the blackest of nights will leave only a muted, ashen-skied landscape within me: just enough light to walk the path my mother has left for me and just enough darkness to remind me I'm without her. So I refuse such a union, as I've made my choice, and it's one that has served me well—night is the current running through me, the moon a sufficient and welcome bit of light; I want nothing else, and other than having her back, I need nothing else.

Responding to my repudiation, my heartbeat thunders in my ears, a sign that the hungry ghost has donned iron gloves and is pounding on the locked door of my consciousness.

Boom. Boom. Boom.

Ceremoniously, I find my steps in time with its knocking, my legs controlled by a bass-heavy, rhythmic thud, and as I navigate the last few stairs, I use the wall for support while my fingers edge along what I surmise is carved wood.

Stepping from the final stair, I lift the candle toward the wall and realize it's constructed of thousands upon thousands of blood-lacquered bones similar to the ones given to me by the creature in my room. Laid with a mason's precision, the bones form patterns in the wall like a macabre mosaic. The intricacies of the bone designs are dreadful, beautiful, and serve to intensify the visceral presence of the whispering dead I sense dwelling within the walls.

With my heart's thunderous beat softening, I move away from the staircase and notice that the hungry ghost is allayed by an impenetrable-looking wall of skulls in front of me. I feel the weight of their eyeless stares daring me to find a way to pass into the Hadean chamber beyond their keeping.

Shifting my focus left, I discover a small inset stone panel and bring the candle closer. I notice a large reversed triangle carved into its surface. Trailing the symbol with my finger, I feel a sharp, jagged stone sticking out from one of the triangle's points and use it to deepen the cut on my finger. Then I repeat the ritual in which Ayalah traced the engraved symbol outside the Hall of Shadows with my blood.

The panel opens to reveal a small stone compartment filled with a single suspended flame. As I watch it sway, it evokes within me a strange sense of protectiveness, and in response, blood flows into my fingers as if seeking its radiating heat.

I reach inside the compartment as the flame slides into my hand and disintegrates into a small pile of white ash at the center of my palm. Again, duplicating Ayalah's actions, I squeeze several drops of blood into the ash and make a thick paste. Refocusing on the wall of skulls, I notice one of them is adorned with a spiked crown comprised of bony inset fingers, the centermost of which is missing, its absence forming a grooved arrow that points to the middle of the skull's forehead.

An image of the skeletal finger lying in my vanity drawer—bones that appear to have been removed from this very wall—flits across my consciousness while I use the paste as ashen ink and trace the symbol from the panel onto the skull's forehead. Once the blood-infused mixture makes contact with the porous bone, the skull rotates counterclockwise, triggering a series of loud clicking noises, like a set of locks disengaging, that mix with the sound of grinding stone until a section of the wall swings open.

Behind the door is pure blackness, and the odor of musty dampness drifting toward me carries with it the unmistakable scent of death. Inside my skin, I feel the souls of those who have perished in this infernal place, as though they're seeking refuge within a vessel of flesh that will shield them from the horrors of being trapped inside a tomb made of their own blood-soaked bones.

As I listen to the dead whispering, begging me for their freedom, my hand sears. When I look down at the ashen paste melting and merging with my skin until it brands a fiery symbol into my palm, I start sweating. With my blood boiling and the taste of ash flooding my mouth, it seems I'm being burned alive, cooked inside my own flesh, and were I to exhale, I'm certain my lungs would release a stream of unrelenting flame, seeing as in this moment, I am a solitary spark raging into full-blown fire.

Painful isn't the word; excruciating is more accurate—even my marrow feels like lava inside my bones. I can't breathe, think, or move. As my candle reaches the end of its wick and dies, all I can do is stand frozen, surrounded by the whispers of the dead while staring into the blackness of the passageway lying before me.

Knowing in my gut that I must move forward, I force my legs into motion, placing one foot in front of the other until I pass through the door and enter an unending tunnel of darkness. Wiping the sweat from my forehead, I'm about to take my next step when I hear the door slam shut behind me and lock with a successive set of clicks. Dread seeps up from the damp earthen floor and lodges inside the joints of my toes like an invading sickness.

I walk forward, fire-filled and heart pounding as my mind floods with scenes from my childhood, the memory vault in my brain feeling as though it's a river of liquid steel dripping into the base of my skull. Step by step, the whispers of the dead are replaced by a scene flickering on the screen of my mind's eye like an old black-and-white movie, a memory long forgotten but vivid nonetheless.

It's just after my mother's death, and I see an adolescent version of myself standing near my father, who sits in his favorite worn wingback chair in front of the fireplace, encircled as always by stacks of his favorite books. Like a living statue, he sits motionless save for the periodic movement required to sip his thick-bottomed glass of whiskey.

On the verge of passing out, he mutters something I can't quite under-stand, so I decide to move closer. As I take a step toward him, the movie shifts perspective until I'm looking through the eyes of my younger self. Making my way across the room, I hear him speaking beneath his breath. "I couldn't get to her in time."

Now inches from him, I notice his hair is too long, his beard untrimmed, his clothes unwashed. He doesn't seem to know I'm here. He thinks he's alone, and in his supposed solitude, he cries as he succumbs to drink-induced sleep. Watching the tears roll down his flushed cheeks and into his beard, I feel my guts tighten as he laments, "The Ferryman...he has her...she is his now..."

An open book lies in his lap, and I remove it from beneath his hands, reading the large heading, "Psyche and Eros." Skimming the text, I focus on a smaller heading halfway down the page: "The Ferryman." Then I read the paragraph describing the instructions Psyche receives before embarking on her journey to the Underworld:

> But you shouldn't go empty-handed through the shadows past this point, but rather carry cakes of honeyed barley in both hands, and transport two coins in your mouth.

The tale speaks of how Psyche uses one coin to pay the Ferryman to help her across the river of the dead, and the other coin to pay for her return. There's an illustration of the Ferryman at the bottom of the page. He is a tall, skeletal figure cloaked in black, with glowing eyes the color of a raging sea; from the front of his boat hangs a small lantern that illuminates the ghost-filled waters he navigates with a long oar made of bones.

Restless, my father stirs, his sleep disturbed and his demeanor agitated. I place the open book back in his lap, and in reaction, he pulls it toward him, causing two small coins to fall from his right hand. Leaning down, I retrieve the coins and notice that both are worn and misshapen.

The front of each coin bears the head of a raven and etched into the backs is a phrase I can scarcely read. Moving toward the fireplace, I use the fiery light to read the script engraved around the edge: DARKNESS SHALL LIGHT THE WAY.

While the phrase echoes inside my thoughts, the movie in my mind's eye flashes and goes blank as I'm pulled into the present with such force it takes me a moment to come back into my body. These were the last words Prayna spoke to me; steeped in lightlessness, with her medallion—a remnant of her splendent soul—around my neck like a beacon in the night, somehow this phrase makes sense. Darkness will light my way, as this penetrating blackness, both literal and figurative, is my chrysalis; for better or for worse, I accept the inevitable fact that I will emerge changed.

Urging myself forward, I feel my skin cool as the ash-inked symbol on my hand smolders inside my palm, a steady reminder that I am forged by the purest of flames. The blood in my veins slows and my furtive steps become determined as I walk hard, in a true, straight line, leaving heavy impressions in the damp soil beneath my feet. With my hands out at my sides sweeping through the air in the hopes of finding anything I may use as a guide, I feel my fingers graze a bone-lined wall to my left.

After veering toward it, I follow its sharp curve, which takes me deeper into the darkness of the passageway. My thoughts drift to the Ferryman, the soulless creature doomed to spend eternity floating upon the river of the dead, shuttling only those who can afford to pay him across the river's blackened waters to the shores of the Underworld. In my mind's eye, I see my mother standing on a bank in front of the Ferryman's boat, speaking to him in a soft, seductive voice. "I need not cross. I only ask to stay with you awhile. We will drift, silently, but together."

To me, it's a strange vision, like a watercolor illustration of the Ferryman reaching out a bony hand to help my mother into his boat. Dressed in white, she is radiant against the dimness of the river's barren shores, and when she steps into his vessel, the train of her dress dips into the death-laden waters. I watch her walk to the single wooden seat at the back of the ferry, the soiled train of her dress dragging behind her like the river's black blood has found a way to infiltrate her purity. She sits while the Ferryman moves them forward, his oar of bones making only the slightest sound as it slices into the water like a knife into decaying flesh.

Standing on the shore watching the lithe vessel approaching, I witness my mother's beauty fading, her dress now a dull, worn grey and her eyes sunken and lifeless, as if a thousand years have passed in mere seconds, the Ferryman sucking the life from her with every stroke of his oar. Just as they're about to pass by, my mother looks toward me and speaks in a raspy, wraithlike voice: "From the prison of fire and earth I shall be freed." Then, without another word, she turns away as the boat disappears into a void of a setting fog.

The words my mother has spoken linger in my mind like smoke-written script. It's a phrase I've read in her diary and one that resonates within my spirit. The earthen symbol on my chest feels heavy, like it was drawn with cemented soil, and the fiery symbol seared into my hand burns; I carry with me, etched into my skin like brazen tattoos, the marks of my mother's prisons.

Yet like an invisible thief robbing me of courage, I'm stopped by the sickness-turned-plague of fear creeping up my legs, as I find the endless blackness around me disturbing and paralyzing. Devoid of bravery, I find it crushing to think of the faith my mother has in me. The hope she's placed in my care weighs upon me like a blanket of stone, and there's nothing more harrowing than the thought of failing to deserve the unshakable conviction she has that I'll be able to see this through.

In my mind's eye, I see an image of her leaning down and offering me an infusion of the wisdom I've long been without. Whenever I was afraid as a child, she would ask me to close my eyes while she placed my hand over my heart, and together, we would take a breath and walk forward. I never understood why, but after just a few steps, I'd open my eyes and everything would indeed seem brighter, more bearable. In this moment, knowing I've no choice but to keep going, I close my eyes, place my blazing hand over my heart, and take a step forward.

I place one foot in front of the other as my hand melds with my chest, like the symbols of earth and fire are seeking resolute wholeness with one another, causing a surge of fiery electricity to course through me, my veins now an interconnected maze of live, fire-filled wires. With my eyes still closed, I walk faster until I'm running and fueled by the force of the two joined elements inside me. I am nature unleashed, if only for a few astonishing spirit-sparked moments.

The soil beneath my feet grows thin until, with another few steps, I'm walking along a smooth, uneven floor. When I open my eyes, take my hand from over my heart, then move into a dungeon-like room, I'm certain I've entered the bowels of an Underworld so hellish, Hades himself would revile its gruesomeness.

The entire chamber has been built with the same type of blood-fired bones used for the tunnel's entrance, but rather than mosaicked and artful, these are haphazardly placed and held together by a dripping tar-like substance that reeks of putrid sugar and rotting flesh. Beneath my feet is a floor comprised of packed skulls buried belowground and crushed into one another, leaving only the tops of their curved heads visible so as to resemble a floor of domed tile; the space between the skulls runs with fresh blood.

Stacks of bloodied human bones and bird carcasses litter the ground along with black feathers that are strewn around the room like a miswoven rug, and beside my feet is a pile of large severed beaks appearing to be those of large crows or ravens. A torch to my right hisses and spits as a drop of water hits its fading flame. When I study the wall on which it's mounted, I notice that it's covered in iron-spiked cuffs and thick chains.

Forcing myself farther into the room, I spot an immense glass globe on a four-legged iron base tucked into a corner to my left. The globe is packed with thousands of small violet spheres identical to those Lukaes ripped from his unwitting victims in the forest, and the sight of its inhabitants causes my very cells to swell until they're rising upward and pushing me toward the corner.

With each step the fiery current within me dwindles, and my heart sits heavily inside my chest. As I watch the spheres floating in circles like comatose fish, I feel Prayna's medallion take on a tenfold increase in weight.

Now standing in front of the globe, I'm aware that my presence has created a shift in the souls' demeanor. From within their glass-encased graveyard, the stolen souls begin screaming inside my thoughts until I can feel their biting voices gnawing at the sides of my skull, begging to be released and demanding their freedom in a violent manner, giving me no choice but to heed their request.

Drawn to them, I reach forward and let my fingers trace the glass while they swirl against my hand. Seeming to sense their liberation is imminent, a group of souls races to one side of the globe and floats above a small sealed door with an iron latch.

Without hesitation, I unseal the door, and like shooting stars, the spheres burst from the confines of the globe, rip across the room, and hover in the far-right corner diagonal from where I'm standing. Then, like changing stations on an old radio, the screams inside my mind subside and are replaced by a static-laden form of conversation, the voices of the souls endeavoring to commune with me and with one another. While attempting to tune in and decipher the chatter, I'm overcome by the feeling that they may be my literal light in the darkness.

To the naked eye, they are a starry formation of spheres hanging in the air like violet fireflies, but in my mind's eye, the many converge into one until they're of solitary consciousness and unified purpose: to guide me. I trust their intentions, and driven by what has become an overwhelming need to be near them, I make my way through a maze of stacked cages toward the opposite corner of the room, feeling Prayna's medallion lighten with each progressive step.

Passing the cages one by one, I notice that most of them are either empty or strewn with bits of rotting tissue and blood, the remnants of someone or something recently slaughtered. When I pass a larger cage on my right, I see an image carved into its iron floor. I lean in closer, realizing it's a large window with a forest of trees visible just beyond the window's etched frame—the very same engraved picture I saw while giving Nikolai an infusion of my blood.

Imagining him here as a child, imprisoned by his own father—his maker—and deprived of light, love, and nurturing is more than I can bear. But before I'm able to ruminate further on the matter, my stomach churns at the scent of fresh blood and excrement.

Continuing to walk forward, I'm almost bowled over by the stench, which is so overpowering I must cover my mouth and nose to stop myself from heaving. Making my way toward the back of the room, I'm aware of the faint sound of breathing—a small, whiny intake of air like that of a frightened child.

The blanket of souls grows silent, then sinks from its position near the bone-encrusted ceiling and merges into a moon-shaped orb of light suspended above a cage at the end of the row. I'm almost in front of it when I see a pair of gnarled hands grip the bars; the creature inside presses its face against the cage, then maneuvers its head so it has an unobstructed view of me with one of its pure black eyes.

Its breathing is frantic and its flat nostrils flare in and out as it shoves its face harder against the inside of the cage. I kneel in front of it until I'm eye level with the creature that's smashing itself against the bars to get closer to me. Lit by the gentle glow of the soul-fused moon, blood is streaming down its face from a gash across its forehead, which is a far lesser wound than the deep cuts covering its body or the missing razor-sharp fingernails that have been torn down to their pulpy nail beds.

The creature has soiled itself, most likely from the brutality of the torture it's sustained or the fear of knowing it's been left here to die. In looking closer, beyond the wounds and blood, I'm almost certain this is the creature that emerged from the shadows of the fireplace in my bedroom. What I thought was a hallucination was in fact truth, and as a result, the settled dust of my exploded world whips up and suffocates my ability to form cohesive thought.

With my mouth dry and my vocal cords feeling caked with soil, I stare into the creature's eyes and sense it's having a parallel experience. Its mouth is trembling, its tight, leathery black lips quivering like it wishes to speak but can't; the only sounds escaping its vocal cords are strained, animal-like whimpers.

Feeling my heart racing, I coax a few shaky words from my throat. "Do you know who I am?"

Reaching its hand through the bars, the creature takes hold of my wrist, then uses a bloodied finger to trace a circle inside the mangled copper strands of my bracelet. As I watch the blood dripping down from the wires into the empty space that contained the stone with my initials—the stone my mother told me was made from the blood of our ancestors—I can't breathe.

In meeting its pleading, black-eyed gaze, I understand we are united. Eye to eye, heart to heart, I'm all but ready to rip the cage apart with my bare hands to tear down the barrier between us when, from behind me, the faint scent of burning sugar drifts over my shoulder and circles the base of my nostrils like a serpent waiting to steal the air from my lungs.

With no idea how to escape this hellish place, I start panicking—I refuse to leave without freeing the other half of my ironbound and beaten soul. We will either flee or die as one. Pulling with all my strength, I attempt to force the cage open, but it's locked with a thick and formidable iron padlock, the sight of which causes my anxiety to increase and my blood to boil.

Perhaps it's my burning blood or the unbalanced state of my mind, but Prayna's medallion seems to be radiating a faint violet light. I shift my focus back to the padlock, take it in my hand, and send all the current inside my veins into the one thing standing between me and a chance to equalize my fractured world.

Like butter to fire, the lock begins to melt, and as molten iron drips from my closed palm and causes a tiny plume of steam to rise when it hits the skull-tiled floor, I nearly pass out from the scorching pain coursing through my body. But with the sheer force of my iron will, I endure the agony until nothing remains of the lock but a puddle of lava on the floor.

The skin on my left hand is burned beyond repair so I use my right hand to throw open the cage and take the creature in my arms while black smoke drifts in from the dungeon's entrance. I move toward the back wall and lean into it only to find that it bows against my weight like it's made of rubber scenery fabric.

Feeling helpless and with no idea what to do next, I'm unable to stop my heart from racing. But when Prayna's medallion grows white-hot, like a sun-infused disk, I watch the souls rush from the corner of the room and form a frame around us before burning a hole in the wall and filtering through it like light-filled militia.

Following their lead, I step into what looks like a corridor filled with misty storm-grey clouds. Upon contact with my skin, the mist drops downward and settles on a wooden floor flanked by high stone walls. A faint silver-blue light shines down from above, like the moon has been covered with a sea-colored gel. Not a sound can be heard save the gentle breeze whipping past my shoulders and tousling a few strands of my hair.

The souls have gone ahead of me, their light growing dim as they disappear deeper into the corridor, and I trail behind, feeling this place is extraordinary, perhaps even sacred. Even though I can't comprehend the purpose of such a passageway, my gut tells me it somehow runs between the bands of space and time.

Distracting me from my thoughts, the mist swirls around the base of my ankles, and the longer I'm in contact with its cloudy fingers, the harder it is to keep my focus. Feeling like my body has a mind of its own, I have an urgent desire to submerge myself in it, compelled to actually *become* mist. Weightlessness takes me over; I hardly feel the pull of gravity even though my legs are still carrying me forward, and with the souls putting an uncomfortable distance between us and them, I start running.

The wooden planks beneath my feet feel more like cotton than wood and I can no longer detect any form of gravity holding me in place. My mind is drifting, firing off random thoughts and memories as if my brain is fighting for its last bits of consciousness.

A booming voice shoots toward me from behind and rips me from weightlessness, sending me back into the solidity of my earthbound body.

"I have her soul."

I stop running and turn around. The creature in my arms grips the sides of my rib cage while, lit by the torchlight of his dungeon, Lukaes steps through the opening and into the passageway. Planted, wide-stanced, and triumphant—the solid outline of his form ominous and leaking bits of smoke from the tops of his shoulders like black flame—I see that in his hand is a violet glowing sphere, the brightest one I've seen and larger than all the others.

Raising his palm upward, he brings the suspended soul to his mouth, taunting me, and although I feel he's lying, there's enough doubt coursing through my thoughts to force me toward him. Yet as I move closer, every fiber of my being is telling me to turn back around and run as fast as my legs will carry me. If ever I were at a crossroads, this is it, and he is the Luciferian puppeteer of a life-altering choice.

As I advance another step, the creature takes my face in its bloodied hands and looks into my eyes, into my very soul. Although it cannot speak, there's no mistaking its cautionary message, and before I'm able to make a final decision, a small cluster of souls flies over my shoulder and hangs in front me, forming a kind of floating blockade.

Praying I've chosen the right path, I take off toward the souls awaiting me farther down the alleyway, and even though a choice has been made, I'm far from assuaged. I fear I may be leaving behind any chance of reuniting the creature in my arms with the life-giving grace of its animate spirit.

Pulling me from the grip of my swirling thoughts, the souls up ahead fan out in a wide circle, like a mighty sun, before scorching a hole into a stone-walled dead end. Feeling the creature clutch me tightly as if urging me to run faster, I push my legs forward and burst through the burned opening like a bullet from a gun.

The souls race past me and disappear in a blinding streak of light, and as I'm thrust into the meadow from which I recently departed, I notice it's covered in a thick blanket of snow. The trees have been encased in a cocoon of ice-crystal threads—like Mother Earth has grown possessive of her forested menagerie and seeks to protect it within her winter-woven womb.

Shifting my focus to the right, I study the marble rose peeking out from a lone snowdrift, its smoke-stained petals in brutal contrast to the diamond-dusted layers of snow being painted by the moon's kaleidoscopic brush of bruised and bloodied light. Walking toward the rose, I feel the charge of its life force with each successive step, my veins growing fat with our shared and soot-laden blood. Moving through the thick snow like an unyielding vessel in a white-powdered sea, I'm certain it's exerting the last of its wild-born will to govern my cells, coaxing them to push me forward until we're again united.

Wading through the snowdrift encircling the rose, like scythe to flesh, an image of Zoran and his Shadowed companion carves a hollowed space inside my mind. Holding the creature in my arms and staring into the rose's snowy center, I hope the stone-carried warriors' blood I placed inside it does, as my mother professed, run through me, as I'm in dire need of the fortitude and faith it affords.

Faith was the platform on which my mother built her life; it was the root of her purity and the source of her power, and in a twist of fate almost cruel in its irony, she bore a child who mirrored her physically and opposed her spiritually. For I am faithless. I'm inconstant, and my relationship with Great Spirit is more one of folly than of faith. Ruthlessly, I used my mother's mirrored allure to serve my own desires and rebuffed her teachings like a clumsy child unwilling to learn the intricate steps of a complex and beautiful dance.

Seeking to distract me, the creature puts its arms around my neck and guides itself upward until its cheek is against mine, causing my cells to sink toward the ground like they're succumbing to the chained weight of unassailable sadness. To say I'm lost in this moment minimizes my current state: I feel shapeless, like I'm floating on an unmoored plane of existence, and with but one chance for an anchor—half of which rests in the hands of my traitorous beast—a sense of hopelessness tugs at the edges of my consciousness and my cells further their descent toward the frozen meadow floor.

Countering the frostbitten night, heat rises in my veins, the rose-infused sacred fire of my ancestors lit and recharging my cells into a forced rally as cold air stings my skin and the blistering burn on my palm sears in response to my lava-like blood. Ignited by the fire coursing through me, my heightened senses detect an electric current in the air, the hairs at the back of my neck standing on end as I feel something hovering just above my left shoulder. Upon turning my head, I find myself face-to-face with the Shadow I left in Zoran's care.

I lower the creature to the ground, then kneel beside it as the Shadow drifts downward until it's floating in front of us and studying the creature's face. The Shadow wraps two inky arms around the creature's neck and presses itself against its leathery skin. In seeing their willingness to unite, I place a hand on both of their backs and push them together; yet rather than merging, they fight rigorously. In my determination to see them fused, I shove them closer until the creature lets out a horrific scream, its eyes bulging from its deep-set sockets while my burnt palm sears, enflamed by the waves of electric shocks emanating from the Shadow's back.

Blood leaks from the creature's mouth and the Shadow pixelates like a fading apparition. Undeterred, I continue thrusting them together, but like magnets refusing to connect, each repels the other, and with the shocks from the Shadow too painful to withstand, I release them and watch as they topple into the snow like strangled kittens.

The scent of pre-rain fills the space behind me like a gentle cloud awaiting its chance to release a quenching mist.

"Only a Guardian's blood can unite them."

Looking over my shoulder, I meet, then hold Daegan's gaze while his tattoos tumble in slow, unbalanced circles.

He's given me hope, but in this, he asks that I commit to the impossible. As the sound of my voice glides into the air like a clip-winged dove, I can scarcely believe what I'm considering. "There's no other way?"

Turning away from him, I examine the two fractured halves of my world lying almost lifeless in the snow, knowing that if I'm to finish what I started, I must will myself to agree.

When I shift my focus back to Daegan, I notice his tattoos have stopped dead, lying at his temples like stone-coiled snakes.

"No. You must accept."

Ire-spiced blood saturates the tissues of my brain as I realize I've no choice but to acquiesce. I all but spit my words into existence. "Then yes."

Refocusing on the creature and the Shadow in front of me, I draw from the memories of my mother's teachings and call upon Great Spirit to lend me the spark of creation from his life-giving hands, while of Mother Earth, I demand the dry riverbeds of my ancestral bloodline be restored with the flowing waters of ageless bounty.

I feel the earthen symbol above my heart bear a charge as the fiery symbol on my hand blazes beneath the burned skin of my palm. When the air around us grows warm, I look up and watch while the domed mini-universe created by Mother's Mystics pulses with renewed, silver-veined life.

Like spirit taking over flesh, a surge of pure creation replaces my humanness. Great Spirit has answered my prayer and granted me the ability to bend the laws of nature, and with a tremendous stream of power coursing through me, I'm quite certain the entire forest would fall to its knees if I commanded it so.

Mother Earth's life-infused blood flows into my veins, mixing with that of my ancestors, and in aligning with the arcane majesty of the warriors who came before me, I raise both the Shadow and the creature to their feet and slam them together like living bricks without mortar.

With my hands burning and my blood about to boil, I can barely hear Daegan protesting behind me, "Wait!"

But it's too late. I've fused them into an unrecognizable, subhuman creature, and as Daegan's words push into my thoughts—"Only a Guardian's blood can unite them"—I lean forward, rip open the unhealed cut on my finger, and squeeze a river of blood into the mouth of the wraithlike being I've just created.

Like child to breast, it wraps its pale fingers around my arm, bares a set of sharp teeth, and bites into my wrist, and I let it feed from me—willingly, gladly, because the longer it does, the more human its distorted, pallid body becomes. It appears to be rebirthing itself from an invisible womb, and like I'm viewing a time-lapsed film, I watch something half-human transform into a female form covered in soft, snowy flesh.

A thick layer of skin covers her eyes and her features are unformed, yet with each passing moment she evolves like she's being shaped from a slab of marble by the hands of Great Spirit himself. In seeing the effect my blood has on the rapidity with which she's developing, I press my wrist harder against her lips and send the life-giving serum gushing into her waiting mouth.

The passing seconds feel like hours until her newly formed lids fly open, and when she focuses on me, I feel my stomach drop, as her eyes are not the warm earthen brown I'd expected, but rather fiery red with pinpoint black pupils. While I stare at her, a sense of dread rises from my guts and spreads through my chest like a plague: nature will right itself, Mother Earth demands order, and, in this vein, I know I'll pay for what I've just done. I've twisted the strands of Great Spirit's loom and woven together something unnatural, and as I look into the face of my wicked creation, my blood runs cold.

Pulling my wrist away from her mouth and wiping the blood from her lips, I watch as she drinks me in. There's an element of heat in her eyes, not born of rage but of pure will, and I know she's fighting through the chaos of her unholy resurrection to find a way back to me.

After maneuvering her upper body into my lap, I let my fingers trace the side of her face, and when she feels my touch, I see a glimmer of recognition in her eyes. It's apparent she comprehends who I am, and in so knowing, I can't wait a moment longer to have her wholly alive and able to speak to me.

I stroke her hair until she inhales as though she's risen from the bottom of a lifeless sea. In response to an infusion of the meadow's ice-coated air, the fiery ring around her eyes fades enough to reveal the warmth of the earthen irises beneath them.

Reaching her hand up to my face, she brushes my cheek and wraps her arms around me while forcing a string of breathy words from her throat. "Little Dragon."

As she pulls me into her, I feel my heart release over twenty years of bottled sorrow, weeping not only for being forced to live without her but also for the barbaric torture she's suffered in death and its hellish afterlife. She is my other half, and with her cheek against mine, I feel whole for the first time since I was a child, a sentiment that forms into words.

"I'm never letting you go."

Locked in our embrace, together we mourn, our tears wetting the skin of one another's cheeks as a faint trace of lilac drifts from her skin and hair, the scent of which plunges me through the raw sorrow woven into the fibers of my being.

Having forgotten what real love feels like, it occurs to me that I've never felt safe in the world since the day she left, and while wrapped in the comfort of my mother's arms, I drink in the sense of security and protection her love provides. Since her death, I haven't let anyone hold me—not like this—and with the weight of what seems like a thousand lifetimes, I anchor into the grounded solidity of her presence.

We rock back and forth, entangled so tightly it's as though we're of the same skin, our hearts beating and breaking as one, neither of us capable of doing anything but clinging to the other.

The yearning for her love overtakes me and echoes along the cords of my fragile voice. "Stay with me." I gather her tighter in my arms and run my hand down her back, feeling the softness of her hair beneath my palm, praying this isn't the last time I'll ever touch her or feel her this close.

She kisses the side of my face and weeps, as do I, for the time we've lost. Though she feels like the mother I remember, I sense there is something different about her, like the pieces I've put back together have been darkly welded, and if I look closely enough, I'll see the hairline fractures where two halves were made whole. Yet with whatever time we have, I intend to let her radiance seep into my spirit until her luminous light reminds me how to accept the love I've refused myself in her absence.

Listening to her breathe in my ear, I feel my body relax into hers as though the air she's inhaling sustains us both. My thoughts drift to the question of who I might have become were I not robbed of her love and enduring support.

She rests her chin on my shoulder. "Forgive him. Your freedom will only come through mercy."

Feeling her body growing stiff, I break from our embrace and find that her eyes are changing.

"Mother?" Frantic, I wrap my arms around her as the pain inside my heart crushes my will to continue breathing. "Please, stay with me."

She is my everything, my soul, and seeing the earthen warmth in her eyes replaced by a ring of blood red unleashes another wave of grief.

"Mother!"

I can't stop myself from becoming manic as I watch her beauty wane, her flesh turning leathery grey, her cheeks sinking inward, and her bones protruding from beneath her skin until it looks like her insides are being sucked from her body. Witnessing the savagery of her deterioration, I beg Great Spirit to stop this from happening. I offer him my own soul if it means she can stay in my arms for even one more stolen moment.

Writhing in my lap, she moans as the tears leaking from her eyes turn to blood, her irises demon-red and her skin dark, sickly grey. Struggling to break free from my grasp, she digs her fingernails into my skin, but I refuse to let her go. I'm prepared to hold onto her even if it means she claws me to death.

Daegan kneels beside me, then unsheathes a small knife on his belt while the wraith in my arms digs into my ribs. "You must release her."

Drops of blood spatter into the air around us as she tears at my flesh, and although I understand that the demon in my arms is not my mother, the child in me cannot bear to part with her. With my body feeling like lead and my ears filling with the sound of my own tormented cries, I force myself to admit that I cannot leave her like this. Great Spirit has granted me the chance to hold her one last time, and now he requests that I send her into the sanctity of his waiting arms.

Seeing her anguish and knowing what unrelenting torture the last twenty-two years have been, I convince myself that what Great Spirit asks of me is the most loving thing I can do. So in a bid to end her torment, I grab Daegan's knife and slit her throat, quick and clean. Blood spills from her neck and covers my legs while I watch the life draining from her fire-filled eyes. After the last spark of spirit leaves her body, I hear a final crackling breath escape the slash in her neck as her lungs fill with fluid.

I've freed her, but in so doing I've also murdered a part of myself and plunged my spirit into darkness. Inconsolable and raped of hope, I scream, acid tears burning my face until my mind succumbs to the blackest of impulses.

Having nothing now, I close my eyes and without hesitation turn Daegan's blade on myself, asking through the bedlam of my thoughts for the Ferryman to take me. I tell him I'll be waiting on the shores of the river of the dead so I may take my mother's place at his side—I'll become a willing apprentice offering solace to the lost souls he ferries across the river.

Feeling the blade's steel piercing the flesh of my stomach, I grip the handle tighter, but before I can plunge it into my guts, Daegan wraps his arms around me and takes the dagger from my hands and I listen to his heartbeat thundering in my ears.

Feeling the weight of the creature in my lap lighten, I force my eyelids open and notice that its body appears almost ghostlike, melting into the air and forming a cloud of fine grey smoke. A warm breeze drifts through the trees and carries the smoke toward the meadow's edge, but just before disappearing into the crystalline forest, the smoke turns white and takes on a familiar shape, a story from my childhood, a tale of one smarter than all the rest: the silver fox.

The fox watches me for a moment, then like a candle being extinguished, its misty form thins into a trail of smoke and vanishes into the forest.

I am broken. Undone.

Daegan turns me toward him, then takes me in his arms, and I slump against him like my bones can no longer support the mass of my crushed spirit. The kindness of his presence is of little comfort to me, and when my mind fills with quicksand, one single thought, one last plea pushes itself up through the muddled state of my consciousness.

Meeting his gaze, I utter the most honest words I've ever spoken. "Let me join her. Please."

Daegan's eyes flash with pain as he takes my face in his hands and puts his mouth to mine, letting his breath float over my lips and imbue me with a lightness that lifts my heavy heart enough to see through the blackness. With his heartbeat pounding in my ears, I feel my own pulse fall in time with the steadiness of his ever-solid rhythm. After sitting me up, he helps me to my feet. As I look out at the landscape that was once cloaked in night, I watch the bruised sky give way to a violet sunrise.

Darkness slips away from the meadow on black velvet feet, and as Daegan leads me toward the frozen forest, I notice the souls hovering above the thick foliage at the meadow's edge. There's a palpable sense of sadness emanating from them, and it appears their light has dimmed to a dull and muted grey.

Letting go of Daegan's hand, I walk toward them until I'm inches away and after a moment of trying to decipher what I'm seeing, I realize it's Zoran who lies beneath the souls' storm-hued glow. He is all but formless, stuck between two mutilated versions of himself, and by the scent wafting up from him, it's evident he's rotting from the inside out.

Along with his labored breathing, I hear my mother's words drifting through my thoughts: "Your freedom can only come through mercy." In seeing him at the threshold of his demise and having already been stained by death on this night, I refuse to accept the responsibility of anyone else's blood on my hands.

Leaning down, I offer mercy, if only to gain freedom. "I forgive you."

Then I open my life-giving veins and let him drink from me until his deadened eyes flicker back to life, one aqua, the other misted black, as if it's been scarred by the fire he braved to save me: my beast, my savior, my traitor.

For whatever reason, my mother bound Zoran and me together, a fact I must come to understand and accept. But for the moment, he shall stay here on the cold ground beneath the watchful eye of the forest while I leave the night behind and walk toward the rising dawn.

61

LIFE, INTERRUPTED

Staring into the vanity mirror, I watch a faint tattoo undulating in a small coiled circle above my heart as if a piece of my mother's spirit has liquefied into misty ink and resides beneath the veil of my snowy flesh. Yet rather than bloodied black, the stain is a faint light blue, which is as Daegan described it, "An indication of a killing born not of rage or hatred, but rather of love." Understanding this, I wonder under what circumstances the sky-hued tattoos at his temples were created.

With my consciousness wishing to submerge the memories of my dreamscape and the events that occurred there, I feel my thoughts growing thin, like watered-down paint, until the only thing my mind can perceive is the clarity of my own reflection. This woman, wearing my face and observing me from the other side of the looking glass, holds a lost piece of my soul. She's an enlightened point of connection to my wisdom-bearing ancestors, and her strength is such that on my darkest of nights, she not only lay with my beast, but also forgave him.

Like an artist studying a muse, I'm struck by her eyes, which are bluer than mine, like a stormy sea that's been calmed by the sun's luminous embrace. Watching her, I find myself wanting to understand and absorb the serenity she exudes. She is radical authenticity embodied, and I'm certain any circumstance with which she's presented is met by the most unflinching of truths; and in this, it's apparent that her desire is for us to become one. She is my better half, my mother's echo, and in feeling her beckoning—her seraphic stillness seeping into my skin and delivering the message that I'm safer with her inside me—I know we should unite.

But my mind intervenes and reminds me that I'm far from prepared to accept such a raw and bonded union. Presently, I can only allow controlled moments of companionship; I will sit with her, together yet apart, absorbing her wisdom and admiring the part of her soul that carries the divine breath of my mother—*our* mother. This minuet between the two halves of myself will, for now, end in a forced parting that allows me to remain separate, feeling the stinging ache of my humanness a little while longer.

Whether I was seeking distraction or anchoring myself to a once-known existence, I've offered myself to those at the forefront of my exploded world: Bill and Mr. Llewellyn, two men who understand the density of loss and in whose company I'll walk stealthily through the pangs of my current circumstances, knowing theirs are no less heartrending.

Like a miniature earthquake, my phone buzzes with a muddled text from Mr. Sumel. "DeAd men tEll no tales…"

Despite Mr. Sumel's claim regarding Malcolm Blackwood, I've elected to follow my gut, which informs me that—dead or otherwise—he has information compelling enough to make the meeting worthwhile. With this as my final decision, I reply, "This one might."

Appearing to convey an opinion of her own, Lucille crawls from beneath the bed, leaps up from the floor, and sits on top of my phone, her eye contact direct and stark like she, too, protests my having accepted Blackwood's invitation. Swiping her tail across the vanity top, she narrows her gaze before looking off to the right, displaying just enough disdain to let me know I'm no longer worthy of her attention.

Knocking, Lula opens the door and walks into the room as Lucille bounds from the vanity and runs toward her.

"You sure about tonight? Both of them?"

"Yes," I confirm.

The sound of the doorbell sends Lula back into the hallway, her steps quiet, as if they're hesitant to carry her away from me. When I hear the door click shut behind her, I feel trapped in my room.

The walls exude a sentience that leaves me uneasy. When I focus on the velvet wallpaper, its flourishes seem to expand, as though the house is breathing, its powerful lungs lodged within the walls threatening to burst free while its ever-watchful eyes burrow into my very soul.

Feeling exposed, I close my robe and apply a layer of bloodred lipstick as I listen to the sound of footsteps coming up the stairs. Yet instead of Mr. Llewellyn's punctuated walk, these steps are light and carefully placed, and rather than his signature woodsy cologne, a sweet-spiced scent seeps beneath the door like a wispy peppered cloud.

Responding to a deliberate knock, I walk across the room, open the door, and find myself staring into the china-doll face of Giulianna Xu, her slate-colored eyes sharp and her voice emotionless as she speaks. "My husband can't make his appointment this evening. I'd like to attend in his place."

Bill stood outside in the cold staring up at the stone steps to her front door. It was moments from snowing, the air around him packed like ice-filled artillery ready to unleash a storm, which only amplified his hatred for winter.

If he had his way, it would always be September, the idyllic few weeks when summer gives way to the crispness of fall and the leaves turn from green to yellow-orange, then fiery red, a reminder that nothing is immune from the cycle of growth, death, and rebirth. In Zoë he'd found an unending autumn: just enough of summer's warmth to draw him in, and the slightest of chills to signify the coming fall.

Letting his thoughts spiral deeper, he felt his chest tighten and his stomach clench with the same sense of uneasiness he'd been experiencing all afternoon. His gut told him change was coming, and he never ignored his instincts, a trait he'd inherited from his father who often quipped, "I could put away every criminal in this city with just my gut."

A frigid gust of wind whipped down the street like a warning. Something powerful was moving beneath his feet, shifting and breaking apart the very sidewalk on which he now stood. It was clear to him that winter intended to force him into the darkness of the unknown, a fact he knew with a certainty that caused the hairs at the back of his neck to stand on end.

The sound of Zoë's front door opening pulled him from his thoughts as a petite Asian woman stepped out into the frigid night and closed the door behind her. Glancing at him before reaching for the railing, she made her way down the stairs, each step calculated—in part due to her torturous stilettos, but mostly because that's who she was: meticulous, vigilant, and exacting. As she reached the last stair, her grey eyes focused on him for a moment before she brushed by him and walked down the street without a word.

The image of her face lingered in his mind. She had a steely beauty, almost cruel, like a rare orchid with silky, poisonous petals, and the spicy scent of her perfume affected him like a paralyzing toxin. In his peripheral vision, he watched her open the door of a black sedan and step in. With her inside the car and no longer in the open air, he could move again, and in an effort to put distance between them, he walked up the steps as her car pulled away from the curb.

Reaching the landing at the top of the stairs, he was about to ring the bell when Zoë, dressed in white silk, opened the door and motioned for him to come inside. Stepping across the threshold into her house, he studied the subtle waves in her hair, which were picture perfect save a few strands that crept down her shoulder and lay tucked beneath the weighted lapel of her robe. It was customary for her housekeeper, Lula, to greet him, which left him wondering if they were alone, and as she closed the door, he felt he'd been caught in the web of a spider more agile than he could ever hope to be.

She watched him, and the longer they held one another's gaze, the more flushed her skin became—everything about her felt wild, unbridled. Taking a few steps toward him, she carried the spicy scent of the Asian woman's perfume with her as she took his hands and ran them down her sides until they rested on her waist. Reaching around to the front of her robe, he untied its silken knot, and when his fingers traced her naked skin, he couldn't breathe. She was the most arresting woman he had ever known.

She brushed her mouth against his, letting him close enough to detect the Asian woman's scent on her lips, and knowing they had been together intimately ignited and infuriated him. Backing her up against the wall, he opened her robe and exposed the fullness of her bare breasts. All he wanted to do was taste her, to know what it felt like to make her lose control, but before he could take her in his mouth, she kissed him.

Like an all-consuming storm, her kiss was deep, ravenous, and there was an unapologetic immediacy to her hunger that drove him mad. Pressing herself against him, she removed his coat, then, piece by piece, robbed him of his clothing like a pickpocket moving through a subway car.

There was no denying the reasons men laid their burdens at her feet. She had a way of making the world disappear, but in this moment, it was clear to him it was she who sought unburdening. The searching nature of her kiss, the inherent urgency of her touch told him this encounter wasn't consort to client, but rather woman to man.

Lifting her up, he shoved her against the wall and let her feel how big he was. Wrapping her legs around his waist, she reached down, took him in her hand, and stroked him until he was so hard it hurt. She lowered her body just enough to put him inside her, and as he entered, an involuntary moan left his lips. The way she received him—eyes closed, head tilted back, mouth open—made him feel like she'd never known the pleasure of a man.

Her strong legs wrapped around his waist as she rocked back and forth against him. She was tight, velvety wet, and it took every ounce of strength he had not to let himself release inside her—just feeling her was enough to push him to the edge.

It was how she was breathing, the way her fingertips massaged the back of his neck or the sheer euphoria of feeling how much she wanted him, but whatever the manner of connection between them, it was visceral. Her kiss was insatiable, and any gentility he'd hoped to maintain was gone. There was no room for artistry, and although the sensuality of her touch was undeniable, he sensed that what she wanted was pure, unadulterated sex.

He pushed himself deeper inside her until both of them cried out, and although he was trying to keep himself under some semblance of control, she preferred him rough. Taking one of his hands, she wrapped his fingers around her neck until he could feel her breathing beneath his hand, and the more he restricted her air, the louder her moans became.

It felt like hot lava ran through her veins; her skin was on fire and the muscles inside her held him so firmly he could barely keep himself from coming. Reaching down between her legs, he ran his thumb back and forth until she was seconds from climaxing. As she arched her back, he took one of her ample breasts into his mouth, sucking and licking until he felt her body tense. She took in a deep breath, squeezed her legs around his waist, then let out a soft cry as she shuddered against him.

Seeing her reach such ecstasy sent him plunging into his own, and with what felt like an electric shock bolting down his spine, he came inside her. The muscles in his body contracted and caved into her as if his very bones sought a home within her skin. His knees were weak, and before he could brace himself, they both crumpled onto the cold wooden floor like rag dolls.

They lay draped over one another, exhausted, and in that moment he knew he'd never felt so close to another person. His gut had been right: she had a piece of him now, and although he'd given it freely, he feared he'd never be the same.

62

BEAUTY IN THE BEAST

Our legs are intertwined, our mouths inches apart. The hair at his temples glistens with sweat and his skin is damp. He sleeps, but I want him again. We'd scarcely made it up the stairs and into my bedroom before devouring one another a second, then a third time. Everything about the way he takes me is perfect—he knows what I need, he meets me wherever I am, and he's not afraid to lose himself in the wildness between us.

Like a thief, I wait for him to exhale so I can steal the air leaving his lungs. I do it because he's pure and doesn't hide who he is, and with his breath floating over my lips and filtering into my cells, I forget how inherently different we are. Lying here watching the firelight dance on his skin, I feel a knot growing in the pit of my stomach. Just as my father's beloved Shakespeare penned, we are a story of ill-fated lovers, out of step with the rightness of time.

Still, what I wouldn't give to fall into the solidity of his adoration, to offer him the care I know he's long been left without. But considering the plight of my current circumstances, the kindest thing I can do is keep him at arm's length, as I'm at the precipice of an unknown life, a new and unfolding existence that will scorch anyone I allow to walk beside me.

The truest of unions should be based on honesty, a space between two people where the veil of their respective illusions is removed, a place where they're free to stand soul to soul. The kind of raw nakedness I will help ensure Mr. Llewellyn and his wife, Giulianna, Gigi, share. With the memory of her visit filling my thoughts, an unexpected thread in Fate's ever-twisted loom, her voice fills my ears. "Tell me about my husband, and I'll tell you about Evan." Tonight, we made a trade, a deal. We are allies.

I suppose the only true union I can allow at this point is with Lula, and although I've kept things from her, I have an overwhelming feeling that she somehow understands, and with her draped inside my consciousness, I realize she has yet to come home. It's unusual for her to leave the house without writing a note, and, come to think of it, I find it odd that she sent Gigi up to my bedroom without so much as a warning. Bill stirs and puts a gentle hand on my thigh as I pull the covers over his waist, wishing I was as deeply asleep as he, but I'm too restless to settle inside my skin.

My mind fills with lines of blurred text that fly in from every direction before breaking apart into single crisscrossing letters. As I attempt to understand what these rogue letters represent, I wonder why they refuse to organize themselves into legible words.

Like bullets, they whizz around the inside of my brain. The more they ricochet, the more driven I am to put pen to paper, as there is a kind of push inside my consciousness telling me I can only decipher what's in my mind's eye by forcing the flying characters into ink-born words.

Recalling that my mother once told me she wrote because her thoughts would only meet her on paper, I untangle from Bill's embrace, put on my robe, and walk across the room to the vanity.

It's clear the letters are being fired upward from the base of my spirit, and when I sit at the vanity and stare at my reflection, I feel the woman in the mirror owns some part of them having been loosed. Taking my mother's journal from the vanity drawer, I open it, flip to the page after her final entry, and pick up where she left off, letting the discharging array of text in my mind fuse into strands of script.

Characters string together and flow into words like a rushing river—line after line, they spill from my pen, my words ink-formed and taking shape as an image of my mother materializes in my mind. She is dressed in white, with streaks of sunlight on her face, she is healthy...she is free.

Her skin is gleaming, her earthen eyes misting over, while with every fiber of my being I feel how thankful she is to be unbound. If I've done nothing else truly selfless in this world, I can nestle a few of my fractured pieces within the softness of knowing that I found the courage to release her from the hell in which she was caged. It's difficult to imagine having the bravery of spirit to endure what she did, and no matter the price or consequence, I cannot choose a path that renders her sacrifice meaningless.

Like a candle's dying flame, my mother's image fades, and although I want to keep her with me, I let her go. She was my light, my grace, and I will never find another person on this earth who will love me as she did. With my hand still carving words into paper, I ask Great Spirit to keep her safe; I beg him to hold her in his arms until I've left this life to join her.

As I write the last sentence inside my mother's journal—*our* journal—I find myself ready to walk the path she forged for me with both her flesh and her blood. Even though I refuse to consent to the role of Guardian and don't believe that the words I spoke aloud on the night of her death have any actual meaning, I will accept the truth of her legacy.

Following the footprints she has left for me may mean giving up everything—a living version of death—but it's from those ashes that I hope to find myself. Maybe then I'll have the strength to let the woman in the mirror leave her glassy prison and take her place at my side. I'll tell her my secrets, she'll tell me hers, and together we'll become my mother's daughter.

Laying down my pen on the vanity, I read my words and feel like someone else has written them. This is the writing of a woman who, for better or worse, has made a definitive choice. She has an unwavering voice, an unyielding conviction, and a sense of groundedness that I've never experienced.

Looking into the mirror, I stare at the woman on the other side of the looking glass, pondering what she sees as she gazes back at me, until my thoughts are interrupted by movement in a shadowy corner of the room.

I'm almost afraid to turn around, but I do, and when I see a man step out of the darkness into brighter light, I stand and walk toward him.

Although his form has changed, his eyes remain the same: one aqua, the other charred grey. With his imposing frame and towering height, I'm taken aback by the size of him, seeing as the man I'd seen in the Polaroid with my mother was far thinner and weaker.

The right side of his face has a vicious burn scar that runs from his strong jawline down the side of his neck, a permanent mark from having shielded me from the inferno I created. As he stands before me reborn, I find myself momentarily able to see beyond my hatred.

Dressed in black as if in homage to his alternate form, his eyes are filled with a palpable hunger that makes me wonder how long he's been hidden in the corner of my room. As he glances first at Bill sleeping in bed, then back at me, I understand these men are both ship and ocean: one built to hold the weight of my soul, the other possessing the liquid strength to carry it away from the blackened waters of the river of the dead and out into the openness of the moonlit sea.

Zoran retreats into the darkness at the room's edge and I find myself wanting to go to Bill and touch him one last time, to feel his skin against mine. But I don't. Instead, heavyhearted and unsure of what's to come, I step into the watery shadows and take my place beside my beast.

63

CAT TALES

Lucille peered outside the sitting-room window as Lula greeted a woman standing on the sidewalk in front of the house. Why had the woman come back?

She never liked her, the woman with the grey eyes. The keeper of riddles. She knew too much about the house—about everything.

Lifting her nose, she took in Zoë's lingering scent. She was gone and the house was empty without her. Leaving the sitting room, she bounded up the stairs, crossed into Zoë's room, and nudged open one of the doors to the antique, built-in wardrobe.

Wading through silken fabrics, she made her way to the back, past a brass plaque that read,

Expressly Crafted for Mr. Cullen P. Hall
by Limerick Woodworks, 1961

Beside the plaque was a small iron lever-like pedal positioned near the wardrobe's corner. She pressed on the pedal, but it didn't budge.

Crouching down, Lucille inhaled each of the scents drifting in from whatever was behind the wardrobe. The strongest odors were of dust, musty paper, and candle wax, while the faintest were of cologne, tobacco, and metal-scented oil.

Trotting from the wardrobe, she leapt up onto the vanity. Sweeping her tail along the smooth wood, she wrapped it around the lower half of her body and studied her unfamiliar reflection.

Shifting her focus from the mirror, she knew the wardrobe would reveal its secrets. But not now…later.

Looking down, she read Zoë's open journal.

> When I was little, you told me there are two wolves in us all, the black and the white. When I asked which wolf wins, you said it was the one I chose to feed. The truth is, I have been a mistress to both.
>
> I have been shapeless, a haphazard form upon a stark-white canvas, a traveler wearing night's chill as a blanket so that I may cool the burning skin encasing my fiery spirit. But your voice is clear now, Mother, telling me to push and stretch my boundaries until I find where they end. Through you, a new life crystalizes. I feel my shapelessness taking form, and in this, I can serve two masters no longer. So, I have chosen.
>
> It is the white wolf's carcass that lies before me. I cut away its snowy fur and wear it as a second skin while, both bloodstained, the black wolf and I set out into the night.

Lucille gazed out the window and watched the bruised night sky giving way to a violet sunrise. A glint of light not to last.

THE END

ABOUT THE AUTHOR

S hannon Denise Evans is an artist, musician, vocalist, playwright, and novelist living in New York City.

Facebook: @VelvetMoonXIII
Twitter: @VelvetMoonXIII
Instagram: @VelvetMoonXIII
VelvetMoonChronicles.com